PRAIS[illegible]

“*Trust Me on This* is a [illegible] of a story, taking us into the hearts and minds of two very different estranged sisters as they travel along bumpy roads to try to reach their rough-diamond father before it’s too late. Full of snarky dialogue and unresolved grief and resentments, with a topping of hope if the sisters are brave enough to reach for it. I was there for the ride from page one.”

—Kitty Johnson, author of *Five Winters*

“With emotional family angst and clever, sharp writing, Parvizi gives us a bingeable road trip up the West Coast with gorgeous scenery, incredible food, and indelible characters. I could not put it down.”

—Sierra Godfrey, author of *A Very Typical Family*

TRUST ME ON THIS

For Meredith -

I so hope you enjoy the ride!

Lauren Parvizi

OTHER TITLES BY LAUREN PARVIZI

La Vie, According to Rose

TRUST ME ON THIS

A Novel

LAUREN PARVIZI

LAKE UNION
PUBLISHING

This is a work of fiction. Names, characters, organizations, places, events, and incidents are either products of the author's imagination or are used fictitiously. Otherwise, any resemblance to actual persons, living or dead, is purely coincidental.

Published by Lake Union Publishing, Seattle

www.apub.com

ISBN-13: 9781662523526 (paperback)
ISBN-13: 9781662523519 (digital)

Cover design by Kathleen Lynch/Black Kat Design
Cover image: © kampee patisena, © tenkende, © Jaswinder Singh, © Zenina / Getty

Printed in the United States of America

To my sisters—Hailey, Sydnie, Nastaran, and Chuckie

1

Zahra

There was always a beat, right before she pulled the pan from the heat, added a final squeeze of lemon, a sprinkle of parsley chopped as fine as the petals on a forget-me-not, watching the tendrils of steam striving upward, when she wished she had someone to serve. Not a romantic someone per se, but another person for whom she could plate the dish just so, and together they could taste, let the first bite awaken their palates, herald the brain's pleasure center to turn on and do that thing it does when you eat something so good everything sharpens—your taste buds, of course, but also the temperature of the air around you, the smells, the colors, the feel of your mouth.

Yes, even Zahra Starling, self-described anti–people person, could admit that food was meant to be shared. Not consumed in feral mouthfuls straight out of the pan from a wooden spoon spotted with burn marks while hunched over the counter.

Even so, she saved the sharing for her cookbook and restaurant clients. Zahra preferred the company of her kitchen tools, the reliable slice of her stainless steel forged Misono chef's knife against a bamboo cutting board, the predictable whoosh of her gas burners coming to life, the dependable scrape of her Microplane against the rind of a lime.

Cooking was an equation she could solve. A pinch of French grey sea salt; a mirepoix of carrot, onion, and celery; or a tablespoon of thick tomato paste caramelized to the color of rust . . . If she did her part, the ingredients never withheld.

If the first attempt failed, the answer was only a matter of recalibration. Eventually—and this, the certitude, was the thing—she would create a recipe she could trust to perform, a promise to be kept if only you followed the steps, one leading straight to the next.

The billboard towered above her, almost too bright to look at in the late summer sun. Zahra shielded her eyes, blinked twice in disbelief.

"You've got to be kidding me," she said through gritted teeth, then kicked the flat tire on her decrepit Prius.

Obviously, the billboard wasn't just any of the many billboards littering the sky above the city blocks. And it wasn't just an advertisement for one of the year's hottest streaming shows, *You, Me, Us*. But a sign, a literal sign that portended something Zahra couldn't grasp. At least, not yet.

It was a September morning, already hot as hell, and she had a trunk full of groceries and a desire bordering on obsession to get back to her kitchen. So it was fitting she found herself stuck on the side of the road, stranded in a run-down parking lot while LA traffic roared past her, releasing a haze of smog thick enough to tickle her nose.

But the billboard was a particularly unwelcome surprise, and Zahra cursed herself. For not seeing the massive pothole that had taken a bite out of her front right tire. For not having the forethought to go to the grocery store last night after she'd finished working. For not choosing any other strip mall parking lot to pull into, without the larger-than-life image of her bright-eyed little half sister, Aurora Starling—pardon, *the* Aura Star—looming over her and radiating an angelic charisma that bewitched everyone.

Everyone except Zahra.

She shouldn't have been surprised to see her there. The universe had a twisted sense of humor she'd come to expect ages ago.

Hadn't she gone out of her way at the grocery store to avoid the magazine rack with pictures of Aurora plastered everywhere? One mistaken glimpse at her heart-shaped face on the cover of *People* and the headline "Aura Star: America's Favorite Little Sister!"—how ironic that she played an oh-so-lovable younger sister on TV—and Zahra had pulled a one-eighty in line, bulldozing through the people behind her with their prepackaged sandwiches and plastic tubs of anemic fruit salad straight to self-checkout, which meant abandoning the bottle of albariño she'd chosen as a reward for completing her latest consulting project.

She could have really used a glass of chilled white right about now.

Sweat pooled on her back. Her forehead pulsed. She shuddered, thinking about the bright-green bunches of cilantro and chard going limp and dull in their bags. The ripe peaches and rosy pluots with their tender flesh softening toward overripe, their delicate fragrance turning thick and sickeningly sweet. The precious blocks of imported Parm and ash-veined Humboldt Fog collecting a sheen of sweat beneath their plastic wrap.

Today was supposed to be a whole day for Zahra to experiment with her own recipes. No double-checking notes on the computer while fielding last-minute email requests. No recipe development for the same trending ingredients. No client work at all. So she wasn't about to waste another second standing here.

And she wasn't going to sit around, waiting for a tow truck with some sketchy driver who might or might not even show.

She'd been twelve years old the last time she'd changed a tire—the one useful thing her dad had taught her before he'd left—but how hard could it be?

Getting to work, she found the lug nut wrench in her glove box and pulled the grocery bags from the trunk, setting them in a shaded corner beneath the billboard. It wasn't much cooler there, but at least they'd be able to breathe.

With the trunk empty, she dislodged the spare and heaved out the jack, all the while praying she wouldn't get some creepy guy offering his help or worse, a do-gooder with a propensity for chitchat. The last thing she wanted to do was make conversation. But she got the car lifted without incident, slapping her dirty hands on her jeans in relief.

Only then did she remember she was supposed to loosen the lug nuts *before* she lifted the car. Her body tightened with frustration, the realization of her mistake sparking the already hot air that surrounded her. Fine. She'd make do, throw some real muscle into it.

A tiny voice inside her wondered if she should have sucked it up and called a tow truck. But no, it wouldn't save her any trouble in the long run. She could handle this herself.

She sopped the sweat on her forehead with the hem of her T-shirt and kept going.

As she fought with the final, insufferable lug nut, her phone vibrated with an incoming call. Probably a client. Maybe a referral. Her spirits lifted. She could always use the extra money. She sank onto the ground, relieved for the momentary distraction. Until she saw the name on her screen.

Dad. Why was he calling?

She hadn't talked to him in . . . what? At least a year, maybe more. They occasionally exchanged text messages, but they were perfunctory proofs of life at the holidays and birthdays, if at all.

Her finger hovered over "Decline."

It's not like she wasn't in the middle of something. She could imagine how thrilled he'd be to know she was changing her own tire. "Guess your old pops was good for something after all," she could hear him say in that slow country voice he had, despite being born and raised in California.

She didn't want to talk to him. But she was curious. He never called. Her finger reacted before her mind could approve.

"Dad?" The line was quiet for a half second too long. The sound of something rustling. "Dad," she said again.

"Hey, kiddo." When he spoke, his voice didn't boom through the speaker the way she anticipated. He swallowed audibly, and she pictured his Adam's apple speckled with five-o'clock shadow rising and lowering and felt a pang of longing for the father she'd never actually had.

But she wasn't a kid anymore. She was an adult speaking to another adult. That's all this was, even if talking to her dad could make her feel otherwise. She put her phone on speaker and set it on the ground so she could get back to work loosening the last lug nut.

"So what's up?" she said, raising her voice so he could hear her over the street noise.

"No small talk, eh? Down to business?"

"I've never been great at small talk. Last I checked, you weren't either."

He snorted with amusement. "Got me there. At least tell me how you've been."

"I'm sort of busy right now."

"Okay, okay. Fine. Have it your way." He cleared his throat. "I'm sick, kiddo. I guess I have been for some time. Lung cancer, but the bastard spread before we could catch him." As if on cue, he coughed from some place deep and ancient in his chest, and she could feel the rattle reverberate in her own. The rhythm of her heart snagged on the vibrations. For a brief moment, her breath caught, and her hand stopped working on the lug nut.

Dom Starling didn't get sick. He didn't fatigue. He was one of those people who only needed four hours of sleep to function. He'd once fallen while fixing the roof, cracking a rib and breaking his wrist, and the next day, he'd climbed back up the ladder, cast and all, and had gotten back to work as if nothing had happened. The man had a few dozen weaknesses, but his body was tough as hell. If he said he was really sick, well . . . Zahra couldn't summon the words to respond. She could barely breathe. The outside glare burned her eyes. Her heart pounded.

She forced herself to find her voice, get back to work. "What now, treatment-wise?"

"I've done the chemo and all that other poison stuff. They said they could give me more, but I don't want it. I'm done with that. I think I'm done with all of it."

The lug nut wrench slipped, and her hand slammed into the edge of the car, catching on a sharp metal edge she hadn't even known was there. She stifled a yelp, gripped her cut palm where blood began to ooze from a dime-size puncture. She was used to cuts from her hours in the kitchen—her hands and forearms were riddled with scars—but this one felt deep.

"You still there?"

Taking a breath, her voice measured despite the pain in her hand, she said, "What are you telling me? You're what? Dying?"

"Yep, you're still a straight shooter alright. I've always appreciated that about you." He snickered. "Don't worry, you're not gonna be rid of me that easily. I've got some time left. If I'm lucky." His voice had no right to be as playful as it sounded, not with her, not during this particular phone call. "God knows I've been a lucky man," he said, setting off another coughing fit.

Holding her injured hand in the other, she sank onto the hot pavement, the rough ground digging through her jeans and into her knees.

For a fraction of a moment, the time it takes to sear your arm on a sheet pan or cleave an onion in half, she was twelve years old again, watching her dad pack his car with no explanation, except to say, "I'll send you a postcard on my way to Seattle. How does that sound?" Like she was a toddler hoping for a souvenir, like he might just be taking a business trip from which he'd return. She sloughed off the memory as fast as it came.

"I figured you'd want to know. Or maybe not. Anyhow, it's not the only reason why I'm calling. There's something I need to tell you." A pause. "It's something I should have told you a long time ago."

She could think of a few dozen things he should have told her over the years. "I love you," or better yet, "I'm sorry for being such a checked-out dad, and I acknowledge it probably screwed you up in all sorts of ways, but you've done okay despite that, and even though I can't take any credit in how you turned out, I'm still proud of who you are." That would have been a start.

"I can't say it like this, over the phone," he continued. "Can you come here so we can talk in person?"

"To Seattle? Like right now?"

"You know, not this second, but yeah, soon as you can. I've had some . . . uh . . . complications, but they should discharge me today or tomorrow."

Discharge him? She couldn't picture her dad in a hospital, let alone in a hospital bed, wearing a flimsy, faded gown with Velcro fasteners curled from overwashing. She wanted to know who was taking care of him at home, but she feared the answer would require something of her she wasn't willing to give.

"Did you hear me?" he said. "Book a flight."

The grunt of street traffic filled her ears as she came back to the conversation.

"I don't fly, Dad. You know that." Of course he didn't remember. Why would he? Her resentment toward him flared and caught, a burn as familiar as the veins that lined her skin.

"You don't—" His memory seemed to come back to him. "Right, yeah, okay. Drive, then. Call Aurora and coordinate a plan." The line stilled for a beat. When he spoke again, his voice was stronger, a hint of the hard-ass she knew. "I need to talk to the both of you. Together. It's not negotiable."

She crossed her arms; the pain in her hand pulsed through her fingertips.

For once, he needed her. He cared enough to call her to him. And still, she didn't want to give an inch. Zahra had hoped the next time her dad called he might finally apologize for . . . something, one of the many letdowns over her lifetime, beginning with what happened the last time they'd seen each other a decade ago. She didn't want him to be sick, but *she* was the one who should have been making the demands.

"I'll think it over," she finally said.

"That's all I ask." Another cough. "But kiddo? Think fast. We need to talk ASAP."

The line went quiet, and when she picked up the phone from the dusty ground, she could see the call had ended. Forgetting herself, she sought out shade in Aurora's oversize shadow, her eyes watering as they adjusted to the change in light.

2

Aurora

Sun-kissed. Sweetheart. Girl next door. Summer girl. Golden-haired nymph. Lackluster nobody. Second best. Second rate. Overrated.

Already, Aurora Starling had been called so many things, described so many ways, that the words had lost their meaning. The only word she trusted was Dillon's.

What had he said the first time they met? "Your aura radiates star power."

Her stage name—Aura—stuck, just like that.

The word he still hadn't used was "love." But she knew what he felt. He'd said as much in not so many words. He'd caressed her hair and called her "baby girl" or "my muse" or "the brilliant beauty." In public he called her Aura Aura, always in duplicate. If someone didn't know better, they might think he was stumbling over her real name, but it was another nickname, a code for the color of her eyes. The crystalline blue, he'd told her, reminded him of the waters in Bora Bora. He'd take her there one day. Once they could finally go public with their relationship.

Her dad had a nickname for her, too: Roar. And the way he said it made her think of a lioness, strong and wise. But Aurora was neither of those things.

"Roar," he'd said, just before their call ended a moment ago, and the word felt like an entreaty she didn't know how to honor. Alone in her dressing room, phone gripped in one sweaty palm, Aurora heard her dad's gravelly voice drumming in her head, and something like a roar began to gather in her chest, a swirling cloud welling up from a place deeper than tears.

Tears threatened, too, but she wouldn't dare, not with a face full of makeup.

She knew how to make herself cry, and she could as easily turn tears off before they began. Replace the picture of her strong, lively father gray in a hospital bed with one of him swinging her over his shoulders when she was a little kid. Box up the fear and remind herself that miracles happened all the time. He could still get well. Sometimes things worked out better than you could even imagine.

Her life was proof of that. Look at where she was. On set for a shoot with *Vanity Fair*! Less than a week out from the Emmys!

But she had that disconcerting feeling again that this was not her real life, that an actor had been hired in the role of her sick father and she was playacting the part of devastated daughter. The sensation had been happening even before her Emmy nomination, like the bigger her career became, the less real her actual life felt, her true feelings cushioned by a cloud of improbability, while as soon as the camera turned on, her character's feelings were exposed wires, ready to spark her back to life.

She'd been staring at her face in the dressing room mirror for the better part of two hours, but her mind had gone somewhere else as she'd spoken to her dad. She'd hardly seen her surroundings, let alone the contours of her own face. She came back to herself now, saw the thick coating of makeup that transformed her patchy, inflamed skin into a smooth, creamy coat; her usual straight, gold-blond hair fashioned with extensions and teased so it looked full and untamed; the dark, brooding eye makeup unlike the bronze and shimmery browns she usually wore—a look meant to contrast with Serena's. If her costar ever showed.

There was a tap at the door, and she took a breath, unpursed her stained lips, and watched them pull into a smile. Maybe this was good news. Maybe Serena had finally arrived.

"Come in," she called.

Her hairstylist tiptoed back into the small room with an apologetic grimace on his round face. He'd stepped outside the second it had become clear her dad wasn't calling just to say hello.

"It's fine; I'm off the phone," she said to him through the mirror.

He returned to her side and began to pick at the strands of her hair. "Everything okay?"

She couldn't quite chirp out the word "yes," but she nodded. "It will be."

Because it had to be. Because she couldn't picture her life without her dad. She wouldn't. There had to be another option, a plan B or C or D. She'd get to Seattle, and they'd figure something out. Just the thought let her heart rate settle. Like Dillon said, when one door closed, be prepared to bust a hole through the wall.

There was another knock, and a moment later, Evangeline entered, head down, half her face hidden behind the sweep of hair she kept chin length on one side, shaved on the other, fingers tapping away at her phone.

"Would you mind checking flights to Seattle? I need something ASAP." Aurora spoke to her assistant's hunched form, still trying to get used to asking someone else to do something she could do herself.

"On it," Evangeline said, her thumbs working even more furiously. "I could get you on a flight next week. But we'd have to move things around. A lot of things. What about the following week? Or the one after that?"

A part of Aurora was drawn to the idea of putting off the trip, avoiding whatever reality of her dad awaited on the other side, but he'd said he needed her as soon as possible, and her dad never said he needed anybody or anything.

No, what he'd said was he needed her *and* Zahra, and she'd promised to get them both there, together. As for how to make that happen, well, she'd think of something. Having an excuse to see Zahra, spend uninterrupted time with her, made Aurora giddy with anticipation. Circumstances notwithstanding, she'd been hoping for an opportunity like this since she was a kid.

"Next week," she told Evangeline. "But make it two tickets. I need to book one for my sister."

Evangeline lifted her head, jaw hanging open, to meet Aurora's gaze in the mirror. "Sister? Who—"

The door swung open and Margot Trainer, Aurora's manager, swept into the room, bangles clattering against her wrists. Despite her petite stature, Margot took up plenty of space, and the stale-smelling dressing room suddenly felt half its size with her inside. Aurora grabbed a paper take-out menu and began to fan her face.

"You look amazing," Margot told Aurora, flinging her left arm in the air, bracelets sounding like wind chimes. Her other arm she kept firmly by her side to hide the two missing fingertips on her right hand, a habit that was the only hint of insecurity Aurora had ever glimpsed in her manager.

"Good news or bad news?" Margot didn't wait for Aurora to choose. "The bad news is Serena isn't coming."

The whirring pressure in Aurora's chest began to gather strength again, but before she could speak, Margot pressed on. "I know, I know. She has the stomach flu. *No bueno.* But don't fret, okay? You're too young for wrinkles."

"The whole point of the shoot is the two of us together, supporting each other. That's the story."

It wasn't Aurora's fault she'd been nominated for a lead actress Emmy. Everyone knew Serena would get the nom, but Aurora's had been a surprise. It wasn't like she'd win, but the media loved to pit the costars against each other. *They play competing sisters on TV, but can these supposed best friends weather this fierce competition IRL?*

Despite the front Aurora and Serena put on for the show, they weren't best friends and never had been, but the truth, the *whole* truth, was more complicated than anyone could guess.

Margot waved her arm, rattled her bracelets, and brought Aurora back to the conversation. "They can do incredible things in postproduction. I've already spoken with the art director and the photographer. They have a fabulous pivot." Aurora tried to keep her face neutral, but Margot must have registered her concern. "You trust me, don't you?"

Of course she trusted Margot. She had to. Her manager ran Aurora's life.

"We were supposed to do lunch after, too," Aurora said. "For the paparazzi shots."

"We'll reschedule for next week."

"Wait, so *after* the Emmys? Doesn't that defeat the purpose?"

It wasn't as if she looked forward to another awkward meal with Serena. In the beginning, Aurora had hoped Serena might become a mentor, but over time, their public interactions had grown forced, their private interactions limited to what the show required of them. The *Vanity Fair* interview was meant to be a fresh start ahead of Season 2. If they ever started filming.

Margot squinted in thought. "You know, a post-Emmys lunch could be strategic. You two still supporting each other no matter the outcome, that sort of thing."

"You mean me still supporting her even after I lose."

"Sure. Or if you both lose." Margot's bracelets clattered as she jabbed her pointer finger toward Aurora's face. "And listen, you never know . . . Everyone loves an underdog."

Aurora didn't care about winning the Emmy. She cared about making Dillon happy, and as the showrunner for *You, Me, Us*, he'd be better off if Serena won and Aurora gave a gracious show of losing to her on-screen big sister.

"So what's the good news?"

"Hmm?"

"You said—"

"Oh, right, right. Wardrobe is ready for Look One. Let's get this show on the road, shall we?" In a half second, Margot spun on her heels and disappeared through the door with Evangeline behind her. Her hairstylist gave Aurora's hair one final fluff, then he, too, was gone, leaving her alone again. She picked up her phone, aware she only had a stolen moment before Evangeline came back to get her. She texted Dillon: Tonight?

The vibration of a text response sent a surge of excitement straight through her. But she read Dillon's words and fear fluttered against her heart.

Meet me outside the house at 11. Park down the cul de sac. Don't text. I'll come to you.

The request wasn't strange, but the location was, so near to Serena. Had she found out about them? Was that the real reason she couldn't make it to the shoot? There'd been that blind item circling on celeb gossip accounts a few days ago, but it hadn't named names. No one could possibly know it was about her and Dillon. Could they?

And wasn't that what Aurora wanted anyway? The truth to come out? Wasn't that exactly what she'd told Dillon? A real relationship; no more secrets. Yet Aurora couldn't entirely shake the clouds gathering inside her. They sat there, hovering way out on the horizon, obscuring the otherwise clear view.

I'll be there, she wrote, tucking the worry away. For the moment, she had a more pressing matter.

3

Zahra

Zahra stood at the worn butcher block that served as the only workspace in her eight-by-six kitchen, slicing sweet red bell pepper into thin strips, cutting chard into ribbons. On the stove at her back, a small pot steamed with the effort of warming seasoned black beans. A sauté pan hissed with excitement, the smell of garlic and onion turning soft and sweet in the heat.

This was decidedly not the kind of inspired cooking she had in mind for the day, but by the time she'd finished putting on the spare, made it to the mechanic, waited for the new tire to be installed, and bandaged her cut, she was too starved to experiment.

She tossed the peppers in the hot pan and gave them a few minutes to blister and brown before she added the chard with a heavy pinch of salt to help the hearty leaves wilt and turn tender. After slapping corn tortillas in a cast-iron skillet to warm, their nutty smell filling the air, she returned to the butcher block to thinly slice avocado.

When everything was ready, she smeared the tortillas with beans and topped each with a scoop of the vegetables, the wedges of slick, salted avocado, and a sprinkle of chopped cilantro. Not bothering to sit down, she leaned against the butcher block, head dipped over her plate to take the first bite. The flavor was good, simple and fine, the combination of textures pleasing, nothing special, but satisfying and reliable, nonetheless. It was the relief she craved, her stomach, loud and demanding, finally settling, the busyness of her mind distracted by the comfort of food.

The kitchen was where Zahra went to clear her head, cooking as a form of active meditation, the most meditation her brain could handle. It kept her busy but focused on the task at hand, one step after another. That's how it was supposed to be, at least. Today, her thoughts were scattered, and she had to keep reminding her hands what to do. The phone call with her dad was like a bad dream she couldn't shake. A layer of discomfort that coated every thought no matter how hard she tried to push the conversation from her mind.

Each bite was a balm, and she ate slowly. The open window above the sink let in the sound of buzzing insects and the distant noise of cars. Zahra's studio was an in-law unit behind a bigger, bungalow-style home. The two properties shared a small backyard with an outdoor living room beneath a wide pergola, shaded with thick citrus trees and wisteria. The plants were overgrown, hanging so low and heavy she'd banged her head on their thick branches a time or two, but Zahra liked the privacy, the feeling of being hidden.

A warm breeze trailed through the small window every minute or so, rattling the leaves outside, and she caught a whiff of Meyer lemons, the floral citrus perfume cutting through the rich smells in her kitchen, mingling not unpleasantly with the scent of the stone fruit she'd piled in a bowl on the counter. Her brain whizzed to life, cobbling together an idea, a new possibility for the Caesar salad she wanted to include in her cookbook.

She abandoned her last taco, opened the dictation app on her phone, and hit "Record."

"Try using preserved Meyer lemon to round out the sweetness. Ask Mom to send a jar. Better yet, ask her to send the recipe. The whole recipe book, actually." Her grandmother's collection of recipes was a cherished heirloom she'd been dying to cook her way through. The ingredient notes for her spiced preserved lemons had the perfect ratio of coriander, bay leaf, and fennel Zahra had never been able to replicate just so. "Remind Mom for the umpteenth time she can't just hoard family recipes."

She stopped, catching herself. She tended to go off when she was talking to herself, a habit that made sorting through her transcribed recipe notes a nightmare.

"Mortar and pestle the lemons into a paste. Mix with the garlic and try tahini for the creamy factor. And"—she needed something punchy and unexpected—"a glug of colatura. The fish sauce will add the anchovy-umami pop." Perfect. "Consider—"

Exactly what she should consider was lost at the sound of movement outside, then the distinctive rap of a knock on her french doors.

She braced herself for an encounter with her landlady. Preeti lived in the big house and had no qualms about padding across the twenty feet between her back door and Zahra's unit for unexpected visits. But when she pulled open the glass doors, it was Aurora who stood before her.

Aurora, in the flesh, her face made up to seem as though it wasn't. You'd have to look closely to see the rough betrayal of eczema Zahra knew lay beneath.

"Hi," Aurora said. "Sorry for the surprise visit."

Whenever she faced her sister, Zahra suddenly became aware of all her own faults and deficiencies, from her unkempt eyebrows to the wrinkles etched on her forehead. But it wasn't just the way Aurora looked. She exuded a sense of vitality and possibility Zahra couldn't chalk up to the nearly thirteen-year age gap between them. She'd been this way since she was born, as if she'd been imprinted with good luck from the great beyond. Zahra tried not to hold Aurora's enviable qualities against her, she really did. But she preferred not to have to confront them either.

"Hi," Zahra finally managed. She'd been seeing Aurora's face everywhere for the past year, but she couldn't remember when they'd last been with each other in person.

Without responding, Aurora quickly shrank the distance between them and wrapped her small arms around Zahra, who stood stock still, her face pressed into Aurora's jasmine-and-sweet-mint-scented hair.

Aurora pulled away but continued to stare at her. "You look good. I like this cut."

Zahra touched the ends of the thick, unruly black hair she'd recently chopped to chin level. "Keeps it out of my way."

Aurora nodded approvingly and, without waiting for an invitation, stepped into the kitchen, like it was the most natural thing in the world for her to pop by for a visit.

"God, it smells good in here. What is that?"

Zahra squared her shoulders and pushed past Aurora to come stand at the butcher block.

"Nothing," she said, despite the obvious signs of a meal laid out in front of her.

Aurora's eyes darted around the small space, and Zahra tried not to wonder what she thought of the metal rack that held her heavy kitchen tools, the chipped flower vase she used for utensils, the towers of canned tomato sauce, coconut milk, and beans lining the only free wall, how it compared to whatever palatial home Aurora was probably living in nowadays. Zahra's bedroom, up a small, narrow staircase to the left of the french doors, was not as cluttered but no less compact or utilitarian, and she suddenly felt embarrassed, even though she wasn't sure why. Aurora was the one who had shown up without so much as a text.

"So . . . ," Zahra started. "You're here."

"Can we talk?"

Zahra led them outside to the weather-beaten outdoor couches, her only sitting area, and perched on one of the armrests, rubbing her fingers across the bandage she'd wrapped around the puncture in her palm.

She knew already why Aurora was there. What other reason could there be? "You wanna talk about Dad."

"I know what he said. But I'm hopeful. Aren't you?" Aurora looked at Zahra expectantly, her blue eyes watery and wide.

"I don't know. It sounds like he's pretty sick."

"Yeah, but we don't have all the information yet. It's not like he's giving us details. You know how he is."

Zahra did and she didn't. Not the way Aurora knew him. For Zahra, her relationship with her dad had been defined by his absence. Even before he'd left her and her mom to start a new family with his mistress—his *pregnant* mistress, as it turned out—he'd never been available, always working, every promise broken the second "something came up." The only thing she could rely on was that she couldn't rely on him at all. She certainly couldn't count on his word.

But Aurora didn't bother to wait for her to respond. "It'll help to see us."

Zahra stiffened, her fidgeting uninjured hand balling into a fist. So that's what this unannounced visit was about.

The cat padded into her line of sight. A plucky stray with a short, gray coat and an insatiable hunger for Zahra's kitchen scraps. The more often she fed him, hoping to plump him and send him on his way, the more often he appeared.

With nothing to offer, she shooed him away, and he scampered elsewhere.

"Look, I told Dad I'd think about it, but I haven't really had time to do that yet," she said. "It's hard for me to drop everything. I have clients." A thin excuse, namely because she was a freelance recipe developer who made her own hours, and having just finished one project, she could easily push her start date for the next by a few days.

But Aurora didn't call her bluff. "Totally. That's why I've booked us two tickets for next Tuesday. That's a whole a week away. I can get through the Emmys. You can . . . figure out your client stuff. And we can be there and back in thirty-six hours."

Zahra reared back. "Wait, what? You booked us tickets?"

"For a flight."

"First of all, I don't fly."

"You don't fly?" Aurora said, her soft brow knitted with confusion.

"No, I don't." Zahra's face tightened into a hard point, a dare for Aurora to push back, but she only nodded with acceptance. "Second of all, isn't it a bit presumptuous to book a flight without asking me first?"

"I thought it would make things easier. Dad said he wanted us to get there together, so maybe we could—"

"He said he needed to *tell us* something together, not that we needed to travel together. And I still don't get why he can't tell us over the phone."

"He said he needs us there. He wants to see us." Aurora spoke with such confidence it almost sounded like she believed their presence by his side would heal him. "He wants to see *you*. And what if it's your last chance to see him?" Aurora implored when Zahra didn't respond. "Doesn't that matter?"

Zahra didn't know how to explain the idea of watching him die filled her with anger, not grief, that he could do this again: abandon her with so little warning. She couldn't bear to see him sick. But she wasn't sure she could bear never to see him again either, and the push and pull left her whiplashed.

Sighing, she relented a little. "I guess if I went, and I'm not saying this for sure, I could leave first thing tomorrow. I'm in between projects for a few days. But I'd need to stop for a night . . ." She could stay at her mom's house in Santa Cruz, get the recipe book and preserved lemons while she was there. That was tantalizing. Two birds. She could make it to Seattle in two long driving days, hear what he had to say, then turn around and . . . She shook her head. It was all happening too fast. It was too much to process.

Things between her and her dad had been status quo for so long, she'd grown used to the distance between them. In some ways, she'd come to rely on it. They weren't close. And yet he remained an anchor in her life, so that some part of her assumed he'd live forever. Even if nothing changed between them, there was comfort in the constancy of their dynamic. Zahra preferred stability to surprises.

While her mind had been at work, Aurora's face had transformed from sorrow to something bordering joy. Her sister's expressiveness made her a good actor. But it was her earnestness that made her so likable, and Zahra could feel Aurora's longing like the burst of heat from an open oven. *Don't you know,* she wanted to warn her, *when you wear your heart on your sleeve, it's easy to break?* Instead, she waved her hand as if to erase what she'd just said. "I just need more time to think."

"Think about what?"

Think fast. Her dad's warning echoed in her mind. How much time did he really have? He'd made it sound as if he might have months. But then why the urgency about coming to see him right away? He'd mentioned something about complications, hadn't he? Why hadn't she made him give her more information?

But she hadn't asked on purpose, to maintain the space she'd spent so long putting between them.

"I don't know," she admitted.

Aurora's mouth parted in a pretty O, as if she had something else to say, then closed again. She released a heavy exhale. "Okay. But promise me you'll text when you decide anything."

"Sure."

"No, promise." Aurora stuck out her pinkie finger, and Zahra looked at her in disbelief. A pinkie swear? Really? Zahra had taught her how to link their pinkies and kiss their thumbs when Aurora was no more than a toddler. It had turned into a secret handshake Zahra used to amuse her little sister, but it had been a couple of decades.

Aurora's pinkie dangled in the air, and Zahra found herself sticking out hers to meet it, pressing her lips to her thumb while her sister did the same, until their heads nearly touched.

4

Zahra

Usually, Zahra was fastidious about putting everything away and washing the dishes, wiping down the counters and sweeping the floor. She didn't have the square footage not to be tidy. Usually, she couldn't think of anything else until her kitchen shone, ready for the next cooking project. But after Aurora left, Zahra had forgotten about the dirty pans and cutting board in her sink, the uneaten tacos, the ripe end-of-summer fruit she'd planned to eat for dessert.

She stayed outside, watching the evening light fade and filter through the leaves of the citrus trees, dappling the ground. The cushions of the outdoor sofa held her like glue, even as the breeze cooled and goose bumps spread across her bare arms. Without looking, she touched the tattoo on her inner forearm—**June 16, 2014**—a habit when her hands were idle.

She'd already lost so much, and now she would lose her dad, too, a final abandonment from which they could never recover. She was thirty-eight years old, still clinging to the secret hope that one day her father might come around and make things right. That things might change between them. Now she knew they never would. A swell of grief rose inside her so thick she gasped as if she were drowning. She fought against the familiar heartache before it could pull her under.

He wasn't allowed to make her feel like this anymore. She wouldn't let him.

She stood with stubborn determination, but before she could decide what to do next, the cat appeared out of the shadows. Beelining toward her legs, he walked with a limp, one front paw held aloft, his delicate shoulder knob craned to a point. She bent down to take a closer look and saw a fresh red mark through his soft pink pad. Her own cut throbbed at the sight.

"How'd you do that?" The cat rubbed his tattered ear against her hand, leaned his body against her. "Lucky for you I have the first aid kit out already."

She left him in the outdoor sitting area and returned a minute later with a gauze pad soaked in the saline solution she kept on hand in case of cooking nicks. She gently dabbed on his paw, and he accepted her ministrations good-naturedly as long as she stopped frequently to scratch his ears. He wasn't bad company. Really the only company Zahra'd had since she moved into her current place five years ago. She preferred it that way, and it was hard to remember she'd ever felt differently.

"There," she said. "I'd use a bandage, but you might get it caught on something out here. We'll keep an eye on it, okay?"

The cat's ears twitched back and forth. Beneath her fingers, his body tensed. A second later, Zahra heard Preeti moving about on her deck. No doubt her landlady would want to hang out.

Zahra tried to shrink herself into the evening shadows, but it wasn't dark enough yet. Could she slink inside before Preeti spotted her?

"Zahra, are you back there?" Preeti's melodic voice singsonged across the yard.

Zahra dared a glance, caught Preeti's hopeful face through the branches. She beckoned for Zahra to come join her. So much for sneaking away.

Normally, she avoided conversations with Preeti for fear of how long they might last, but she'd worn out her resistance speaking with her dad and Aurora.

For once, the cat watched her walk away without following. "Smart cat," she mumbled.

"Here," Preeti said, shoving a glass of wine in her hand before she reached the top of the steps to the deck. "I hate to drink alone. Cheers." She tapped her glass to Zahra's.

Zahra took a polite sip, expecting the taste of something unexceptional—a butter-bland chardonnay, the sharp acid of a cheap New Zealand sauv blanc—but she was surprised by the complexity of the flavor, the mineral finish.

She swirled her glass. "This is good."

"I have to introduce you to my wine friend, Marisol. She's a genius. I basically don't buy anything without her approval." Preeti's eyes widened. "Oh my God, we should do dinner, the three of us. You can cook, she can pair, and I can . . . host?" She winked at Zahra, then laughed.

Zahra took a gulp of her wine, leaned against the deck's railing. The scent of something herbal and medicinal wafted from Preeti's screen door. She had a specific incense she burned when she did yoga, which Zahra only knew because Preeti had described her daily yoga practice in detail, trying to get her to join her at the mat. On various occasions, she'd invited Zahra to her book club, to an aura reading, to Thanksgiving, to the opening of one of her movies. Preeti was a voice actress who'd been in at least a half dozen animated blockbusters, but always, as Zahra understood it, in a small role. She did audiobooks, too, and she'd recently finished a stint in a recurring part for some animated kid's show. It had only lasted a couple of seasons.

"But still," Preeti had said, as if those two words were their own consolation prize.

The expression grated on Zahra. She could imagine herself saying the same thing. She had no culinary degree, no experience at a Michelin-starred restaurant, no cookbook of her own despite the many recipes she'd created for her client's cookbooks, *but still*, she cooked for a living. That was enough, right?

She gulped her wine. Preeti waggled her eyebrows. "Refill?" she asked, already lunging toward the sweaty bottle on the patio table.

"No, thank you," Zahra said. "I should probably—"

"Not to sound like a nosy fangirl, but was that your sister here earlier?"

"Oh, um . . ." Zahra paused. She'd slipped up shortly before *You, Me, Us* released, back when all the first promo billboards were going up over winter, and mentioned to Preeti she was related to one of the leads. Then realizing her mistake, braced herself for a slew of annoying questions, or God forbid, the request for an introduction, but Preeti had been surprisingly discreet about the whole thing. She hadn't brought it up again. Until now. "Yeah, I guess it was."

"Wow. Is she freaking out about the Emmys? I would be. I heard there's some sort of drama with Serena Kelly, too."

Zahra looked at her blankly.

"Her costar? The other sister on the show?" Preeti said. "I'll be devastated if those two have a friend breakup."

Besides the facts of their childhoods, Zahra hardly knew anything about Aurora's personal life anymore. Even after Aurora and her mom had moved from Seattle to Southern California to pursue Aurora's acting career, Zahra hadn't spent much time with her half sister. They'd done a handful of gift exchanges at Christmas and a few coffee dates where Aurora told Zahra about her latest auditions. But since Aurora's star had begun to rise, even the random texts she sent had become rare, a change that came mostly as a relief for Zahra. Aurora's incessantly bubbly personality had long vexed her. They were perfectly mismatched in that way. But it was also that Zahra couldn't reconcile how different their lives had been, despite having the same father. It was easier not to try to reconcile it at all. She and Aurora may share 50 percent of their DNA, but as far as Zahra was concerned, she was an only child in all the ways that counted.

"She didn't mention it," Zahra said, too embarrassed to reveal she'd failed to ask about the Emmys, let alone acknowledged the nomination. "Our dad's sick. We were talking about that."

"Oh no! I'm so sorry. Is it—" She mouthed *cancer*, as if it were a dirty word, and Zahra, nodding in return, supposed it was.

Preeti bit her bottom lip and shook her head. "My mom died of breast cancer when I was thirty. We knew it was coming, and even so, I couldn't believe when it actually happened. I wonder sometimes who I'd be if she were still here. But the grief changes you." Her voice caught, and Zahra's chest hitched in response. She looked away while Preeti fanned her eyes. "Look at me go. Even though it's been nearly twelve years, sometimes it feels that fresh, you know?"

Zahra cleared her throat. "I'm sorry about your mom. Really," she said. "But you were probably close, right? That's much harder. My dad and I, we're not . . . We don't really have a relationship. That's actually why Aurora was here. He wants us to go see him together. But I don't know if I can . . . I mean, I'm not sure . . ." Even to explain that she was debating whether to go felt shameful. What kind of person didn't race to go see their ailing parent?

She clenched her glass, staring at the last drop of wine circling the bottom. When she looked up, Preeti nodded knowingly, even though Zahra never managed to finish her thought.

"You poor thing. I understand completely." Preeti released a dramatic sigh. "This is one of those times when it's so important to have someone, right? *Your* someone."

When Zahra had moved into the in-law unit, one of the things she'd quickly realized her landlady liked about her was her single-girl status. It seemed for Preeti to be a great unifier, them both being "single by choice." In the time they'd known each other, Preeti'd had at least a half dozen short-term relationships, while Zahra'd had none.

Zahra never let on she'd been married in her twenties, back when she'd still been unseasoned enough to feel hopeful about her future. In that sense, she supposed, she was not "single by choice."

"It's not that," Zahra said flatly.

Preeti closed her eyes, then opened them again and stared at Zahra. "I mean this with love, but your energy is . . ." She waved her hands toward Zahra, her long face pinched with concern. "You're like a great big ball of friction. But you know what?" She pulled Zahra's free hand into hers, traced her bandage gently like she was reading Zahra's palm. "The very fact you don't want to see him is the reason you need to."

Zahra pulled her hand away. She winced as the movement inflamed her cut.

"See, see! There it is. The resistance. Trust me, life is so much easier as a sponge than as a Brillo pad. My first therapist told me that. Life changing. Anyway," she continued, "point is, you need the connection even as you fight against it. Let yourself be held, my friend."

Zahra's eyes blinked twice as her mind struggled for equilibrium.

She didn't need to be held. She just wanted to be left alone, without everyone expecting something from her. "I'm fine how I am," she snapped. The wineglass clattered against the table with the unintended force of her hand.

Preeti blinked, her face immobile. Silence dragged between them, and Zahra almost apologized for her sharp tone. But she swallowed down the *Sorry* resting on the tip of her tongue like a bitter horse pill. She didn't want to talk about this anymore. She couldn't. Eventually, Preeti shrugged as if coming to some inevitable conclusion, a sad smile on her face.

Back in the safety of her kitchen, Zahra cleaned the counters, washed the dishes, dried and put them away. She scoured the sink and mopped the floor. From the fridge, she pulled the remnants of a roasted chicken she'd used for the client development project she'd just wrapped up, plucked a bit of meat, and set it in a small dish, which she carried outside and placed near her french doors. A moment after she turned on the patio light, the cat appeared, limping toward the bowl. His head bobbed with each bite, his mouth smacking with satisfaction.

She glanced in the direction of Preeti's. The deck was dark, but brightness poured from inside, the blinds left open, her private living space laid bare.

Zahra regretted how their conversation had ended. She hadn't meant to sound so harsh, but her anger had a way of lifting to the surface before she could stop it, sneaking out like steam from a kettle. It wasn't Preeti's fault the call from her dad had riled her. Although Zahra wouldn't admit it aloud, her landlady hadn't been entirely wrong either.

What had she said? That Zahra needed to see her dad *because* she didn't want to? It sounded like a bunch of self-help nonsense, but if Zahra squinted hard enough, she could spot a kernel of truth there.

Maybe it was time to have the conversation she'd been avoiding for the last decade, for her entire adult life, really. After all, she was the only one looking out for herself, and she deserved an apology. Barring that, she deserved an acknowledgment of what a letdown parent he'd been. If he wanted some kind of last-second absolution, he'd have to work for it.

So fine, she'd go. She'd go.

The decision came with relief. Purpose. Even if she wasn't entirely aware of it, she'd been headed in this direction all along, waiting for her outsize rebellion to snag and deflate, or in this case, catch the wind and pull her along.

If she left first thing, she wouldn't even have to delay her client work. She had a new tire, but she'd have to get gas in the morning, and there was the matter of letting her mom know she was coming, *why* she was coming. That conversation could wait until they were in person. In the morning, she'd send a text telling her she was on her way. As for her dad, she'd tell him once she got there.

Leaving the cat to finish his meal, Zahra returned inside to pack. It wasn't until late in the night, right before she drifted off to sleep, that she realized she hadn't texted Aurora.

Whether Aurora could meet her there wasn't Zahra's problem. Her dad could tell her what he had to say or not, but she wouldn't let him use it as an excuse to avoid what *she* had to say. She would make him listen. For once, he would hear her.

She pulled her phone from the bedside table and typed a message to Aurora.

I'm going. Leaving in the morning and stopping at my mom's for the night.

Against Zahra's will, an image of Aurora in some fancy Hollywood Hills house flashed through her mind: a big white bed with overpriced bedding, a clutch of tissues in her sister's hand like a small dove about to take flight, and her fervent, unmet wish to have a different big sister, the kind she could call for support.

In another life, Zahra might have liked that, too. Someone she could turn to who understood how she felt. Someone who shared more than a bloodline. Because she and Aurora had nothing in common. Not their childhoods. Not their personalities. Not their interests or outlooks. Not even their dad, not really. He may have fathered them both, but he'd only raised one of them.

Zahra had always been, and would always be, on her own.

5

Aurora

Aurora was nowhere near her bed. Or her home, not a Hollywood Hills mansion at all, but a three-bedroom, sixteen-hundred-square-foot West Hollywood apartment in a Mediterranean Revival building with brick walls and arched doorways she'd chosen solely for the vintage Tinseltown aesthetic. She had the third floor to herself, and she'd imagined running into the tenants of the four other units, exchanging small talk in the elevator. But she'd seen only hints of life: packages gathering in the lobby that soon disappeared; notes of laughter in the stairwell fading as quickly as they came; once, a pink umbrella left at the bottom of the stairs despite weeks of blue skies.

There were nights she was certain she was the sole person in the great ornate building, a thought that left her checking the locks twice before bed, gripping her phone in her sleep, even though the only person she could think to call—the only person she knew up late enough to answer—was Evangeline.

Her assistant was her friend, but a *best* friend? She hadn't had one of those in a decade, not since her mom had decided she should drop out of tenth grade to study for her GED.

The two of them had moved from Seattle to SoCal after her parents' divorce, and despite Aurora's protests that she *liked* school, her mom didn't see any point in enrolling her in a new high school, not when her career had so much potential.

She supposed her mom hadn't been wrong, but in the process, Aurora had also lost all her friends. Watching their young adult lives unfold online, she never commented, never DMed. She was forbidden from posting anything her mom didn't vet first. It was all about perception, her mom explained. *Do you want to be a normal nobody?* Aurora knew better than to answer honestly. She'd stopped following most of them by then anyway, so she wouldn't have to watch them graduate, go off to college without her.

Most of the time, Aurora preferred to be away from her lonesome WeHo apartment. But not tonight. Tonight, she would have happily settled for a night in, alone, listening to the sounds of the neighborhood's booming nightlife gather and crescendo outside her windows.

Instead, Aurora sat in her quiet SUV on an empty, rather exclusive residential road, the darkness edging closer every time she blinked. Night had come on slow, a curtain inching toward the stage as summer made its mid-September exit. Now the sky was black, the slivered moon swallowed by a bank of clouds.

Another minute passed. She fiddled with her hair between her fingertips, brought the ends to her lips, straining her eyes to see past the gate that led to Dillon and Serena's sprawling estate. Dillon and Serena Kelly, co-owners of Kelly Productions, *You, Me, Us* showrunner and lead star. Aurora's lover and her supposed bestie. It sounded so salacious, except Dillon and Serena hadn't been a real couple for a long time. They were only together for appearances, for the sake of the show.

It was a brand thing, Dillon had explained to her once. Aurora didn't understand how it worked really, but she understood enough to get that Dillon and Serena must know more than she did. They were older and way more experienced in relationships, business—life, in general. After all, Dillon had been Aurora's first *everything*. If she didn't want to lose him, she had to be patient.

To calm herself, she straightened and closed her eyes, forced her leg to rest. She inhaled and held her breath—*one, two, three, four*—then exhaled and held her breath again—*one, two, three, four*—visualizing a safe box she could tuck herself into, like a neat square of tissue paper.

Her phone vibrated. Anticipating a text from Dillon, she abandoned her breath work and hurried to swipe open her messages. But it was from Zahra.

Aurora smiled. Her sister would drive to Seattle! But as quickly as her smile appeared, her lips fell into a frown. *Tomorrow* morning? She'd never be able to leave tomorrow. How could she justify going anywhere with the Emmys in five days?

Before she could fully digest this update, a flash of movement caught her attention. Dillon snaked his way down the driveway and toward her car, his stark-white pants hardly subtle in the black of night. But then again, nothing about Dillon was subtle. He commanded attention. Magnetism, her mom called it, but for Aurora it felt like magic. She'd grown up with the kind of parents who always made her feel special, a precious gold nugget to be molded and shined. But with Dillon, she was a diamond, strong and glittering. When his light radiated upon her, she sparkled.

He opened the passenger side door and slipped inside, leaned over the console and kissed her cheek, cupped his palm to her chin, his warm skin tender against hers. His scent of sweet spice and cool rain filled the car.

She let her head rest in his hand. When she was with him, all the fuzzy parts of her life—like whether she really wanted this career or what it meant to love a married man, one so much older than her, or now the matter of her dad's health—all those worries she held at arm's length, just out of sight, faded away entirely.

Nuzzling against him, she said, "I missed you."

"Me too. You know that. But . . ." He moved his hand and she lifted her head.

"What?"

"This blind item. It's bad news."

"Who says it's about us? It's so vague."

A well-known director with a mega popular wife—and new TV show—known to "canoodle" with a costar in his off hours. It could have been about anyone.

"Even so, rumors are circulating." Gazing at her, his eyes dry and tired, the webbing at his creases pronounced, he looked, she realized with a start, old. All his forty-nine years and then some. She quickly glanced away. "Someone's caught wind of something. An assistant, maybe."

"I would never tell Evangeline." But when she thought about it, Evangeline *had* been the one to bring the blind item to her attention.

"They always know more than you think they do," he said. She wasn't sure if he was talking about assistants or the media or the general public. It didn't matter. It was true of them all. "If this gets out, it would be terrible. A PR nightmare. The tabloids will eat you alive. You'd be a liability. Your career would effectively be over before it began," he continued, putting words she didn't want to hear to quiet fears. "It's one thing to be caught cheating with a married man, but an older married man who happens to be your director and the husband of your costar, your supposed best friend?"

Cheating. The word banged through her like a door slamming open. That wasn't what their relationship amounted to. But if that's what everyone thought, then it might as well be the truth. And what did it say about her if it was?

She flicked away the question as quickly as it appeared. In the beginning, their secret rendezvous elicited thrills and guilt in equal measure. The initial thrill had faded, but the guilt lingered, a circling gnat Aurora had to shoo away time and time again, even though she knew what they were doing was *technically* wrong.

"Maybe we should finally tell Serena the truth," she ventured. It was the right thing to do, wasn't it? Come clean? So they could finally be together publicly, but also for Serena's sake. There had to be a way to make things right.

"You don't get it," he snapped, his warmer countenance replaced with his bossy on-set tone that left no room for debate. "You're still so new. You don't understand how all this works. If this comes out, you would be over. We would be over. The show—" Stopping himself, he sighed. "I'm not trying to be cruel, but I can't sugarcoat this for you." He took a breath, then began again more gently. "I'm sorry. You're wonderful. You don't deserve to deal with any of this. I hate that I've done this to you."

Dillon rubbed the space between his eyebrows the way he did when he was getting a headache. She hated when he stressed. He'd told her once that being with her was like dipping into a hot bath on a bitterly cold day, numbness giving way to the zip of his nerves coming back to life. Running her hand along the nape of his neck, she let her fingers slide through his short, feathery brown hair.

"You haven't done anything wrong," she said.

"It's just . . . I have a lot on my mind. The studio heads are breathing down my neck right now. We've had to push back shooting."

"Again?"

"It's a temporary setback, manageable. But we can't let anything else derail us." Season 2 production had been delayed initially because of the previous year's writers' strike. The second time was over an internal contract dispute. Now what? She knew better than to ask right then.

"What do we do?" she whispered into his ear.

He shuddered and briefly closed his eyes. When he opened them, he took her hand from his neck and held it in his lap, letting his fingers graze hers.

"I think it'd be best if you went away while we make sure the story gets killed," he said. "Just for a couple of days. I'm so sorry. I know with the Emmys it's asking a lot. But I have to protect you."

She gave nothing away, but possibility bubbled inside her. She *could* go away for a few days. She could leave tomorrow. She'd make this right for her and Dillon, and she'd be with her sister. Before Zahra could ghost her entirely. Because eventually, Zahra would. Aurora knew it. The same way she'd known Dillon was going to change her life.

That Zahra didn't fly was news to Aurora. A question mark among the many she'd collected about her sister the way other girls might gather mementos in a keepsake box. She'd have to find a way to convince her to drive together. Something would come to her.

In the meantime, she'd give Dillon what he wanted. And the whole thing would tip in her direction. Even if the story broke, he'd see that it made more sense for them to go public than to keep hiding.

"Actually, there's something I need to do in Seattle. My dad is, sort of, like"—she tripped over her words—"sick."

Her manager would never let her go, but if Margot didn't know until it was too late to stop her . . . Better to ask for forgiveness than permission, right? Evangeline could move her schedule around, and it was only Tuesday. She'd be back with a full day to spare before the Emmys on Sunday.

"Perfect," Dillon said. She gave him a look, and he grimaced. "No, no. I mean, I'm deeply sorry to hear about your dad. I know you're close, but think about it—the timing is right. Maybe this is the universe's way of looking out for you."

She nodded, letting his words sink in.

"But avoid the media, okay? No pap shots. No social media. Seriously. Wear a disguise or something."

"A disguise?"

"Hat, sunglasses, whatever. Just don't attract attention." He lifted her hand, kissed her knuckles. "Have faith, pretty girl. I'll be in touch when things calm down. I promise." Just before the door clicked shut, he stopped. "By the way, it's probably better you don't text me. I'll text you. Once it's safe."

Then he was gone, and she'd forgotten to ask about Serena's no-show at the shoot, if she really had the stomach flu. It didn't matter now. She wouldn't be seeing Serena until they walked the red carpet.

What time? she wrote back to Zahra, willing the three dots to appear. She wasn't above waiting outside Zahra's place all night, but it'd be so much easier if she knew when to get there.

A minute passed, another. It was late now; maybe she'd gone to sleep. Aurora tried again in case Zahra was thinking about ignoring her text.

> I have something important to bring but I can't fly with it. I was hoping you could drive it up. I can drop it off before you leave.

Just when she was about to give up, a response.

> No later than six. It's not illegal, right? Because I'm not about to be your mule.

Aurora's rosy lips buttoned into a small smile. That was ridiculously early, but she could make it. She was used to call times before dawn.

> Heh no! Just can't fit in my carry-on. See you then. Night!

She leaned her head back, let a hit of excitement wash over her. Dillon was right about the timing. If she trusted him, everything would be okay.

6

Zahra

Zahra woke extra early, scrambling to get dressed in the dark, shins knocking into the edge of her dresser, warm legs fighting a cold pair of jeans. She'd need sustenance to motivate her through this solo drive, so with the sun still hidden beneath the horizon, she entered the kitchen. First, clicking the start button on her Moccamaster. The machine burbled and spit before she heard the first drips smack against the bottom of the glass pot, inhaled the nutty scent of coffee.

In the quiet, she assembled tangy-sweet red and gold pickled peppers, the final bits of meat from the roasted chicken, and shredded clover-green little gems leaves into a ciabatta roll spread with a quick chipotle mayo.

That was lunch. She'd need breakfast, too. Something else handheld.

She scrambled eggs with a splash of cream and a dose of chopped cilantro. Adding the leftover beans and veggies from last night, she rolled all this up in a warm tortilla and wrapped the whole thing in foil for the ride. Potatoes would have been nice, carby and absorbent, but she was good at working with what she had.

After pouring the coffee into a travel mug, she began to clean up, pausing only to consider the last flecks of cilantro clinging to her chopping block. There was an idea.

She opened the voice record app on her phone. "Herby preserved-lemon dressing? Cilantro, dill, or mint? Or all three?"

She glanced at the time; it was only five thirty. An extra-early start would have been nice—she was eager to get to her mom's, have a visit, a little time to play with the Caesar idea, scope the recipes from her grandmother's binder—but she'd told Aurora six.

Zahra wasn't sure why Aurora's request rubbed her wrong. Maybe it was because she hadn't bothered to *ask* if Zahra would mind carting something across three states; she just assumed it was fine. But that was Aurora; she expected everything to go her way.

While Zahra waited for time to pass, she dished a bowl of water for the cat alongside an extra tin of salmon, since she'd be gone a few days. It was hours before she normally fed him and he didn't come running, even when the bowl clattered against the pavement outside her doors.

She'd planned to keep an eye on his injured paw, but surely he'd be fine without her, like he'd been fine all the days before he'd first appeared. Maybe he'd even give up on her and find a new human to ease his hunger pains. The thought gave her a surprising prick of sadness, but it was better that way, for both of them.

Zahra rubbed her arms in the cold morning air and peered toward the dark house. A night owl, Preeti usually slept late, and Zahra would probably be halfway up the coast before her landlady noticed she'd gone. Well, that was for the best, too. She was glad to avoid her for a while longer. She'd drop off a plate of brownies when she returned.

At the thought, her stomach grumbled. But the sensation was more than hunger. Agitation. She was off to see her dad for the first time in ten years. The last time she'd seen him, she'd been the one in the hospital, watching him turn his back on her and walk out the door. She'd decided then and there whatever tenuous relationship they had was effectively over.

But she didn't have to forgive him to see him again.

Nudging the cat bowl with her foot, she whispered into the gray dawn, "So long, cat."

❦

She waited until six on the dot. When Aurora still hadn't shown, Zahra lugged her bags and mini cooler down the long driveway that led from her unit to the sidewalk, the divide between night and day casting a hazy, surreal hush over everything, the air sweet and damp.

It took her a moment to realize there was a car blocking the entrance to the driveway. A massive SUV, some kind of sleek electric beast that looked like it cost more than Zahra's rent for a year. Neither she nor Preeti used the driveway, but what kind of jerk risked blocking someone in? She muttered an obscenity under her breath and had barely made it past the car when the driver's door flung open. She jumped back, heart in her throat.

Aurora's face appeared, hidden beneath a black trucker hat.

"What the hell, Aurora? Are you trying to scare the bejesus out of me?"

"Oh my God, I'm so sorry. I've been sitting out here for a while. I guess I got excited to finally see you."

"Why didn't you come to the door? You could have just dropped it off." Zahra lugged her duffel higher on her shoulder, tried to strengthen her hold on the cooler. "What is it anyway?"

Aurora smiled, her biggest one, all perfect white teeth and lips stretched wide. Her high-wattage smile, their dad called it. "It's me," she said, throwing out her arms. "Surprise. Sister road trip."

"Wait, what?" She couldn't be serious. Could she?

"I'm going with you."

Zahra's brain stuttered to recalibrate, and her muscles tensed, the jerk of her grip spilling a splash of coffee from the mouth of her travel mug. "You made it up, the whole I-need-you-to-take-something-for-me story?"

"Only because I knew you'd never agree to go with me."

Unbelievable. "So it's okay to lie to get what you want?"

"It was a white lie, I swear."

That explained why Aurora hadn't come to the door. This was an ambush, the trap sprung, Zahra strung up by her ankles, dangling before her captor.

Eleven hundred miles. Two days one-on-one with Aurora. She couldn't. She wouldn't. They'd never spent that amount of time together, and Zahra didn't want to start now, not with the weight of seeing her dad hanging over her. It was too much forced closeness. Too much of Aurora's sunny disposition to take. Too much space for conversation when all Zahra wanted to do was be by herself.

She had to get out of this.

"You don't want to drive." Forcing herself to stay calm despite the mounting pressure in her chest, she groped for an excuse, anything that would make her sister get back into her car and drive straight to the airport. "You'll save so much time if you fly. What about the Emmys?"

"Exactly. I have so much going on right now. I need a minute. And I'll fly back with plenty of time before Sunday."

Something slipped around Zahra's ankles, and she glanced down to see the cat, hobbling at her feet.

"The cat!" she practically shouted, unable to keep the desperation out of her voice. "He's . . . injured. I have to take him with me."

Mini lines briefly appeared across Aurora's forehead. "Oh, okay . . ." She sounded chagrined but corrected immediately. "Well, I love animals."

"What about your allergies?" Zahra remembered how much Aurora had wanted a pet as a child, how the little girl who got everything couldn't even have a hamster because she was so allergic to dander.

"It's fine. I'll get an antihistamine." She looked down at the cat, and a flash of wariness crossed her face. But when her eyes met Zahra's again, she gave her that high-wattage grin.

DAY ONE

7

Aurora

This was really happening. They were together and on their way.

Aurora couldn't believe Zahra hadn't put up more of a fight. After some audible grumbling about being most comfortable in her own car, she'd even agreed to take Aurora's SUV.

"Consider reliability. It's a safety issue," Aurora had said, nodding toward Zahra's old Prius, and sure enough, appealing to her sister's practical side had swayed her.

The cat had been a plot twist, but nothing an allergy pill couldn't fix.

The only real snafu had been when Aurora said they had to make a quick stop at her mom's house. Aurora might as well have slapped Zahra across the face. She'd reared back in her seat and grabbed hold of the door as if she might throw herself out. "Lucy? Oh, no way. I don't think so. I did not agree to that."

"Don't be so dramatic."

"Says the actress," Zahra muttered, still holding tight to the door.

"It'll be in and out."

"Does your mom know I'm coming with you? You know she prefers to forget I exist, right? She's never liked me."

"That's not true."

Zahra released something between a laugh and a scoff. "Either you really do deserve that Emmy or you're purposefully being naive."

"How could she not like you? You're her stepdaughter."

"Ex-stepdaughter," Zahra corrected. "During one of my visits, she actually made me stay in the guest room while she and Dad had people over. I'm sure you were too little to remember, but she told me it would be easier if she didn't have to 'explain' me. Meanwhile, she brought you out for one of your performances."

Aurora frowned. She didn't remember Zahra being hidden away in her parents' guest bedroom like an embarrassing secret. But Zahra was right, she *had* performed for her parents' guests. A routine her mom made her practice, "On the Good Ship Lollipop." The song was like nails on a chalkboard for Aurora now.

She preferred to remember the tickle of delight every time they went to pick up Zahra from the airport, the zipping joy of riding home in the back seat beside her, then waking up the next day knowing she was there, her sister. Her presence back then had made Aurora part of a unit, a whole instead of a half, a complete set.

"She's just in Calabasas," Aurora said. "And the Target right by her house opens super early. We can get a cat carrier there."

"Fine," Zahra conceded.

But since then, her apprehension had taken the shape and heft of another passenger, and she hadn't uttered a word since they'd gotten on the freeway. She wasn't even looking at her phone, just sitting there with her arms crossed, staring out the window.

In hindsight, Aurora never should have agreed to stop at her mom's. Never should have told her mom she was passing by in the first place. Not until she was a hundred miles past her exit.

But the notion that Aurora might not tell her mom where she was going was too impossible to entertain. Lucy Starling knew where her daughter was at all times—minus Aurora's stolen hours with Dillon. Even then, she told her mom where she was and who she was with, just not what she was doing. Lucy might raise an eyebrow and ask, "Another dinner meeting with Dillon?" but that was all. Time spent with Dillon didn't require explanation.

Aurora had texted her mom that morning, right before she texted Evangeline, while she waited outside Zahra's. To her assistant, she'd written that she had a family emergency and would be gone for the next two days. Could Evangeline please adjust her schedule accordingly, book her on a flight out of Seattle the day after tomorrow, and most importantly, avoid mentioning anything to Margot?

Evangeline hadn't responded yet, but her mom, being an early riser, had fired off a string of increasingly agitated messages Aurora let collect until they came to their inevitable conclusion:

I don't understand. What do you mean sick? How sick?

He can't be sick this week. You have the Emmys.

Wait, you're driving? To Seattle? That's ridiculous!! It's called a plane!! You could be there and back in a day!!!!

If you're coming this way, you better stop by. I want to see you.

Aurora had protested, although meekly: I can't.

Her mom's response was swift and definitive: Yes you can.

The sooner Aurora agreed and got it over with, the sooner she and Zahra could get back on the road. It was the price for taking the 101 so far north, a toll like any other.

She didn't know how to explain that to Zahra. Or that she had her own reason for needing to swing by her mom's before they went on their way.

Aurora sniffled and lifted her sunglasses to her head. No one was going to recognize her on the highway anyway, and the dim dawn light made it impossible to see. That and the inflammation in her eyes. Blinking the irritation away, she poked her pinkie finger at the corner of her itchy, swollen eyelid and stifled a yawn.

She'd barely slept last night, but she wouldn't let her discomfort show. One thing she'd learned from auditioning: never let them see you sweat.

Reflexively, one hand grazed her chin, feeling the rough, raised patch of eczema beneath her makeup. If she didn't get an antihistamine soon, her neck and chest would break out in red splotches, too, and she'd have to pull out the bottle of foundation from her makeup bag to coat her skin the way she had her face. Anything could set off her eczema, and she lived in a constant state of either trying to prevent its appearance or hide the telltale red welts.

Traffic ground to a crawl, and Aurora repressed the desire to accelerate, go as far and as fast as she could. As soon as Margot caught wind of her disappearance, she was going to be in a heap of trouble.

Without thinking, she reached out and swiped her phone, checking for a text from Evangeline. The car bucked under her tight grasp of the wheel.

The movement roused Zahra. "Maybe I should drive. If you're going to be texting."

"I'm not." So her sister was still speaking to her. That was good. That was something. She just had to keep the conversation going. She put her phone out of her mind and swung her thumb over her shoulder toward the cat in the back seat. "What's the little guy's name?"

"Hmm? Oh, him? He doesn't have one."

"Seriously? What do you call him? Cat? He definitely needs a name. What about Fluff?"

"He's not mine to name. But if I did name him, I can assure you it wouldn't be Fluff."

"What do you mean he's not yours? Did we just kidnap a cat?" Aurora feigned a look of horror, but Zahra ignored her.

"He's a stray," she said. "I'm looking out for him, that's all."

"Even a stray deserves a name, doesn't he? I'm gonna call him Fluff."

"Don't you dare."

"Give me something better."

Without responding, Zahra shifted in her seat, bent down, and fiddled with something at her feet. They caught a break in the traffic and began to gain speed.

"Hey," Aurora said, deliberately changing the subject. "Do you remember how you taught me to tie my shoes? A piggyback ride every time I got it right?"

Zahra turned to look up at her, and for a half second, their eyes locked. "I did?"

"Yep. And I taught you how to French braid."

"I don't know how to French braid."

"Well, you did once." Zahra had long, thin fingers. Her nail beds came to rounded points, and Aurora could still remember the gentle way they'd glided over her scalp, so unlike her mom clawing her hair to make a neat part.

"I don't remember." Zahra sat up and shoved something warm and foil wrapped into Aurora's hand. "Breakfast burrito. Or half of one at least."

Zahra had peeled back the foil, and the savory smell sent Aurora's stomach galloping. She normally didn't eat gluten or dairy, but she wouldn't say no. She took a bite, the flavors flooding her palate. "Wow," she said, midchew. She was suddenly ravenous, unable to remember when she'd last eaten. "Is this one of your recipes?"

"It's not a recipe. It's eggs in a tortilla."

"I mean, is it going in your cookbook? Because it's really good. I'd pay for this."

"My cookbook?"

She could feel Zahra's eyes bore into her. "Didn't you tell me once you were working on your own cookbook?"

"It doesn't sound like something I'd share, but I guess I must have." Zahra clicked her small cooler shut. "But it's just a hobby. For my eyes only," she said in a way that told Aurora she was done with conversation.

Aurora didn't take it personally. That's just how Zahra was. All things considered, they were actually off to a promising start. She just needed to get her schedule with Evangeline resolved, make the stop to see her mom, and she'd be golden.

A second later, a short staccato vibration rattled her phone, and she risked a quick glance to see the flash of a Google alert land in her inbox.

Username: Elly Spills All

Bio: Serving tea with a side of hot goss

A close-up of popular video gossip queen Elly Belly with the GlamAnon filter obscuring her facial features appears over an empty green screen.

"Yesterday, *You, Me, Us* hottie Aura Star posted some fun behind-the-scenes pics from her *Vanity Fair* shoot."

The pictures behind Elly change to show Aurora posing for a photographer in front of a white screen, then one where she sticks her tongue out toward the camera.

"Girl looks to be living her best life with a *VF* cover story and the Emmys on the horizon. As she should. Except . . ."

Elly's face takes over the screen as she cups her hand over her mouth conspiratorially.

"An anon source tells me that the shoot was *supposed* to be for both Aura and her *YMU* costar, Serena Kelly, but Serena bailed at the last minute because she had the flu. In case you've been checked out, or I don't know, maybe on one of those holier-than-thou social media hiatuses people are always posting about, both Serena and Aura are going up against each other for the best lead actress Emmy."

Elly moves away from the camera and the picture shows a red-carpet photo of Serena and Aurora standing side by side.

"Even though the two claim to be as close as OG Ben and Matt, I, for one, have never really bought it. I'll repost my original video where I present evidence to prove my theory.

"But anyway, back to today's tea. Anon source says the fake-feuding sisters have real-life drama. Rumor or truth? Consider Exhibit A."

She points to a new picture behind her, one of Serena walking down a nondescript LA street on a sunny day.

"This was taken yesterday afternoon, the very same day as the photoshoot she couldn't make. Hmmm . . . Rather strange to be seen out and about when you're supposedly home sick with the flu. Note, she's clearly been crying. She's all red and blotchy, just like she is when she cries on the show. Then she catches sight of paparazzi . . ."

The green screen image changes to another one of Serena looking directly at the camera.

" . . . and puts on a pair of sunnies. Here's the thing: my source tells me Serena wasn't actually sick, she just didn't want to attend the shoot with Aura. Could this be why they recently postponed filming for *YMU* Season 2? Or something . . . bigger?

"I'll give you one more parting gift to chew on. How about a warm bun in the oven?"

Elly gives a devilish grin. The green screen image changes again. Serena Kelly opens the door to a black car.

"This profile shot of Serena might reveal something I've been wondering since they pushed Season 2 a couple of weeks ago. Could there be a Baby Kelly on the way? Okay, my little amateur internet detectives, do your thing. I'm dying to know what you sleuths dig up."

8

Aurora

It had taken all Aurora's willpower not to look at her phone while they drove. All her willpower and Zahra's watchful company. After pulling into the Target parking lot, she'd begged off coming inside and asked Zahra to grab her a box of dark-brown hair dye, the wash-out kind. Zahra had raised an eyebrow at the request but didn't ask any questions.

The second Zahra passed through the automatic glass doors into the store, Aurora had swiped open her phone. She'd been waiting to see if the new alert she'd set up caught anything new about the blind item. Her chest fluttered with nerves as she'd read the top headline: *You, Me, Us* Sister Drama: Does Serena Kelly Have a Secret? The link led her to a celeb gossip forum, one of those shadowy hostile places on the internet she'd avoided since making a name for herself, where someone had posted a video from a popular social site and a user whose name Aurora vaguely recognized.

By the time Zahra strode back toward the car, Aurora had watched the video a half dozen times. At the sight of her sister, Aurora quickly closed her browser and jammed her phone into its holder. But her ears buzzed, her sweaty palms slipped against the steering wheel.

Speculation about the nature of her friendship with Serena was nothing new, but a pregnancy rumor?

It wasn't true, obviously. It couldn't be, but no one except her, Dillon, and Serena could know that. The photog had caught Serena looking a little bloated after a bout of stomach flu. Aurora knew how easily pictures could mislead. Yet the timing, on the heels of the blind item, felt significant, a foreshadowing she couldn't quite push from her mind.

A fuse had been lit, and she had no doubt something would blow. But what?

The question sparked its own panicky explosion inside her, and the fallout nearly made her want to spill the whole thing to Zahra.

But she could never do that—risk pushing Zahra further away—not when she finally had her so close.

They'd never talked about it openly before, but based on various barbed asides Zahra had made over the years, Aurora sensed her sister took particular offense to the fact that their dad's relationship with Lucy, and Aurora's conception, had begun while he was still a married man. If Aurora confided about her relationship with Dillon, she could easily picture Zahra connecting imaginary dots, sticking Aurora in the same lowly category as she put Aurora's mom. Even though it wasn't at all the same. For one thing, Dillon didn't have a kid. And Aurora was nothing like her mom. But the details wouldn't matter to Zahra, of that Aurora was certain.

As her sister neared the car, Aurora hit the button to open the hatchback. The second the door started to lift, the cat leaped and bounded toward the opening as if he'd been waiting for his chance to escape.

"Shit, shit."

She hit the button again, then winced, envisioning him getting caught by the door coming down. Luckily, his injured paw slowed him, and he'd only just made it to the wayback before the door clicked into place.

Zahra jerked open the rear passenger door. "What the hell?"

The cat's movement unleashed a wave of dander that clogged Aurora's lungs, and she coughed into her fist. "Sorry," she choked out, unsure if she was apologizing for opening the door in the first place or closing it before Zahra could get there.

"Come on, cat," Zahra said, lifting him. His legs splayed out in protest as she struggled to get him into the top of the small carrier she'd bought. "He won't go."

"It's fine," Aurora said. "We'll deal with it when we get to my mom's."

Back in the front seat, Zahra dropped an armful of items on the console. Aurora grabbed the allergy medicine, tore open the box, and popped the blister pack. She swallowed a pill dry, then gestured at a cat collar and leash. "Bold move."

"It was either that or setting up a litter box in your car," Zahra said. "Which would you prefer?"

"No, I mean, it's smart."

It was only as they got back on the freeway that Zahra spoke again. "I know I don't know anything about Hollywood, but isn't it really weird that an Emmy-nominated actor would box-dye her hair a few days before the big night?"

The last two words were spoken with a hint of apprehension. But before Aurora could respond, a text from Evangeline flashed on her phone, then a series of others:

Good one.

Wait, you're joking, right?

Oh my God, you're not joking, are you?

A second later her phone began to ring.

Gunning the SUV up the hill that led to her mom's house, Aurora tried to ignore the live wire that tangled its way through her chest the same way she'd ignored the call from Evangeline—and the two that immediately followed. She couldn't have that conversation in front of Zahra. It would have to wait until she could get a minute alone. A "low mileage" warning message flashed on the car's display, and Zahra flung a finger toward it.

"What does that mean? The car's running out of power?" she asked. "Don't we need a full charge to make it to Santa Cruz?"

"Don't worry; it's fine," Aurora said, tapping the screen to close the message. "The censor's faulty or something. It's been doing that off and on for a few weeks." The car was close enough to fully charged, but either way, they'd have to stop to charge along the way. She should look up a good place to stop. Before the reminder could take root in her mind, another text from Evangeline appeared.

So sorry to bother you, but would you mind calling me when you can?

Aurora took a deep breath through her nose, counted to four. Released, counted to four. Took another.

"Why are you breathing like that?" Zahra asked. "Are you okay?"

"Good," Aurora chirped, pulling into her mom's driveway. She cut the engine and hopped from the car to prove just how good she was, but Zahra didn't follow.

"I'll wait here."

"You sure?"

Zahra nodded. Fine, Aurora would leave her to stew. She would have liked to hide in the car, too, but here was her penance for driving instead of flying—for booking out of her life when she had no business going anywhere—and she was about to be in for a serious show of contrition.

"It'll be quick," she told Zahra, wondering if she could get away with leaving the dye in her hair for half the time.

"Mom," she called as she stepped through the unlocked front door, her voice lost among the house's clutter.

Her mom had bought this place shortly after Aurora signed with Margot, around the time Aurora had moved into her own apartment. Whereas Aurora had hired a decorator and asked that everything be kept as simple and clean as possible, her mom dove into the project of interior decorating with the zeal she'd applied to Aurora's growing career. The result was a busy collection of competing colors and textures that made Aurora's heart sink every time she saw it, a painful pity for her mother she couldn't quite understand and didn't want to examine, preferring to tuck it under one of the thick Turkish carpets her mother called "classy."

"Mom!" she tried again, making her way toward the kitchen.

A door opened and shut down the hall, the slap of slippered steps followed. Aurora turned to greet her mom, gritting her teeth while she smiled.

Her mom pulled her into a hug, her head tucked near Aurora's chin, her arms nearly cleaving Aurora in two.

"You shouldn't be here," Lucy said as they came apart, smoothing her white V-neck shirt and picking a piece of lint from Aurora's sweatshirt in one fluid motion. "I know you must have something better to do."

Her mom always had an uncanny way of saying so much without saying much at all. After a bad audition, she never spoke an unkind word to Aurora, never demanded to know why she hadn't done better. It was, "You tried your best," delivered deadpan. From her dad, those words could have sounded encouraging, but her mom stated them as a sad fact.

Lucy stomped into the kitchen and Aurora followed. She recognized the light-wash ankle jeans her mom wore, a recent hand-me-down. Her mom lived in Aurora's old clothes. Home decor notwithstanding, Lucy hated to shop, preferring to wear whatever Aurora didn't want anymore, her middle-aged figure trim enough to squeeze into Aurora's size-small wardrobe.

In the kitchen, Lucy opened a cabinet. "You want a Nespresso?"

"I'm not staying too long, okay?"

"If you're here now, let's have a proper visit. I haven't seen you at all lately." Her mom popped a Nespresso pod into the machine, hit a button, and took a long, appraising look at her.

"Why do you look all . . . puffy? Have you been eating dairy again?"

Aurora's jaw tightened. The kitchen smelled like stale coffee and something sickeningly familiar, the cloying tang of her mom's perfume and cut melon rotting in the trash. "I saw you last week."

"*Pfft.* That was barely a full lunch."

"I have something I need to do real quick, and then we have to get back on the road."

The Nespresso machine hissed as Lucy pulled a bottle of almond milk creamer from the fridge. "Who the hell's 'we'?"

"Me and Zahra. We're driving together. She's waiting in the car."

Lucy shook her head, aghast. "So this seems like the appropriate week for a little scenic excursion, does it? This week of all weeks. I can't believe Margot would sanction this."

"She didn't, exactly."

Her mom's eyes grew wide. "What? You didn't tell her?" She lifted her phone. "I'm calling her right now. We need to—"

"Mom, no. Please. You promised you'd back off for a while."

"Right, so you could learn to manage things yourself. This joyride is hardly evidence of sound business judgment. Why have we worked so hard for so many years if you're willing to sabotage yourself when we're *this close*"—she pinched her thumb and pointer finger together—"to finally achieving something?"

Aurora's confidence wavered. Her mom had officially stepped down as Aurora's manager when they hired Margot, but the choice had been Lucy's, calculated ahead of time. She'd been the one to screen and vet replacement of high-level managers, to negotiate the contract. Her mom didn't technically make business decisions anymore, but she didn't have to. Her influence was like the bracing winds that whipped across the Grapevine on I-5. You didn't have to see her influence to feel its power.

"I'm not sabotaging anything. It's not like I asked Dad to call me. He needs me."

"Oh, he does, does he? What about when we needed him? Where was he then?"

Aurora gripped the counter for support. She knew what her mom was referring to, and she hated to talk about it, hated to think of her dad as a criminal just because he'd made one—admittedly illegal—mistake. It didn't match the idea she had of him, and the inconsistency was like the eczema that blighted her otherwise smooth skin. But no matter how much Aurora avoided the topic, her mom couldn't let it go. It wasn't enough to have divorced him and moved her and Aurora eleven hundred miles south to Southern California; she had to keep bringing it up, ten years later.

"Mom, stop. He served his time, and he did his best under the circumstances. Can't you finally forgive him? He's sick."

But Lucy either didn't hear her or didn't care.

"Your father is a felon, Aurora. And you're a fool when it comes him. You still put him on a pedestal. And as for Zahra . . ."

"What about her?" Aurora's heart thrummed. Maybe Zahra was right, maybe her mom didn't like her. But Lucy shook her head and sighed, the aggression leaking away.

"I know you want a relationship with her, but it's not happening. If she was gonna come around, she would have already."

Aurora let the words fall over her but didn't react. Her mom came to stand in front of her, cupped her cheek.

"You always see the best in people, honey. It's a gift. But you can't expect to rely on other people like you can on me." Her mom broke away, her voice hardening again. "Not everyone has your interests at heart."

"My interests?"

"Yeah, you know. Your priorities. Your career."

The sound of the front door slamming startled them both, cutting their conversation short.

"Hello?" Zahra's voice called into the ensuing silence.

9

Zahra

The leash had been a big fat fail.

Zahra had managed to get the harness around the cat's chicken-boned body okay and clipped on the leash without issue, but when she placed the cat on the ground, he wouldn't budge. Even a gray squirrel zipping up the knotted oak tree that hung over the front yard didn't draw his attention.

But the leash had been the least of her dumb decisions that morning. If she'd known she'd wind up outside her former stepmother's home, she never would have agreed to drive with Aurora at all.

The house was one of those Spanish Colonials with terra-cotta tiles on the roof and a creamy exterior with arched windows—a home too large for any single person but befitting Lucy's personality. She'd always cared about appearances. Another reason Zahra could never understand her appeal. She was nothing like Zahra's mother, Nasrin, who preferred an unassuming life, the pleasure of a home-cooked meal, the company of the same good friends. But maybe that difference *was* Lucy's appeal. Dom had clearly wanted a different life, a different sort of wife. A different type of daughter.

It's not that her stepmom had been all bad. In her own way, she'd tried to keep Zahra content during her visits to Seattle, dragging her to the nail salon and sending her back to California with an assortment of new clothes, even if they were things Zahra would never wear. And she'd never been outright mean. It was more like she found Zahra's existence a nuisance, a built-in cabinet original to her home she had no use for, taking up valuable space. Zahra had been well aware of what an inconvenience she was in her dad's new life, and Lucy had only made it worse.

"C'mon, cat. Just walk," Zahra said, launching into a string of cutesy kitty talk that embarrassed her.

When words of encouragement didn't work, she carried him to various parts of the yard. The immaculate lawn, a river of wood chips flanking a bed of flowers, a pile of round white rocks beneath a small faucet. But he sat impassively wherever she put him as if he were waiting for her to figure out the error of her ways.

Eventually, she filled his dish with water from the tap. He lapped languorously, but then, once again, took a seat. Maybe he just didn't have to go. Maybe the litter box would have been a better idea.

But he was an outdoor cat, for God's sake, half-feral; this shouldn't be asking too much.

The leash must have been to blame. The indignity. He'd been tricked into this road trip, just like Zahra.

It didn't take impressive deduction skills to assume the oversize house had a backyard to match, enough room for the cat to roam, do his business. The side gate was locked. Zahra stuck him back in the car and barreled her way to the front door, annoyed at the hassle, at her impulsive decision to bring the cat in the first place.

The door was ajar, but she knocked anyway, waited, then knocked again.

"Hello?" she said, tentatively, as she pushed the door open. The entryway had a two-story ceiling, but despite its size was somehow cluttered and gaudy as hell. The heavy rug covering the softwood floor absorbed the sound of her steps, and she was about to call out again when she heard Aurora's voice. "Can't you finally forgive him? He's sick."

She went still, strained to hear more. As she listened, the excessive decor took on an eerie edge, like she'd stepped into a fun house. It wasn't that she disagreed with Lucy's opinion of her father, obviously. It was the opposite. That they shared any set of beliefs was wrong somehow, off-putting, a disturbing blip in the space-time continuum. It frazzled Zahra's synapses, made her want to distance herself from the connection. Made her want to—of all unimaginable things—come to her father's defense.

But she couldn't announce herself now, crouched as she was in the entryway, eavesdropping.

When she heard her own name, her body went rigid. She scurried away, opened the front door and closed it with a slam.

"Hello?" she shouted, louder than necessary. The voices stopped at once, and a moment later, both Aurora and Lucy found her standing with her back against the front door.

"Zahra," Lucy said. "Hi."

"Hi," Zahra said, training her eyes on Aurora. "Can I take the cat into the backyard? The leash isn't—"

"What?" Lucy snapped. "You're traveling with a cat? No wonder you look so awful," she said to Aurora.

Aurora gave her mom a look. "Go ahead," she told Zahra.

"Don't bring it through the house." Lucy glared at Zahra as if everything were her fault, as if she were the one who roped Aurora into this stupid plan and not the other way around. Just like old times during Zahra's visits to Seattle when she'd get stuck babysitting while Lucy ran errands, then end up in trouble because Aurora had talked her into serving ice cream for lunch or pulling out every one of the hundred dolls she owned. Whose fault was it she had so much stuff? "You can go around to the side gate. I'll unlock it."

Lucy led Zahra through the side yard with the flick of a wrist, as if Zahra was hired help.

The quiet backyard was as huge as Zahra had guessed, but less excessive than the rest of the house. She dropped the cat beneath a purple tree heavy with shiny plums.

Sensing Lucy's appraising gaze on the side of her face, she turned to find the woman standing only a few feet away.

"So how've you been?" Lucy said, and then in the same breath, "Still in LA, I take it. Still cooking? New someone in the picture? It's been a while."

Of course she knew Zahra had divorced, but did she really have to bring it up? Leave it to Lucy to poke Zahra right in the sensitive bits under the guise of pleasantries.

"I'm doing well, thanks. Yes, I'm cooking, and no, no . . . anyone." Zahra kept her attention on the cat as he prowled the yard. She didn't want him getting any ideas about hopping the fence, and she had no patience for small talk.

"That's too bad. But you're still young from where I'm standing. There are other fish."

"I'd rather be alone."

"*Pfft.* You always were your father's daughter."

"We're nothing alike," Zahra bit back.

Unfazed, Lucy chuckled. "I remember on your visits how you'd show up all sullen and moody. Dom used to say, 'I'll cheer her up,' and even in the early years, I knew it was a lost cause. I could see how deep you'd dug in your heels. But still, he was like, 'Just watch me.' He'd drag you everywhere to try and impress you: Space Needle, fish sandwiches." She waved a hand in the air. "And later it was all those fancy restaurants, whatever everyone was talking about. But either you flat-out refused or else you went and came home even angrier than before. Do you remember that?"

Before this conversation, Zahra would have said she didn't remember, that she couldn't recall a single outing her father had taken her on in Seattle, but Lucy had jarred her memory. There had been a few times, dinners out with just her dad, at restaurants so upscale they made her feel awkward and embarrassed, with their white tablecloths and varying-size forks and soft music. The last types of places she'd wanted to go. Though she understood now they must have been the highest-reviewed restaurants in the city, the places her dad read about in the newspaper.

"And then, of course," Lucy continued, "that left Dom the moody one, stomping around the house, working long hours even though you only had a few days before you left. I swear, you guys were opposite sides of the same tug rope."

Despite her desire to ice Lucy out, Zahra was drawn in, the words escaping before she could stop them, words she'd wanted to say for a long while—and when would she ever have another chance? "Didn't you feel guilty, stealing a father from his daughter?"

Zahra might have expected Lucy to deny stealing anyone at all, to attack Zahra for implying that Dom hadn't walked away from his first family of his own free will. Instead, she said without a hint of derision or, for that matter, guilt, "I stole a father *for* my daughter. That's the difference. And it wasn't the deal I thought it'd be. I can tell you that."

It came back to Zahra then that the last time she'd seen Lucy was right before her dad surrendered himself to the Northern California Federal Correctional Institution, where he faced a nine-month incarceration for securities fraud. Zahra and her husband, Wes, had just relocated to San Francisco so he could take a new tech job and she could finally start at the Culinary Institute of America in Napa, but she'd made the time to take the rare trip to Seattle to see her dad, to say her goodbyes, so to speak.

Perhaps part of her also wanted to make sense of why a man who'd always put his career first—who'd often bored Zahra talking about his "fiduciary responsibility" to his clients with the air of a peacock fluffing his feathers—would do something so catastrophic. But there had been no great revelation.

The visit had been stilted and uncomfortable: Dom waffling between pretending his impending prison time wasn't imminent and making light of the whole thing, as if daring anyone to call his bluff; Aurora her usual upbeat self, the audience to their dad's jokes, the fill-in entertainment when the jokes grew stale; and Lucy in an attention-seeking state of disbelief that should have come with a fainting couch and a bottle of smelling salts. Zahra had hardly been surprised when Lucy filed for divorce only days after his sentence began.

"Look," Lucy said. "My job is to look out for Aurora. I don't know what she's told you, but for the record, this is an important week for her."

"I gather that," Zahra said. "But I'm not the one who asked her to drive with me. This was her idea. *For the record.*"

It took all Zahra's fortitude not to point out that Aurora was a twenty-five-year-old adult and perfectly capable of looking out for herself. She let the silence grow thick and heavy until Lucy finally broke. "I'll go see what's taking Aurora."

The cat tiptoed through a bed of blazing-yellow black-eyed Susans, stopped to sniff the ground. Lucy pointed at him as she walked away. "Do not let that creature shit in my flower beds."

As if on cue, as soon as Lucy was out of sight, the cat squatted for a moment, then kicked at the dirt with his back legs.

Oops. Zahra smiled, just a little.

10

Aurora

Aurora used the guest bedroom's en suite to set the dye in her hair. She had to sacrifice one of the robin's-egg blue hand towels her mom had stacked on a shelf, but oh well. She and Zahra would be back on the road by the time Lucy saw its stained carnage.

She roped her thick hair on top of her head with a clip, dug out a shower cap from beneath the sink, and put it over her head, the chemicals tickling her nose. At least the antihistamines were working. The itch had gone from her eyes and lungs, and the redness had faded to an unpleasant shade of pink.

Zahra was right. Coloring her hair wasn't the smartest choice right before the Emmys. Or at all. Aurora wasn't supposed to change her hair while under contract for *You, Me, Us*. But it was temporary. Her colorist would kill her, but she could fix it. And Dillon *had* told her she couldn't be seen. Aside from her face, her hair was her most recognizable asset. Glasses, hat, and dark hair, and no one would be the wiser. If it meant proving to Dillon how serious she was about making their relationship work, she'd do just about anything.

Hiding in the bathroom, Aurora sank to the side of the tub and returned Evangeline's phone call.

After a single ring, her assistant answered, high pitched and in a tizzy. "Thank you so much for calling. Okay, so I can book a flight from Seattle to LAX for Friday afternoon, and I've been going through your schedule. Some things are easy to move. Like I can push your dress fitting to Friday evening—"

"That's great." Aurora caught sight of herself in the mirror, the shower cap blooming over her head like some kind of spotted mushroom. "Oh. I'll also need an appointment for my hair."

"It's already on the schedule for Sunday. Emmy-morning prep, right?"

"No, I need color, too."

"Um, okay," Evangeline said, sounding confused. "I guess I can carve out time on Saturday. But there are some other things that I don't think I can—*should*—move without letting Margot know."

Aurora sighed. It was delusional to think her manager of all people wouldn't find out she'd left LA, but she couldn't deal with that now. The longer she could hold off, the better.

"Tell Margot's assistant if you absolutely have to, but just say I'm sick or something. Be vague."

The sound of her mom's calls reached the room.

"I don't know if—"

"Look. I trust you, okay? You'll handle it. You always do. Gotta go," she said, slipping back into the bedroom and shutting the bathroom door behind her, hopefully trapping the worst of the dye's smell. "Text me if it's an emergency."

"But—"

She ended the call right as her mom stepped into the bedroom.

"There you are." Lucy cocked her head and sniffed. "What is that?"

"Just a hair mask."

"It doesn't smell like a mask. It smells like—"

"It's specially formulated to . . . revive," Aurora lied.

She took a seat on the bed, and Lucy joined her.

"Well, it *was* looking a little lifeless. *You're* looking a little lifeless, honey. Are you okay?" Despite her word choice, her mom spoke with unexpected warmth. Aurora knew it wouldn't last; her mom's soft side went as quickly as it came. But for a moment, she imagined what it would be like to have the sort of mom she could talk to—not just regurgitating stories and parsing gossip and discussing logistics, but real talk, the emotions Aurora kept stored inside. The truth about Dillon.

The notion was impossible. Her mom would go off. She'd start obsessing about the potential damage to Aurora's career. She'd organize a ten-point plan to fix the problem, and she'd definitely loop in Margot. She'd never grant Aurora a smidge of personal freedom again.

"I'm fine," she said. "It's just . . . I know how you feel about him, but I'm worried about Dad. He doesn't sound like himself."

"Of course you are. I know I was harsh before, because I'm thinking about you, not him. This week is so important for you; I don't want anything to derail it."

Aurora opened her mouth to speak, but her mom raised her hand. "No, I get it, okay? Let's not rehash that argument. You're on your way, and there's nothing I can say to stop you." She paused. "Is there?"

"Sorry."

"In that case, there's something I need you to do."

Aurora looked up, curious. She hoped her mom would ask her to tell her dad something from the heart, like the corny things she used to overhear them say to each other when she was really little. She wanted to convey this message of forgiveness to her dad; she wanted to be the one to bring him this good thing. "Sure," she said. "What?"

"Since it's on your way, I need you to stop by Hannah's new restaurant in Ojai. It's their soft opening this week, and you know how hard they've been working to get it off the ground. Any publicity would be huge for them."

Hannah was her mother's best friend, although Aurora didn't think Lucy had any others. They'd both gone straight to Hollywood from Washington state after graduating high school. Neither had succeeded as an actress for a whole bunch of reasons—ones outside their control naturally. Reasons Lucy would list for anyone who exhibited the slightest interest. "But I applied everything I learned to Aurora's career," her mother would say with a kind of rueful joy.

"Seriously?" Aurora could feel the dye sinking into her sensitive skin. Her scalp began to itch, and she resisted the urge to bring her nails to her head.

"I'd never ask otherwise, but the timing is perfect. Since you're already headed that direction . . . ," Lucy said, as if the request were Aurora's own fault. "What's another hour or two?"

But it wasn't the extra time Aurora was worried about. "I can't have my photo taken right now."

Her mom gave her an odd look, and Aurora realized her misstep. "With the Emmys, it's too much right now."

Lucy seemed to accept this answer, chewed it over for a moment. "That's fine. They'll get a quote about how delicious the food is, take a photo to post on their social channels next week, after the Emmys. You'll create a little local buzz, that's it."

Aurora hated when her mom asked her for these kinds of favors, but this was the first time every cell screamed at her to refuse. The timing was, in fact, all wrong.

The itch beneath Aurora's hair had evolved into a harsh burn, the heat building with each second. She had another fifteen minutes to wait for the dye to set, but she didn't think she could bear it much longer. She could practically feel the eczema rising from her epidermis like a fungus beneath her mushroom cap.

"Can I tell Hannah you'll be there soon?"

Aurora couldn't think straight anymore. The burn was too much. Her scalp ready to burst into red flames, she gave in. "Okay, sure." She was never really going to say no anyway.

Lucy's flash of a smile gave way to a grimace. Her nostrils flared. "Okay, seriously, what in the hell is that smell?"

Aurora couldn't take another second. She rushed into the bathroom, her mom barreling in behind her.

"What did you do?" she shrieked as Aurora dove toward the tub's faucet.

11

Zahra

Back on the highway, Zahra sensed they'd both barely made it out of there in one piece. Beside her, Aurora's eyes were trained on the road, her mood more subdued than it had been earlier that morning, or maybe it seemed that way because she'd managed to go a whole five minutes without talking.

God, her hair. Zahra still couldn't get used to it, seeing Aurora's golden hair transformed to a muted, shoe-leather brown.

She didn't actually care why Aurora wanted to color her hair with cheap, store-bought dye when surely she had the best hairstylists at her beck and call, but it was odd.

Still, Zahra gave her credit for a bold choice, and for the effect it had on her mom.

Lucy had feigned a heart attack, literally gripping her chest in horror as she walked them out to the car. "What have you done to yourself?" But Aurora just laughed, kissed her mom on the cheek as if it were all a prank.

Watching them closely as they climbed back into the Beast, Lucy's eyes narrowed. "You've never looked more alike," she'd said, not intending the sentiment as a compliment to either one of them.

But that was Lucy. How Aurora could bear to have her mom so enmeshed in her life, Zahra could never understand. All she knew was that it had been a bad idea to stop there, and she'd have taken satisfaction in being right if it weren't for the aching pit in her stomach she'd come away with.

They trudged through morning rush hour. Music Zahra didn't even recognize dribbled through the speakers. She pulled out her phone. Now that they were finally on their way, she needed to text her mom.

I'm coming home for the night. I have Aurora with me. It's a long story. I'll tell you about it when we get there.

That was good enough for now. Her mom wouldn't need to know more. She wasn't like Lucy. A minute later her phone vibrated, a long text filled her screen.

That's a surprise! But the timing's great. There's something I want to tell you too. I have a class tonight. Maybe you can join?

Zahra read the words twice. What could her mom possibly have to tell her?

As far as Zahra knew, nothing had changed for her mom in over a decade. Not since Zahra's grandparents had died when Zahra was in college and her mom finally had the time and money, a small chunk left to her from her parents, to build out a kitchen studio in the backyard. Nothing fancy, it was mostly IKEA cabinets and cupboards, but big enough to accommodate a small group of cooking students with room for their own workstations. Nasrin lived in the same Northern California college beach town her parents had moved to from Iran when she was sixteen, in the same house she'd grown up in. She had the same couple of friends. Walked the same route around the neighborhood every evening.

Her mom had still been a young woman when Dom left them, but it was like she'd decided she'd had enough drama for a lifetime. Within a year of him leaving, Nasrin had moved both her and twelve-year-old Zahra back to her parents' house, where the mornings smelled like sea life and the fog hung around like a shroud, and let her life shrink down to the basics. Zahra admired the way her mother had tucked the blankets in on the bed of her life and hospital-folded the corners.

Now what? She shoved the question from her mind, ignored the request to join her mom's cooking class, and tapped out a response: Just south of Ventura. See you later this afternoon.

They probably had another solid five hours without any more stops. It seemed they were fully committed to taking 101 and sticking to the coast for a while, instead of the more efficient but hideous I-5. Fine. Zahra could live with that. Except—

"Wait, wait. Where are you going?" she nearly shouted as Aurora veered off 101.

"Uh, I have to make a quick stop." Aurora spoke as if coming out of a stupor, as if she weren't the one behind the wheel, as if she hadn't already made a quote, unquote quick stop. "My mom's friend has a restaurant opening in Ojai this week or something. She asked me to go, as a show of support, I guess. To be honest, I'm not totally sure."

"And you didn't think to mention it to me?"

"I just didn't wanna stress you out. But it's basically on the way, and it's still early. We have plenty of time to get to Santa Cruz."

Zahra's molars caught against each other; her whole skull felt tight, her throat constricting with frustration. "It's not *on the way* if it means going a different way than the way we were going."

"I just meant it's in the same direction."

"The direction being north? Because there's a lot north of here, like most of the continent."

Zahra kept her eyes glued to the passing scenery, but she had half a mind to demand that Aurora pull over, leave her on the side of the road. She'd call a rideshare; she'd hitchhike if she had to. Well, she wouldn't go that far, but a part of her wanted to, to prove she wouldn't be strung along like some kind of groupie.

"There are things I want to do at my mom's. I had a plan," she protested. She didn't have to work on the Caesar dressing, and her grandmother's recipe book wasn't going anywhere, but Aurora's lack of consideration needled her. She felt tricked, again, by another one of Aurora's so-called white lies, in this case, a lie of omission.

"I know, okay? I'm really sorry," Aurora said. "But my mom needed me to do this."

"And you couldn't tell her no?"

The car jutted over a dip in the road, and they both bounced in their seats. "You might find it interesting."

Zahra turned and glared. "I won't."

Aurora continued as if she hadn't heard. "So Hannah, my mom's friend—did you ever meet her? Anyway, she ended up marrying this old legit rock-star guy, like one of the really old ones with the big hair. But now he's a restauranteur, I guess."

"Restaurateur, not restaurant-er."

"Whatever."

"And every old rocker is a restaurateur now."

Aurora shrugged. "It's a free meal, at least."

As it happened, Zahra never trusted a free meal.

12

Zahra

The restaurant was in a wooden building that was either old and warmly worn or built new to look that way. It was so hard to tell these days. A hand-painted sign above the open door aptly read Out of the Way Café. They tromped inside, Aurora in her trucker hat and oversize sunglasses, somehow looking nothing like herself and still like a movie star, and Zahra lugging the carrier against her hip because she wasn't about to leave the cat in the car when the inland morning air had already begun to heat.

"I can temp-control the car," Aurora had said when Zahra explained why she was bringing the cat.

Of course she could. The Beast was a spa on four wheels. But Zahra stubbornly dragged the carrier—and the cat—with them.

The café was exactly the kind of place Zahra hated: faux wood everything and mason jars everywhere, customers parked at about half the wobbly-looking tables, waiting on food or service or both. Not a great sign.

Aurora approached the hostess stand. "Hey, there. We're here to see Hannah. She's expecting us."

"Oh! Hi!" The young woman who stood by the desk perked up immediately, her eyes studying Aurora's face. "She just ran out to talk with a vendor, but she told me to seat you when you got here. Is that alright?"

Aurora agreed, and they tucked themselves at a corner two-top that offered a pretty good view of the dining room. There were two sets of older couples, a group of middle-aged women, what looked to be a younger mom-and-daughter duo, and a single guy, dark haired, head dipped over his phone and a heavy-duty camera hanging from his neck. Zahra noted him, and then without her permission, her eyes swiveled back in his direction to get a second look.

"Can I get you something to drink? I have strict instructions to take real good care of you two, so just tell me if you need absolutely anything at all whatsoever," the hostess said.

"Hmm . . ." Aurora glanced over the menu. "Just a peach iced tea. No sweetener."

"I'll try the strawberry lemonade," Zahra said. "And one of the cardamom date milkshakes."

The woman nodded and hurried away. Aurora looked around while Zahra fiddled with a glass jar set with a fake tealight. The cat meowed.

"It's cute," Aurora said, after assessing the room.

"That's not a compliment."

"Yes, it is."

Zahra sat back in her chair and crossed her arms. "Food isn't meant to be cute," she said.

"Oh yeah? What about cake pops and marzipan and bento boxes . . ."

The guy set down his phone and scanned his camera's screen. His arms were strong and tan, his tendons moving each time his fingers tapped the camera's buttons. He was the most out-of-place person in the joint, but he looked like he owned it, like he'd never been more comfortable.

"It should be passionate," Zahra said. "Intimate, maybe, but not precious. Simple, but never basic, you know? It's desire. It's . . . lusty, even. Satisfying. That's what it should be. But it should demand your attention, too. The best bites are the ones you're not expecting, the ones that give you a taste of something you didn't even know you wanted until—"

"Oh my God." Aurora tipped her head toward Zahra's, her voice at a high whisper. "Are you staring at that guy?"

Realizing she was, Zahra jerked her head in the other direction. "What? No."

"Yes, you were." Aurora laughed. "You like him."

"What are you, twelve? How could I possibly like someone I've never spoken to?"

Aurora looked him over, but the guy was oblivious, or at least appeared to be glued to the contents of his camera. "He's a snack for sure," she said with an approving nod.

Suddenly his head turned, and for a brief second, he and Zahra locked eyes. Her heart rate jumped as his mouth slipped into a grin, his eyes squinting closed. Then just as quickly, he looked back at his camera.

Aurora began to snicker. "He totally just checked you out."

"He did not." Zahra picked up the food menu, but the words swam across her vision.

"Did too."

Before they could go back and forth again, the hostess appeared with their drinks.

"Milkshake's on the way," she offered. "Can I get you anything else?"

"Sure," Zahra said, scanning the menu, forcing herself to focus so that her heartbeat would slow. "I'll try the burger and the chicken sandwich. The carrot soup sounds interesting. And I'll do the Caesar, too."

Aurora gave up her menu. "I'll share with her." As soon as the hostess was gone, she said, "You just ate half a burrito. How hungry could you be?"

"I like to try things. It's research."

Tasting her lemonade, Zahra decided it was a touch too sweet but at least fresh. She stirred the muddled bits of strawberry at the bottom and most definitely didn't look at the guy.

A moment later, a woman with white-blond hair tied into a high ponytail beelined to their table.

"I'm sorry I'm late, hon," she said as she approached, bringing Zahra's milkshake with her. Aurora stood and the two hugged. "So good of you to stop by, what with your schedule and"—she hid her mouth behind her hands—"the Emmys." Before Aurora could respond, the woman turned to Zahra. "You must be the sister."

"Half sister," Zahra said. "And you must be the owner."

The woman winked. "Half owner."

As soon as the introductions were over, Hannah hooked her arm over Aurora's shoulder and pulled her aside. While she slurped her milkshake, Zahra heard Hannah say, "I have a friend who works for the *Santa Barbara Gazette*. I know if you'd give her a quote, she'd do something fun with it. You could just say how much you love everything. How it's the place to be if you're ever in Ojai, that sort of thing. Listen to me, feeding *you* lines. I'm sure you'll say it so much better than I ever could." Hannah laughed. "Gosh, I can't get over your hair. Gorgeous. But what a surprise! Your mom must be beside herself. You pull it off, though. You really do."

Zahra coughed and reached for her throbbing temples as the cold ice cream caught up with her. How could Aurora stand this kind of interaction? The fawning, the manipulation, the ass-kissing. It was so fake, and that's what Aurora looked like, standing there with an uneasy grin on her face: as fake as could be. The whole thing made Zahra recoil, and at the same time, an uncomfortable impulse to speak up on Aurora's behalf overcame her. Suddenly queasy, she shoved her milkshake away.

❦

By the time Aurora and Hannah had floated away, Hannah saying something about giving the full tour, Zahra had downed her lemonade.

"Another?" the server asked when she dropped off the food. Zahra nodded and jammed her napkin on her lap.

The burger was overdone, but the miso caramelized onions were a nice touch, if not a little cloying. She took a single bite of the chicken sandwich and immediately knew it was too dry and underseasoned to warrant another. She pushed it away as if it didn't deserve a place on the table.

Next, she dipped into the soup, a silky carrot-curry broth enrobing thin slices of tender carrots, with a refreshing layer of cilantro and scallions on top. She liked the flavor, but it wanted heat and acid. "Way more lime," she muttered under her breath. Finally, the Caesar. She'd liked the sound of the crispy capers and enjoyed the pop of them on her tongue, but it was like most Caesars: ho-hum.

She pulled out her phone and opened her recording app: "A Caesar needs unexpected crunch. Not croutons. Too obvious. Try a pangrattato in place. Maybe flavored with . . ."—she searched for an idea—"za'atar? The floral-herbal flavor of the blend could be good with the preserved lemon dressing."

"Sounds delicious," a voice said, catching her off guard.

Beside the table's edge, someone knelt to peek into the cat carrier. Not someone. Him. The guy!

She choked down the last bite of macerated romaine in her mouth and eked out the final drop of lemonade to dislodge any green bits from between her teeth. He smiled up at her, his eyes crinkled with amusement.

"Sorry. I was saying hello to your cat, but I couldn't help overhear you . . ." He cocked his head.

Not that it was any of his business, but she gestured to her phone. "I'm recording notes."

"About the food?"

"Sort of."

"Are you a food critic?"

"God, no."

"A chef?"

She shook her head.

The server returned with her second lemonade, and she gulped at the drink as if it were a lifeline. Now was his opportunity to walk away.

"I love cats," he said. "Dogs too. But I'm not home enough to have a pet. Mind if I pet him—or her?"

"Him," she said. And taking that as permission, the guy pulled out the chair Aurora had sat in only a few minutes before and cracked open the carrier a few inches to make contact. The cat began purring at once.

"Is he yours or your . . . friend's?"

"She's not my friend." She chided herself for sounding like a catty schoolgirl. "Half sister."

He zipped up the carrier and pressed his palms to the table, but he didn't move to leave. He just sat there, camera hanging around his neck, calling attention to where it rested against his broad chest. She averted her gaze to the sad chicken sandwich, the arugula wilting out the sides. She'd completely lost sight of Aurora, and they really should get back on the road.

When her gaze landed on him, his eyes did the funny-perfect squint thing again, and the right side of his mouth hitched into a smile. God dammit. Why was he so good looking? Why was he sitting at her table? Best to nip things in the bud.

"Just so you know," she said, "I'm not interested."

He laughed, lifted the camera's strap over his head, his sleeve snaking up toward his shoulder, revealing a line of ink twirling like a chain and disappearing beneath the fabric of his shirt. She followed it with her eyes as far as she could, then looked away fast. She was a sucker for a little ink. Not too much, nothing like the chefs she'd met over the years, full sleeves on every limb, but something small and meaningful. "Interested in what, exactly?"

"You. Anyone, for that matter."

"Lucky for us, the feeling's mutual." He held up his camera. "I'm a travel photographer. Settling down isn't really my thing."

That explained the camera. She asked him why he was there, and he told her he was on assignment for a magazine, a feature about driving from SoCal to Southern Oregon. While he spoke, she couldn't stop staring at his features, the perfectly just-crooked bridge of his nose, his hazel eyes shiny with amusement.

Zahra was used to seeing beautiful men; LA was crawling with them. Although she knew they were objectively attractive, she was never attracted to them. Not since she'd sworn off men a handful of years ago, after spending the preceding few years as a new divorcée sleeping her way through all the dating apps.

When she decided to do something, she did it, and giving up men hadn't been hard. By then, she'd learned she was better off alone anyway. This was after her life fell apart, after she'd dropped out of culinary school, after she'd learned how Wes had betrayed her. She'd worked at a wine bar without even a proper kitchen, trying to decide what to do next—or rather, trying *not* to decide what to do next. She'd been drinking too much, eating nothing but leftover mixed nuts and plates of rethermed flatbread topped with out-of-season tomato bruschetta and preshredded mozz, hating herself and lonelier than she'd ever been.

It had been pure relief when she'd woken, for what felt like the hundredth time, in the bed of a stranger during a honey-hued April sunrise that happened to herald her thirty-third birthday, and realized she was done.

Done with lust.

Done with men.

Done with expecting anything to fill the void inside her.

It couldn't be filled, and accepting that as truth meant she could learn to live with the void, learn to give the gaping black hole a wide berth, tiptoeing around its blurry contours only if she had to. And, it turned out, if she sealed herself off, dispensed of relationships and people and things that demanded she give too much, she didn't have to go anywhere near it.

If she was going to be lonely, wasn't she better off alone?

After that April morning, any lingering carnal resistance in her loins never asserted itself. That part of herself was all but gone, a limb lost to nerve damage, a numb reminder of another time when she'd been a different person.

Whatever was happening now, this most unwanted, rampant sexual attraction, she needed to squash, stat.

"What about you? Are you from around here?" he asked.

She shook her head. "LA," she squeaked out. "Road trip."

"Where you headed?"

"Seattle."

"Funny. We're headed in the same direction," he said.

With a great sense of relief, she heard Hannah's voice as she and Aurora returned to the dining room. Zahra just had to get Aurora's attention. But she wasn't the only one who'd clocked Aurora's reentry. The young mother-daughter couple at a nearby table had begun to titter and trade glances in her direction.

"So . . . ," the guy started, but before he could ask her another question, she cut him off.

"So, a travel photographer," she said, half her attention still trained on the mother and daughter watching Aurora. "Does that mean you spend your life flying from one place to the next?" The thought of all that air travel helped to cool the heat running through her veins.

"Yeah, I love to fly." She couldn't help herself from visibly shuddering. "Not a fan, I take it?"

"That's putting it mildly. You actually *like* to fly? You're probably one of those weirdos who loves to jump out of planes for fun, too."

He full-body chuckled, his eyes squinting, her skin vibrating in return. She really needed to leave. Instead, she sucked at her straw, looked anywhere but at his face.

The mother and daughter clambered out of their chairs and nudged each other over to Aurora. The daughter asked Aurora for a picture. "I'm not doing pictures today, but I'd be happy to sign something for you," Aurora said. The daughter spoke too softly for Zahra to hear, then walked back to her mother.

"I told you it was her," the mother hissed. "Go back up there, and I'll get a photo."

"Is your sister famous or something?" the guy asked, noticing Zahra pause to take in the exchange.

The mother had pulled out her phone and raised it toward Aurora. "Go on," she stage- whispered to her daughter. "Run up there, and I'll get a picture before she knows it."

Now, that wasn't right. The woman had clearly heard Aurora tell her no. What kind of jerk would take her picture without her permission? The need to speak up overcame her. Zahra placed her hands on the table, ready to tell the woman to back off, but something deep and heavy stopped her, a chain she'd been carrying for a long time, coiled and weighted. It wasn't her responsibility to protect Aurora. If the woman took Aurora's photo, that wasn't Zahra's fault.

The daughter dashed to Aurora's side, and the woman held up her phone again, angling for a picture.

"Oh, I don't—" Aurora started.

"Got it!" the overbearing mother practically hollered. "See? How easy was that?"

Aurora had a smile pasted on her face, and Zahra looked away, guilt flaring as she saw the clear worry in the quick blink of Aurora's eyes.

"Okay, then," the guy was saying as her attention returned to him, "Miss Not-a-Food-Critic, Not-a-Chef, what's your unprofessional assessment of the food?" He grinned at her, waiting for an answer.

Was he flirting? Did she want him to be?

No. Absolutely not. She'd told him she wasn't interested, and she wasn't. But her body, fluttering with the tantalizing tingle of forgotten sensations reawakening, didn't seem to agree.

"It doesn't excite me," she said too quickly, before realizing the words could sound like an innuendo. Blood rushed to her cheeks.

His eyes flashed. "What does excite you?"

Okay, now he was definitely flirting.

She swabbed her hand across her forehead. God, she was perspiring. She had to get out of there before her emotions completely took control. She jumped out of her seat, the cat shuffling as she lifted the carrier. "I have to . . . do something," she muttered, abandoning the table without a second look.

Striding toward Aurora, she said, "I need the keys."

"Oh. Okay." Aurora stuck her hand in the pocket of her jeans.

"Does that mean you need to leave, Aurora?" Hannah asked, sounding disappointed.

"Yes," said the sisters in unison.

The second Aurora had the keys in her fingers, Zahra snatched them and took off toward the door. "I'll meet you out there," she called over her shoulder as she left.

In the driver's seat, she turned on the car, and after struggling with how to work the display, pressing all sorts of things she probably shouldn't have, she managed to get the AC blasting. Good. That was better. With the cool air on her face and the steering wheel beneath her hands, she could think clearly again. The attraction she'd felt toward the guy wasn't a big deal. It was purely physical. It didn't mean anything.

Back in her right mind, she wasn't about to let Aurora get behind the wheel and take them on another side trip. A moment later, Aurora emerged, looking harried, her strange, dark hair falling from her hat in uneven clumps. She hurried toward the car, took note of Zahra in the driver's seat, and made her way to the passenger side.

"Let's get out of here," she said.

Zahra jammed the car into reverse. Aurora steadied herself with the grab bar. A plume of white dust gathered behind them as Zahra yanked the wheel toward the road.

13

Aurora

Aurora had the worst feeling inside her, like something trapped was trying to find its way out through her organs.

She'd let her picture get taken, the one thing Dillon had asked her not to do. Granted, it hadn't been a pap's shot, but sometimes fan photos could be worse.

She should have marched right up to that woman and demanded she delete them. Zahra would have. But not Aurora. Aurora would be labeled an ungrateful brat who didn't care about her fans. Though it wasn't only that. The woman had reminded her too much of her own mom.

But just because the woman had pics didn't mean she'd post them, and even if she did, her social accounts were probably private or had a total of fifty followers, who wouldn't know—or care—who Aura Star was. As for the daughter, Aurora could only hope she'd be too embarrassed to share them herself. It would probably be fine. It usually was.

If it wasn't?

Last night, the thought of her relationship with Dillon coming out had tantalized her, that they might *finally* let their love out of the dark and into the spotlight. The farther she traveled from LA, the more that seed of hope gave way to fear. Dillon's steady voice in her ear had already become a whisper. But she had to stay the course. Stay strong for him. No matter what happened. It was about loyalty and responsibility; sometimes you had to sacrifice for the people you loved.

"Thanks for rescuing me back there," she said to her sister's unreadable profile. She didn't mind riding shotgun. It seemed more natural this way, with Zahra in the driver's seat.

They were on a winding stretch of highway, headed west toward the coast. Out the window was mostly scrub grass, scraggly bushes, and olive-brown hills. The bluest sky you could imagine reflected in a placid lake that disappeared into the distance.

Zahra cut her a quick glance. "Rescued you?"

"That mom was beyond. I had to get out of there." She exhaled in frustration. "I knew going was a mistake."

"Then why we did we just waste an hour?"

"Because my mom promised me it would be fine. She convinced me it wouldn't be a big deal."

"Knowing your mom, she's probably thrilled you have fans wanting their picture taken with you. Any publicity is good publicity, right?"

The iced tea slushed unnervingly in Aurora's belly, and for one awful moment, she wondered whether her mom and Hannah had planned the whole thing or, at least, hoped for it. Lucy didn't know about the blind item. She didn't know Dillon had sent her out of town, so it wasn't inconceivable she'd assume there was no harm in a random, and convenient, sighting of Aura Star at her friend's new restaurant.

It's not that her mom used her. But Lucy liked to enjoy the "perks of the job." Whether she meant Aurora's job or her job as Aurora's mom wasn't clear. It didn't matter. Aurora owed her mom her life, and anyway, her mom would never set her up like that.

"Is it a big deal?" Zahra asked.

"No, it's not," Aurora shot back. "I just didn't feel like having my picture taken." She brought a lock of hair to her lips, but the off-putting fragrance of the dye irritated her nose and she recoiled. "My hair," she told Zahra. "I look awful. And if the photo goes viral—which it probably won't, but you never know—then it's going to be a whole thing."

"People really care about your hair?"

Zahra couldn't have sounded more incredulous, but Aurora didn't know how to explain to a person who made it a point to avoid people what it was like to live under such intense scrutiny, to know at any given time someone might be watching, formulating an opinion about you they had no qualms presenting as fact to everyone they knew—or didn't know. All she could manage was, "It's a breach of contract for the show. Changing my hair."

"Seriously?" Zahra said. "How absurd. You're not a doll."

"It's just the way it is."

"I don't know how you stand it. Not being in control of your own life. Your own hair!"

Aurora shrugged. What other choice did she have?

There'd been a time during her late teens, when every "yes" she got was for a role that seemed to set her further back, typecasting her as the sunny but vapid best friend or the pretty-popular girl in a show dedicated to the losers. She was there but unimportant, earning a little money but not enough, building a clip reel but not an impressive one, and she'd started imagining herself going to college. It was silly at first, just a little idea. But it grew bigger over time, the desire for spacious lecture halls and brick buildings and a library with those green-and-gold table lights.

In secret, she'd researched programs that would consider someone who only had a GED, schools far enough from SoCal she could justify leaving the business, her mom's expectations. Even though she was already older than most college freshmen, she wanted to know what it felt like to blend in with a crowd. To discover something about herself no one knew, not even her.

But then she'd met the Kellys and got the part on *YMU.*

Zahra had said something, interrupting her thoughts.

"What?"

"Why'd you dye it, then?" Zahra repeated. "If you weren't supposed to."

Aurora noted with some pleasure that her sister sounded almost concerned for her. She wished she could tell her the truth, that she could turn to Zahra the way you were supposed to rely on your older sister. Maybe she would understand if Aurora could just explain the situation. The words welled in her throat, but before she could get them out, her phone vibrated. Worry rattled inside her, catching on the bits of self-doubt that had begun to collect.

"Uh, I just needed something different," she said, grabbing her phone, choking down her confession. She couldn't risk ruining this road trip, this precious window of time when she finally had Zahra's attention. "A breather from my character, you know? But it'll look good for the Emmys."

"Okay . . . The timing seems intense. But I guess I get that. Wanting to do something for yourself."

Distracted, Aurora made a noncommittal "mm-hmm" as she swiped the screen. But it wasn't news about the blind item or the photo showing up online. Just another check-in from Evangeline: Your new schedule is set. Nothing from Margot yet 🤞

See? Everything was fine. Under control. She just needed to think about something else.

"You and that guy at the café," she said. "You were vibing for sure."

Zahra's eyes narrowed. "No. No vibes. Nothing at all."

"Then why'd he ask for your number before I left?"

"Tell me you didn't."

Her silence was confirmation enough.

"I don't even know him," Zahra said, exasperated.

Aurora had been delighted to share Zahra's number, hadn't given it a second thought when the guy asked. Why would she? Her sister was single. Had been forever. Aurora had been . . . what? Fifteen, when Zahra divorced? So that was, basically, a lifetime ago.

"Isn't that the point of him asking for your number? So you can get to know each other?"

"It wasn't for you to decide."

"It's just a phone number. With the way you were looking at him, I thought you'd be happy."

"You don't know what I want, Aurora. You don't know me."

Aurora felt the sting at once, the truth of their relationship flicking around the car like a trapped bug.

An uncomfortable silence settled over them, lasting so long it was almost a relief when Aurora's phone began to vibrate again. Almost. Until she saw it was Evangeline calling. That couldn't be good.

She answered, sounding as upbeat as she could, ignoring the whoosh of dread in her belly. "Hey!"

"Aurora, I'm so sorry," Evangeline sputtered through tears.

"What's happened?" For a brief second, Aurora could see her career coming apart like a sweater in the wash. Dillon wouldn't want her anymore if she damaged the show's reputation. Oh God. "What is it?"

"Margot saw some pictures of you online, I guess, and her assistant just called me, and she made me tell her where you are. She *made* me. She knows you're going to Seattle, and she's pissed."

Username: Elly Spills All

Bio: Serving tea with a side of hot goss

A close-up of popular video gossip queen Elly Belly with the GlamAnon filter obscuring her facial features appears over an empty green screen. She claps her hands.

"Ask and ye shall receive! Earlier today, I started to hear reports of Aura Star going rogue right before the Emmys *and* right after that weird drama with Serena Kelly and the *VF* shoot. Well, before I could even share what I'd learned with you all, I managed to hunt down the magically disappearing Aura Star. And she's dyed her hair apparently? Sus much?"

The green screen flashes to a photo of Aurora in a trucker hat with dark hair, giving an awkward smile beside a young blond girl.

"User Girlmomknowsbest and her daughter sent me this snap of Aura at a restaurant that just opened in Ojai of all places. According to Girlmom, who spoke directly with the restaurant owner, Aura is northbound to see her sick dad in Seattle. She's traveling with a mystery friend, who may or may not be her real-life sister. Aura has never referred to a sister in public, and as of this posting, her Wikipedia entry doesn't mention a sister. But I guess a family emergency would explain her hasty Hollywood departure."

Elly pauses, zooms in on her blurred lips. "Or does it?"

The camera pulls back to show her whole face. "Guys, I've buried the lede because we have even bigger gossip to unpack here today. I'm getting reports of an apparently legit blind item swirling among those in the know about a married TV showrunner having an affair with his successful series' young costar. It's vague, sure, but trust me, I've been around this particular block a few times, and where there's smoke, there's always fire. And this particular four-alarm is supposedly about"—Elly makes the drumroll sound—"Aura Star and *You, Me, Us* creator Dillon Kelly. Yes, *that* Kelly, husband to Star's costar, Serena. Serena, who canceled her *VF* photoshoot with Star at the last second and may or may not be sporting an early pregnancy pooch. *Eeek*, y'all!"

Pressing her hands to her cheeks, Elly shakes her head. "If it is true, I hope Aurora really is traveling with her sister, because she's gonna need family support to get through this mess. Especially since it appears the Kellys are putting on a united front."

The green screen changes to a picture of Dillon and Serena walking hand in hand down a tree-lined street. Dillon leans toward his wife, who wears a loose T-shirt. The picture switches to one of the couple stopped on the same street, Dillon holding Serena's head while he kisses her cheek.

"Yep, that's Dillon and Serena out and about, with a side of PDA. A power couple notorious for their privacy. But methinks someone doth protest too much, and that someone is Dillon trying to downplay any links to the blind item.

"You're gonna need to do better than that, Mr. Kelly, because we're not convinced. Are we?"

Elly's face gets super close to the camera, distorting the filter.

"As for Aura, you can run, but you can't hide. Godspeed, girl."

14

Zahra

Zahra sort of had to pee—all that lemonade—but she wasn't about to be the one to suggest stopping now, no way. She'd hold it and plow on through. The fancy electric Beast wasn't half-bad to drive. Certainly a step up from her Prius, not that she'd ever say so.

After Aurora got off the phone, a quiet so thick descended on the car it made even Zahra itchy. She had no idea how to turn on the radio, and she hadn't thought to connect her phone to Bluetooth, so she sat there trying to focus on the road and definitely not on Aurora, whose usual golden-retriever energy had transformed into Chihuahua anxiety as she obsessively scrolled through her phone.

Aurora had spent a minute on the call reassuring whoever was on the other end of the line that everything was fine, nothing was their fault, and Aurora wasn't mad, she promised. Which meant that it probably was their fault and Aurora should have been mad.

It was like that awful mom at the restaurant. Aurora had every excuse to put her in her place, but she never would until she learned how to stand up for herself. Zahra had been right not to intervene. That's what Aurora was used to, other people taking care of her. She'd never learned how to deal with anything hard. She couldn't even admit their dad was dying.

But Zahra was a little curious what the call had been about. If it hadn't sent Aurora into such a tizzy, if they hadn't had that exchange about Aurora giving away her number to the guy right before, she might have asked.

He wouldn't call, would he? Probably not. He'd said it himself, he wasn't interested in anything serious. The request for her number had likely been nothing more than a machismo move masquerading as chivalry. She hadn't even given him her name, though it didn't take a psych degree to assume Aurora had coughed that up, too.

She would put the whole thing out of her mind. Some random guy was the last thing she needed to deal with right now.

Back on the coast, they neared Santa Barbara. The country terrain had given way to four lanes of Highway 101, the blue sky to an overcast gray. To the west, the Pacific Ocean came into view, improbably placid from afar. Suburbs and palm trees peeked from behind the retaining wall to the east; on a teetering marquee, a vet clinic and a liquor store advertised their services.

Aurora swiped frantically across her phone, the constant movement nagging at Zahra's peripheral vision.

"Hey," she said. And when Aurora didn't respond, "Hello?"

"Yeah?"

"Did you happen to tell Dad we were coming?"

"Not yet. Good point. I'll call him."

"Wait—" But it was too late. Aurora was already dialing. Why couldn't she just send a text like a normal person? Zahra hadn't intended to speak to him again until they got there. She just wanted to know if he was expecting them. Her body tensed as the ring sounded through the speaker of Aurora's phone.

"Hey, Roar," their dad answered, his hoarse voice subdued but upbeat, the same as it had been when Zahra had spoken to him the day before.

"Dad, great news. Zahra and I are in the car and on our way."

"Already?" He sounded genuinely surprised, like he wasn't the one to have instigated this whole outing in the first place. "But don't you have the fancy award show this weekend?"

Zahra couldn't suck down her irritation; in a bare whisper, she mouthed to Aurora, *He made it sound like we should drop everything.*

Aurora held the phone aloft in her hand, her wrist bent at a right angle as if she carried a plate of hors d'oeuvres. She flung the speaker in Zahra's direction for her to chime in, but Zahra waved it away.

"Yeah, well," she said. "Zahra wanted to get a quick start. I decided to tag along."

"Good, good. That's really great. The sooner the better. When do you think you'll be here?"

"Not until tomorrow evening at the earliest," she said, turning in Zahra's direction for confirmation. Zahra nodded.

"That's fine. They've still got me here at the hospital. Observation or something. But I'll be discharged tomorrow."

Zahra cut in without meaning to, without *wanting* to. "You have someone taking you home?"

"You're on speaker, Dad," Aurora said.

"Hey there, kiddo. Glad you made it." A pause stretched across the call. "Anyway, yeah, I got some help. A home aide or whatchamacallit. A fancy nurse that comes to your house. But he's a nice guy."

A weary tenderness rattled his breath, and something he used to say came back to Zahra like a kick. *I don't get worn out or worn down, kiddo. I'm worn in, like a good pair of jeans.*

Aurora must have heard it, too, because she said, "You sure you're okay?"

"Oh yeah, I'm good, sweetheart. A bit tired, maybe. Can't sleep in this damn bed with all the noise and interruptions."

The way he called her sweetheart. The way he still protected her, even now. Because Zahra was pretty certain he was not entirely okay. Zahra had always been the strong one. The one who could look out for herself. "Walk it off," her dad would tell her when she skinned her knees. "Crying's for babies and funerals." She steeled herself again.

"You'll be home soon," Aurora said. "We'll see you then."

"You will." The words inhabited a sigh that would have sounded like defeat from anyone other than Dom Starling.

"He sounds good overall," Aurora said after the call ended, at the same time Zahra was thinking he didn't sound good at all. She'd long been practiced at seeing through her dad, sniffing out his half-truths. But she saw no point in disabusing Aurora of her fantasy right then. They had too long left to go to start snaking that drain. Another four hours until Santa Cruz.

"Hey." Aurora interrupted Zahra's thoughts. She thought she might be about to explain her strange call. That, at least, would be interesting. Instead, she said, "Wanna play a game?"

"If you say I Spy, I swear—"

"What about the karaoke game?"

"No singing."

"Okay . . ." She thought for a moment. "Sweet or Sour? You remember, don't you? Where you wave to people and see how they respond. Sweet if they wave back. Sour if they don't. You taught me that one."

"I did?"

"When we went to Mount Rainier that one time. Remember?" As if just repeating the question might unlock Zahra's memory.

But Zahra didn't remember. Not the way Aurora did. All those visits to Seattle to see her dad and his new family—because that's how she thought of them—had lumped together in her brain, a stew cooked too long and hard, not a single element remaining recognizable, the memories having become only one indistinguishable, immovable gray mass.

Except, as had happened before when Lucy mentioned those dinners out, Aurora's prompting dislodged an unspecific and hazy image. Nothing about the ride or a car game, but a set of sun-bleached picnic tables with splintery edges. The way the snowcapped range before them loomed so much larger than how Northern California's coastal mountains inclined with a casual shrug, as if they knew the height of their peaks would always be dwarfed by the redwood trees that grew from the top. At the picnic tables, they'd pulled from cloudy plastic bags sandwiches Lucy had made that morning. Tuna without mayo, a sacrilege her dad declared inedible. Zahra agreed. Lucy huffed with hurt feelings, while Zahra and her dad split a bag of potato chips, and for those few minutes, they'd been on the same team.

"I can't believe you don't remember," Aurora said, breaking the finespun thread that held Zahra's memory. "That was such a fun trip."

Zahra shook her head. "No, nothing."

They hadn't been back on the road an hour when Zahra's phone rattled in the cupholder where she'd left it.

They'd veered east, abandoning the coastline and the game of peekaboo they'd been playing with craggy crescents of sandy beach and jagged rock formations covered in outcroppings of ice plant bursting with purple blossoms that, up close, Zahra had always thought resembled sea anemones. Even after you turned inland and glimpses of the steel-blue Pacific gave way to flat pockets of scrubland and knobby hillsides, you could still smell the sea, taste the salt on your tongue when the wind was right, at least for a little while.

When Zahra didn't reach for her phone, Aurora did, plucking it from the cupholder. Since her weird call with the mystery person earlier, Aurora had ignored a half dozen others, not declining them, but overtly silencing them so they could ring out and go to voicemail. And yet, here she was, invested in Zahra's notifications.

"Want me to check?" Aurora asked, already halfway to doing so. Zahra knew the way to her hometown from just about anywhere in California, but even so, she'd mapped it like she always did, and the foolish decision to leave her map app running gave Aurora full access to her phone without needing a password.

As Zahra protested, Aurora swiped at the screen. Zahra stretched her right arm to pull the phone from Aurora's grasp. But Aurora leaned into the passenger side window, and Zahra couldn't give chase without potentially running them off the road.

"It's a text from a number that's not in your contacts," Aurora said.

"It's probably just a client."

"Your clients send voice texts?"

"Huh. Weird." That even piqued Zahra's curiosity. She didn't think she'd ever received a voice text before. She was certain she didn't know how to send one. "Play it."

A voice had already begun to come through the speaker. She recognized the low tone at once. It was him. The guy from the café. The one with the tattoo that curled up his bicep, that smirk Zahra wanted to find off-putting but couldn't.

"Zahra, hello. I thought about sending a regular text but then I remembered you prefer audio, and anyway, it's easier this way while I'm driving. I'm on the coast, staring out at the big blue Pacific Ocean, almost to Santa Barbara now. I have a stop to make in Big Sur, then Santa Cruz, but I'm planning to make it through to San Francisco before nightfall. I love to cross the Golden Gate Bridge right when the sun is setting; there's this way the light glints off the towers that really gets me. If it isn't foggy. Have you seen it like that?"

He wasn't far behind them on the road, but she was glad for the distance. Just the sound of his voice kicked her heart into high gear, a somatic response she found most irksome.

"You're probably rolling your eyes about now, wishing your sister had never handed over your phone number, right?" He laughed a little, and that unwelcome sizzle of desire in Zahra made itself known again. Her body betraying her.

He paused for a few seconds, and when he spoke again, he sounded a touch more serious. "I never did get to learn anything about you. Where are you from? Why are you headed to Seattle? And what's what with the food notes?" Another pause. "If you message me back, I promise to tell you my name."

The message ended and Aurora practically squealed. "Oh my God, what a little flirt. You *have* to voice text him back."

"Are you nuts? What about me would give you the impression I'm interested whatsoever?" In truth, Zahra couldn't believe he'd reached out. Was that kind of follow-through creepy or endearing? "What's the point anyway? It's not gonna go anywhere."

"Would you want it to?"

"No." Zahra certainly did not want it to go anywhere, but the yearning inside her had already grown louder, more insistent. The best thing to do was to shut it down completely. "Definitely not."

"I know things didn't work out with Wes, but don't you ever feel like trying again? You could still have a family."

Zahra gripped the wheel, the leather hard and unyielding beneath her hands. The way Aurora spoke so nonchalantly, the brutality of her careless delivery. But it wasn't her fault. She'd been too young to understand what Zahra's life was really like before.

Zahra had been so close to that once—the happy marriage with the picket fence—so close she could still feel the warmth of it the way you did when you stepped out of a hot shower and the cold air left you shivering. But Wes had left her in the worst possible way. After what they'd been through together, his betrayal cut like a knife straight through her belly.

She didn't want that life anymore. Didn't want to risk losing everything all over again. *Don't you ever feel like trying again?* Aurora's words echoing now as the highway lengthened ahead of them.

Aurora thought everything was so simple because it had been for her. Sure, yeah, Zahra was beginning to see how her optimism served her, but it wasn't the same for Zahra. Hope only led to heartache. Believing the best could happen only made the worst more likely. She'd learned her lesson enough times.

"No, I don't," she finally said. "Not at all."

"Then it can't hurt, right? With this guy. I mean, maybe it's just a little fun on the road. Would it be kind of freeing? To just go for it?"

"Easy for you to say." She paused, prickling like a porcupine. "Everything's easier for you."

"Easier how?"

"Look, I get there are aspects of your life I can't understand, industry stuff and whatnot, but you're young and beautiful and things always work out for you."

"My life isn't as *easy* as you think." But before Zahra could ask her to explain herself, Aurora continued. "Anyway, don't worry, I kept the message. In case you decide to respond. Or just wanna listen to it," she said, in a teasing voice, "again and again and again."

15

Aurora

The trouble started somewhere past Nacimiento, where the terrain flattened and there was nothing but oak trees and dry grass, the nearest next town nowhere in sight, Santa Cruz still two hours away.

Aurora, feet kicked up on the dashboard, had managed to tumble headlong into an anxious doze. In her half consciousness she'd lived a dozen uncomfortable phone conversations with her manager. Each time one ended, she'd briefly wake before slipping back into a dream state, only for the whole thing to start over again.

When she heard Zahra unleash a string of expletives, she dragged herself awake, relieved to realize they were still on the road, her only interaction with Margot a slew of missed calls she would respond to once she was alone.

Trying to get her bearings, she rubbed the corners of her eyes.

Zahra shook the steering wheel. "You've got to be kidding me."

"What's happening?"

"I can't accelerate." Zahra flicked on the blinker and pulled into the right lane, just as Aurora noticed the battery indicator on the display.

"It can't be dead already." But, of course, it could be—Aurora was supposed to look up somewhere they could stop for a charge on the way. She'd meant to do that.

"We just need a charging station," she said, determined to stay upbeat in the face of Zahra's rising panic.

A big rig passed, jostling the car. "Do you happen to see one of those out here in the middle of nowhere?"

The only things surrounding the stretch of highway were low rolling mountains to the west and a great big expanse of nothing but grass, train tracks, and barbed wire fence to the east. This wasn't the ideal place to end up on the side of the road.

"Here." Aurora pressed the car's screen. "It'll show us the nearest charger."

But after a few moments of fiddling with the navigation, she knew there was no way they'd make it. The car would shut down shortly.

Aurora sighed and gestured at the next exit, a short off-ramp that led straight down to a frontage road. "You better get off here."

Straining her eyes to see down the frontage road, she weighed their options. Someone around here might let them bum some power, but there was nothing nearby. "The bad news is we're not gonna make it to a charging station. The good news, it could be worse."

The car began to drag, and Zahra clutched the wheel as it slowed and they glided to a stop on a rough gravel shoulder. Then everything cut out, and the only sound was the rush of cars on the highway.

"Oh yeah?" Zahra said. "How could it be worse?"

"I don't know, exactly, but it always could be."

Zahra's head was turned toward the window, looking up at the highway's embankment in the distance where more functional vehicles sped to their destinations. Her frustration radiated off her like heat on asphalt. "You said the car was charged."

"It was. I mean, maybe not fully—"

"Are you serious right now?"

Aurora pulled out her phone. "Didn't you notice the battery indicator? It shows the remaining mileage."

"You said the display thingy was broken. You said to ignore it, so when it kept appearing, I closed it."

"Yeah, the warning message. Not the battery indicator."

"Are you really trying to pin this on me, the person who was told the car was fully charged?"

The problem was that no matter what Aurora said, this was her fault. It was her car; she was the one who had made Zahra drive with her. She checked her phone but didn't have any service. Still, she could get them out of this. She just had to think of something.

Before she could, Zahra shrugged off her seat belt. "I can't just sit here," she said. A moment later, she hopped out, then opened the back door to grab the cat carrier. Aurora hurried to follow.

"Where are you going?" The only house Aurora could see was probably a mile away.

"I'm not about to hang around, waiting to be rescued."

They trudged along the tall grass beside the frontage road, the earth packed and hard underfoot. Aurora grew swampy and her legs wobbled after so long in the car, but she swallowed her complaints.

The details of the house were visible now, a sizable farmhouse maintained but rough around the edges. An American flag, tattered to half its size, swung near the front door. A chain-link fence surrounded the cleared yard, home to an assortment of sun-bleached plastic kid toys, and beyond that, a graveyard of some half dozen vehicles and a small tractor that looked like it hadn't moved in a few years. A large dog circled the yard, sniffing at the fence posts.

"I'll ask to use their Wi-Fi," Aurora said definitively. "I'll call a tow truck."

Zahra shaded her eyes and took a moment to examine the house. "I doubt whoever lives here will be inclined to help."

"Can't hurt to ask."

She expected Zahra to argue, but her sister followed her down the long dirt driveway with nothing more than a curmudgeonly grunt as she shifted her bags around. The dog began to bellow as soon as he caught wind of them. A man stepped out of the garage wearing paint-stained cargo pants and a tie-dyed T-shirt.

"Can I help you?" he called when they were still at least two dozen yards away, the question not particularly friendly. "Quiet," he yelled toward the dog.

She could sense Zahra ruffle beside her, but Aurora raised her hand and waved. "Hello, there!" she hollered with a smile. "We sure hope you can."

As they neared, Aurora could see the man was working on a truck, hood open, its insides scattered on the ground. She pulled her hat down a little on the unlikely chance he recognized her.

"So sorry to bother you," she said in her sweetest voice. "My sister and I broke down back on the road, and our phones aren't working. Could we borrow your Wi-Fi?"

The guy looked back at the house, scratched at the side of his nose, then shrugged. "My wife's napping with the kids. But sure. She'd probably kill me if I turned you two away."

They followed him up the front steps onto the porch and sat on a set of faux wicker chairs coming undone at the edges, the plastic jabbing into Aurora's back every which way. He gave Aurora the Wi-Fi password and asked if they wanted some water.

"No," Zahra said, at the same time Aurora said, "Yes, please. We're super thirsty."

The screen door closed behind him. The dog's barks tapered to an unenthusiastic woof.

"You should always accept the offer," Aurora whispered.

"Maybe you do. I sure as hell don't."

Aurora opened her phone, searched local tow-truck services, but as it turned out, "local" was still twenty miles away. "I don't know. A tow truck could take a while," she said, thinking aloud. "And then we'd still have to wait for the charge. But we can't exactly Uber to Seattle."

"No shit." Zahra hopped to her feet and paced the porch, the wood squeaking beneath her sneakers.

The man returned with two glasses of ice water and a small bowl. "For the cat," he said, pressing it toward Zahra.

"Thank you."

At the sight of his human, the dog went off again. "Sorry about that. Pretzel's a sweetheart, but she's not well trained."

"Any chance you know of a car rental company around here?" Zahra asked.

"Back in Paso, probably." He headed toward the steps. "Let me grab Pretzel so she'll quiet down."

"Good idea," Aurora said, already googling the nearest car rental place. "We can Uber back to Paso Robles, then rent a car from there. That was only, like, what? Thirty minutes back?" She googled that, too. She could have Evangeline arrange a tow home for her car. That would cost a small fortune, but fine.

"Sure," Zahra said. "Two separate cars. You can go straight to the closest airport, and I can go home."

"You're serious?"

"This isn't working, Aurora. I think the universe is sending a message, loud and clear."

"And what message is that?"

Zahra stood, hands on hips, staring down at the carrier. The cat lapped audibly. "That this was a major mistake." The attitude in her voice was gone, replaced with something quiet and unnerving.

She wouldn't really make them get separate cars, would she? She wouldn't actually turn right back around. But even as the thoughts crossed her mind, Aurora knew she would. Zahra didn't say things for the sake of saying them. It was a miracle Aurora had gotten her into the car to begin with.

"That's not the message." Although Aurora had to admit things weren't going great. "I'll call the car rental company," she said, buying time until she could think of something better.

The man returned, his fingers hooked under Pretzel's collar. Zahra drew the cat carrier toward her.

"Can I use your bathroom?" Aurora asked. "I promise I'll be super quiet."

❦

The house was as old and worn as it looked from the outside, cluttered but tidy. Bins overflowed with tired-looking toys, a stained play mat sat in front of the couch. The man led her to a door just off the main hallway, a small bathroom with Pepto Bismol–pink tile floors and a rusted claw-foot tub scattered with neon-colored plastic boats.

After she peed and washed her hands, Aurora considered her next step, the number of the rental car company at her fingertips. A vivid image of her sister hopping into a car and driving away rushed through her mind. She had a choice to make, and she was sure neither option was exactly right. But when you wanted something badly enough, sometimes you had to go all in; that's what Dillon would say.

She wouldn't call the rental car company. She had another idea.

Back outside, Aurora found Pretzel curled up at Zahra's feet, the cat in her lap. Her sister looked awkward and anxious, like she was ready to make a run for it, and Aurora felt a surge of certainty for what she was about to do.

"What'd the rental place say?" Zahra asked.

"No luck," Aurora lied without so much as a blink. "Nothing's available until tomorrow afternoon. But I'm gonna get us back on the road."

Before Zahra could say anything else, Aurora hustled down the porch steps and to the garage, where the man had his upper torso ducked beneath the truck's hood.

"Do any of those cars out there actually drive?"

He cocked his head, an amused look on his face. "Sure, they do. That one at least." He pointed to a gold box of a car. "'95 Volvo station wagon. Two hundred and fifty thousand miles. The trunk's latch won't stay locked, and it could use some new tires. I haven't had time to replace the serpentine belt, so you can bet the AC's gonna be a joke, and it whines like a sugar-fed toddler when the engine starts. But it still runs."

The sound of footsteps behind her brought Zahra to her side.

"And how much does a '95 Volvo station wagon in need of a tune-up go for these days?" Aurora asked.

"No way. We can't drive that to Seattle," Zahra said, jabbing her in the shoulder.

"It looks in better shape than your Prius."

Zahra made a noise, but that shut her up fast.

"That's a premium vehicle," the man said. "I'm not even sure I'm willing to part with it. But I'd say at least three grand, given its potential resale value."

"I'll give you five," Aurora said.

His mouth dropped open. "You got that kind of cash on you?"

"I'll Venmo you right now."

"Venmo? I'm not—"

"We'll take it," the wife called from the porch.

16

Zahra

While Aurora worked out the car sale with the couple and called her assistant to have the SUV towed, Zahra sat on the porch cradling the cat, giving him a few minutes of freedom before he'd have to be confined again.

On the wooden slats of the porch, discarded in a heap, lay a small baby's receiving blanket, the kind they gave at the hospital, the familiarity of those blue and pink lines pulling at the threads of Zahra's awareness so hard she had to look away, fight back the memory trying to rise to the surface. She burrowed her hands into the cat's fur, and his muscles twitched beneath her fingers. If she let go, it would take only a half second for him to leap from her lap and race to the ground.

"Sorry, cat," she whispered into his fur. "I can't lose you out here."

She was getting used to the feel of his warm weight, the soft tufts behind his ears. Maybe she was an animal person after all. Maybe she didn't know everything about herself there was to know.

Without thinking, Zahra pulled out her phone and opened the Messages app. If she could figure out how to send a voice text, then fine, she would. Otherwise, she'd let it go, consider the whole thing no great loss.

After scanning a quick online tutorial, she located the "Record" button.

"Hey," she said into her phone. "This is me messaging you back. You owe me your name."

Short, sweet. She sent the recording at once, then immediately felt ridiculous for doing so. She had no logical reason to message him back. No reason to engage whatsoever. And yet here she was, intentionally ignoring the question of why she'd been inclined to respond in the first place.

❦

They bumped along a route gutted with divots and holes just off the frontage road, the Volvo squeaking and creaking with effort. Each jerk sent Zahra's bladder screaming. She really had to go now, and she clenched her pelvic floor and gripped the overhead bar for dear life.

Aurora clutched the wheel at ten and two. "It's like driving a bus."

Aurora had ended up in the driver's seat again, which felt fitting to Zahra, given how this road trip was going so far. Although the idea of renting a car and heading home had cheered her, when that turned out not to be possible, she'd actually been relieved Aurora figured out another option.

"I told you it'd be fine," Aurora said, as if reading her mind.

"I can't decide whether your optimism is useful or delusional."

Aurora threw her head back and laughed. "Maybe both?"

Another massive thump. The pressure in Zahra's abdomen heaved. "God, I'm about to wet my pants."

"Why didn't you pee at the house?"

"Are you kidding? I wasn't about to walk into some stranger's home and use their bathroom."

"They were nice strangers with a nice home and a clean bathroom."

"Yeah, well, those nice strangers just took you for a ride." Zahra patted the car's scratched and discolored dashboard.

"I *offered* them the money."

"And they took it! Right after he said it wasn't worth that much. C'mon, that's not right."

"Sometimes right isn't as obvious as that."

"Sometimes people aren't as decent as you'd like to believe. It's not all sunshine and rainbows out in the real world."

"You can pee when we get gas," Aurora said. "He said it'd be right . . . There it is." A small building, unassuming and uninviting, stood in front of an old single gas pump. But Zahra couldn't care less what the place looked like as long as the bathroom was a step up from a porta potty.

The second the car lurched to a stop, she leaped from the door and rushed inside. At a counter near the back, a woman stood sentry, fiddling with the long black braid that hung over her shoulder, studying something before her.

"Hi. Where's your restroom?"

The woman looked up, face set in stone. "You planning to buy something?"

"We're pumping a tank of gas."

She dropped her braid and glanced at her computer screen. "I don't see anything."

"Well, she's about to," Zahra said, jaw tight, Kegels engaged. "You can go look."

The woman didn't move. "The store's for paying customers."

"Fine, sure, I'll buy something. Just let me use the bathroom first."

Zahra could see now the woman had in front of her a collection of tarot cards laid out like a Christmas tree; at the tippy top, the card closest to Zahra had, appropriately, a yellow, eight-pointed star and a nude woman pouring water from two jugs that only made Zahra's bladder clench. She smacked her hand down upon it.

"Look, lady. This is a legit emergency."

Hostility crept across the woman's face. "You know what that card says? It says you feel sorry for yourself. Because nothing goes your way, does it?"

Case in point. Zahra was about a minute from running outside and popping a squat in the dirt.

The woman poked her finger into Zahra's hand, and Zahra whipped it away from the cards as if she'd been touched with a lit cigarette. "But you know something? You're the only one standing in your way."

"At the moment, *you're* the one standing in my way." Zahra grabbed a pack of gum off a small metal stand near the register. "Here. I'll take this."

The woman took the crumpled bills Zahra handed her.

"So where's the bathroom?" she asked, shoving her wallet back into her bag.

The woman gestured to the small doorway at her back. "But you'll need the key."

Zahra's chest tightened with frustration. "Can I have the key, then?"

"I'll tell you what. I don't like your energy one bit. Around here we do things differently than wherever you're from. It's called common courtesy. So no, I don't think I'll be giving you the key." She flung the braid behind her back to punctuate the point, an action that only served to incense Zahra.

A white-hot flame erupted around her so strong she temporarily forgot about her bladder near bursting and wanted only to open her mouth and let the fury building inside her burn this store to the ground. But before she could, a hand dropped on her shoulder, and Aurora said to the woman, "Hi, Maggie."

Maggie appeared to be as surprised as Zahra, her eyes taking on a deer-caught-in-the-headlights look as she tried to parse the sudden appearance of this new person and her intentions.

"Do I know you?"

"Not yet. I'm Aurora. This is Zahra. Brent sent us this way."

"You know the Manns?"

"Nicest family, right?" Before she could refute or agree with the claim, Aurora barreled on. "Listen, Maggie, my sister and I are sort of in a tough spot. It's already been a long day, and we have a lot farther to go. I was thinking maybe while she uses the bathroom, you could give me a quickie card reading?"

As her heart rate slowed, Zahra's bladder came back to life, pulsing with a fervent SOS message. Her weight shifted from one foot to the other then back again.

"Oh," Maggie said. "I could pull a card for you, I guess."

"Would you?" Aurora reached beside the register and grabbed a key affixed to a miniature wooden baseball bat. Why hadn't Zahra seen it sitting there? She'd been blind with her own frustration. "Here," she told Zahra before turning her attention to the cards. She waggled her finger over the Christmas tree tower. "Now what does this all mean?"

Zahra jogged back to the bathroom, their voices fading.

The relief was powerful and immediate. She stood and zipped up her pants, feeling a half ton lighter, her mind clearer. At the sink, she scrubbed her hands, steadied herself for a moment before she went back out there.

She wasn't sure what, exactly, had rubbed the cashier the wrong way, but the night before with Preeti came back to her. Zahra bungled things. She said what she meant, but she said it all wrong. Like an affability deficiency she didn't know how to fix. Aurora had no qualms about saying what she wanted, but there was a kindness to her Zahra didn't possess. Zahra didn't know how, but it worked for her, as if all Aurora's soft parts actually made her stronger.

17

Aurora

The second Zahra had disappeared inside the old gas station's storefront, Aurora had peeled off her sweatshirt and dialed Margot's number. With the phone between her ear and shoulder, she slid her credit card into the machine and fit the gas pump into the Volvo.

The only way to mitigate this issue was to address it head-on or, at least, as far as she could without revealing the real reason for her sudden departure.

So maybe not head-on, then. More like directly adjacent to the truth. Still, Aurora's heart ratcheted up a notch with each ring.

But she could do this. She would stay calm. Positive. It really wasn't *that* big of a deal. A minor schedule blip in the scheme of things. She glanced at the building's door. She would have to make this quick before Zahra reemerged.

The line connected and she took a deep breath. From the flatland surrounding the store, a warm, wispy wind picked up, blowing the smell of pavement and gas into her nose. Her nostrils twitched.

"Aura," her manager barked into the phone.

She exhaled. "Margot, hi. So sorry we haven't been able to connect until now."

"What, pray tell, is going on? You decide to leave town, *this week*, without telling me? You're ignoring my calls? And now you've, what? Dyed your hair? Please tell me I'm hallucinating."

She forced herself to smile before she spoke. Even if Margot couldn't see her face, the expression would color the sound of her voice. It would convey an air of confidence. "It's only temporary, I swear."

Margot made a grunting sound. "It better be; this whole thing better be."

"It is, I swear. I'll be back the day after tomorrow. I had to do this for my dad. He's"—she'd readied herself to deliver this excuse, but she couldn't bring herself to say the actual word—"not doing well. He needs me right now and he doesn't have anyone else. Not really. Not since my mom and he—"

"Okay, okay. I get it." That was about as close to compassionate as Margot came. The woman was allergic to vulnerability, and it wasn't the first time Aurora poked this sore sport to her advantage. "The timing couldn't be worse, but you know that or you wouldn't be sneaking around. Anyway, Evangeline assures me she's managed to reschedule everything. God knows how. As long as you're here by Friday—"

"I will be."

"—and come back ready to be on. And I mean the *minute* you step off the plane . . ."

"Yes, yes, for sure. I'll be so much more focused when all this is behind me."

As Margot's intensity receded, Aurora's heart rate slowed. The wind pawed at the wild ends of her hair.

"But you can't lie to me anymore," Margot said. "Our relationship is built on trust. Mutual trust. I'm looking out for you, and I need to know you're looking out for you, too. So if there's something I should know, you need to tell me. Got it?"

"Right. I absolutely agree," she told Margot, willfully overlooking the giant secret she was keeping, unexpectedly grateful the blind item hadn't turned into anything more. Dillon was right. If they went public . . . She caught herself. *When* they went public, it needed to be on their terms, with the power of a PR game plan behind them. She'd need Margot on her side, and now was clearly not the time to broach the subject.

"Stay in touch," Margot said, and the call ended.

That out of the way, Aurora experienced a rush of relief. She inhaled the breeze, the potent scent of gasoline replaced with the sweet smell of wild grass.

After she replaced the pump, she scanned the storefront for signs of Zahra. What was taking her so long?

Inside the building, she'd followed the sharp sound of Zahra's voice to the back of the store, where she saw her engaged in a clearly hostile interaction with the shopkeeper. Leave it to Zahra to piss someone off in under ten minutes. Her sister had zero chill.

Before either Zahra or the shopkeeper caught sight of her, Aurora considered getting out of there, letting Miss Independent work things out on her own. But she could see her sister practically prancing with discomfort, so she found her smile again and approached the counter, noting the name tag the woman had pinned at her midline.

She had no interest in a tarot reading from Maggie. She only trusted her psychic in LA, a woman Dillon swore by. Once Zahra was off to the bathroom, Aurora deflected the reading by asking Maggie how long she'd been doing them.

"This is mostly a hobby," Maggie explained. "For me or my friends. Don't get me wrong, I have the sight. Passed down from my Meemaw, but I've never felt a calling to use it professionally. It's just part of my identity." Her chest swelled a bit. "I'm actually finishing my training to become an end-of-life doula."

A draft fluttered across Aurora's skin, raising the fine hairs on her arms.

"A what?"

"Death doula. It's like a baby doula, except you're helping people pass out of this world instead of into it."

"Whoa. That sounds kind of dark," Aurora said. What it sounded like was awful. Perhaps the most depressing job in the world. "And you like it?"

"Well, I've only assisted so far. And it's hard to say you *like* someone's final moments, but it's an honor, you know? To be there. To bear witness."

Aurora didn't know. She'd never been good at endings, avoided them as far as one could, choosing, instead, to throw herself into new beginnings.

"We can't shy away from the hard things, can we?" The woman tilted her head, managing to look both solemn and proud. Aurora could see how she might be good at her job. "I, for one, have no desire to glaze over the surface of life."

"Oh sure, sure."

Aurora was glad when Zahra's return interrupted the conversation, but Maggie stopped them before they could leave.

"Beware, ladies," she said, tapping the deck of cards. "You're both in a lot of trouble. I can sense it. You better decide soon if it's the good kind."

18

Zahra

"The good kind of trouble? What's that supposed to mean?" Zahra said.

She'd taken the driver's seat for the last leg to Santa Cruz and felt better already. Even the car felt right. Her best friend growing up had been gifted a hand-me-down family Volvo station wagon on her sixteenth birthday, and car-less Zahra had spent many hours as chauffeur on the nights when Sarah drank too much to drive or just didn't feel like it. But Zahra never minded. She had always loved to drive. She knew the statistics, but no matter what the numbers said, she felt safest behind the wheel, knowing she could take herself wherever she needed to go.

"Who cares?" Aurora said. "If I believed every negative thing someone said to me, I'd be too depressed to move."

"You sure did a good job making her think you cared."

Aurora shrugged. "I mean, I wasn't trying to trick her or anything, but it was either that or someone having an accident."

"I would have been fine," Zahra said. "I wasn't above running behind the building."

"Wasn't it nicer to use the bathroom?"

"I guess."

"You could just say 'Thank you.'"

"How about we call it even?"

"Fine." Aurora pushed down the visor and eyed herself in the mirror, tucking her hair back into her hat. A second later, Zahra's phone vibrated, and despite her determination not to care, her heart jumped at the thought of a new voice text.

"Where is it? In your bag?" Aurora began to riffle through Zahra's bag on the middle console.

"Please don't—"

"It's fine; I'm not gonna go through your stuff."

"Seriously. Don't."

Aurora held up the phone. "Look."

Zahra automatically complied, inadvertently unlocking the phone with her face. *Dammit, Aurora.* She never took no for an answer.

Before Zahra could demand she put the phone away, Aurora squealed. "Um, hello, he texted again."

"Don't play it—"

"Hi, I guess I'm surprised you actually responded. In a good way." The voice coming through her tinny phone speaker sounded both smooth and playful, as if he spoke with a smile.

Aurora paused the message. "Um, wait a minute, you ho. You texted him back already?"

"Excuse me? You did not just call me what I think you called me."

"It's a compliment," Aurora said, Zahra's reprimand rolling right off her back. "I'm impressed."

Zahra shook her head. Communicating with her sister was like trying to decode a message without the cipher.

"Well, can you . . ." She flung out her arm, hoping Aurora wouldn't think she was seriously interested in him just because she was curious what he had to say.

Aurora pressed "Play" and the message started again. "I was driving along, thinking, *What are the odds she doesn't think I'm a weirdo, or at least gives me the benefit of the doubt?*" He paused. "Though, I have to admit, your response was . . . brief. Not that I'm complaining. I like a challenge."

To prove how ridiculous she found the whole thing, Zahra made a big show of rolling her eyes, snorting her disapproval. But inside, the word "challenge" tickled her.

"Anyway, since you earned it, my name's Elian. Elian Scott. I'm aware it has a whiff of pretension." It was exactly what she'd been thinking. Elian. *Elian.* She repeated his name in her head.

"Let's just say, growing up, I stood out among the Christophers, Michaels, and Joshuas. But I've always enjoyed extra attention. Call it middle child syndrome."

She could hear that smirk again but couldn't relate. Zahra had never been shy, but she'd always been an introvert who preferred less people to more, and her own company to most.

The sound of the wind rushed through the recording.

"Sorry about that," he said. "I'm standing at the edge of the world on a crusty patch of cliffside in Big Sur. I've been here plenty over the years, but every time it's like the first time, like I've stumbled upon the most beautiful place on the planet, and I wonder, why would I ever leave? But I always do, I guess to be certain there isn't someplace better than this. Wow, that sounded kind of . . . lame. I'd delete that last part if I could, but I try not to give in to regrets. You can't change the past, only plow forward, right? Then again, I don't normally do *this*. Ask for numbers from random women. Or send voice texts. Between you and me, I had to google which icon to use."

He released a soft chuckle that fluttered against Zahra's own rib cage.

"That probably tells you about how old I am. I'm counting on you being the same age, give or take. Not that you look old—aw, damn. I've already put my foot in it, haven't I? Would it help if I said I thought you were beautiful? Not manufactured beautiful and not unassuming beautiful, but the kind of beauty I'm staring at right now, the kind I don't think you can ever get tired of looking at. Jeez, there I go again.

That really sounds like a line, doesn't it?" A beat. "Well, this is bad and getting worse."

Elian cleared his throat. "I'm gonna cut myself off before I say something else weird. Now you know my name. You know I'm a middle child. You know a little more than I meant to share, truth be told. So it's your turn."

The message ended, and Zahra stared at the road, waiting for the unexpected desire inside her to pass. Or maybe it wasn't desire but something hungrier even than that. Whatever it was, she bit it back.

Aurora set down the phone. "Wow. He really likes you. You have to respond."

Zahra shrugged noncommittally. "Maybe. Probably not. It's a waste of time."

"Oh c'mon."

"No way." When she responded—*if* she responded—she'd do so without an audience.

Aurora sighed in defeat, put on some music. "I'm starved. I should have picked out a snack at the store."

"Grab the cooler from the back."

Aurora looped her belt off her shoulder and leaned over the seat back to grab the cooler. When it was on her lap, she opened it to reveal the sandwich Zahra had packed that morning. She handed half to Zahra and took a large bite. Between chews she said, "I don't normally eat bread. Is it always this good?"

"If you buy it from a decent bakery and soak it in good olive oil, yeah, it's always this good." With one hand on the wheel, Zahra tasted the sandwich, too. It was tangy and bright, crunchy and fresh from the lettuce, a little pop of heat and salt from the pickled peppers. But pickled onions would have been nice, too, a smear of pumpkin seed pesto, maybe. She'd have to think on that. "So you don't eat bread. What else don't you eat?"

"Dairy and sugar. I avoid most grains and beans, because of the bloating. But man, this is so delicious. Do you always eat like this?"

"Sort of."

Aurora meant the food itself, but Zahra thought of the company. She wasn't used to eating with another person. She often had Zoom calls with her cookbook clients when they tested recipes and tried them at the same time. She did tasting demos for the restaurant groups she worked with sometimes. But that was different.

She couldn't remember the last time she'd shared a meal with someone. A proper meal. Probably not since she'd visited her mom over the holidays. It always altered her perception, the awareness that someone else was eating at the same time, having their own physical response, the same ingredients distilled in a different way on another set of taste buds. The shared intimacy unnerved her, left her exposed and tender, the last plum abandoned on an otherwise bare tree in November.

It hadn't always been like this. She'd grown up at her grandparents' kitchen table, eating dinner with her family every night. Sharing whatever dishes Maman Joon decided to make, always a feast, the leftovers diligently packed at the end of the evening to be reheated at lunch, reinvented for breakfast. Even before her dad left, she and her mom spent most evenings with her grandparents, but once he was gone and Zahra and her mom moved in with them, those meals became sacred, a kind of sanctuary in Zahra's young life, her grandmother's love and the flavor of the food so intertwined until she couldn't think of one without the other. Until even the smell of kabobs or lasagna could make her feel as if she was in her grandmother's arms.

But over time her sense of safety had frayed, like the kitchen injuries she amassed on her hands and forearms, one nick and burn at a time. Now, she knew when it came to others, she wasn't safe at all. Not at the table . . . and not with her heart.

19

Zahra

It didn't matter how long her grandparents had been gone, the house in Santa Cruz—the chipped white fence and wind-tattered siding, the uneven stone path as familiar as the contours of a loved one's face, the crooked street numbers hammered by her grandfather above the salt-beaten garage—would always make Zahra think of them, the only two people whose love had ever felt uncomplicated. Easy to bear and impossible to lose.

But on this visit, something had changed.

Zahra noticed it right away. The once busy living room, a shrine to her grandparents' eclectic assortment of decorations, had been cleaned out and rearranged. Where was the little horse figurine whittled by her grandfather's brother Zahra would pull down to play with as a girl? Or the bud vase her grandmother kept filled with either a stem of dried baby's breath or a single rose in the spring?

When she'd asked her mother, Nasrin had shrugged. "I boxed them up," she'd explained. "I need a fresh start."

What followed was a big show about how Aurora would have to sleep in Zahra's old room and Zahra would sleep on the couch because the guest bedroom had been converted into a gym. Nasrin hadn't been expecting the cat, but the neighbors would probably have an old litter box lying around. She would run over and ask.

Zahra nodded, gave a murmur of gratitude, but she was hung up on the gym.

The guest bedroom had originally been her mother's bedroom, before *and* after her marriage. After her parents died, Nasrin moved into the big bedroom, leaving the third bedroom empty aside from an extra bed. It wasn't odd that her mom would want to use it for something else. But a gym? It was about the last thing Zahra expected from a woman who'd never shown any inclination toward exercise other than long walks on West Cliff.

Zahra sniffed something in the air she didn't recognize, too. Not a food scent or a cleaning product. It wasn't unpleasant, exactly, but it caught on Zahra's tongue, leaving a bitter residue in the back of her mouth. What her mom had said in her text, that she needed to talk about something, came back to Zahra. A sense of uneasiness she couldn't shrug off wound its way over her shoulders.

After settling on sleeping arrangements and procuring a dusty litter box and some litter from the neighbor's garage, Zahra, Aurora, and Nasrin gathered in the kitchen. Under the table, the cat munched his dished can of food with a ferocious hunger.

Aurora exchanged pleasantries with Nasrin, while Nasrin fixed them a plate of cut fruit, nuts, and cookies, and a pot of cardamom tea that would keep Zahra up all night, the small talk growing so loopy and high pitched Zahra didn't think she could stand another minute.

A cursory visual assessment of the room didn't reveal any sign of the recipe book she'd come for. But then even here, she had the disconcerting sensation things had shifted.

"Mom? Where are Maman Joon's recipes?" she interjected during a lull in the conversation.

"Oh. Hmm . . . Let's see . . ." Nasrin bit her lip, then pointed to the bulky wooden armoire that stood in the kitchen as steadfast as an appliance. At least that hadn't changed. "Maybe there."

Zahra stood and dug through the items on the top shelf. Under an antique green glass cake stand, she found the album, the recipes inside tired and yellowed but kept safe like pressed flowers between plastic sheaths. Flicking through the pages, Zahra scanned the dish names, the loose scrawl of notes in her grandmother's writing. She could almost see the hazelnut knots of her grandmother's knuckles as her fingers slid across the paper.

"Did you hear what I said?"

Her mom stood in front of her, offering a cup of fragrant black tea.

"Sorry," Zahra said. "What was it?"

"I wondered if you could go through those last boxes in your room while you're here, to make space."

"Are you redecorating or something?"

"I'm making some changes." Nasrin had turned back around to pour her own cup, so Zahra couldn't read her face.

It wasn't just the house changing. Nasrin's hair, usually in a neat bun near the base of her neck, hung long and loose, the jeans and simple tunics she favored replaced with a flattering, cotton V-neck dress patterned with bright flowers. Distracted, Zahra took a sip of the steaming tea and scalded her tongue. *Damn.* She hated that, hated to think of the damage to her taste buds.

"You said you wanted to tell me something." She set down her mug. "What is it?"

In the few seconds of silence that followed, Zahra prepared herself for something terrible. It was the house, she just knew it. Her mom wanted to move.

Nasrin sat down, pushed the plate of food toward Zahra and Aurora. "Do you remember Rodrigo, who I told you about?"

Zahra pulled a cookie from the plate, hoping the busyness of chewing would calm her, the sugar might reset her heart. "Rodrigo? You went on a few dates with him, right?"

"That was ten months ago. Since then, things have gotten more serious."

"Good for you, Nasrin. That's so great," Aurora chimed in, her chipper voice scraping against Zahra's sensitive insides. She could barely swallow the bite of cookie in her mouth, the crumb scratching all the way down her throat. She didn't visit her mom often enough, taking for granted she would always be right here if Zahra needed to come home. She had no claim to the property, but the idea of Maman Joon's old kitchen in some other family's care—redesigned to meet some other family's modern sensibilities—made her nauseous.

"Thank you. I'm really happy," Nasrin said.

"Is it the house? Are you planning to sell?" Zahra blurted out.

Her mom's eyes widened. "The house? No, no. I'm planning to be here as long as possible. But . . ." She paused. "Rodrigo is moving in with me."

Her mom had dated on and off over the decades since her dad had left, but there'd never been anyone of note. She certainly hadn't expected her mom to meet someone, not after all this time, not at sixty-two years old.

"Everything feels *right* with Rodrigo." Nasrin blew on her tea, took a sip, and tucked a strand of her hair behind her ear. "We're happy. He makes *me* happy."

"The gym was Rodrigo's idea?" Zahra asked.

Nasrin smiled. "We use it together."

Zahra stood, dropped the remnants of her cookie in the trash. She wanted her mom to be happy, but she'd thought her mom *was* happy, all this time. She'd thought she and her mom were the same that way—independent women, fine on their own. It was as if her mom's decision to start a new relationship threw Zahra's life choices into question, even though rationally she knew one had nothing to do with the other.

While they'd been talking, the cat had begun to explore the kitchen. He jumped from the trash can he'd been perched upon, his feet meeting the floor with a soft thump. Zahra stooped to pick him up, rubbing behind his ears until his familiar purr revved beneath her fingertips.

"Aren't you worried you could make all these changes only to not have it work out?" she asked, trying to sound more neutral than she felt.

"I can't know what the future holds. But I'm getting older, and I want companionship again. It was never my plan to live by myself forever, but when your dad left, I needed time to find myself again. I got married so young, you know," she said, more to Aurora. "Then my parents were getting older, and once they were gone, I had to recover from those losses as well."

The talk of loss reminded Zahra why they were there in the first place. She hadn't considered how she would tell her mom about her dad. Her parents didn't have any kind of relationship anymore, but she understood they'd cared about each other once, no matter how much time had passed or how much hurt they'd shoveled on top to bury those first feelings. "Mom? I have to tell you something."

The news clearly shook her mom, her vibrant energy dimming to a subdued glow after she heard what Zahra had to share, but she pulled herself together, asking questions about his health neither Zahra nor Aurora had the answers to yet. After a few minutes, Nasrin stood and began to collect their cups. "It's already a quarter till. My students arrive soon. Zahra, will you join me?"

"Maybe another time." She wasn't up to more socializing. She had no patience for the kind of teaching her mom did.

"Could I?" Aurora asked.

Nasrin brightened. "Of course. That would be great."

"Aren't you worried you'll be recognized?" Zahra said. "That's three hours in a small space with nowhere to hide."

Aurora frowned. "You're right. Maybe I better not."

"Just wear a mask," Nasrin said. "It's not as if it's unusual anymore; I doubt anyone will think twice."

"A mask." Aurora tapped her forehead with the pad of her hand. "Duh. Why didn't I think of that?"

"It's settled, then." Her mom unwrapped her apron and set it on the counter, back to her no-nonsense self. To Zahra, she said, "I guess that gives you the evening free. Can you dip into those boxes? I'm happy to toss or donate what you don't want, but I need you to make sure there's nothing important in there."

"Sure," Zahra said, not sure at all.

"And what about dinner? Maybe you could cook one of your recipes for us."

"Ooh, yes," Aurora said. "I vote for that."

Zahra continued flipping through the recipe book while they headed out the sliding glass door to the kitchen studio in the backyard, the cat eyeing the exit with interest.

She gave him a tender squeeze. "Don't even think about it."

A half second later, her phone vibrated with a notification. A voice text.

"Zahra, hey, me again. You didn't respond yet, which means either you already blocked me or maybe there's hope and you haven't had an opportunity to message me back yet. So I guess this could either win you over or freak you out enough to block me now. Good thing I prefer to live on the edge.

"I've landed in Santa Cruz. Decided I'd make a pilgrimage to see the redwoods. But photographing these giants is no joke. I took some trunk shots, a few straight up through the middle of the grove, and I still can't do them justice. Their magnitude defies a camera's lens. I feel that way about people, too. It's why I don't do portraits. At least, not anymore.

"I heard once there's more life in the canopy of the forest than on the floor. Everyone knows how tree roots are interconnected, but this is different, because it's not just the trees, it's other species interacting, and feeding the tree, too, completely hidden from view. It's a nice thought, isn't it?

"I've been thinking about stuff like that a lot lately, trying to mentally note things, even the smallest things, that make me feel better when the world gets too heavy. When life feels too hard.

"Something bad happened last year, really bad, and it shook me up, changed me to be sure. I got back to traveling and living my life, but I haven't felt the same. Until I ran into you today. I know we don't know each other at all, but talking to you makes me feel a little more like me.

"I was thinking about that since I sent the first voice text. How it can be easier to share yourself with someone you don't know well, who doesn't have context for your past, for your foibles, for your default settings. Or maybe it's that you can start to see yourself differently through the eyes of someone else.

"Speaking of, maybe you could just tell me what you see right now."

20

Aurora

The kitchen studio was small but with high ceilings and tall windows that let in a ton of light. A perfect place to take a selfie, and Aurora couldn't help herself. She pulled out her phone, teased her dark hair, and snapped a photo. Usually, she might take fifty shots to get a single one she could post to her socials, but since she wasn't posting anything, she shoved her phone in her back pocket, glad for once not to have to care how she looked.

Arriving at Nasrin's house had come as a relief, the whole place disarmingly normal, Nasrin a regular sort of mom. Aurora had forgotten a bit about normal and regular. It started before she even had her own money, her mom always imploring her to dress for the job she wanted. For a long time, they'd lived just beyond their means, faking a level of success Aurora hadn't yet achieved. After the faking became real, she'd quickly lost track of the difference, of what came before. The other life she'd begun to hope for.

Nasrin handed her a heavy canvas apron. "Cook much?"

"Not at all," Aurora said, tying the apron's straps behind her back. "Just one of the ways Zahra and I differ."

Nasrin opened a fridge hidden beneath the countertop and began to paw through it. "You have a dad in common. I'd say that's significant."

"I don't think Zahra would agree."

"She may have a different relationship with her dad than you do, but it doesn't change the facts. You know, I'm relieved you're both going to see him. It'll be good to have you both so close. It'll be good for Zahra."

"Pretty sure Zahra would disagree with that, too."

Setting several plastic tubs and trays onto the counter, Nasrin released a sardonic grunt, sounding not unlike her daughter.

"Even if I don't always understand her, I know she has her reasons for how she feels," Nasrin said. "It's not just your dad, you know. She's been through a lot."

For a second, Aurora wondered what Nasrin could be referring to, but then Zahra's divorce popped into her mind. She'd never known the details of what happened. Trickle-down information had led her to assume her sister had married a nice guy but the wrong one. It happened all the time. Incompatible people who weren't willing to make compromises. Look at her own parents. Look at Dillon and Serena. That's why Aurora had waited for a boyfriend. Long past the point when her peers had kissed and had sex and fallen in love for the first time, Aurora had held out for someone special.

Except maybe there was more to Zahra's story than she knew.

"I try to respect her"—Nasrin looked up, groping for the word—"boundaries? I owe her that much after her rocky childhood. I wasn't always there for her. Even after Dom left, I was in my own world."

Working together, they began to set out the trays in front of each workstation. Nasrin directed Aurora to the utensils and knives.

Thinking aloud, Aurora said, "Do you think Zahra blames herself?"

"For what?"

"For our dad leaving? The character I play, Sloane, she blames herself for their mother's death. Because she was a little girl, and she didn't know how to call 911 like her older sister would have known how to do. It's a whole . . . thing." She waved the thought away with her hands, her eyes darting from Nasrin's blank stare. "I'm just saying the character *wrongly* blames herself, you know? But it influences every decision she makes. It's at the heart of her story and her relationship with her older sister."

Nasrin's brows wrinkled together. "Has Zahra told you that?"

"No, no way. She doesn't tell me anything. I just thought maybe it might be something similar. Wires get crossed when you're a kid."

In Aurora's earliest years of auditioning, the ones she could remember anyway, her mom used to say things like, "We got this, Aurora," or "We'll nail it. I just know it," or "We're gonna make it big, girlie, wait and see." Her liberal use of the plural pronoun led Aurora to believe that both she and Lucy were trying out together, that when her mom's lips moved in sync to the lines Aurora had to deliver, she was practicing for her own audition. When Aurora had found the courage to ask her mom about this, Lucy had nodded seriously. "I am performing. In a way," she'd said, serving to further Aurora's confusion for another couple of years after she was old enough to know better.

Nasrin had stilled, her eyes glazed over in thought. Finally, she shook her head. "You know, I'd never considered that possibility before." She plucked a set of cards from a file folder and handed them to Aurora. "Here. Can you set out one each of these recipes, too?"

Aurora studied the cards, grateful to be steered away from the heaviness she'd inadvertently waded into. "Persian food?"

"Persian inspired. Based on my mom's recipes, but I take liberties with them. For that matter, *she* took liberties with them."

"From the recipe book Zahra wanted?"

"Mm-hmm. My mom collected a huge number of Persian dishes before she came to the US, and a whole bunch of other recipes once she'd lived here awhile. It's the strangest mix, but it works because it's all delicious."

"She passed a love of cooking down to you, and you down to Zahra. I wish I had that with my mom. She loved acting, but I don't think she really passed down the passion to me. More like the determination."

Nasrin shook her head. "I didn't teach Zahra how to cook. My mom did. She taught both of us. But you know, we don't always get to choose what we inherit. Or what we pass down."

❦

Nasrin had a natural presence in front of her pupils that commanded their attention—and affection. It wasn't unlike performing on camera. Aurora could totally see her fronting a cooking show.

Aurora had been paired with a girl a few years younger than her who was attending the class with her parents as a belated birthday gift for her mom. Was this really the kind of thing families did together? Even when her parents had still been married, they hadn't done much as a unit outside of their home. They'd dragged Aurora along to the occasional dinner out with friends or her father's business associates. A few trips to the waterfront, some weekends around the Pacific Northwest. Mostly, she spent time with them individually, smothered with care by each, if not necessarily at the same time, and yet she felt as if she was the one doing for them, presenting herself as their precocious little girl, such good company around adults.

Aurora shook off these uncomfortable thoughts and concentrated on the clumsy feel of the knife in her hand.

Violet, the girl beside her, chopped a carrot and a piece rolled off the counter and onto the floor. "I don't know what I'm doing."

"Good. Me neither," Aurora said. Behind the mask, she could be herself, falling into an easy rapport with Violet when they weren't listening to Nasrin's instructions.

"Do you go to UC Santa Cruz?" Violet asked. "Or wait, you seem older. Did you already graduate?"

"Oh, actually, I didn't," Aurora said, self-conscious despite the fact this girl didn't know who she was. "I mean, I haven't graduated. Yet."

"What year are you?" Aurora didn't correct Violet's assumption but let her keep talking so she wouldn't have to respond. "I'm a junior. Biz

/ econ major, which is super boring but good for getting a job, I guess. My parents begged me not to"—she threw up a pair of air quotes—"waste my degree, or whatever. What's your major?"

"Um. Film?"

"That's so cool. I would love to do something more creative."

"I might change to English lit, though." And just like that, Aurora found herself falling into the role, a walk-on part, nothing special. Average College Student chatting with a friend. "Or psychology?" she said, trying the idea on for size. She liked the notion of working with people who were different from her. She was good at that.

When Violet complained about her parents' involvement, how over she was living at home, Aurora could even relate.

"Once I graduate, I can get a real job, save up some money, and find a place of my own," Violet said. "I can't wait for my life to start, you know?"

Aurora's life had already begun, the foreseeable future spotlighted as her path ascended. But if she stopped to look back at where she'd come from, she could see there'd been a fork in the road she'd missed, an opportunity to go left along some unknowable, overgrown trail, and she'd gone right into Dillon's arms instead.

"Yeah, we want freedom," Aurora agreed vaguely. "I don't live with my mom, but I see her all the time. She's still a force."

"That's almost worse. Because how do you make the break then, right? You're trapped." Violet seemed to catch herself. "I don't mean *you* you."

"No, it's fine. It's exactly how I feel. Trapped." Aurora hadn't known that was the feeling until she said the word. A few hundred miles away, a whole team of people were planning her future. There was a whole show's worth of writers and actors and production members depending on her for their salaries.

If they ever got to shoot Season 2.

Did she even want to?

The question hit her so unexpectedly she nearly fell off her stool. Of course she wanted to. And even if she didn't, which she definitely did—this was a dream job, *the* dream job—she had to. There was too much at stake. Her mom and her team. Dillon. Her whole future.

"But it's fine," she told Violet. "Because I'm really, really lucky."

"Oh, totally," Violet said. "Count those blessings, girl."

And Aurora did. She had it all. She just had to hold on to it.

21

Zahra

During her undergraduate years, before Zahra had even begun to consider applying to culinary school, she would come home from UCLA to cook in her grandmother's kitchen, their hips touching as they stood at the stove. If she complained about not getting something just right, Maman Joon would poke her in the ribs. "How can there be right or wrong? It's just flavor," she would say as Zahra scoured the recipe's directions, wondering where she'd screwed up, what she could improve the next time.

"It's technique," Zahra would explain.

She had told herself that Maman Joon didn't understand because she'd fallen into her place in the kitchen by gender and necessity. But, of course, her grandmother had always been so much more than a home cook.

Lying open on the counter, Maman Joon's recipe collection was a book of spells propelling Zahra around the kitchen. She was working on the preserved lemon Caesar dressing that had been on her mind the last couple of days, a recipe not found in the pages of the makeshift book, which instead had things like Shirazi salad with the typical tomato, cucumber, lemon, and parsley, as well as briny olives and cubes of salty feta, or a recipe for green goddess dressing made with the traditional licorice bite of tarragon but also Maman Joon's addition of maple-y fenugreek and ground pistachios.

Out of practice navigating her grandmother's kitchen, she had to open every drawer and cabinet to find a mixing bowl, a Microplane, a hand-size mortar and pestle. When she visited the family home in Santa Cruz, she let her mom do the cooking, a minor point of contention between them. Hence, her mom's request that Zahra make dinner. Tonight she just might.

Her mood had lifted since her mom and Aurora had left. With a knife in her hand and the smell of garlic on her fingertips, she was in control again. Everything was fine. Even if the kitchen was changing. This day would soon be behind her. This whole trip.

So her mom had a serious boyfriend. And a home gym. So what? She wasn't selling the house. Zahra was getting used to the idea of Rodrigo living there. She knew she wasn't great with change, but this was her mom's change, not hers.

And there was that voice text. She was trying not to think about it. Him. Elian Scott with the syrup-thick voice she pictured the shade of dark purple, like the skin of a perfectly smooth eggplant.

But it was just a voice. A voice attached to a body nowhere near hers. This method of communication had its benefits. Though the fact that he was also in Santa Cruz never left the back of her mind.

From the fridge, she pulled out a glass jar cloudy with the spiced preserved lemons, the white pith feathery and sea creature–like in the salt brine. She plucked out a half lemon and finely chopped the softened rind, the knife a bit dull but tapping pleasantly along the board, before she paused to add the yellow bits to the mortar. A food processor would have been faster, but she preferred the gentle grind of working by hand to the mechanical whir of a machine.

She tossed in a fat dose of garlic and a pinch of salt, grateful her mom's culling hadn't extended to the kitchen's coffers. With the mixture blended, she spooned it into a bowl with a dollop of tahini, a splash of fish sauce, and a few glugs of olive oil. She whisked, ignoring the pain from the cut on her hand, her wrist hardly moving as her tendons on her forearms engaged, the punch of the garlic catching her in the nose.

There. Done.

Now, the moment of truth. She dipped a teaspoon into the dressing and brought it to her mouth.

Immediately, her lips pursed, her nostrils flared. She took another bite to be sure. No, no, that wasn't right at all.

Somehow the flavor was both too pungent—the heat of the garlic too hot, the funk of the fish sauce too funky—but bland at the same time. She'd been trying to avoid the basic salt-bomb quality of a creamy Caesar, but this one popped in all the wrong ways. The preserved lemon wasn't bad, but it wasn't doing any favors; she couldn't tell it was there. Damn. She thought she'd been close. She thought she had something special, but this was going to require a series of tweaks to get *right*. She didn't have it in her. Not tonight; maybe not ever.

She didn't usually quit so easily. It was her job, after all, to keep calculating the ingredients until they added up to something exceptional. But as she stared down at her grandmother's recipe book, the thought of her own growing file of recipes on her computer, the ones for her supposed cookbook that she'd amassed since dropping out of culinary school, which she'd so painstakingly made and remade over the years, shamed her. All that work had added up to nothing so far. *A hobby,* she'd told Aurora. What a waste of time.

Zahra's grandmother's recipes had first come with her from Tehran, but then she'd expanded her repertoire, inspired by dishes from other immigrant mothers she met when she came to California; from the working white ladies down the street with their shoulder pads and pantyhose and the dump-and-stir casseroles their Midwestern mothers had made; from the backs of the boxes she bought at the supermarket and clippings from the newspaper; and from the ones she'd cobbled together on her own out of curiosity. But they'd all been made to be enjoyed, not perfected.

And yet, Zahra couldn't help herself. Even now, some engine in the back of her mind was already toying with a new plan. Back to the usual anchovy instead of fish sauce, more preserved lemons, a bit of fresh lemon juice, too, to balance the salt. Even this subconscious habit scratched at her shame. As if her efforts mattered at all for anyone other than her.

She abandoned the whole bowl of dressing in the sink, the contents splattering across the stainless steel, and pulled out her phone to open her recording app and add another note about another culinary fail. Instead, she found herself opening the Messages app, pressing "Record."

"You wanna know what I see? No big wide view here. No redwood trees. Even though I am partial to them. Growing up beneath them, they've always felt holy to me. But I just see an old kitchen with a mess I have to clean up, and a cat with a bum paw." She glanced around the room, her eyes settling on a patch of wall near the doorway. "There are some lines marking my height over the years. The apron my grandfather sewed for my grandmother looped over a hook. No one wears it. It just hangs there and has for the last twenty years.

"Every time I come home, I never wanna leave, and at the same time, I'm desperate to get out of here. Have you felt that way before? Like you can't leave, and you have to leave." She caught herself. "Oh wait, you're probably the guy who always wants to leave, right? On to the next thing, the next place, the next woman."

Was that too coy? She didn't care. The words flowed, the failure in the kitchen fading from her mind as she spoke. She paced the room, the cat watching her with ticktock eyes.

"What you said about being able to be more open with someone who you don't know—I'm not sure it's true for me. Sometimes I feel like I don't even know the people I do have the context for. Or maybe the problem is I have the wrong context . . . You know, I used to have this best friend. We were capital-letter BFFs, with those split-down-the-middle heart necklaces and everything. Even when I was at UCLA and she was at UC Davis, we stayed in touch—phone calls and voicemails and emails back and forth every day. And then . . . then she fell in love with my husband.

"God, when you say it aloud, it sounds like something from a soap opera. But that's exactly what happened. Well"—she shrugged—"technically, he was my soon-to-be ex-husband. But it doesn't matter now, does it? And since I know you're wondering, yes, they're still together. Married, actually. Does that make it better? No, it does not. Not that I'm hung up on him. Or her. I hardly even think of them anymore."

That was true. If her brain went rogue and tried to *go there*, she'd usually jerk herself away as if her fingers had grazed a hot pan.

"Anyway . . ." She began to wander down the hall, heading to her old room, the cat following at her heels. Aurora had abandoned her suitcase on the floor, but otherwise there was nothing in there besides the neatly made bed, and beyond that, stacks of boxes and giant plastic bins gathering dust against an empty wall.

"I'm in my childhood bedroom. It's probably more accurate to say that I'm in my adolescent bedroom. My *childhood* bedroom was in another house. Another lifetime. The first time my life was split into two, before and after, I was barely twelve. I don't think that's unusual for kids whose parents get divorced. But it felt unusual. It felt as if the rug was pulled out from underneath me. Even though it shouldn't have been a surprise. I could never remember a time when my parents got along. My dad traveled for work, but when he was home, it was almost worse than having him gone. Because he so clearly didn't want to be there, with us."

Setting her phone down on the floor, she lifted a box down from the top of the pile and knelt beside it, her hands scraping against the cardboard edges as she pulled back the flaps. The cat tiptoed around the pile, rubbing the length of his chin against one of the box's sharp corners.

"I was very angsty in this bedroom," she said. *And lonely.* "I don't know why I'm telling you this. I guess I'm still pretty angsty." Her skin prickled, as if she'd been stripped of her clothes on a cold day, and she rubbed at her arms. All that she'd revealed to him seemed to hover around the room as if the private inner workings of her mind were on display. So fine, he *was* right that sometimes it was easier to talk to people who didn't know you, even for her. "By the way, a ring of redwoods is called a cathedral, not a grove." She paused. "Tag, you're it."

After she pressed "Send" she felt both pathetic for responding again and eager to hear back from him. She was, in fact, acting like an angsty teenager. Being home brought that out in her, even at thirty-eight.

To distract herself, she began to dig through the boxes. In the first, she found nothing but clothes, all black, unrecognizable without pulling them out. She couldn't imagine why she'd hung on to them.

A few minutes later when her phone vibrated, she broke into a smile.

"I'm picturing your childhood bedroom and imagining . . . what?" Elian's voice trickled through the speakers, clear as cool water. "*The Craft* poster and a bedspread with something unexpected—tiny daisies, maybe? A throwback from your younger years you couldn't bear to part with."

He was factually incorrect but also not wrong. The bedspread was black with eyelet lace trim.

"No, but I know what you mean about your life splitting in two. My parents aren't divorced, still very committed to being unhappy together, and given their shining example, I've never been interested in marriage. But that's exactly what it was like, this very bad thing that happened. One day I knew one set of rules about the world, and the next, the game had completely changed, and the only rule is there are no rules. I guess it's a good thing I never really liked rules anyway."

He said this as if it were a punch line, but there was no smirk there. She sensed this was a line he'd doled out to comfort himself, like the SSRIs she'd taken for a while until she found they muted her appetite.

Background sounds she couldn't make out filled a brief silence.

"Sorry. I'm walking back to my car, getting ready to leave Santa Cruz." He paused as if she could interject, ask him to stay, and she could almost imagine herself meeting him somewhere, hopping in the car when Aurora and her mom were none the wiser, feeling that rush she'd felt before at the café. But that was Hollywood magic, not real life.

Finally, he said, "You never did tell me why you're headed to Seattle. But I feel like you and your sister aren't traveling together for the sightseeing . . . Not that sightseeing is the only reason to travel. I booked my first flight the day after graduating from high school and spent every minute and dollar I had before college started seeing what I could. I convinced myself I was running toward adventure. Based a whole career on it. But that was in the Before times. Now I'm not sure what I'm working toward." He sighed, the rush of air like a gust of wind. "I don't think I've ever admitted that to myself," he said. "So it's only fair you tell me something no one knows about you . . ."

The recording ended and she resisted the urge to respond right away. She'd give him time to leave town first.

Aurora wanted to know why she couldn't have a little fun. Zahra was skeptical of fun, but she could see the appeal of a good distraction. Something to hang her mental apron on that had nothing to do with herself or the conversation she needed to have with her dad. Or the running list of things she had committed to *not* thinking about.

Shoving one box of clothing aside revealed another. Inside this one, her culinary school uniform, a chef's coat emblazoned with CULINARY INSTITUTE OF AMERICA in green stitching across the left shoulder. It was pristine; she'd barely worn it in. Beneath that she found a shoebox, the sight of which roiled her stomach. How could she have forgotten?

But she hadn't really, had she? She'd intentionally redacted the knowledge of its existence, a big black swipe across her memory, and that was different from forgetting.

She stared at the old shoebox a long time before lifting it into her lap. She didn't have to open it. She could stick it back in the box and leave the whole thing for her mom to toss, go back to pretending it never existed.

But the stubborn part of herself reared up, overcoming her fear.

"It's just a box," she told the cat, who had curled up among the cardboard, his tail flicking as he watched her.

A box filled with boxes. Matchboxes. Each one a tiny work of art, outlined in delicate beads or lace, or both. Each lid a hand-drawn image or a painting in miniature, impossibly detailed. The undersides of the matchboxes were unadorned, except, sometimes, for the name of the restaurant from which they'd originally come; on the side, "A. Hayes," written small and light with the flick of a sharp pencil.

Childhood wasn't the only time Zahra's life had split in two; it had happened again in her twenties, each time like severing the end of a finger. For a time, she'd been Zahra Hayes.

An image of her ex came to her unbidden, his beautiful smile, so easy to come by. The way his sharp canines gave him the appearance of an edge he didn't have.

She had fallen in love with Wes Hayes like she'd fallen in love with cooking, over time without her even noticing. Until giving it up would have been like asking her not to breathe.

With Wes's family, however, it was love at first sight.

That happy, close-knit crew welcomed her when she was a sullen college girl Wes had met in Econ 101 at UCLA. To save money, he lived at home and commuted from Sherman Oaks, and soon she lived there, too, sleeping beneath his parents' roof somehow an improvement over the crappy apartment she shared with five other girls she hardly knew and didn't particularly want to know.

But it was Ann, Wes's mother, she'd loved the best. She was eccentric, an artist living as an elementary school teacher. Ms. Frizzle, her students called her, and she delighted in the reference to *The Magic School Bus*. When she got sick, it was like the earth cracked open, the beginning of the end, but they didn't know it then. Zahra and Wes had been out of school a few years, talking about marriage down the line, but suddenly it was imperative they get married soon so Ann could be in attendance.

They had, and the chemo and the surgery seemed to work. Ann retired early from her job and began to spend her precious free time recreating found objects into things wholly unexpected. A pointy-toed shoe might become the base for a lampshade. A set of espresso cups glued together and repurposed as a candelabra. But the reimagined matchboxes were her favorite. "It reminds me how small we all are," she told Zahra once. "There's comfort in that." By the time the cancer returned, metastasizing to her lungs and liver, Ann had created dozens of matchboxes, to be split among her children, and Zahra, too. "A legacy of empty space," she'd joked.

She made everyone promise to fill them.

Zahra and Wes had known right away what they'd use theirs for: a love note to their unborn child tucked into each box. Right after Ann died, Zahra had looked down at the two lines on a pregnancy test and felt a rush of fear and longing like she'd never known before. She was a few months into culinary school, and a baby was in no way part of the plan, not right then, but maybe there was a reason for all this. That's what Ann would have told her and Wes, something they couldn't see yet. And Zahra had been foolish enough to think that for once the universe might be looking out for her.

Now, here the matchboxes were, filled with a future that had never come to pass, the letters she and Wes had taken turns writing during her pregnancy undelivered.

She picked up each box, light as air, and held them between the tips of her fingers. She couldn't open them, but she couldn't bear to part with them either.

The last she lifted rattled in her hand, and this one she did push open, her heart taut as an overfilled balloon. She stared down at her wedding ring. Ann's wedding ring. A square diamond, not just for tradition but for the April birthday they happened to share, set between two emeralds on a gold band.

She hadn't realized she'd kept it. Or perhaps she had. Perhaps she hadn't wanted to let it go when she'd already lost everything else.

A pin was pointed at her heart, and she knew she couldn't bear a single prick. She set the ring back in its matchbox and returned it to its place among the others, closing the shoebox and carrying it to her things in the living room, where she shoved it into the empty cooler, airtight and out of sight.

Back in the bedroom, the cat had relocated, sprawled himself on the bed beside her phone. Zahra stared down at the remaining boxes and made a decision. If there was anything else in there that mattered, she'd rather lose it forever than find out what. She wished she'd never looked at all.

Elian wanted to know something no one else knew about her, but he didn't mean it. Some things were better boxed and shoved away for good. Some people, too.

22

Zahra

The sun had nearly gone, casting an orange light through the sliding glass doors, by the time Nasrin and Aurora returned to find Zahra in the kitchen, opening boxes of Pizza My Heart on the counter beside plastic tubs of salad. Yes, yet another Caesar that added nothing new. She didn't know why she couldn't give up, her drive in the kitchen sometimes more like a compulsion than a passion.

"I ordered in," she told them unnecessarily. She'd removed any evidence of her attempt at cooking, wiped down the mess in the sink, put the preserved lemons back where she'd found them in the fridge.

Her mom nodded. "I can see that."

They settled at the table, the cat in Zahra's lap. She scratched behind his ear. She'd rewrapped her hand with a new bandage and checked his hurt paw, too, but it looked like the cut was healing okay. He licked at it halfheartedly before settling.

"Class was great," Aurora said, even though Zahra hadn't thought to ask. "Your mom is such a pro. The rest of us were totally clueless, but we had fun. I'm barely hungry." The massive bite she took said otherwise. "What'd you do?"

"Not much," she said. "But Mom? You can get rid of the boxes. I don't need any of that stuff anymore."

Nasrin shook her head. "Isn't it amazing how much you can accumulate in a lifetime?"

"But I'd like to keep the recipe book." Before her mom could disagree, Zahra added, "I'll take good care of it and can make you a copy. A nice bound one."

Nasrin set down the slice of pizza in her hand. "I never felt ready to part with it before, but I do now. You're right; it belongs with you."

She'd gotten what she wanted, but the ease with which her mom had given up unbalanced her. "Oh, okay. Well, thank you."

"You know what's funny." Her mom wiped her mouth with a napkin. "Maman Joon didn't care about the food."

Zahra swallowed. "How can you say that? She loved food."

"She loved to eat and cook, but she wasn't concerned about how the food turned out. Not really. And she hated to talk about it at the table. When you sat down to eat, you were meant to enjoy it, enjoy each other, not critique each bite."

Her mom's words echoed her own thoughts from earlier, and the reminder only served to raise Zahra's defenses against an unnameable force.

"She cared about the recipes," Zahra said, unsure whether she was trying to convince herself or her mom. "Her recipe book is proof of that."

"Food was a means to an end. A reason to gather. She wanted what she made to taste good. Good enough to keep people lingering in her kitchen, at her table. That's all."

Zahra couldn't argue but she wanted to. To lecture her mom on flavor and technique. Ingredients and appetite. But what was all that for, without a table to share it? That's what Maman Joon would want to know.

Zahra shoved another bite into her mouth without tasting it.

"I'm glad you have the book now," Nasrin said. "I hope you cook from it."

"Maybe you can put some of the recipes into your own cookbook," Aurora said.

Zahra didn't respond, just chewed, chewed, chewed.

After dinner, Aurora made an unnecessary to-do about cleaning up, even though the mess was minimal. Zahra followed her mom from the kitchen to the living room, where Nasrin began to turn the couch into a makeshift bed.

Zahra lifted a corner of one of the heavy wool blankets her grandparents had brought with them from Iran, its weight as close as she would ever again get to feeling her grandmother's arms encircle her. "Let me help."

They worked in quiet for a bit, until her mom cleared her throat. Zahra recognized the sound as the beginning of a conversation. She and Nasrin weren't practiced in deep talks, and immediately a surge of discomfort washed over Zahra.

"You know, I've been thinking about your dad," Nasrin started.

Zahra's eyebrows shot up. "Yeah?"

"When we had you, we were so ill prepared."

"Well, sure," Zahra said. "You were so young. Though Dad was almost thirty."

"He was barely twenty-seven and as clueless as I was, as far as parenting goes."

Zahra waggled her head as if to say, "What's your point?" She knew this already. She'd heard the story a dozen times, back when she used to beg her mom for the details.

Her parents had met at Cowell Beach, before pollution and an endless influx of tourists had dirtied its crescent-shaped shoreline. The shy young woman on break from her retail job at the wharf and the strapping man who'd driven down that morning from the Sacramento Valley had fallen hard for each other right away, or so the story went.

Zahra had never managed to glean what had kept them together after the initial moment of attraction, or whether it had only been the gravitational force of two stars doomed to collide.

It's true Dom Starling wasn't the last young American man Dariush and Fariba Sadr would have chosen for their daughter. Clean-cut and driven, he had not only a college education but also an MBA and a lucrative-sounding job as an investment banker. His Central California family were fourth-generation farmers, as wary of their son's career path as they were of Middle Eastern immigrants, but the Starlings' prejudices never entirely eclipsed their manners.

The problem wasn't Dom's background. It was his personality.

Bullheaded, brash, and unreliable, the traits "baked in from birth." That's what Dom's mother had said to Nasrin the first time they met, a warning about her youngest son. Dom was accustomed to being the smartest guy in the room because he usually was. He was also charming, chivalrous, and old-fashioned in how he peppered his speech with formalities like "sir" and "ma'am" and "pardon me," the way he carried a pocket watch and smelled of spicy aftershave.

Intuiting her parents' response to Dom, Nasrin had intended to keep him a secret until an unexpected pregnancy derailed that possibility. At first, she didn't tell her parents about the baby, just that she'd met a man and they'd decided to get married. That went over about as well as you'd expect.

Nasrin's parents never entirely came around, and they weren't sorry to see Dom eventually go, even though they still found divorce unsettling. But the baby—that was another matter. They loved being grandparents. Their devotion to Zahra had no barriers, no caveats.

Zahra stuffed a pillow in a pink floral case. Nasrin sat down on top of the blankets, patting at the fabric as if feeling for something small and lost underneath.

"You know, when your dad left, I didn't have a kind word to say about him. I guess I didn't have much to say at all, I was so mired in self-pity. I should have made a point to check in with you more. I realize now if I had been more open with you then, maybe today you might be . . ."

Nasrin trailed off, clearly trying to collect her words. Zahra's eyebrows pinched together, trying to figure out where her mom was going with this.

"I'm sorry. I'm not good at this. We haven't practiced talking to each other very much, have we? I'm trying to say there's more to the story you should know."

From the kitchen came the rush of the faucet. Dishes clanking against the sink. Aurora humming an unrecognizable tune.

"We hadn't been good together for a long time—ever, really," her mom continued, looking first at Zahra and then down at her lap. "But I . . . I had something happen with one of the men I worked with at the restaurant where I waitressed. It wasn't a real affair. We didn't sleep together or anything. I just wanted to be admired again."

Zahra resisted the urge to plug her ears and close her eyes. Thinking about Rodrigo moving in was weird enough; she didn't want to unpack her mom's sex life. They didn't have that kind of relationship.

"He flattered me, is what I'm saying. We had a connection of some kind. It went on for a few months, and in the heat of one big fight with your dad, I admitted it to him."

Her parents' fights clung to Zahra's memory with the potency of static on plastic wrap. But they were strangely shapeless like that, too. She couldn't remember a single specific accusation or insult they'd thrown at one another, only the volume of their voices bouncing off the walls. The heavy stomp of her dad's gait to the front door. The way the glass panes on the windows rattled with the slam.

Nasrin looked contrite, and Zahra only understood right then that her mom was in the midst of some kind of confession. Her throat tightened in response. She willed the sink to shut off, Aurora's humming to quiet as she marched into the room to interrupt them. At the same time, she gripped the pillow tighter, leaned in to hear what her mom had to say.

"I told him to hurt him," Nasrin went on. "Not to assuage my guilt. Not even because I believed coming clean was the right thing to do. That's how I thought back then—an eye for an eye. And of course, it did hurt him. So he hurt me back. We were both very immature. It can take a long time to grow up. Much longer than you could possibly believe when you're young."

"You didn't drive him away," Zahra argued. "He cheated on you for real. He got another woman pregnant. He left us without looking back."

"I know. I'm not condoning what he did, what he established with Lucy behind our backs, but what *I did* came first."

"Just because he's"—Zahra glanced toward the kitchen to make sure Aurora wasn't listening and lowered her voice the way a person might to spare a child's ears—"dying, it doesn't change the facts."

"Not the facts, no. But our perspective maybe. Your perspective?"

"He's not suddenly a better man."

"I'm not saying that it's okay, him leaving the way he did. But it's not as black-and-white as you believe. You need to understand . . ." Nasrin took a breath, and when she looked at Zahra, her yellow-flecked eyes had gone dark. "I told him to go. That's the cold truth. When he confessed, I told him to pack his things. I said we—*you*—were better off without him, and I couldn't stand to look at him again. So he went."

Pressing the pillow to her chest, Zahra tried to compute this new information, align it with her memories. "Neither of you thought I deserved an explanation?"

"It's not about what you deserved. We weren't thinking about that. *Neither* of us. But don't you see? You blamed him and forgave me."

"You didn't leave."

"But I told him to go without saying goodbye. He wanted to talk to you, and I said no."

Nasrin's hands gripped the blanket, and Zahra fought a churlish desire to toss the pillow on the ground and stomp out of the room. "Why would you do that?"

"I was so angry. So ashamed to have to go back to my parents with my tail between my legs. I didn't leave you, but I checked out, didn't I? We were both selfish in our own ways."

Had she ever had this frank of a conversation with her mom before? The limitations of their relationship were like the thick black outlines in a coloring book, and Zahra had always been the type to prefer staying in the lines. In a single moment, Nasrin had not only colored outside the lines but also ripped the page from the book.

Zahra had seen her mom's failings and forgiven them, because at least she had her mom there to forgive, and because Maman Joon had filled the void until her mom had come around again. By the time Maman Joon died, she and her mom seemed to have found an unspoken understanding. She appreciated the distance between them. It made Zahra trust her more, the way you trust that a wild animal's disinterest in you means they won't suddenly attack.

They talked about food and work and restaurants, but harder topics they broached briefly with surface-level details. It had worked fine enough. Or so she'd thought.

It wasn't just the house changing, or her mom's appearance, it was her mom, too, as if someone had put a step in Zahra's home where there hadn't been one before. She couldn't tread the same worn floors without tripping.

Nasrin didn't seem to notice the awkwardness that had come over her daughter. She said, "By the time I stopped feeling hurt and realized his leaving had been a mercy for me, you were in high school, and I thought it didn't matter anymore what had happened. I'm sorry for how it affected you. I want you to know that."

Zahra shook her head. "It doesn't change anything. He could have made other decisions. It's not like he was Father of the Year before he left."

"No. That's true. I can't argue with that. But I know he loves you."

She stifled a scoff as Aurora bounded in from the kitchen.

"All done," she said, eyes twinkling, the cat trailing at her heels, limping on his hurt paw. "What'd I miss?"

On the couch with the cat pouncing around the room and onto her feet, Zahra found it impossible to sleep. Her thoughts were in knots from the conversation with her mom. That and knowing the matchboxes sat so near, the unread letters in each emitting a low-frequency buzz she couldn't seem to tune out.

Fine. She'd escape the living room and sleep on the floor of the so-called gym. But when she dragged her blankets in there, she discovered the stationary bike and yoga mat she'd envisioned were accompanied by a weight bench, a towering pyramid of hand weights, and a massive treadmill that took up half the room.

Scuffling back to the couch, she ran into Aurora in the hallway. "What are you doing?" she hissed, ears pulsing from the scare.

"Sorry," Aurora whispered. "I had to pee. What are you doing?" She glanced behind Zahra. "Quick late-night workout?"

"Trying to find somewhere else to sleep. But unless I want to sleep on top of the treadmill, it's not happening in there."

"I did that once. Slept on a treadmill. Not recommended."

Zahra squinted in the dark. "When? Why?"

"High school party."

"You went to parties?" With her best friend Sarah leading the way, Zahra had gone to her fair share of awful high school parties, but she didn't remember Aurora as a typical teenager, let alone someone who would show up to a party.

"Before I left high school." Aurora shrugged. "I mean, it was only the one time. When my mom found out I spent the night there, she forbade me from ever going again."

"How she'd find out?"

The whites of Aurora's eyes flashed in the dark. "She told me I could tell her anything."

"Oh my God, and you believed her?" Their stage whispering had begun to intensify. The house creaked, making them both jump. Why were they even talking about this? "I'm going to sleep," she said, moving down the hall.

"You can stay with me. If you want? The bed's plenty big."

Zahra thought about shrugging her off, but the humming was still in her ears, and she knew it would only grow louder. She'd end up spending the whole night wide awake, waiting for the first hint of light to sneak through the blinds.

It was just one night. And it's not like they were going to snuggle to sleep.

"Fine," she said. "Thanks."

Once they were in bed, it took them a while to get comfortable, each shifting in micromovements so as not to disturb the other.

"Is your alarm set?" Aurora said into the quiet.

"Yep."

"Long drive tomorrow."

"Mm-hmm."

"If you let me drive part of the time, I promise not to detour us again."

Zahra snorted. "Maybe the second half."

A few minutes passed, Zahra nearly on the edge of sleep when Aurora spoke again. "You still awake?"

"No," she grumbled.

"Do you really think he could be okay? Dad?"

Zahra didn't think it was likely he was going to come out of this one unscathed. It felt unnecessarily cruel to blurt that out right now, but she didn't believe in Aurora's little white lies either.

"I don't know," she finally said. "I'm not psychic."

"What do you think he has to tell us?"

"Honestly? Nothing. I think it's all a ploy to get us both there."

"Yeah," Aurora said. "You're probably right. But what if it's not? What if he really does have something important to say?"

Zahra couldn't imagine what it might be, but then in the space of a single day, there'd already been too many surprises. Her phone lit up the room with an incoming voice text. She resisted the urge to press "Play." She owed Elian a response, but she didn't want to listen with Aurora lying a foot away. It would have to wait.

"I guess we'll find out tomorrow," she said into the dark.

"Zahra, I'm trying not to take your lack of response to heart, and I had half a mind not to message you again. Or to at least wait until tomorrow. But then I looked at the time—I'm in a hotel in Mendocino—and I saw it's past midnight. Effectively tomorrow already, and I've always been inclined to jump first, think later.

"If you were attempting to ghost me, then you probably won't bother to listen to this, and I can say exactly what I want to. So I'm wondering what you were cooking earlier today—er, yesterday, that is—and I'm wondering how a man leaves a woman like you, for her best friend, no less. And I'm wondering what that does to a person. I could see how it might make you hesitant to trust people—say, like strange men who start sending you texts out of the blue.

"Fair enough.

"You might be wondering what my intentions are, and I . . . Well, all I can say in my defense is I like talking to you. I meet a lot of people while I travel, and it's given me the ability to work out right away if I want to keep talking to someone. I can't say exactly what it is, but sometimes you just know, you know?

"I've never regretted striking up a conversation, but on occasion, I've regretted not striking up one. Because there's always something there. Something in talking to someone else that makes life more interesting.

"Anyway . . .

"Tomorrow—today—I drive home to Portland. I'll do the Southern Oregon portion of my assignment in a few days. If I head back home first, then I don't have to rush it. The thing about a coastal road trip is you have to take the long route. All those twists and turns add miles and time. I don't mind. You still get where you're going, even if it takes longer. You see things better that way. There's more time to tune in. Is it the same for food?"

DAY TWO

23

Zahra

Zahra took a turn too fast, splattering the contents of her coffee cup all over her hand and the Volvo's torn seat cushion. "Dammit to hell."

They were an hour and a half into their daylong drive, passing through Silicon Valley on their way to the Central Valley and onto I-5, which would take them the whole way to Seattle. It was only six thirty, but they had eleven more hours to go.

Aurora pulled her sweatshirt sleeve over her hand and used it to wipe up the spill. "Someone woke up on the wrong side of the bed."

"No kidding." Zahra had slept fitfully, the conversation with her mom replaying in her head, her lower back aching from the old mattress.

But if they wanted to make it to Seattle by nightfall, they had to get an early start. They'd woken long before daybreak, each groggily gathering their things and packing them in the back of the Volvo, careful to make sure the hatchback latched. In her half-doze haze, Zahra had dreamed of the busted latch coming undone on the drive, their bags bumping out the back. In the rearview mirror, she could see their belongings strewn across the highway, the matchboxes crunched into oblivion by the crush of tires.

She'd sloughed off the strange feeling that followed while she got the cat settled into his carrier and Aurora made a pot of coffee. Hidden in the bathroom, she'd listened to Elian's voice text but felt too agitated to message him back just then.

Bleary eyed and clutching her robe, Nasrin caught them right before they headed out the door. She looped an arm over Aurora's shoulder and gave her a squeeze, then pulled Zahra toward her.

"I'm glad you're going," she said. "I didn't set the best example, I know, when it came to forgiving your dad, but everyone deserves another chance. If not him, then at least you do."

Zahra didn't know what one had to do with the other, but there wasn't time to ask.

From the passenger seat, Aurora cleared her throat. "It's a really long drive, so if you wanna talk about anything . . ."

"I don't want to talk. And no games either." But the matchboxes, the letters they held, still buzzed, like she had a hive of bees locked in the trunk. She could hear the hum radiating through her body, synchronizing with the flow of her blood. She ordered Aurora to put on music, but even that didn't work. Maybe the lack of sleep had heightened her emotions. Whatever it was, she couldn't seem to tamp it down. As the ugly expanse of highway flowed outside their windows, the sensation became too much, a terrible itch that had to be scratched right then.

"This isn't gonna work," she said.

Aurora looked at the map on her phone. "It'll be tight for sure. But as long as we're there before it gets too late."

"No. I mean, I have to stop," Zahra said.

"You want me to drive?"

She grabbed her phone from the cupholder and held it out to Aurora. "I need you to look up a contact in my phone. Wes Hayes."

"But that's—"

"Yes. Now, please. Can you? I need his address."

"His address—"

"Aurora, please!"

Aurora quieted and scrolled through Zahra's phone. "Okay, I have it. Petaluma?"

"Map us there."

"You have to go there right now? We're in the middle of a twelve-hour drive."

"I just need to drop something off. It'll be fast." She paused, took a deep breath. "Please. It'll only push us back an hour, hour and a half tops. I really need to do this." Then, as if to wipe away the earnest request, "And anyway, you owe me a stop."

"I thought you said we were even."

"I changed my mind."

Aurora relented with a sigh. "I should at least text Dad." She tapped at her phone and a vibration followed. "He says it's fine. He says he still doesn't know what time he'll be discharged. Also, he says to drive safely and not to rush."

"Coming from the guy who used to take me off-roading in his Jeep when I was too short to reach the overhead hold bar."

"He did?" Aurora asked, incredulous. "I can't imagine that."

"He was more cautious with you."

Zahra thought of the time when she was sixteen, stuck on a visit to her Dad's and left to watch four-year-old Aurora while Lucy was out.

They'd both been bored, so Zahra had bundled them up, stuck Aurora in her stroller, and walked her a few blocks over to the park. She hadn't thought to leave a note; they'd be back long before Lucy got home, and she could turn on the clunky Nokia she had in her backpack in case of an emergency. She puffed with a measure of pride as they walked. She'd remembered to pack snacks, take Aurora to the bathroom before they left.

But when they got back, their dad paced the sidewalk in front of the house. He pulled Aurora from her stroller, the straps catching on her arms and causing her to cry out.

"Where the hell have you been?" he demanded, his tone as dangerous as venom.

Zahra floundered. What had she done wrong? They'd actually had an okay time, hadn't they? It hadn't ended with Aurora in tears, until now. "We were at the park."

"You don't take a child from their home without telling their parents," her dad said, like he was accusing her of kidnapping someone's child.

She, Zahra, was someone's child, too. His child. In that moment, the final thread that stitched her to her father seemed to break, and she'd no longer felt like *his* or a child.

"God, whatever. Don't ask me to babysit *your child* then," was all she could think to say. Not even a hint of her real hurt rising to the surface.

Anger could cover so many wounds.

Whenever she thought of her weakness that day, the way she hadn't told her dad how she really felt, not letting him know how he hurt her, it dissolved all the strength she'd built over the intervening years. But not this time. This time she would muster her courage. She just had to unload some baggage first.

Zahra pulled off the road but stopped short of turning down the long, winding driveway. Instead, she parked on the dirt shoulder, left the engine running.

They were tucked between two small hills. The sky blue and white striped. The air heavy with the scent of earth, grass, the tangy bite of manure. Late-summer's heat stained the hills brown and yellow, except for pockets of green where irrigation systems kept the grass high for herds of lumbering cows, a patchwork quilt of farmland.

The house, Wes and Sarah's, was partially visible from the Volvo's vantage point, albeit nestled behind a small crest and surrounded by a grove of soaring, gray-green eucalyptus trees. It would take only a minute to get there by car.

Zahra turned off the ignition. "I'll walk the rest of the way."

She needed the extra time to collect herself. And if they were home, and she suspected they might be given the early hour, she didn't want them to see the car. She wanted to leave the matchboxes and slip away unnoticed.

"Do you want me to come?" Aurora asked.

Zahra shook her head. "I won't be long."

"I guess I'll wander a bit and see if I can get service."

Aurora's assistant had called as they were getting into the valley. When she'd tried to answer, the call dropped, and Aurora had been obsessively checking her phone since, trying to find service.

They were both, it seemed, untethered.

"The cat," Zahra reminded her.

"I won't go too far."

Zahra went to the back of the Volvo and pulled out the shoebox, ignoring Aurora's curious stare. She didn't have to explain herself, and even if she'd been inclined to do so, it would require too much. Too much time. Too much of her.

She plodded down the long driveway, watching her step to avoid the large ruts in the dirt track, trying to convince herself they could have left for work already. But she didn't have a clue what their schedules might be, if Sarah was still a nurse, if Wes's job still allowed him to work remotely.

What she knew of her ex-husband and her ex–best friend was limited. During a particularly masochistic period right after her divorce, she'd tortured herself by following their movements online. But in recent years, she'd only learned small bits of information from her mom, who sometimes ran into Sarah's parents in Santa Cruz, and from Wes himself, who sent her a quick email maybe once a year or so. His most recent had come a few months into the pandemic when he'd told her they were moving from San Francisco north to Petaluma. Why not, when he could work from home and Sarah's shifts were only three days a week? Why not, when they'd always wanted to live on a plot of land?

She hadn't known that Wes wanted to live in a more rural area. She'd thought he was a city person through and through. Wasn't that why they'd decided to stay in LA after graduation when she'd wanted to go back to Santa Cruz? Or why they'd moved to San Francisco instead of somewhere in Wine Country before she started her ill-fated culinary program? It was the use of the word "always" that hurt her the most. "Always" implied Wes and Sarah had decided this from the beginning. But *when* was the beginning? Had they discussed this shared affinity when they'd been Zahra's boyfriend and her best friend?

She hadn't been able to respond to that email, and he hadn't emailed again since. Somehow four years had gone by. But she'd kept his address, updated his contact information in her phone. Just in case.

In case of what? she'd wondered at the time, disgusted by her inability to let go, once and for all.

Now she knew.

The three-story home was one of those country Victorians with a wraparound porch as wholesome as graham crackers in milk. An SUV was parked in a carport to the side of the house. Her heart began to pound, and a potent wall of heat descended on her. She paused midstep, unsure whether to move toward the porch steps or reverse course and take off running back to the Volvo. She wouldn't have the heart to come back here. It was how she felt about seeing her dad. Propelled by a tank of pent-up fuel she didn't know she had. It would burn up, one way or the other, and she didn't want to go down with the flames.

She had to do this.

Her throat tightened and her gut twisted as if she might vomit, and she *never* got sick, thanks to the cast-iron stomach she shared with her dad. As she neared the porch, she decided she would set the box at the top of the steps and hurry away.

Finding her usual strength waning, Zahra tapped into her reserves of stubborn defiance and forced herself to place one foot onto the first step, then the other. The wood creaked beneath her weight, and she winced at the sound. But she was so close. She'd leave it, then go. The final step groaned worst of all, and she nearly dropped the box before tripping her way back.

She'd just made it to the bottom when she heard the click of the front door opening, the sound of footfall.

"Zahra? Is that you?"

She'd recognize that voice anywhere, no matter how many years had passed.

"No," she responded nonsensically, barreling forward, feet crunching on gravel, hands balled into fists flinging back and forth to get her away.

"Zahra, wait," Sarah called after her. "Please."

A loud thump and a grunt stopped Zahra in her tracks. She turned around to find Sarah on her butt at the top of the steps, hanging on to the railing, her frizzy red hair in her face.

Without thinking, Zahra moved toward her. "Oh shit. Are you okay?"

"I think so. My backside took the hit." She pulled herself upright and stared at Zahra, green eyes round with disbelief. "It is you."

But Zahra couldn't speak, couldn't breathe. She grabbed her abdomen with a wave of nausea. Sarah mirrored her movements, rubbing her hand over her protruding belly.

"Oh," Sarah said, her face whitening with fear as she saw Zahra looking at her, taking in the sight of her pregnant body.

"I have to go—"

"Zahra, please don't leave—"

"I shouldn't be here."

"But you came," Sarah said.

Zahra moved backward, but she couldn't look away. Sarah was eerily unchanged from a decade ago. Except for the new expanse of her body, the bottle-cap mound of her belly button visible beneath her stretchy black shirt.

"How far along are you?" Zahra couldn't help herself, couldn't deny the curiosity she didn't want to feel. She wanted to know everything and absolutely nothing. She wanted to pull Sarah into her arms and scream in her face.

Sarah closed her eyes for a long second, and when she opened them, Zahra could see the tears welling over her lids. "Twenty-nine weeks."

"Girl or boy?"

"We wanted to tell you, but we didn't know how. We didn't know if you'd want to know. We've been thinking about you constantly. *I've* been thinking about you. I miss you." She spoke fast, her face desperate and pale.

But Sarah wasn't allowed to miss her, not when she was the one to break her. Not when she was the one who got to have the baby. And yet Zahra split in two, could almost hear herself returning the sentiment, could feel the words forming in the back of her throat, catching before they could slip from her tongue, because God, she missed her best friend, too, missed being someone's best friend.

"Girl or boy?"

"Girl."

Zahra nodded, swallowing down a sharp rock of pain. Part of her wanted to wail. It was so unfair. But a stronger part of her stopped the cries that gathered in her throat.

"I'm so sorry," Sarah said through tears. "I wish things could be different. I really do."

"I had to return something to Wes." Zahra gestured to the shoebox. "It belongs to him. I shouldn't have held on to it so long."

Jutting her head toward the front door, Sarah said, "You can give it to him yourself. Let me get him."

Zahra shook her head. "I can't do this."

"Do what? Zahra, we just want to see you. Talk to you."

At that exact moment, the door flung open. "Sarah?" Wes's voice came from inside the shadowed house. Sarah didn't respond, her eyes glued on Zahra. When he stepped from the door, the sight of his sturdy shoulders walloped Zahra in the heart. She'd loved those shoulders once, believed those shoulders would carry her.

Recovering, she squared her own shoulders, the familiar anger she'd hefted around so long fitting over her chest like a bulletproof vest.

"Zahra," he said. "What are you—"

She nodded at the shoebox. "I was just dropping that off."

He bent down to pick it up. Lifting the lid, his expression transformed from confusion to disbelief to sadness. Had a small, petty part of her been hoping for this moment? To witness his heartbreak? It seemed possible, and if so, she didn't care. She knew now; he had everything.

"The ring's in one of those, too. Now you can pass it down. Your mom would want that, I think." She let out a breathy exhale, throat still as tight as a lid screwed shut. "Anyway, my sister's waiting."

She stepped from the staircase and began walking to the car as confidently as she could, despite wishing the ground would open and swallow her whole. If they weren't watching, she would have taken off at a run.

"Zahra, wait," Wes said, feet pounding down the steps. But she wouldn't. She'd already come too close.

24

Aurora

Aurora walked down the county road they'd driven in on, first one way then the other. She'd had a signal before, long enough to get the call from Evangeline but not long enough to take it. Now her bars kept shifting from three to one, and every time she tried to load her browser or make a call, the whole thing conked out.

Her head itched beneath her baseball cap. The cheap dye had dried out her sensitive skin. At home she had a hydrating masque to apply to her scalp when her eczema flared. Home. She might as well have been thinking about another planet, another way of life. Even though they'd only been on the road a day and hadn't even made it out of the state yet, she felt a million miles away. That was the point, of course. To get off the grid. And here she was, totally deadzoned.

It wasn't a great sign that Evangeline had called again. But that didn't necessarily mean it was a bad one either. She was probably calling to ask about a schedule change. Or maybe there'd been an update from Serena's camp, a denial of the pregnancy story or confirmation that she would still smile and nod with Aurora on the Emmys' red carpet.

Unlikely, but it was possible. Stranger things had happened. Like that Aurora had met Serena at all. Right when she'd gathered the courage to give up acting.

She'd been catering at a party for extra cash, like the cliché of a wannabe actor she was, her prime years disappearing in a malaise of modest and middling roles that would never amount to anything life changing, when up walked Serena Kelly of contemporary rom-com fame, the other half of Kelly Productions, holding an empty wineglass. With gazelle-like proportions and grace, Serena set the glass on Aurora's tray, and the goblet broke right off its stem.

"Wow, major Hulk move," Aurora blurted out.

Serena, still perplexed by the glass perhaps, cocked her head one direction then the other, examining Aurora's face before she burst out laughing.

"I've never been compared to the Hulk before," she said. "You're an actress, aren't you?" Of course she was, along with the rest of the staff. "You know, my husband and I are working on a project you could be perfect for."

That was it. The entire course of her life changed forever. Everything she'd been working toward since before she could remember, all the embarrassing roles and disappointing auditions, and in a split second, here was her future handed to her on the cheap silver platter she'd carried around that night.

Aurora wasn't surprised, not really. Big breaks happened. But she certainly hadn't expected Dillon.

She craved the sound of his reassurances. He could talk anyone off a cliff, and the more time that passed without hearing from him, the closer she felt to some sort of edge. She closed her eyes, saw the way his mouth softened when he looked at her, the hazel flecks of his irises staring straight though her. If he were here, he would tell her she needed to keep her head up. Put the noise out of her mind. "Criticism is either fuel or fumes," he would say. "Let it propel you or pass right over you."

A car whizzed by her, blowing wisps of hair into her face and thrusting her back into the moment. When she looked back down at her phone, she suddenly had four bars. Her voicemail dinged, followed by a series of text notifications. Then more. Each one like a punch to her chest.

It couldn't be.

She refreshed the browser window she'd been using to search her name. Her brain went fuzzy as the results loaded, the headlines nearly knocking her to the ground.

> Bestie Gone Bad: Aura Star of *You, Me, Us* Caught Cheating with Costar Serena Kelly's Producer Husband Dillon
>
> Aura Star and Dillon Kelly Affair Rumor Confirmed!!
>
> Everything We Know (So Far) About Aura Star and Dillon Kelly's Affair
>
> Aura's Star Falls: Source Reveals *You, Me, Us* Actress Cheated with Costar's Husband

Dazed, she found herself at the Volvo without remembering walking back there. She couldn't remember what Evangeline's voicemail said either, something about Margot demanding they get on a call immediately.

Standing on the side of the road, refreshing the page and watching the headlines collect, she'd gone from a sweat-drenched panic to numb acceptance. Any second, her phone would start ringing and it wouldn't stop.

The numbness would last as a shield for a while, but it didn't grant her the power of invisibility.

Only spotty cellular service stood between her and complete mayhem.

No one knew where she was right then. No one could begin to guess. She couldn't disappear, but she could turn off her phone. Evangeline would have a panic attack. Margot would lose her shit. And her mother would kill her. But it would only be for a little while. Until they made it to their dad's tonight. Enough time for the dust to begin to settle and everyone to chill.

But first, she composed a text to Dillon: Tell me what to do. I need you.

Without giving herself time to second-guess, she fired off a another: I love you.

As soon as the text had sent, she turned off her phone. There was still no sign of Zahra, but she was in no rush now.

Opening the passenger side door, Aurora blinked against the harsh sunlight. Sweat collected at her temples, and the rash on her scalp started hollering. She took off her hat and ground her fingers over her head, grateful for the temporary relief, the pain of her nails a preferable alternative to the itching.

Before she was even settled in her seat, she heard the cat's cries.

Leaning over the center console, she tried to see into his carrier on the back seat. "What's wrong, kitty?"

He meowed in response, his narrow body pushed against the carrier's mesh side so that his gray-brown fur poked through each hole in fluffy little tufts.

"You really are a Fluff, aren't you?"

She let her fingers trail along his fur and his lithe body pressed harder into her. The poor guy. Removed from his home, stuck in a cage, craving contact.

"What do you need? What can I do?"

Back outside of the car, she banged on the broken hatchback's latch until it popped. She opened a tin of cat food and carried it around to the back passenger door. Her plan was to free him from his carrier, give him a bit of food, hold him for a while. Pet him until he calmed down. Until she calmed down.

But the moment she unzipped the carrier, the cat moved like a flash, launching himself not just out of his small enclosure but straight from the car, darting into the tall grass and overgrown bushes that ran along the side of the driveway.

She gasped. "Oh no."

Her forearms and jeans caught on a bramble of blackberry bushes as she gave chase. The plant's spindly branches were knitted into a tangle, and despite her effort, she couldn't get very deep. She elbowed her way back out to the Volvo and grabbed the cat food. Positioning the can on the ground, she began to elicit a series of desperate, fruitless coos.

He could be anywhere. But she would find him. Even if Zahra didn't know it herself, Aurora could see her sister had an attachment to the cat. The thought of losing him felt like losing the one chance Aurora'd ever really had to connect with her sister. She wouldn't let herself screw this up. She'd comb the countryside if she needed to.

Things might have been blowing up back home, but this she could fix. She had to.

Username: Elly Spills All

Bio: Serving tea with a side of hot goss

A close-up of popular video gossip queen Elly Belly with the GlamAnon filter obscuring her facial features appears over a green screen photo of Dillon Kelly with an arm hooked over Aurora's shoulders. The two are dressed in black and clearly attending a large event. Rather than looking at the camera, they're looking at each other.

"In news that will surprise absolutely no one who knows how the celeb gossip mill works, that blind item we thought might be about *You, Me, Us* showrunner Dillon Kelly and Aura Star has been confirmed. By no less than, and I quoteth, "an extremely reliable insider source." I have my money on Dillon. But it could be coming from Aura as a way to punish her two-timing paramour who's made sure the paparazzi have captured him out with his wife this week no less than three times."

The green screen flashes to a picture of Dillon and Serena dining outside. Dillon holds what looks like an iced tea, while Serena's back is to the camera.

"This might be a record for the Kellys, a notoriously private couple. Fun fact: they met when Serena was eighteen and Dillon was thirty-five. Serena took a screenwriting course at USC that Dillon was guest teaching, and the couple married a few years later. The impending divorce rumors have been swirling ever since.

"Meanwhile, we've had no new Aura sightings. Given the timing with the Emmys only days away, we know she has to make an appearance soon. Now we wait for statements from one or both parties, but seeing as how both Serena and Aura are nominated for Best Lead Actress in a Drama Series for the same show—yikes!—I have a feeling we'll see more drama before Sunday."

Elly raises her hand and crosses her fingers. "One can only hope."

25

Zahra

"I wish we'd known you were coming," Wes said as he and Zahra tromped down the driveway, glare glinting off the roof of the Volvo where it waited down by the road.

Zahra couldn't see Aurora anywhere. She hoped that meant she was back in the car, ready to make a run for it. She glanced at Wes. Beyond the shade of the house, she could see that he had bags beneath his eyes and his shoulders had grown a little hunched. They'd both aged. So much time had passed since they'd first met.

She could still remember the way she'd felt with him at the beginning, held snug by an invisible sling between them.

But early love always transforms into the mythical once it's over. A cloud city that only you and your lover have ever been invited to. In reality, there was nothing novel about falling in love. Staying in love, staying *for* love—that was the true fantasy. An imaginary proposition Zahra had discarded ages ago.

"I didn't stop by for a visit," she said.

"I know. Look." Wes held her arm and brought her to a stop. "Thank you for bringing the matchboxes. And the ring. You didn't have to do that, but it means a lot to me. Feels like a little nudge from Mom."

Zahra looked anywhere but at him. "For me, being here has been more like getting socked in the face with a bag of quarters."

"I'm sorry I didn't email to tell you about the pregnancy. It's just when you didn't respond to my last one, I figured maybe it was best to give you space." They fell into silence. "I still think about her, Zahra. What might have been."

"Don't." She couldn't bother to hide the hurt from her tone.

"C'mon. You know I would never have chosen things to turn out the way they did. Ever."

She frothed with anger, a ragged rage that had been fermenting for years.

He'd always been so damn kind. So damn thoughtful. So damn positive. Measured, in a way that made him impossible to argue with. Zahra had always been the problem, the instigator, the one prone to lashing out. He'd made her feel so irrational. But his rationality dripped with condescension. How could he ever be in the wrong when he never so much as raised his voice? But his calm, his reason, even his kindness added up to a form of manipulation. A defense mechanism that left no room for Zahra's feelings. "We'll try again," he'd said after they lost their baby. As if they'd been trying their luck at a carnival game, their daughter a prize easily swapped for another.

Try again. She hated those words.

"You can't have both," she said now. "You can't wish things happened differently without wishing away the life you have. It doesn't work that way."

He shook his head. "You always see things so black-and-white. There's so much in between."

"It's easy for you to say when it's all worked out just fine for you. When you get a whole do-over."

"A do-over? There are no do-overs."

"A new wife. A new life. A new"—she could barely utter the word—"daughter."

"That's not how it is. I didn't want a new anything. At first. I wanted you. I wanted *us*. I wanted to get through things together, but you made it impossible. You shut me out, over and over again."

Accusations from their last fights came back to her with brittle clarity, another unopened letter tucked into the matchbox of her mind. He kept asking if she was okay; he wanted to know how she felt, and she wanted him to understand how she felt without having to tell him.

No, she wanted him to *feel* how she did. Brokenhearted. Hollow. Bereft.

What he wanted was for her to feel better.

"These things happen," he'd said at the time. "Who knows why? But it wasn't meant to be." As if something as mundane as the offer for a house they wanted hadn't been accepted, as if lives hadn't been lost, her daughter's and her own, the version in which everything didn't fall apart. "You think you're keeping yourself safe by pushing me away, but you're keeping yourself broken."

"I'm not broken," she shot back.

"And I'm not your dad. Stop treating me like I am. I'm not going anywhere."

"What does he have to do with anything? Don't bring him into it."

"Let me in."

They'd gone back and forth, and then despite all that, or maybe because of it, he'd left anyway after a couple of months of barely speaking. And here they were, a decade later, standing an arm's length from each other, the same argument still on the tips of their tongues.

"I needed time," she said.

"But you never told me that. You just kept pushing me away. With your attitude and your sarcasm and all your little digs. I tried to take it. But I'm not tough like you."

She recognized the truth in his words even as she fought against them. He'd left her. But only after she'd shoved him away. After she'd told him she didn't need him anymore. She remembered what her mom had said about how she'd pushed her dad away.

As all this washed over her, Zahra trembled, overcome with everything she felt but couldn't manage to articulate. Salt burned her eyes even though she stood miles from the coast. The wind that whipped off the water could travel that far, sometimes, when the conditions were right.

Finally, she managed, "You left me when I needed you most. You left me for my closest friend. You got to move on. I didn't just lose my baby. I lost a part of myself I can never recover. Ever." A part of herself who had believed life could be one way but came to understand her life would now be another. A part of herself that had believed in hope but now knew better. This part of her had been an idiot, she told herself. She, of all people, should have guessed how things would go. Hadn't she known deep down hope was for other sorts? People like Aurora. Hadn't she already learned the only thing reliable about people was they disappointed you?

He opened his mouth to protest, but she raised her hand, cutting him off. "Don't say anything, okay? There's literally nothing you can say."

He nodded, and they were quiet, Zahra lost in the deepest grooves of her brain's darkest neural pathways, the ones she had thought she'd boarded up a decade ago. It wasn't that she didn't think about the baby she'd lost. She thought about her all the time, but abstractly, the way something important you needed to do might flutter its way in and out of your awareness all day but never land, so that despite it being on your mind, you might fall asleep without having ever put your attention to it. It turned out, you could do this for years if you needed to. If you felt you had no other option.

Zahra's phone vibrated, breaking her trance. Coming to a stop, she pulled out her phone to find a text from Preeti. But it was only eight thirty, way too early for Preeti's usual midmorning wakeup.

Hey, the neighbors are complaining about one of the outdoor lights attached to your unit. They stomped over here first thing claiming it lit up their bedroom all night 🙄

Outdoor lights? No way; she never left those on. But then it came back to her. The way she'd rushed back inside to get a can opener for the cat food after Aurora's unexpected arrival yesterday morning, flicking on the bank of lights by the french doors. The one for the entryway, but also the one for the floodlight on the other side of the unit that looked over the driveway—and the neighbor's back bedroom. She must not have turned them off.

I ended up going to see my dad. I won't be home for a few days.

No worries. I can let myself in and flick the switch if it's okay with you.

She didn't want Preeti in her place when she wasn't there, but what choice did she have? She was the one who had angered the neighbors, sent them banging on Preeti's door when she was surely asleep.

Sure, that's fine. Thank you.

Good luck with your dad. Thinking of you.

As if good thoughts were going to get her through this nightmare. Zahra shoved her phone back in her pocket without responding.

"Everything okay?" Wes asked, but the sound of a car door slamming called their attention toward the Volvo. In the distance, Aurora appeared, pacing alongside the car. When she caught sight of them, she lifted her arms and began to wave frantically.

Really? She had to go for the dramatics right now?

"What is she doing?" Zahra asked.

She kept waving and soon they caught the sound of her voice.

"I think she's yelling for help," Wes said. Then Zahra heard it, too, her sister's cries carrying on the breeze.

They took off together, running in her direction.

26

Aurora

Zahra came barreling down the road, the man Aurora recognized as Zahra's ex-husband at her side. "It's the cat," she called when the two neared. "He escaped."

"You have a cat in the car?" Wes said, brow wrinkling with confusion.

"Well, not anymore." Aurora directed her attention to Zahra. "It's my fault. I know; I'm a total idiot."

She braced for her sister's scathing assessment. Whatever she said, for once Aurora really deserved it. But even the worst of Zahra's ire would be better than what was building elsewhere. A welcome distraction, even.

But Zahra only held her hand to her chest and examined Aurora with wide, hollow eyes before leaning on her thighs to catch her breath. Facing the ground, she said, "Holy hell, Aurora. You scared me. I thought something had happened to you."

It has, Aurora wanted to say. But that was the last thing Zahra needed right now.

"We'll find him." Zahra lifted herself upright and began making noises to coax the cat from wherever he'd hidden himself. She grabbed his cat bowl and began to tap it with the car keys. Aurora joined her efforts, and Wes forced his way into the bushes.

But even with all of them calling, the cat didn't appear. Twenty minutes passed, followed by another. They both knew they needed to get back on the road, but Aurora couldn't bear to say so with Zahra as frantic as she was.

"Where is he?" Zahra said, her voice pitched with desperation. "We can't just leave him."

A great wave of shame rose up in Aurora.

She was so careless. She never thought things through. She never thought about the consequences if things went wrong, because she assumed everything would turn out fine. *Things always work out for you.* Zahra's words taunted her like a curse. Her sister would never forgive her for this mistake.

"Look," said Wes, picking cattails and burs from his shirt. "We live on four acres and our neighbors live on ten. There's a lot of open space here. We could search all day and still not find him. But I'll keep looking on and off, okay? I'll ask the neighbors to keep an eye out."

Zahra nodded grimly and described the cat as best she could when his only notable physical characteristics were his short gray coat, the hurt paw. "He's an outdoor cat, but he always shows up, looking for a meal. I'll leave his food and his bowl. He's not skittish, so if he comes running, you can pet him." Biting her lip, she stared out at the wide field, then glanced to the main road, where cars whizzed by. "He likes to be scratched behind his ears," she added quietly.

"He'll turn up," Wes said.

"Yeah," Zahra said, sounding unconvinced. "Thank you." The two exchanged a quick goodbye. Their hands grasped, but they didn't come together in a hug, and Aurora wondered what had transpired between them, what her sister had needed so urgently to drop off. But Zahra walked back to the Volvo, her face mournful in a way Aurora didn't recognize, and she knew she couldn't ask.

Zahra tossed something in Aurora's direction. "Here. Catch."

The keys landed in Aurora's outstretched palm.

"Would you mind driving? I'll take the next leg. I'm not feeling up to it right now."

They settled into the car. Aurora checked the rearview mirror but left the seat as it was. Being the driver might be a good thing right about now. No way for her to break down and turn on her phone. Until she looked again, it was almost like the story didn't exist, as if Dillon had texted her back. What did they call that? Schrödinger's cat?

The thought of the cat sent her spiraling again.

"I'm so, so sorry about Fluff," she said, then corrected herself. "I mean, the cat."

"It's not your fault. You were right. We should have named him."

Aurora was so bewildered by Zahra's simple forgiveness, for a second, she couldn't formulate a reply.

"We still can," she managed. "Something better than Fluff."

Zahra brought her hands to her face. Aurora didn't think she'd ever seen her sister cry before, but when she spoke again, Zahra was subdued but not shaky. Her eyes stayed dry. "I should never have brought him. It was selfish."

"You were looking out for his paw. You were trying to take care of him."

"No, I wasn't. I only brought him because it was an excuse for us not to drive together."

"Oh," was all Aurora could think to say. It's not like she hadn't known her sister didn't want to drive with her, but she was surprised by Zahra's admission, by the lengths her sister would go to avoid spending time with her.

"It was stupid," Zahra said. "I wish I could take it back."

Aurora prepared herself for what she was sure was coming next, how Zahra regretted coming at all. How she wished they'd never ended up on this road trip together to begin with. How this was all Aurora's fault. But instead, Zahra said nothing more, clearly lost in her own thoughts. Aurora should have been glad that Zahra wasn't angry, but somehow it was worse to have Zahra blame herself. She tried to think what to say that could make it better, but for now, it seemed better to say nothing at all.

Other than when Zahra nudged Aurora with navigation instructions, they sat in silence, the Sonoma countryside sweeping past them.

Aurora had no idea how much longer they had to go from here. The entire rest of the day, that was for sure. It seemed impossible they would make it to their dad before late in the night, long after a sick person should be waiting up, but Zahra didn't say one way or the other, and Aurora was content not to know. To keep moving forward. But even though it was irrational, she couldn't stop herself from looking back the way they'd come, glancing into the rearview mirror like some kind of criminal on the run.

It wasn't a crime to fall in love with a married man, but it might as well have been. Except instead of jail time, she faced the court of public opinion.

She thought of her dad when the FBI had shown up at the house. It was a memory she would have preferred to delete from her brain, but there it remained, waiting for her defenses to fall. She could still picture the officers knocking on the ugly red door, displaying badges, serious, set jaws. What she couldn't picture was the expression on her dad's face. Did he feel remorse? Shock? Guilt?

"Like Martha Stewart," he'd explained to Aurora later.

"Martha Stewart? The cooking lady?"

"She went to prison for insider trading."

The air had left Aurora's lungs. "You're going to prison?"

"Probably."

He pulled her into a hug before she could study his features, and she realized her own were wet with tears, soaking through his shirt.

"I'll be okay," he told her. "You don't have to worry about me."

But Aurora, a hormonal teenager at the time, was worried for herself, for how her life would change, and the implication that she should have been thinking of him shamed her so that she resolved not to think of it anymore. He would go away and come back, and they'd never have to talk about it. Eventually, they could pretend it never happened at all. Pretending had always come easily to Aurora. Her parents' divorce had upset her, but moving to Southern California and focusing on acting had been a good way to take her mind off things.

"Hey." She spoke without realizing she would. "Do you think Dad felt guilty for what he did?"

Zahra grunted. "What do you think?"

"I think I wanted him to feel guilty. I think in my head I told myself that was the case. That he regretted it and would take the whole thing back if he could. But now I'm not so sure."

She sensed Zahra studying her but didn't turn her head to see.

Finally, Zahra said, "I don't think he wanted to go to prison. That part he regretted for sure."

"Well, yeah."

"He wished he hadn't been caught, that's what I think."

Aurora thought of Dillon, how he wanted to keep their relationship secret and in the same breath claimed his marriage was over, and she'd let it stand. She'd never demanded anything of him. Just like she'd never even asked her dad why he'd done something he knew was illegal, something he knew could ruin his career. Then she'd gone and followed in his footsteps. If her dad was a cheater, then didn't that make her one, too? She loved Dillon, but was that enough to justify their relationship?

These questions disturbed her, and they lingered, despite her usual tricks to put them out of mind. Aurora had long ago convinced herself it was better to only ask questions you wanted to hear the answer to, like she never asked Dillon outright if he loved her, but she might say, *Do you love being with me? Am I the only one you want?*

But maybe she'd been wrong all along. Maybe what you didn't know could hurt you.

"In one of the letters he wrote to me while he was away," she said to Zahra, "he told me how his dad had been . . . What was the word he used? 'Indifferent,' maybe. He said his dad disciplined his older siblings with a belt, but by the time Dad came around, the man had been worn down. One time he said to him, 'You're not even worth the effort of lifting my arm.' Or something like that. Dad said it made him want to see what he could get away with."

Zahra sat up a little straighter, adjusted her visor. "He wrote that to you? He never told me anything about his childhood. Not really."

"Same. Other than that." Aurora could remember how reading the letter had left her uncomfortable. She'd wished he'd left that part out. When she wrote him back, she didn't mention what he'd written at all, but it struck her now that he'd been trying, in his way, to convey something important. She still didn't know what. Maybe when they got to Seattle, she'd finally be brave enough to ask.

27

Zahra

The cat would have bedded down in her lap, his soft body a contrast to the hard shell she'd built around herself.

But the cat was gone, and Zahra could only level the blame at herself. She would have taken her chances and run, too, given the circumstances. *You can't count on people,* she wanted to tell him. Of course, he already knew. That was why he'd left. She'd let him down.

Zahra would have sworn she wasn't attached to him. He was never really hers, belonging solely to himself, but his disappearance upended her. She'd taken him from his home, against his will, and lost him four-hundred-odd miles away. The farther they drove, the worse she felt.

"I can't stop thinking about Fluff," she admitted.

"That field's full of mice and little birds, right?" Aurora said. "Snacks for days."

"Yeah, rodents galore," Zahra replied, but what she was thinking was: What about the road so nearby? And the coyotes that come down the hills every night? She pictured the cat limping on his hurt paw, his three-legged gait no match for a predator.

She looked down at the bandage on her own hand. The pain had stopped, but the skin was still broken beneath there. What if the cat's cut got infected?

At least the weather seemed to be cooling a little, and there was plenty of shade. He was wise enough to go to one of the houses for water.

They hadn't yet made it back to Highway 101. The two-lane road they navigated wound over hillocks and around bends, and Aurora drove like someone being chased.

Zahra braced herself against the door as Aurora took a turn a little too fast. She corrected and slowed before Zahra could say anything.

"He's scrappy, right? Tougher than he looks," Aurora said. "He has street smarts."

"I know you're trying to make me feel better, but I can't right now with the whole Pollyanna thing."

"Who's Pollyanna?"

"Seriously?" When she determined by studying Aurora's face that she was, in fact, serious, Zahra sighed. "Being around you makes me feel about one hundred years old."

"Sorry."

Zahra waved away the apology. "It's not your fault. You're young."

"I'm not *that* young," Aurora protested.

"Only young people get offended when they're called young."

Aurora was quiet after that. Zahra released the car door, let her body shift along with the turns in the road, her head bobbling back and forth, her thoughts, too.

"You know," she started, "I was married at your age."

Aurora waved her hand. "Whoa. Wait. Is that right?"

"Wes and I got married less than three years after graduating, so yeah."

The timeline seemed impossible now. Something from another era, and it was, in a way—her own era of innocence. But she'd been so sure that *this was it.* There hadn't been anyone to tell her otherwise. Her grandparents had died by then—first her grandfather in her second year of college, then her grandmother her senior year. Her mom would never interfere. And her dad?

It came back to her then, like a bucket of cold water over her head, the way he balked when she told him about her engagement. What did he say? That he was disappointed. No. That wasn't it, exactly. He'd said, "I expected more from you." More what, she'd wanted to know?

If she'd had any doubts about Wes, and she supposed she could admit now that she'd had a few—because it did feel fast, and because she was young and had never been in another relationship, and because she sometimes wondered who she might be with someone else—she'd decided in the face of her father's judgment to put them aside. Prove the man wrong. He didn't know her. He had no claim to any of her decisions.

In the end, she'd proven him right.

Aurora interrupted her thoughts. "I mean, you seemed so grown up to me at the time. Your long white silk dress, the way you wore those gold bangles up your arm."

They had opted out of a traditional wedding, choosing a backyard celebration at Wes's parents' house instead—easier for his chemo-ill mom that way. Dom had come, towing a teenage Aurora with him. Together they'd been the life of the party. *That charming father and daughter* everyone talked about all evening.

"You looked beautiful," Aurora continued. "I wanted to be you so badly."

Aurora's admission made Zahra squirmy. The earnestness too much to bear. Or maybe it was the compliment she couldn't stomach. And yet Zahra pocketed it to consider later, like the peach and date pits she found in the front pouch of her apron, the wine corks that bore the faint smell of a perfect bottle.

"Be glad you're not," she said. "Learn from the error of my ways. When you meet someone."

Aurora released an awkward laugh. "Is that what you think? That Wes was a mistake?"

Zahra could never regret Wes, because to regret him would be to regret what they'd made together. And at the same time, she wished she could roll back the years and try another path. An impossible want. Like she'd told Wes, you couldn't have it both ways.

You always see things so black-and-white. There's so much in between.

"They're having a baby," she said before she even noticed the words were on her tongue. "A girl." Zahra was so tired of keeping everything inside, stuffing it away and out of sight. It was never out of mind. And this bit of information cracked her open.

"Oh, wow." Aurora paused. "And that's bad news . . . ?" she ventured.

"Not for them. They're thrilled."

"But you're not. You're . . . what? I mean, I thought you didn't care about having a family, kids."

Zahra bristled. "Are you seriously this obtuse, or are you just being mean for fun?"

"I'm not trying to be mean. I just don't get it. You already knew he'd moved on. Is the fact he's having a baby making it feel more real or something?"

"Aren't actors supposed to be good at empathy? Aren't you Emmy-nominated for putting yourself in someone else's shoes?"

Aurora let out a frustrated exhale. "If you think I'm such an idiot, why don't you spell out what the problem is with you and your ex? Because he seemed perfectly nice, and it's not unreasonable to assume after a decade or whatever you might be over it by now."

"Over it?" Zahra sat up, flung her hands down on the seat, anger overriding every brain cell. "My husband left me for my best friend after I'd lost our baby. It's not something you just *get over.* Unless, I guess, if I were more like you and could magically"—she waggled her hands in the air—"manifest the silver lining to anything."

"What the hell are you talking about? A baby? I don't—"

"Jesus, Aurora. She still counts, even if . . . Why are you acting like you don't know this?" Suddenly, Zahra's brain fizzed and short-circuited; a dark hush whooshed through her, and pressure began to build in her head.

The reality hit like an airbag to the chest, punching her in the lungs, flattening her. "Dad didn't tell you, did he?"

"Wait, you're serious? No, I didn't . . ." Aurora trailed off.

When Zahra could speak, she said, "Ten years ago, I gave birth at thirty-four weeks to a baby who never took a breath."

Not *a* baby, *her* baby.

She and Wes had been debating a short list of names. But when the time came, the names they'd decided upon slipped her mind entirely, and Zahra, alone, had made a snap choice. In a pamphlet the hospital social worker had given her afterward, with grieving parent groups and coping suggestions, Zahra had read how other mothers longed to hear their baby's names said aloud. But Zahra kept the name hidden close to her heart, as if the name itself were the glue holding her together.

A long pause settled between them as Aurora took this in. "Zahra, I didn't—"

"And Dad failed to mention it to you."

"I mean, I was a kid. I don't know; maybe he was trying to shelter me."

"You were fifteen." A young fifteen, but still. "And your age doesn't explain why he wouldn't have at least told you I was pregnant."

"That was when Dad was . . . away, right? So maybe—"

"Maybe what? Didn't you talk to him on the phone all the time? Letters? And he wasn't 'away.' He was in prison. Let's call it what it was."

Aurora's lack of response was proof enough she had no way to defend him, and for once, Zahra wished she would. She wanted there to be an explanation to justify his decision, other than the only one she could think of: he didn't care enough. He never had.

If he'd been that way about everyone and everything, Zahra might have been able to write him off as another absentee dad. Nothing special. Nothing to see here—just your average father wound. But that hadn't been the case. She'd witnessed how he cared for Aurora.

"I just don't understand," Aurora said, clearly struggling, shaking her head, her face scrunched with stress.

"It was right after Dad got out," Zahra said. "I was in culinary school, and I flew from SFO to see him. I started spotting on the plane, but I'd been on my feet all week in the kitchen, you know? I'd thought sitting for a couple of hours would be good, forced rest. But . . ."

She hadn't recounted this story for ages, and in retelling, the memory of the knife-sharp pain worked itself through her all over again. A pain she'd never be able to describe. It wasn't just her body in agony, but her soul, racked and splayed. She forced the feeling away.

"I took a cab to the hospital when we landed. Dad met me there, but then he up and left. Left me *alone* at the hospital."

Zahra waited, let Aurora catch up. "I thought seeing Dad that time would be different. I really believed he might have changed, and I was changing, too, because I was going to have a baby. I was happy. I'd been so hopeful for once. So do you see why it's hard for me to hear about Wes and Sarah having a baby daughter? Do you get why I wasn't keen on rushing to Dad's bedside? I mean, the hypocrisy that he demanded I come, after everything."

"But why? Why did it happen?"

"Placental abruption. She lost oxygen. It was like . . ."

But she couldn't explain what it was like, the hell too excruciating to say aloud, too complicated.

She ran her fingers over the tattoo of the date on her wrist, where her baby's head had, for a brief moment, rested, and the horror that gripped her by the throat each time she remembered her daughter's swaddled body being lifted from her arms came back to her in a rush.

It might as well have been her heart they carried out the door. Zahra had been two, and then she was none. A void.

She scrunched her eyes, closing herself off from memory. Wes wanted to know why she couldn't open up to him, but she had brought herself back to life the only way she knew how, building walls around herself, a protective cocoon. The shell that had begun to crack.

"I just can't believe he didn't tell you," Zahra said. There'd been a moment when Aurora told her what their dad had written about his own dad's indifference where Zahra thought she might be able to understand him, to make sense of *his* indifference to her. But then this, a slight beyond indifference. She wished she were standing before him right then. Forget an apology. *Explain yourself,* she wanted to shout. *Explain yourself so I can stop wondering why I am the way I am.*

"But," Aurora started, "why didn't you . . ." Zahra watched her shake her head as if ridding herself of whatever she was about to say. "Never mind."

"What?"

"Nothing."

"No, just say it," Zahra demanded, not unkindly but firmly.

Aurora waited a beat, then said, "Why didn't you tell me yourself?"

Zahra blinked against the question's implication, trying to gather her thoughts. The truth was that back then it wouldn't have even occurred to her to tell Aurora something like that. She was a kid, and she wasn't on Zahra's radar anymore, not really. Zahra had been so caught up in her own world, she hadn't considered what that same time period, with their dad going to prison and Aurora's parents divorcing, would have been like for an impressionable teenage girl.

"You were . . . I was . . ." She floundered, trying to land on a better explanation. After a second, she gave up. Zahra didn't want to hurt her feelings, but those were the facts, and she couldn't change them. "We weren't close, obviously. I had my life and you had yours, and you were getting settled in SoCal and doing the acting thing for real, and I wasn't exactly looking for an opportunity to talk to your mom again. I guess I didn't think about it."

Aurora seemed to take a moment to digest this.

"I assumed you would hear," Zahra added when Aurora didn't respond.

"No, I get it. He should have told me," Aurora finally said. "I understand why you feel about him the way you do."

A consolation prize, but that was something, understanding.

"It's confusing, because it's like you're talking about a different person than the dad I know."

And Zahra, too, understood what she meant. Reconciling the wrongs committed by the people you loved could drive a wedge into your spirit. It could make you second-guess everything. Even yourself. Especially yourself.

She hated to cry. Hated the way it made her feel like someone was peering into the window of her soul, lit up on a dark night. Hated how it left her loose and sniffly and red-cheeked. Hated how it let anyone see the private pieces of her broken heart.

After losing her daughter, Zahra had cried for a week straight. She'd cried on and off all day, and even in the night, she'd wake up with tears streaming down her face. Then as if she were a well that had run dry, the tears stopped entirely. Her sorrow became lodged somewhere deep and unreachable, enclosed in a white-hot hull of anger. Releasing the anger felt better, more powerful.

It had been suggested to her by a certain ex-husband that perhaps she got stuck in the anger stage of grief. But he couldn't understand that accepting their loss was exactly the thing that made her see red. It was so unfair. Such a cruel twist of the knife by the universe. Rage was the only appropriate reaction. Not Wes's placid disappointment. She hated him for that, how he talked so easily about the future. She didn't want another baby; she wanted the girl she had lost. Who could blame her if she'd pushed him away? But then, who could blame him for leaving?

The anger had shielded her once he left. The same way it protected her when her dad left. Each time, the soft parts of her hardened a little more until she was encased in armor so thick she could hardly move.

It was still there, as she sat in the car, but somehow, even though she would never give in to the unwelcome tears that pressed at the backs of her eyes, her sadness had snuck back through. The mix of feelings, their potency, overwhelmed her, and there was nothing she could do to relieve them but talk.

While they drove the long, boring expanse of I-5, Zahra told Aurora about the matchboxes she'd found at her mom's house, the collection of letters tucked into each once. Aurora listened. She didn't try to make things better or console her or put a positive spin on anything.

"Right before we left, Wes stuck one of the matchboxes in my hand." Zahra opened her fingers to reveal the small token. Red indentations cut through the lines in her palm from where she'd gripped it so tightly.

Aurora glanced down, then back at the road.

"What are you going to do with it?"

"I don't know. What do you think?"

"You need to let it go."

"Yeah?" She'd been expecting Aurora to offer a more sentimental reaction. Something saccharine she'd immediately have to refuse.

"There was a reason you took them to Wes. You couldn't hold on to them. You said that yourself."

"True. But now that I have it, I can't throw it away."

Aurora's mouth pinched in thought before brightening. "I have an idea. Another detour, but this one is important."

28

Zahra

They'd been on the road for over three hours, just south of Mount Shasta, when Aurora pointed to a sign for a trail access. A few minutes later, they'd parked and walked far enough along a marked path that the only sounds were birdsong, the rustle of small critters in the undergrowth, the crunch of their own feet on the dried pine needles that blanketed the ground.

The pine trees surrounding them seemed to reach beyond the sky, their bark like the lined backs of Maman Joon's hands. Zahra craned her neck but couldn't make out the tops of trees, only patches of blue. It was cool beneath the canopy.

"It's fire season, so a ritual burn is out of the question," Aurora said.

"I'm not even going to ask you what a ritual burn is."

"Here's what I think we should do: you'll read the letter, so you never have to wonder what it said. Then we bury it in the dirt. Symbolic release."

"Isn't that littering?" Zahra said, possessive of the matchbox and its contents despite trying to be rid of them both a few hours earlier.

"It's a piece of paper. It's just going back where it came from. Like compost."

"Pretty sure that's not how composting works. And what about the matchbox? I don't think I can bear to abandon it."

"Don't worry. I have another plan for that."

Aurora opened her hand and after a long second, Zahra set the little box into her sister's palm. Gently, Aurora pressed open the interior and plucked the folded note from its hidden den. She held it out to Zahra.

Zahra shook her head. "No. You do it."

Aurora looked surprised, but pocketing the matchbox, she unfolded the piece of paper. She cleared her throat, held the paper as if she were reading from a script.

"'Dear Little Flame—'" Aurora's nose wrinkled. "Little Flame? What's that mean?"

Zahra swallowed hard. "It was a nickname. When I first found out I was pregnant, it really felt like a warm flicker of life inside me. A spark of a match. It wasn't possible to feel her that early, but I did. I swear I did."

Aurora considered this, then turned her eyes again to the letter.

"'Dear Little Flame, Today, you're the size of a pomelo, bigger than a grapefruit and even more underappreciated. The originator of the grapefruit, the pomelo, is one of the few citruses we have today that wasn't born from a hybrid. Its flavor is similar to a grapefruit, but it's the pomelo's gentle bittersweetness that makes the fruit so exceptional. Like all citrus, it can go sweet or savory, but with a pomelo you have to work a little harder to get past the thick rind, utilize the flesh.'"

Aurora snorted in amusement. "Leave it to you to include a brief history of fruit."

Zahra shot her sister a look.

Aurora shrugged and continued, "'I feel a bit bittersweet myself these days. I'm thrilled you're here, but I've never felt worse. When I'm not nauseous, I'm eating everything I can.'"

Zahra let the words wash over her, tried to remember what it was like to be practically Aurora's age, expecting this baby to change her life but not knowing in what ways. She could barely fathom it, that the person who wrote this letter used to be her. It might as well have been uttered by a stranger. Is this what it meant to lose yourself?

Aurora smiled. "'I picture you reading this sometime in the future. You will be short and gorgeous or tall and cute. Brassy and sassy or quiet and content. A collector or a creator. Either way, you'll have a sharp tongue but the wisdom to know when to use it. We'll cook together and watch movies together and fight the patriarchy together. And if you don't want to do any of those things, we'll do something else.'"

Zahra watched Aurora speak and recognized a kind of poise she could only have hoped for her in a daughter, a gentle spirit she had never possessed and never would. For the first time, she understood that the daughter she'd imagined had been a hybrid of her and Aurora, some amalgamation of the best of them both, the only two little girls she'd ever known intimately. Even the secret name she'd chosen was like a hybrid of theirs.

"'The point is,'" Aurora continued, "'I want to be there for all your parts, the bitter and the sweet. I'm not going anywhere. Hugs, owner of your watery womb.'"

Womb, tomb. Zahra couldn't hear one word without hearing the other. The loss depleted what was left of her energy.

"Okay," she said, sagging to her knees. At the base of the tree's trunk, the earth was dry and hard, roots poking out like bones. She clawed, sharp pebbles catching on the underside of her nails. Aurora dropped down to help. And they both attempted to carve out a small hole, but the packed dirt wouldn't yield.

"This is impossible." Zahra slouched back on to her heels, looking down at her dirty hands, the black lining her nails. "So much for a symbolic release or whatever you called it."

Aurora stood up and looked around. Her gaze homed in on one tree in particular. "There," she said. She pointed to a small hollow. "Stick it there."

"Now, that's definitely littering."

"It's all in your perspective. I prefer to think of it as nest fodder, a gift for the birdies."

"That's one hell of a spin."

Aurora shrugged. "One piece of paper isn't going to hurt anything compared to, you know, ExxonMobil. But it could help you. Every rule has an exception."

Zahra held back a laugh. She was starting to appreciate her sister's loose logic. Without giving it another thought, she rolled up the letter and slipped it into the gap in the tree. The white paper disappeared out of sight.

"I really hope I didn't just trash a squirrel's living room or something." Zahra looked over her shoulder toward the tree as they followed the trail back the way they'd come. "I feel like I'm fleeing a crime scene."

"You have no idea," Aurora muttered.

"What does that mean?"

"Nothing."

"That's it. Fess up. You've been acting weird this whole time. All the cryptic phone calls and notifications. Not to mention your hair. What is going on? Because I'm not about to pull a *Thelma & Louise*."

"Who?"

"Uh, hello, the classic road-trip movie?"

"Oh, right. That's from the seventies or something?"

"God. How young are you?"

"Wait. What happens in that one?"

"They kill a man and end up driving off a cliff."

"Thanks for the spoiler alert," Aurora said, a halfhearted attempt at humor. "It's nothing like that. It's . . . Never mind. It's not even worth talking about."

They'd reached the car and Zahra stuck out her hand for the keys. "I'll drive but give me a minute. I need to send a text first."

She pulled out her phone, leaned against the car while Aurora climbed into the passenger seat. Once she heard the car door click shut, she hit the "Record" button on her Messages app.

"Do you ever find yourself doing weird stuff when you're on the road? Stuff you'd never do in your regular life? And I don't mean BASE jumping or whatever. We've already determined you're an adrenaline junkie. I mean something you said you'd *never* do." She shook her head. "Forget it . . . I just wanted to say, I should have responded earlier. I wanted to. I *meant* to, but it's been a really intense day so far."

She looked around at her surroundings. The turnout was more like a small dirt parking lot for the trail and the quiet state park they'd stumbled upon. Another parked car baked in the sun, but otherwise, there was no one around, the road empty, the highway too far away to hear.

"At the moment, I'm reconnecting with my love of the great outdoors. I've considered myself a city person for a long time, but now I'm wondering if that's not entirely true. Just another story I told myself.

"The earth looks so parched out here; there's this strange sepia cast to everything. There're no redwoods, but these pines aren't so bad. I think we're about an hour from the Oregon border. A state I've never actually been to, if you can believe it. I've flown over it a dozen times. That's one part of why I hate flying. Not Oregon. But all those flights I had to take when I was a kid. To visit my dad and his new family. He didn't want me there, but he still demanded I come, and every time I did, I felt like a package more than a person, something he'd ordered to be delivered. I never felt more alone than I did sitting on those flights. More out of control of my life."

She'd never shared that with anyone. Hardly admitted it to herself. She paused. "So anyway," she said, "you asked if it was the same for food, if going slow gives you more time to tune in, and the answer is yes. But I haven't cooked like that for a while. I'm always doing client work on deadlines, and it sounds so much more glamorous than it actually is. But my grandmother and I used to spend a whole day in the kitchen making a single meal, and the food tasted better that way. I haven't thought about that in a while, the way it made me feel to take the first bite at my grandmother's table, like everything was right in the world or might be one day. But it's come back to me in the last day how food is a conduit for meaning, how the meals we share anchor us to the past and remind us to be present in the here and now.

"So this is me officially *not* ghosting you. This is me keeping the conversation going, if it's not too late."

She hit "Send" and settled into the driver's seat, not bothering to adjust the rearview mirror or the seat. She and Aurora seemed to have settled on a neutral position that worked for both of them, a benefit of being about the same height, a similarity Zahra had never registered before.

"Here." Zahra handed Aurora her phone with the map she'd pulled up. "You're the navigator now."

Aurora frowned. "It says we won't get there until after ten."

"Really?" Zahra said, even though she wasn't surprised, wasn't remotely disappointed to put off confronting her dad for another day. "We can still be there to talk to him first thing. It might be easier to talk in the morning anyway, right?"

Aurora nodded. "I should call him."

She fiddled with her phone while Zahra got them back on the road and headed toward the highway.

A moment later, a dozen notifications buzzed from Aurora's phone, one after the other. "Okay, c'mon, what's all that?" Zahra asked, alarmed.

"Nothing," Aurora said. "Messages. Here. I'll put us on speaker."

They listened as the phone rang. Right before it seemed like he wasn't going to pick up, the line connected and the sound of a woman's voice surprised them both. "It's Nicole, one of your dad's nurses. Here he is."

The rustle of movement crackled over the phone, then their dad's voice.

"Roar." Her nickname released like an exhale.

"Dad? You okay?"

"You caught me lying down. But I can't rest here anyway, not with all the prodding." The last comment clearly directed at Nicole. Sure enough, a muffled voice responded on his end. "Yeah, okay," their dad said, before breaking out in a horrible cough that left Zahra's chest aching. She had a strong desire to put an end to the sound, make it turn off and stop grating her eardrums, the way she sometimes hunted down landscapers in her neighborhood when the grind of their gas leaf blowers wouldn't shut up.

"You don't sound good," she said instead.

His coughing started back up, less furious this round. He caught his breath. "Nature of the beast, kiddo," he scraped out.

"We're on our way." Aurora brought the phone near her mouth. "But we're running behind. We won't be getting there until late. Really late. What time are they releasing you?"

"Not today. They're gonna keep me overnight again for observation. So it's fine."

"Oh, okay," Aurora said at the same time Zahra said, "How come?"

"Fluid in my lungs. It keeps coming back."

"Fluid?" Aurora spoke the word as if she'd never heard it before. "What? Like when you're drowning?"

A beat of silence fell across the phone and the car, and Zahra imagined a drowning man on dry land.

"Don't worry, sweetheart. I'm fine. It's nothing unexpected. They're overly cautious. I'll break down the damn doors if they don't let me out in the morning." This last part was spoken stronger, as if it was said for the benefit of Nicole or whatever other medical staff might be in range. He sounded almost normal.

Aurora laughed, mollified. And Zahra believed him, too, or *wanted* to believe him. Either way, she let herself be convinced.

"Well, maybe we can meet you at the hospital, then, and help you home," Aurora said. "Or get the house ready for you."

"This hospital food's rot. I could use a home-cooked meal."

Zahra understood this statement was meant for her, and she rolled her eyes, but it was mostly habit. Her subconscious jumped into menu-planning mode. He'd need something hearty. Chili would do, a sheet of cornbread she could slather with extra butter to help him make up lost calories. A rich chicken soup, made with fortified broth and egg noodles, a quick stir of spinach leaves at the end.

When she didn't respond, Aurora said, "We'll go grocery shopping before you get home."

"Don't go to too much trouble. You still have a key, right? To the house?"

Aurora nodded. "Yep. I brought it."

"You can stay there tonight. Or maybe you better stop along the way and get some rest. I don't want you driving too late. Okay?"

Zahra had never had a key to her father's house, had technically never needed one, but the gesture, not simply opening his home to Aurora but allowing her to step in at any moment without permission, symbolized a sense of belonging she couldn't fathom. Aurora was his daughter, and he was her father, while Zahra's position remained stuck in the mud of a murky middle.

She was so distracted by her own thoughts, it took her a moment to notice the call had ended. Still, Aurora held the phone, keeping it at arm's length as if the thing might jump out of her hands and take a bite of her face.

"I'm so screwed," she said.

Then Zahra watched in shock as her sister opened the window and launched her phone out of the car.

29

Aurora

"What is *wrong* with you?" Zahra yelled, braking hard and pulling the Volvo to the shoulder.

With the on-ramp to the highway a ways off in the distance, the road they found themselves on was devoid of another vehicle, the brush lining its edges dense and waist high.

Zahra jumped from the car and waited for Aurora to follow. But she couldn't move.

It had been foolish to throw her phone out the window, impulsive and immature. But when the call to her dad had ended, Aurora had seen the slew of message notifications and missed calls she'd avoided earlier, and it was like she'd been holding a stick of dynamite, the fuse lit and smoking.

All those messages and no word from Dillon. She should have heard from him by now. The story had broken hours ago.

Something wasn't right but she didn't know what. The flush of possibility she'd experienced at the thought of their relationship going public had vanished in the face of reality. That bubble of excitement that they could finally be together, really together, a real grown-up couple at last, transformed into a tangled hot mess in her gut she couldn't name.

When she didn't budge, Zahra came around and banged on the passenger side window.

"I can't," Aurora said, through the glass.

Zahra yanked open the door. "What do you mean, you can't? It's your phone. Your phone!" She might as well have said, "It's your life." And she wouldn't be wrong. Aurora had thrown her life out the window. She couldn't face finding the mutilated pieces scattered on the ground.

Already the web of awfulness had knitted itself into a tight ball. She bent over her knees and forced herself to breathe in for four.

"What the hell are you doing?" Zahra said.

Out for four.

"Hello?"

In for four.

"Aurora!"

When she found the strength to speak, she sat up, watching Zahra's face pinch with concern. "Are you hyperventilating?"

Aurora shook her head. "Box breathing. Calms the parasympathetic nervous system." Zahra stared at her, waiting for a better explanation. "I did something bad," she finally admitted, her sister's unwavering attention like swallowing a truth serum. She couldn't keep it in any longer. "Now the story's out and Dillon won't respond."

Hanging on to the car door, Zahra bent down so their faces were on the same level. "Listen. I'll help you, okay?" The compassion in her voice surprised Aurora, and she sat up slowly, let Zahra clasp her hands and guide her up and from the car.

"But who the hell is Dillon?"

After attempting to call the phone a dozen times without luck, they combed through the grass in tandem, lifting their knees high, bending their necks low, sun cooking the tops of their heads.

Aurora told her story, as best she could, from the beginning. From the *very* beginning. Her first encounter with Serena. The meeting that followed with Dillon and Serena. If Serena was cool and aloof, like some kind of bird of prey studying her movements, Dillon was warm and engaging. The Kellys never touched—Aurora noticed that right away—but she assumed they were trying to convey a level of professionalism. And either way, Serena didn't seem the touchy-feely sort.

Aurora knew the part was hers even before the screen test. She could feel it in her bones. A certainty she'd never had before or since, an assurance from some unknowable place within or beyond. Whatever it was, she sensed its power, but it went as quickly as it came.

After that, there were a few innocent lunches where Serena swung by but had to hurry away early. Then dinners. Then the less-innocent dinner when everything changed. Dillon never had to talk her into anything, but he'd also been the one to suggest they rent a room. She hadn't said no. She couldn't say no to him. Or she didn't want to. It was hard to tell which was which.

The first time happened *after* she got cast. That fact seemed important to maintain. She hadn't slept her way into the role. By then he'd confided in her a little about his marriage. The Kellys hadn't been really together for years, but it was important for both their careers, their new production company, that they respect the brand.

Aurora couldn't argue. Under her mom's guidance, she'd been making all sorts of decisions to support her future brand. Graduating high school early, staying away from kids her own age who weren't in the business, no late nights out, no public behavior that might be construed as promiscuous or inappropriate. She had to be likable at all times. "You never know who's watching," her mom would say.

She took Dillon at his word, and he'd never let her down. Even when he asked her to leave town, he'd been doing so for her well-being—and the show, too, obviously, but in a way, that was also for her. He always thought ten steps ahead.

But as she'd described their relationship to Zahra, it sounded so *ick*. So clichéd.

"So that's why you were so eager to drive with me," Zahra said once Aurora had caught her up.

"Yes. I mean, not just that, but yeah."

"And the hair dye and the hat."

"Mm-hmm." She squatted down to sift through the fragrant blades of sweetgrass and braced herself for whatever judgment awaited her. She'd gotten a pass for losing poor Fluff, but this, she knew, Zahra would never let slide.

"And the mother and daughter at the café. You couldn't get your picture taken because—"

"Yes, exactly." She flung her hands up, silencing Zahra. "I'm awful, I know. The *other* woman."

Zahra dipped her head and began to trawl through the grass once more. Aurora took a hard seat in the dirt, the grass tickling her skin, and swallowed the lump in her throat. All this time, she'd focused on how others might judge her relationship with Dillon rather than acknowledge what the relationship really was. But she couldn't avoid the truth anymore: love didn't matter if he wasn't hers to love in the first place.

"Admit it," she said. "You think I'm just like my parents, right? A pathetic, selfish cheater who deserves what's coming to her."

"Jesus, Aurora. You're not your mom. Or Dad, for that matter." Zahra sighed, sounding resigned but not angry. "People make mistakes. In your case, it just happens to be a matter of public interest. Why people care about celebrity gossip, I will never understand. No offense."

"So you don't think I'm the worst?"

"The worst? Hardly. I think you're human. Totally average, very basic."

"But what about what happened with Wes and your old friend? How can you just forgive me after all of that?"

"Wes and Sarah?" Zahra said, confused, but then understanding registered across her face. "I don't know if I even blame them anymore.

But it's not the same anyway. All these situations are so different. And you . . . you'd never hurt anyone on purpose. It's a relief, actually, to know it's not perfect for you all the time. It makes me—I don't know—trust you more or something."

"Really?" It was exactly the kind of backhanded compliment she'd expect from Zahra, but the sentiment filled her, nonetheless. For the first time since the story had come out, she felt like she might not suddenly disintegrate when she thought about it.

"I mean, it makes me relate to you more. Maybe your fans will feel the same way, once things die down."

"I don't think so. Everyone loves Serena, and I . . ." Her eyes darted around the grass. "I betrayed her. I broke every girl code. Basically, set feminism back a hundred years." Zahra didn't say anything. Aurora hurried to fill the silence between them. "But it's not as bad as everyone thinks it is, I swear. If he'd just explain, then maybe . . ."

"Explain?"

"Their marriage was over—"

"Was?" Zahra asked, with a raised eyebrow.

"Is! They have to put on a show for the media, but he knows I know that. It's just complicated. And now there are these wild pregnancy rumors about Serena making it worse."

Zahra went still. "She's pregnant?"

"They got a *supposed* bump shot. But there's no way."

Zahra gaped at her.

"What?"

"Aurora, c'mon. Serena and Dillon, they're still married. They still live together, don't they? What if the rumor is true?"

Aurora closed her eyes and shook her head. She refused to admit the same thought had occurred to her, even for an instant. "Dillon wouldn't do that to me. If he said they're separated, then they're separated. He doesn't live his life like other people. He doesn't conform to social norms." Her voice quivered with uncertainty, one of her "tells," Dillon called it, when she said her lines without really feeling them.

She was repeating his own words, but they'd lost the power they'd once held over her. "You don't know him. You don't. He's special," she said, searching for conviction she didn't possess.

"I just wish he'd call you and explain."

"He said he would. I know he will." She had to believe he would.

"Okay, okay." Zahra raised her hands in surrender and walked farther down the road. "Whatever you say."

Aurora heaved herself up and shuffled her feet, kicking at loose rocks and sticks, pretending to look. Just as she was beginning to think there was no way they would ever find her phone, and maybe that was a good thing, maybe it was the universe looking out for her again so she could disconnect until this whole mess blew over—never mind that her mom would still find a way to hunt her down, that Margot would absolutely lose it, that she had the Emmys to go to—Zahra let out a celebratory yelp, bent over, and came up waving the phone above her head.

"Not even a scratch," she shouted. "You got lucky."

She'd always been lucky. So why did it feel like her luck was running out?

Back on the road, the Volvo's tired AC blasted tepid air in their faces. They fanned their armpits with their shirtsleeves to cool themselves. Aurora fought the impulse to rake her nails across her scalp.

"Working AC would be nice," Zahra said, but not with bitterness. Aurora clutched the cracked leather seat, her palm slick with sweat. She'd stuck her phone in the cupholder, but even though her notifications were silenced, it sat there, taunting her.

"Just look," Zahra said. "Your phone can't hurt you."

Aurora didn't know about that, but she swiped open the screen, avoiding her notifications and voicemails, to send Evangeline a text. A dozen unread messages from her assistant had collected, but she ignored those, too.

My service has been spotty but I got your voicemail.

Evangeline's response came immediately.

Margot won't stop calling me. Have you talked to her yet?

I can't right now. It'll have to wait until tonight.

What am I supposed to tell her?

Tell her the truth. I'm on the road and you can't get ahold of me. Bad service.

Ellipses appeared, then disappeared, then reappeared, before disappearing a final time, followed up by Evangeline reacting with the thumbs-up emoji.

Great. Now she'd even managed to piss off her assistant.

She rolled down her window, let the loud rush of the highway drown out her thoughts.

The open, rocky shoulder led to forested land in the beginning of regrowth after a wildfire. The remaining trees were blackened, their lower branches bare and spindly. But new plant life poked from the ground with purpose, big bushes of purple flowers and dried summer grass reaching skyward with determination.

"I think your phone's vibrating," Zahra said, raising her voice above the sound of the road.

Aurora startled. She'd planned to turn off her phone, but even though she didn't want to admit it, she'd been hoping to hear from Dillon. That happened sometimes; they'd try to call each other at the same moment. Or he'd pop into her head and a second later, he would text. But it was only her mom, and she slouched with the letdown, sticking her feet on the dashboard.

She could keep ignoring Lucy's calls, but it would be easier to give her mom what she wanted, so she answered.

"Honey, where are you? Are you okay? I've been calling for hours but it kept going to voicemail."

"We're still on the road. We're almost to Oregon, I think."

Her answer must have disarmed Lucy, because for a second, her mom didn't respond.

"But haven't you seen the news?"

"Yes, I know."

"My God, Aurora, it's absolutely everywhere. Your name is everywhere. A national story," she said with fear or awe, Aurora couldn't tell. "How are you holding up?"

"Fine. Really."

"What does Margot say? The timing is awful with Sunday, and we don't even have Season 2 locked in yet. She must be beside herself. We can't let them paint you as some kind of homewrecker, I know that much. We need to own this. Have you talked to Dillon?"

Lucy hadn't asked if the story was true. She hadn't needed to, of course. It was obvious to Aurora now that Lucy had known about her and Dillon all along, and if she'd known and never said anything, that meant she'd wanted it to happen, that she'd seen some benefit to the arrangement. A chill followed the trail of sweat down Aurora's back. Her mom must have believed the same thing she did, that if the story broke, then Dillon would be forced to come clean, publicly declare himself to Aurora. The thought sickened her.

"I haven't talked to Margot. Or Dillon."

"What?" Her mom spit the word with ferocity. "How is Margot not all over this? You need a strategy, a statement, maybe even media training. With Emmys coverage, this is about to be huge."

"I have a call with her soon," Aurora lied. She couldn't bear another minute of her mom's tirade, which would end with Lucy demanding she call Margot that very second.

"Soon? Where the hell is she? You should be her only priority right now. In the meantime, you need to get your butt back to LA—"

A loose strand of hair whipped across Aurora's face and caught in her mouth. She rolled up her window. "Mom, please. Your intensity is too much right now."

"Aurora, this is important. The future of your career is on the line. We've worked too hard to screw things up now, and this sort of thing can either make or break you, depending on how—"

Aurora sighed and held her phone away from her ear while her mom kept speaking, until Zahra ripped the phone from her hand.

"Hey. Hello? Lucy?" A pause. "Yeah, it's Zahra. Aurora has to go now. She'll talk to you later. Bye!"

She ended the call, and Aurora stared at her sister with wide eyes. "Did you just hang up on my mom?"

"Only because you wouldn't."

It's true, she never would have hung up on her mom, but she'd wanted to. "Thanks," she said, turning off her phone again. "Helpful."

So much had gone wrong in the last two days, but at least this, *them*, was going right. She could never say so to Zahra, too nervous to scare her away, but she felt that today, despite everything, or maybe because of everything that had happened, they'd become something like friends. Being true sisters, in the way Aurora had wanted since she was a little girl, might be too much to ask, but friendship? That seemed attainable. She hadn't had a real friend for so long.

"The Volvo's really become one hell of a confessional." Zahra released a breathy laugh. "I'm sort of glad the rental car place didn't have anything. I've grown attached to this tank." She patted the dashboard.

Aurora's heart jumped. She'd forgotten she'd lied about calling the rental car agency. She couldn't come clean now, not when Zahra was glad for once. Not when they were finally getting closer. Better never to mention anything at all.

"Yeah," she said. "Me too."

"What do you say we stop for food when we cross into Oregon?" Zahra asked. She nodded to her own phone. "Check the map and see where we are."

Aurora used Zahra's phone to zoom in on their route. "We're really close. We could stop in Ashland. It's . . . maybe forty-five minutes from here." She paused as a new notification popped up. "You have a new message."

"See if it's Wes. About the cat," Zahra said. "Oh God, that would be such a relief."

"It's from Elian. Another voice text!" She couldn't help getting excited.

"Don't open it."

But Aurora desperately needed to take her mind off herself, and so it was too late. She'd already pressed "Play."

"It's funny you mention the city mouse / country mouse thing, because I've put some thought into it, and for me, choosing a side would be like asking you to choose between . . . I don't know, two delicious foods. How does one choose between bread and cheese? Cookies and ice cream? Mexican and Italian? You don't, right? That's the trick. You refuse to choose. I've based my whole life on that philosophy, and it's worked well so far.

"But I also believe that even nomads need a home base. I chose Portland because it's West Coast but far enough away from where I was raised that I don't feel compelled to visit home much. That probably sounds terrible. My parents are good people, but things back on the home front are rough and I'm not inclined to go there if I can help it.

"Anyway, Portland feels like home now. It's a good place for my mail to collect, to share a meal with friends. Which, so . . . Yeah . . . On that note, I imagine you'll be scooting by my city later today on your way to Seattle, and I had this thought. Now it's sort of out there. But humor me, okay?

"I was in Thailand with a writer friend of mine recently. We're sweating through our T-shirts when out of nowhere, this local guy shows up and gestures for us to follow. We tried to nudge him off, but he was insistent, and we were curious, I guess. So we go with him and end up at this home where there's a tiny old woman and a massage table.

"She brings me inside, and at first, it's a normal massage, or not exactly normal because it's the best massage of my life. I'm pleasantly surprised. But then we get to the end. The woman takes my hands in hers, presses into my palms like she's feeling around for something.

"She says, 'I know this terrible thing has happened.' Which it had, that bad thing I mentioned before had just happened. That's why I'd joined my friend in Thailand, even though I wasn't on assignment. I couldn't face anybody. Basically, she tells me, 'You run but you're not letting go. You're carrying it around with you like a heavy backpack. Set it down.'

"I'm thinking, 'This lady is nuts. Get me out of here.' But at the same time, I start crying, full-bodied sobs. I hadn't cried when the terrible thing happened, or the other little terrible things that led to the big one. It came out all at once, violently. And then it was over, and my whole body was lighter, I swear.

"I gave her a fistful of cash, and my friend and I scurried away, and he goes, 'Whoa, man, that was one hell of a diversion.' That word, 'diversion,' felt completely off the wall but totally right. That's why I'd gone to Thailand in the first place.

"I'm sure you're wondering where the hell I'm going with this, so here goes: What if you and I got together for a meal in Portland? I know what I'm proposing doesn't make a lot of sense, practically speaking, and you seem like a practical person, but what do you say? I'd sure love to watch you order way too much food and make snarky comments about it into your phone. We wouldn't have to call it a date because it's more like a . . . diversion. A nice little diversion from the main drag. See what I did there?"

30

Zahra

"Why not go?" Aurora held the excessively large plastic-encased menu in front of her masked face. They sat at a booth in the back corner of the diner, the light cascading through the windows falling over her loose locks. Zahra was reminded of how her golden hair used to capture the light like a painter's strokes. The dull brown she had now was no match for the sun, and yet still, there was something about Aurora that held a person's gaze and had nothing to do with her looks.

"We're sort of on our way somewhere."

Zahra dropped her own menu onto the Formica table. The diner they'd found in Ashland was all wooden walls and peeling leather booths and a glass case with at least ten types of pies displayed on the shelves. The clientele was a mix of about what you'd expect, with a few young families and some groups of teenagers, backpacks piled at their feet, thrown in.

"But we're not in a rush anymore. You heard Dad. At this rate, we won't get to Seattle until way super late, and we're not gonna just barge into his hospital room while he's sleeping. He told us to come tomorrow. I don't think he wants us hanging around the hospital anyway. Seeing him like that, I mean."

Zahra didn't disagree. She didn't want to see him like that either. Their conversation with him earlier that day replayed in her mind. His scratchy voice missing its loud boom.

They were keeping him for observation, he said. But why? What happened if they couldn't clear the fluid from his lungs? She wished now she'd set aside her resentment for the moment and just asked. Demanded an answer, the way she planned to demand an apology. She gave Aurora a hard time for playing an ostrich, but she did it, too, in her own way.

She'd come all this way to get her dad to atone, but now she would have accepted one honest conversation, one time where she could say exactly what she felt, not push him away with her anger but hold him close with the truth, *her* truth.

But even if they weren't going to see their dad tonight, that didn't mean she wanted to make plans to meet up with some random guy.

Except he wasn't a random guy anymore, was he?

He was Elian, a thrill seeker with a velouté-smooth voice and a perfect smirk. He was cocky, sure, but also smart and thoughtful. He was nothing like Wes. Nothing like the kind of person she'd once told herself she needed. She didn't *need* him at all. But want? Want was a whole separate matter. The idea of talking to him, in person, sent her heart racing.

Their back-and-forth these last couple of days had added up to . . . something.

Still, she held herself back.

What was the point of a date? Why bother at all? They had no future, and the only reason she could think he'd want to see her again was so he could sleep with her. She could already imagine Aurora saying, "So? Would that be a *bad* thing? Aren't you kind of due?" Imaginary Aurora did have a point.

"Don't you have a flight home tomorrow?" Zahra dumped out the packets of sweeteners and began to organize them by type. "Isn't that a lot to cram into a morning? Get all the way to Dad, talk to Dad, get to the airport, fly home?"

"I don't fly out until the afternoon. And I can have Evangeline push it to a later flight. If I need to."

"Can you?" Zahra asked pointedly. "Aren't you urgently needed in Southern California?"

"They'll let Dad out first thing, we can get him settled with some food, talk about the thing he needs to tell us, and then . . ."

Go their own ways. Back the way they'd come. But separately. That was the plan. Zahra in the Volvo, if it could make it. Aurora on a plane.

Despite herself, Zahra found she wasn't much looking forward to the return trip anymore. It would be a long drive home by herself. "Yeah, maybe."

"You can go on your date—"

"Please don't call it that."

Aurora lowered her menu and raised her eyebrows. "Fine. Your *diversion* with your hot photographer—"

Zahra crammed the sweeteners back into their dish. "Oh my God. Stop."

"I'll get us a hotel room, we get up at the butt crack of dawn, back on the road by six, and we're at the hospital by nine. Or we go straight to the grocery store to stock up and then directly to Dad's. Whichever makes the most sense depending on when he's discharged."

The server, a wiry septuagenarian with big, white-blond curls and pink lipstick, appeared at the edge of the table. "What'll it be, ladies?" she asked.

"I'll have the garden salad but add chicken," Aurora said. "And an iced tea with lemon."

The server turned toward Zahra. "For you?"

"I'll do the turkey club, a cup of the broccoli-cheddar soup, the Caesar salad—but no chicken—the patty melt, and"—she tapped her lips in thought—"a slice of berry pie. No, wait: lemon meringue. Shoot. Actually, let's just do both."

"Anything to drink?"

"Coffee, please."

Aurora gazed at her with wild eyes, but the server just tapped her pen on her notepad, took their menus, and left.

"How are you going to eat all that?"

"I just want to try it all. Plus, I have a feeling you're going to want more than the garden salad." She zipped her pointer finger in the air in front of Aurora's face. "You're gonna have to take off your mask to eat."

Aurora glanced around the room. "I think I'll be okay," she said, peeling the loops from her ears.

"Do you still have your phone off?"

Aurora nodded, looked down at her hands. Zahra had spent the last forty-five minutes of their drive trying to convince her sister to call her manager. But Aurora maintained that she had to talk to Dillon first. Zahra had to bite her tongue. She'd known immediately the guy was bad, bad news, that even if Aurora didn't want to see it, the imbalance between the two of them was staggering.

Aurora had been right to think that Zahra couldn't help but compare this situation to what had happened between her dad and Lucy, even Wes and Sarah. Maybe a couple of days ago, she would have held this against Aurora. But after spending time with her sister, Zahra understood it wasn't the same. The difference was Aurora didn't seem to understand how *she* was the one being hurt. Zahra had no idea how to get Aurora to realize that without destroying her.

It was too much like the time when Aurora was nine and Zahra had told her that Santa Claus wasn't real. She'd been visiting her dad over winter break, just before Christmas, and Aurora had come home crying because her classmates were making fun of her for still believing in the big guy. Zahra thought she'd been doing her a favor by telling her the truth, but the news had nearly broken the poor kid and given Lucy another reason to dislike Zahra.

"How will you know if he responded if you don't check?" Zahra asked.

"He will."

"But—"

"I'll check at the hotel. When you're on your date."

Zahra grabbed a sugar packet and launched it at Aurora's perfect nose. "Way to change the subject."

The server brought their drinks. She glugged a splash of cream into her mug and refocused her attention on Aurora. "When was the last time *you* saw Dad? Because it sounds like he's been sick for a while but you didn't know."

Aurora sucked from her straw. "Probably not since last Thanksgiving," she admitted, looking uncomfortable. "But we talk on the phone a lot. And text. I don't know why he wouldn't tell me."

"Maybe he didn't think you could handle hearing what he had to share. You seem to shy away from this stuff."

She frowned. "What stuff?"

"Hard stuff. Sad stuff."

"Only because I believe in the power of positive thinking. It works."

Why did being an optimist always sound like such a gimmick? But then, it didn't seem the glass-half-empty approach had done Zahra any major favors. They were both saved from the direction of the conversation by the sound of Zahra's phone vibrating against the grime-outlined table. She half expected a new message from Elian. Half hoped for one. But it was a text from Preeti.

> I finally got into your place to turn off the light, and there's a total fruit fly infestation in the kitchen. Hundreds of them! Looks like you left some fruit going bad in a bowl on the counter.

Fruit flies? *Oh God.* Zahra cringed, remembering the stone fruit she'd brought home from the store and stuck on the counter, the ripe pluots and peaches that had sat in the heat while she changed her tire. She'd been so meticulous—cleaning out the fridge, putting away the dishes, and taking out the compost—but she'd left the fruit behind to rot.

When she didn't immediately respond, Preeti added: I tossed the fruit, obviously. And set up a dozen traps. Nontoxic. I've got the perfect dish-soap-apple-cider-vin formula.

The thought of someone in her small home without her there disturbed her. She wanted to tell Preeti not to bother. But she couldn't stomach the idea of coming home to her kitchen in such a state. If only she could deal with it on her own, but she sat an entire state away, every vantage point surrounding her unrecognizable, the miles they'd logged in the car like years of her life, taking her farther away from a version of herself she could recognize. She had no choice but to rely on Preeti.

Thank you for handling that on my behalf.

Happy to help. What are landladies for? 😉 I'll get it sorted before you get home.

This is all temporary, Zahra reminded herself, reacting to Preeti's last message with a heart emoji. They'd talk to their dad tomorrow, and she could get back to her life. At the thought, she realized her urgency to get home had dissipated, the stability of her usual routine had lost its pull.

By the time the server unloaded the second tray of food, the plates took up the entire table.

Starving, Zahra dove in, taking a few bites from each before moving on to the next. The turkey club was good if not exceptional, the soup was rich, but the patty melt was delicious. When she got to the Caesar she slowed down, used her fork to pick up a piece of lettuce and examine the way the dressing coated the leaves. It was creamy and looked mayonnaise-laden, which she guessed would be the case in a place like this. She put a bite in her mouth, enjoying the flavor and the texture with the broken bits of crouton. It was overdressed but not in a way she minded. The parmesan was powdery and excessive, but she enjoyed this, too. It wasn't the kind of Caesar she was going for, but there might still be something to be gained. She'd been trying to play with the ingredients in the dressing, but she hadn't focused on the ratio of dressing and cheese to lettuce. Maybe it was a case of more is more.

She pointed to the plate with her fork. "Try this," she said to Aurora. Aurora paused as if she was considering, then took a bite.

"Do you like it?"

"Sure, I like it. Tastes like Caesar salad from my childhood."

"Okay, good. What do you like about it?"

Aurora took another bite, chewed more slowly this time. "I like that it's salty and cold. Really crunchy."

"Crunch," Zahra repeated. What else could be cold and crunchy? Thinly sliced fennel or celery?

"So what's the deal with the Caesar salad obsession?" Aurora asked, attempting to stab a wily crouton.

"It's not an obsession." She shrugged. "It's more like a quest."

"A quest, huh?"

"Caesar salad is kind of like the white whale of recipe development." Zahra took a bite. "That's a *Moby Dick* reference, BTW," she joked.

Aurora stared at her blankly. "Moby who?"

"Oh my God, you can't be serious—"

At once, Aurora's face transformed into a wide smile. She barked a laugh. "Got you."

Zahra pursed her lips. "The point is, Caesar salads are everywhere, and they're mostly sort of good, except for when they're really bad. But they're rarely great. I just want to make the best version possible. But surprising, too."

"What if the best version isn't surprising at all? What if what makes it the best is that it's nothing special?"

"I don't even know what that means."

"The best things are usually the ones that appeal to the most people, and not everyone wants their food to be innovative."

Clearly, she didn't get it. Leave it to Aurora to value generic appeal above an acquired taste. Zahra stabbed a lettuce leaf with her fork, then abandoned it on her plate, suddenly losing her interest in the salad.

"Speaking of," Aurora continued, "you're the only food person I know who doesn't post on social. Don't you need followers to get a cookbook deal?"

"What? Like I'm supposed to be an influencer?" Zahra chomped down on her patty melt. She'd long had the argument with herself that she should be putting herself out there more. But she didn't want to. "I can self-publish. I just need to save up some money." She had a vision for a simple chapbook of recipes with photos, something on heavy paper you could fit in your back pocket.

"But you still want people to know it exists, right? Make the food and eat it?"

The right answer was yes. That was the whole point. But she couldn't make herself admit it. As if to do so would acknowledge that she not only needed people to like her food but also needed help finding those people. She needed those people to like *her*.

"I could help you with the marketing," Aurora said, reading her mind. "We could set up some social accounts for you. You wouldn't even have to put your face up if you didn't want to. Though I have a feeling it wouldn't hurt."

"I'm not sure," she said.

"We could do it tonight. Since you won't be on a date."

"Are you trying to get me to go?"

"Is it working?"

Zahra chuckled. Actually, it wasn't working. A day ago, the idea of spending the night with her sister was enough to make her want to flee to the state border, but now it didn't sound so bad. The thing was, though, she wanted to see Elian. And why not? It was just one night. Then they'd never have to see each other again. One night couldn't hurt.

"Either way, we should probably get a hotel in Portland, get some rest before tomorrow."

"Fine. I'm gonna run to the restroom before we go," Zahra said.

"I'll find us somewhere to stay," Aurora called as Zahra hopped to her feet and hurried through the diner toward the bathroom.

When she got there, she paused before going inside and sent Elian a text.

31

Zahra

In the few minutes Zahra'd been gone, the air around Aurora seemed to have changed. It was charged now. Her sister had her mask and glasses back on, her cap pulled down low. Most of the plates had been cleared, a wad of cash left on the check. The slices of pie sat untouched.

Zahra sat back down, looking around. "What happened?"

"Those teenagers. I think they recognize me." Aurora's chin gave an almost imperceptible nod to the table where the kids were gathered. Zahra glanced back. They did indeed seem to be looking in Aurora's direction. Zahra could feel the panic building beneath Aurora's disguise. At any moment, one would aim their phone at her. She definitely wasn't going to be able to get out the front doors.

"Did they get a pic already?"

"I don't think so," Aurora said, sounding pained. "But I only noticed them a minute ago. I wasn't paying attention."

At the café yesterday morning, she'd left Aurora to fend for herself. She wanted Aurora to be strong, like her. Independent, not beholden to assholes like Dillon or people reliant on her for their salaries. But maybe, just this once, it was okay to offer help. Maybe doing it on your own all the damn time was overrated. Maybe it was okay for her to lead by example.

She stood up from the table and picked up the plate of pie.

"What are you going to do?" Aurora asked.

"A peace offering. While you get out the back."

"The back?"

"I saw a door through the kitchen. Go like you're headed to the bathrooms, then duck in and make a run for it. Keep your back to the kids. I'll meet you at the car."

Aurora nodded, slinging her bag over her chest.

The teens piped down as Zahra made her way toward them. They were curious, she could tell.

"Hey," she said. "Want some pie? We're too full."

One of the girls tugged at the ends of her too-short denim shorts and leaned in on her sharp elbows. "That's Aura Star, isn't it?"

Zahra kept her expression blank and dared a glance behind her. Aurora had just slipped back down the hall to the bathroom. "Who?"

The group snickered.

"It definitely is," Denim Shorts said. "We zoomed in on her cheekbones. Dead giveaway. And the hair. I can't believe she dyed it brown."

"I'm obsessed with *You, Me, Us*," the other girl said. "I've watched it, like, five times, and I'd recognize her anywhere."

"You took a picture of my sister?"

The girls shrugged. Zahra's palm was slick beneath the plate of pie. She hadn't accounted for what to do if they already had evidence. She knew it didn't really matter. The story was already out, and another photo or video online wasn't going to spare Aurora from whatever fate awaited her career. But it was about loyalty. It was, she realized, about amends. It was her turn to make things right.

"She's not whoever you think she is."

"She's totally Aura Star," one of the guys said. "She's hot." The other boys chimed in to agree.

"Okay, now I'm curious," Zahra said, as casually as possible, trying to hold the plate steady in her slippery hands. "Show me what she looks like?" she asked Denim Shorts, who'd half admitted to taking a picture.

The girl took the bait, typing into her phone. She held up the screen toward Zahra, her chipped, bitten nails breaking Zahra's heart. She was truly sorry for what she was about to do. She leaned forward as if she were going to study the picture.

"The resemblance *is* uncanny. Let me look closer." The girl released her grip on the phone. As it met Zahra's hand, she tipped the pie plate straight onto the teen's cropped white shirt and denim shorts.

"Oops," she said.

"Oh my God," Denim Shorts said, right as the other girl yelled, "She took your phone."

Zahra was already to the glass front doors. She heard the thud of the boys' feet as the door shut behind her. She had maybe a three-second head start. The Volvo was parked on the other side of the building, and as she ran, she swiped through the girl's phone to her Photos app. Sure enough, the last half dozen stills were either images or videos of Aurora. She deleted them in a flash, but then realized with a breath-catching slug to the chest she'd need to remove them from the deleted folder, too. Her thumbs flew over the screen as she pounded the pavement, the guys gaining on her.

"We're calling the cops," one shouted, his voice too close for comfort.

Just as they neared, she found the folder and managed to remove the images, giving a small thanks to the universe that the girl's recently deleted folder wasn't passcode protected.

"Catch," she said, tossing the phone behind her toward the boys.

The second it was out of her hands, she bolted around the side of the building. But the space where they'd left the car was empty. The Volvo was nowhere in sight.

"Shit." Where had Aurora gone?

Before she could completely panic, she heard the loud squeal of the Volvo's dilapidated engine from the street behind the diner. She took off across the parking lot, flung open the passenger side door, and hopped in. Aurora hit the gas and Zahra watched for the kids as the diner receded behind them.

Her joints buzzed with adrenaline, a cramp stitched into her side. "How'd you know to get on the street?"

"I had a feeling we were going to need to a quick getaway."

Zahra let out a laugh, and then they were both cracking up, one wave of giggles leading to another.

Aurora wiped at her eyes. "Stop making me laugh. I can barely see."

Zahra got ahold of herself. "You know, I was thinking: What if we made a deal?"

"What deal?"

"I'll go on the date if you call your manager and come up with a plan."

Behind her sister's hat and glasses, Zahra couldn't read her expression, but she was stone still and quiet for a long few seconds.

"Fine," she said. "But this is a way better deal for you."

"You can't keep running."

Aurora nodded. "Are you going to text him?"

"Yeah, I already did."

"Wait, what? When?"

"Back at the diner."

Aurora gave the steering wheel a playful smack. "You totally tricked me."

"You're too easy, Aurora. This is what I keep telling you. Don't believe everything people tell you."

"Except for you."

"Except for me. You're just lucky I'm looking out for you."

"You're giving major older sister vibes right now," Aurora said, a smile in her voice.

Zahra didn't respond, but she was surprised to find herself smiling, too.

32

Aurora

She realized her mistake as soon as they made it to Portland and Zahra asked where their hotel was. Oh, right. She was supposed to book a place to stay. There was no Evangeline to do it for her. For the past year and a half, she'd been uncomfortable having Evangeline do things on her behalf, but she realized, with a lurch, her discomfort was just another disguise, one she'd forgotten she was wearing. She'd grown accustomed to the help, to the ease of depending on someone else.

That's all acting was, really. One disguise after another. She'd built up layers of personas, for each audition and the smattering of roles they amounted to over the years. And underneath all that? She wasn't sure anymore.

"We'll head downtown and see what looks good." Outside the car window, the city streets were scattered with fallen leaves. A breeze picked them up and tossed them about.

"See what 'looks good'?" Zahra repeated in what Aurora found to be a disturbingly accurate impression of her voice. "You shop for hotel rooms like I scan the final sales shelf at the grocery store. I can't necessarily afford what you'd define as 'looks good.' Somehow, I don't think there's a Motel 6 in the heart of downtown."

"It's on me. Consider it a repayment for the save back there."

Zahra shifted in her seat. "I don't need a handout."

"It's not a handout and I'm very well aware that you don't need me at all." When Zahra didn't reply, Aurora elbowed her in the side. "The appropriate response is, 'Thank you.'"

"Thank you."

"You're welcome," she said, as chipper as possible. "Here. This looks nice. Central."

She pulled into the loading zone in front of what looked like a boutique hotel.

Twenty minutes later they were in the elevator headed to the eighth floor, their bags abandoned at their feet. Zahra had drawn a line at letting the bellhop bring up their things.

"Have you heard back yet? From Elian?"

She watched Zahra nod in the mirrored doors. "We're meeting in some neighborhood, I guess, for dinner."

"Don't sound too excited."

"Guys like to try to impress a woman who cooks. It gets old."

"And you know this from your extensive dating experience in the last decade?"

Zahra glared at her as the elevator came to a stop and the doors squeaked open. It felt good to razz her sister a little. Zahra was still Zahra, but they had a rapport now. At the door to their room, Zahra tapped her key card against the lock. The light flashed green, and she pushed their way inside. It was a single-bedroom suite, but the living room was huge with high ceilings and a spacious sitting area framed by bookcases. Glass doors led out to a balcony with cityscape views.

"This is what you book for an overnight?" Zahra asked, forehead scrunched.

"It's all they had on such short notice." Aurora dropped her bag and flopped down on the couch.

Zahra went to the glass doors and stared out at the view. "It's gorgeous. And it's also really annoying to see how the other half lives."

"So what are you planning to wear?"

Zahra looked down at her jeans and T-shirt, spread out her arms, and turned around to face Aurora. "Um, this?"

"Can I make a gentle suggestion?"

"No."

"Your hair looks like it could use a wash." Zahra opened her mouth, but Aurora cut her off. "And you don't smell bad, but you don't smell good, and it's just good etiquette to make yourself smell nice before a date."

"I can't go on a date with wet hair."

"Well, duh. But here in the twenty-first century, they have these fancy things called blow-dryers that work wonders."

"Funny. I don't do hair."

"Lucky for you, I do. Now go." She shooed Zahra from the room with a quick flutter of her hands.

"And you'll check your phone?"

After Aurora made a noise that sounded like an affirmation, Zahra darted into the bathroom.

With her sister out of the room, Aurora set her dark phone on the coffee table but didn't turn it on. All this worry and brooding was so not her style. Zahra must be rubbing off on her. But then again, she'd never been in a situation like this.

When she heard the shower running, she powered on her phone, and a moment of silence followed when she could almost pretend everything was as it should be. But then the notifications began to roll in, the numbers in her text messages and social sites, missed calls, and voicemails ticking up, up, up. From Evangeline. From Margot. From her agents, her hairstylist, her clothes stylist, her mom. From people she'd met once. From numbers she didn't know. And still, nothing from Dillon.

She saw it play out like a movie in her mind. The chance encounter with Serena, the meetings with Dillon that followed. The way he made her feel like anything was possible. She'd put all her faith in him and what they had together. It'd paid off, hadn't it? But what came next?

Even though it'd been only a few days since they'd spoken in the dark outside his home, she could no longer hear his voice, couldn't conjure what words he might use to console her. She was losing him.

In the kitchenette, she pulled a small bottle of tequila from the minibar, unscrewed the cap, and swallowed a painful gulp. The liquid burned like fire all the way down her throat and into her belly, before mellowing into a soothing warmth. Another thing she didn't usually do: drink. If there was ever a time for liquid courage . . .

After a second shot and a fiery sigh, she returned to her phone, prepared to call Evangeline and brace for the slow-motion car wreck she could no longer escape. But before she could, the shower cut off. A minute later, Zahra appeared wrapped in a towel, steam trailing her.

"Did you do it?" she asked.

Aurora waggled her phone screen. "All under control. My assistant will set up a call with my manager," she said. It wasn't a lie, more like a minor fudging of the timeline. Soon she would talk to Evangeline and face the dreaded call with Margot but not just yet. "Now let's get Cinderella ready for the ball."

Even though she'd put back on the same worn jeans and a tired-looking sweater over another plain T-shirt, Zahra had a little extra pep in her step when she left for her date. It was the hair, Aurora was certain. There was something about styled hair that made a person feel like a package waiting to be opened.

Good for her.

But the hotel room was too quiet now. She needed background noise. She switched on the TV to a show she recognized but didn't watch, then returned to the minibar for a second bottle of booze. She took a shot, let the numb heat work its way throughout her body. Settling on the couch, she pulled out her phone. She could do this.

Dialing Evangeline, she twisted a strand of hair and brought it to her mouth, biting down on the ends. Her assistant picked up on the first ring. "Oh my God, Aura, where are you? Margot's been calling me nonstop. I told her I couldn't get ahold of you, but she wouldn't believe me. She kept asking me which hospital your dad is staying at. I think she wants to fly up there and get you herself, except I told her I didn't know—"

"Evangeline?"

"Yeah?"

"Breathe."

She listened as her assistant took a shaky, shallow breath, then another. Aurora's chest felt tight against her lungs, but she breathed as deeply as she could, too.

Evangeline cleared her throat. "Sorry. This day has been nuts. Are you okay?"

"I'm good. Totally fine. I'm used to rumors, and this story is . . . Well, it's not the whole truth. Dillon and I—"

"You haven't seen the statement yet, have you?" Evangeline asked, cautiously, as if she hoped she were wrong. Aurora's body went cold.

"What statement? I haven't released a statement." She paused. "Have I?"

"Not you. Dillon's statement. And Serena's. They released one together, less than an hour ago. I thought you would have seen it by now."

Her assistant's admission oozed pity, but a statement from the two of them didn't seem like the worst thing in the world. Dillon would be looking out for Serena, for the good of the Kelly brand. The two of them could refute the rumors together. Sure, it meant he wasn't willing to go public with their relationship yet, but it also meant their relationship was still salvageable.

"Okay . . ."

"I'm texting it to you now."

A second later, her phone vibrated with the incoming text. She clicked on the link and the headline turned her stomach. It couldn't be.

> Dillon Kelly Admits to "Sordid" Affair, Shares Wife Serena's "Miraculous" Baby News

The room tipped sideways, and Aurora couldn't feel her legs. The sound of blood rushing through her head drowned out her own voice when she spoke. "I don't understand. He wouldn't do that. This is just damage control. Or . . ."

Or what? And what about protecting her? There had to be a bigger plan. Why hadn't she heard from him yet?

"You really need to talk to Margot," Evangeline said. "Can I set up a call?"

She'd run out of options. Margot wouldn't care about her feelings for Dillon, but Margot would care about fixing things, and that meant she might be able to reach out to Dillon's camp. Aurora could get through to him that way. It was a last resort, but it was the only option she had.

"Okay," she agreed. "Yeah."

Dillon Kelly Admits to "Sordid" Affair, Shares Wife's "Miraculous" Baby News

Dillon Kelly has turned confessional in a shocking new social media post. The married *You, Me, Us* creator, 49, has been under fire since allegations of an affair with 25-year-old Aura Star came to light following the publication of an incendiary blind item last week. Star currently costars in *You, Me, Us* with Dillon's wife, Serena Kelly, 33. The flames were further fueled by photos of Serena sporting what some speculated was a baby bump.

Kelly addressed both rumors when he took to his Instagram Thursday evening to share a candid photo of him and his wife snuggled on a couch, together cradling the actress's round abdomen.

In the post, Kelly writes, "A good man can admit when he was wrong, and I'm trying to be a good man. What happened between me and Aura Star was a sordid misunderstanding that compromised my integrity, my marriage, and the show that my wife and I have worked for ages to create. I have no excuse that can condone my mistake. A hard couple of years bringing *YMU* to life and a prolonged battle with infertility took their toll and caused me to act out in inappropriate ways and respond to advances I would normally never have humored. I want nothing more than to put this ordeal behind me. To be clear, my emotional investment in Aura has been and remains strictly professional."

Kelly adds, "My loving wife has forgiven me, and I hope fans can, too. For now, Serena and I ask for privacy as we rightfully turn our attention inward toward our growing family. We're in this together for the long haul."

A rep for Serena Kelly says, "After a rough year, the Kellys have never been more in love and eager to put the past behind them. All that Serena wants is to enjoy this miraculous pregnancy in peace."

You, Me, Us, nominated for four Emmys, including Best Lead Actress in a Drama Series for both Star and Kelly, has had no shortage of rumors surrounding it since the wildly popular series first aired. Star and Mrs. Kelly were initially linked as close friends, but there had been recent speculation of a falling-out. An anonymous source connected to the show once described the Kellys' marriage as "purely for appearances" and said the *YMU* set was known for its "whisper fights" between the two.

This is the first time members of the trio have publicly commented on the rumors. Calls to a rep for Star have not been returned.

33

Zahra

Elian had offered to come pick up Zahra at the hotel, but she had no interest in conforming to the usual practices of a capital-*D* date. It was better to make her own way.

Or it should have been. Where he'd asked her to meet him was across the Willamette River, only a few miles from their downtown hotel. But she had an impossible time getting a car. Two rideshares canceled on her, and the third was stuck ten minutes away for a solid five minutes before she canceled the request and opted for standing in the taxi line at the hotel behind a white-haired Southern couple wearing matching Seattle sweatshirts who wouldn't stop talking to her and insisted she share a cab with them.

The talking went on and on, until she faked a drop-off point and had the driver leave her on the side of the road still a half mile away from the neighborhood where she was supposed to meet Elian. By the time she hoofed it there, her clothes stuck to her sweaty skin and her blow-dried hair had frizzed, poofing from her head every which way. While she walked, the evening had faded into a deep-purple dusk, and she fought a preposterous feeling that she might never reach him.

She should have let him pick her up. Why did she have to be so stubborn? Why did she have to make everything harder on principle? What was she trying to prove? And to whom?

Aurora had told her to always accept the offer; surely it wouldn't kill her to do so once in a blue moon. When it made practical sense.

I'm here, aren't I? I came.

She had, and there was Elian, illuminated beneath the bright halo of a streetlight.

He was turned away from her, scanning his phone, his back broad beneath his fitted sweater.

The sight of him shut down her inner monologue at once. Every brain cell had to work to process his presence. Her skin flushed; her body seized with pure attraction. She'd let that germ of desire infiltrate her system, and it could not be quieted any longer.

She hadn't noticed before that his hair was nearly black, trimmed neatly at his tanned neck. She imagined setting her fingers at his hairline, the skin warm and smooth.

Perhaps sensing her watching, he pivoted until they were facing each other.

"Hi." His mouth, upturned in a half smile, had the disturbing effect of bringing one to her face, too.

"Hi," she said.

"What?" He swiped a hand across his features. "Do I have something in my teeth?"

She was staring at him, but she couldn't help it. She had to integrate the sound of him to his face all over again. The stubble running over his cheeks contrasted with the smooth way he spoke, but his dark eyes matched the depth of his voice.

Gaining control of herself, she batted her hand. "Nothing." But her legs called her bluff, shaking as she stepped toward him. But no, she was fine, only tired from the walk here after so long in the car, her muscles rebelling.

He narrowed his eyes. "Don't clam up on me now. Do you want to pull out your phone? Talk into it while we walk? Would that make you more comfortable?"

"Oh, so now he's funny?"

"C'mon, I haven't made you laugh? Not one time so far?"

"Were you trying to?"

His face erupted in a full smile, his eyes squinting with amusement. "You're tough, you know that?"

She did know that, but she wasn't sure she wanted to be tough all the time.

He nodded down the street. "Ready?"

They walked along the sidewalk, so close their arms jostled against one another. The heat of his body radiated toward hers, and at first, it was all she could do to remember how to move her legs and talk at the same time. But as they fell into an easy conversation, she found herself taking in the neighborhood, the sweet storefronts and comfy houses with porches, green front yards with big trees.

They paused at the next corner, a bicycle whistling past them, and she was grateful, all of a sudden, to be far from LA. "It's a beautiful place."

When she glanced at him, he was staring at her. "It is."

A tickle ran up her neck, her cheeks growing warm, and no doubt pink, without her consent. She quickly turned her attention back to her feet and started walking again. "I don't even feel like I'm in a city."

"Yeah, it's one of those small-town cities." He gestured to a door she hadn't noticed. "The restaurant is another block away, but the reservation isn't until eight forty-five. I thought we could grab a drink here first."

The humble storefront looked more like a converted house than a commercial building, but inside it was busy, buzzing with voices and the energy of people in conversation. He pulled her past the bar and through a screen door that led to a small yard spotted with tables and heat lamps. Like magic, there was a free two-top tucked in the corner beneath a fence strung with lights.

When she stumbled on the brick patio, he caught her arm with a firm grip, and she had to fight the urge to cling to him as she righted herself.

"Okay?"

"Fine," she said, taking her seat, even though she didn't feel fine at all. She *felt* too much. For a brief moment, she closed her eyes, tried to focus on the cool night air and not the man in front of her.

Once she had her bearings again, they took turns passing the drink menu back and forth before Elian stood, pointing to a small satellite bar set up near the back door they'd come through. While he was gone, Zahra got ahold of herself. She was getting bent out of shape over nothing. A one-off date. At most, a one-night stand. She was out of practice, that was all. *Fun,* she reminded herself. She just had to keep her guard up.

He returned with two frothing IPAs. "So," he said, setting one of the beers in front of her, "how's the road trip been?"

"It's been . . ." She took a sip off her drink, unsure how to describe their trip so far. "A ride."

He laughed. "That good, eh?"

"Not bad, actually."

"You're going to Seattle?"

"To see our dad," she admitted. "He's sick. Aurora can't even bear to say it, but he's dying, really. He wants to see us before . . ." She trailed off.

"That's really rough. How are you doing?"

"We're not close. Never have been."

"Yeah, but sometimes that can make it harder. You're still hoping there's a chance you'll finally get the relationship you've always wanted. Or they'll miraculously become the person you always hoped they would be. Right?"

His accuracy struck an arrow through her chest. She *did* want to forgive her dad. She wanted things to be different.

"Our dad says he has something he has to tell us in person. That's technically why we're going. But it's not why I'm going. I want him to apologize for all the ways he let me down. It's the least he can do at this point. In case you're thinking about defending him, it's worse than that, because he was a good dad to Aurora. He showed up for her. Which means he had the ability all along, but with me, he just couldn't bother. Wouldn't."

"I wasn't going to defend him. I get why you'd want an apology."

She sensed he had more to say. "What?"

"No, you deserve an apology, but . . ." He sighed. "You might not get what you want."

Her hackles went up. "And you know because you have experience with that?"

"My parents are both still alive," he said, as if that answered the question. But he spoke with such sadness, she found her irritation retreating as quickly as it came.

She studied his impassive face. "What do they think about their son, the world explorer?"

He squinted. "They'd probably say it's exactly what they'd expect from me. There's this story they like to tell about how they left me in the yard to play with my brother, and I escaped under the fence. I think I was four. They searched for hours, had to get the police involved, and then a group of kids found me in their treehouse a mile away. It happened once, but it's taken on mythological proportions, as if it's been my destiny to disappear."

"Is that what you do? Take off with no warning?" She crossed her arms over her chest and frowned. The notion twisted at the complex tendrils that were holding her together.

Giving her a long look, he said, "I've sort of built my life around the concept. But I thought it meant I was headed toward something meaningful. I'm not sure anymore. So yeah, maybe I've been disappearing recently."

"Or maybe it's both," she said. As much as it pained her to admit, Wes may have had a point: things weren't always as clear cut as they first appeared. Two days ago, she'd been in her tiny in-law unit with nothing on the horizon but her same routine, and now here she was, standing before a whole new person in a place she'd never been before in a state she'd been convinced she would never visit.

Maybe the right person could step into your life at the wrong time. Maybe a road trip could take you the last place you planned to go.

Elian interrupted her thoughts. "I guess if I'm getting pulled in two different directions, that means I'm really just stuck in the same place."

"You know what I do when I'm stuck?" she asked.

"What's that?"

"Eat."

The sweet scent of caramelized onions and aromatic spices toasting, the heady char of peppers over an open flame, and a splash of wine deglazing a pan of wild mushrooms. Zahra inhaled the rush of mouthwatering aromas as they stepped inside the restaurant, visualizing the bustle of activity in the kitchen.

She'd loved the way foods would yield to the heat and release their essential selves into the air. *What smells so good?* The constant refrain in her grandparents' home was always spoken with reverence and longing. The smells promised pleasure, an appetite sparked and satiated.

The place Elian had chosen was tinged with wood fire and salt, burnt sugar, and lemon. It was warm throughout. Warm, neutral tones. Warm bodies close to each other in the small space that felt more like a home dining room. Zahra peeled off her sweater before they even sat down. Elian did the same, and she snuck a glance at the bottom of his stomach as he did so. A bare patch of happy trail inched toward his belly button and down below his jeans. She jerked her gaze away and back to the menu the server handed her.

"Let me know if I can get you anything to drink."

What she needed was a cold shower, but she'd have to settle for a cold beer. Elian ordered the same and smiled at her across from the table.

"I can't believe you thought I was just going to take you to some novelty food experience," he said.

"When you work in food, people try to woo you with weird things. They think 'strange' means 'innovative.' I'm not really into the whole gimmicky food world. I get the appeal, but I'm more interested in classic flavors, the bedrock dishes of cuisines, that sort of thing. But then taking them and making them new. Why reinvent the wheel?"

"You like to put your own spin on it?" he said with a smirk.

She gave him an exasperated look but laughed anyway. "I see what you did there."

"I'm sorry. Keep talking. I like hearing what you have to say."

"Do you like food?"

"I like to eat it."

"You know what I mean."

"I'm not a foodie."

She made a face. "'Foodie'? What year is this?"

He kicked her feet under the table, then let his foot linger so their ankles barely touched. The sensation sent a charge of excitement straight to her head.

"You know what I mean," he said, purposefully echoing her. "I can't cook. I'd love to learn but I'm never home long enough to stock my fridge properly. But I respect that it's an art form. For me it's either pure function or pure pleasure. There's no in between." He turned a little pink around the collar, and she laughed. "That sounded way more intense than I intended."

"And tonight is . . . pleasure?" She couldn't help teasing him. He made her feel lighter, excited, like she was sitting on the edge of a coiled spring. It was dangerous; if she didn't hold on, she might go flying.

"Definitely," he said, his voice low. Now it was her turn to get nervous, but luckily, the server appeared with their drinks, and Zahra used the opportunity to sit up a little straighter and pull her feet back toward her side of the table.

Elian took the hint and righted his posture, taking a measured sip of his beer.

"You two ready or do you need another minute?" the server asked.

"You choose," Elian told her.

"But you're the one who's been here before."

"So? Impress me."

She quickly scanned the menu and started a running list of share plates, until the server cut her off.

"How hungry are you guys?" the young woman said, amused.

"Hungry," they both said in unison. The server laughed, but Elian and Zahra just looked at each other, her own hunger reflected back in his eyes.

"Is it okay if we let the chef decide the order the dishes are served?" the woman asked, interrupting the moment.

Zahra handed her the menus. "Please. Thank you."

"Let me get this straight," Elian said once they were alone again. Though they were surrounded by people, their table felt like a cocoon built for two. "You're not a chef. You're not a food critic. You're definitely not a foodie or a food blogger. Is all this food stuff just for fun, then?"

"It's"—she searched for an appropriate explanation—"my whole life."

He raised an eyebrow.

"It's how I was raised, alongside my grandmother in the kitchen. My parents had a not-so-great relationship. It was either loud, angry arguments or impenetrable silences that lasted for days. I spent as much time as I could with my grandparents. And then when I was twelve, my dad left for good, and my mom and I moved in with my grandparents officially. Food was how Maman Joon communicated. Like when you were sad, she fed you *fesenjoon*—a Persian dish with chicken, walnuts, and pomegranate. Maman Joon claimed the pomegranate would perk you up. But if you had something to celebrate—and it didn't take much, like an A on a test was good enough—she'd make this amazing cheesecake with a thick layer of her strawberry-rose jam."

"So your mom is Persian, then?"

She nodded. "My grandparents immigrated with her and her sister when they were teenagers."

"And your dad is . . . white?"

"Very. Grew up near Sacramento in a farming family. Managed to wrangle a scholarship to Cal. Rode that smart, handsome-white-guy energy straight to the top. No offense to any smart, handsome white guys in the room."

"Does that mean you think I'm handsome?"

She gave him a look but didn't respond.

"And your parents weren't compatible?"

"You could say that."

What she couldn't say was how their incompatibility had both confused and hurt her as a child. How the lack of real love between them left her questioning whether they could properly love her.

"Anyway," she said, changing the subject, "my grandmother didn't have proper cooking technique or whatever, but she taught me how to play and explore, because when it comes to food, you can't know if something works until you taste it. She taught me about building flavors and how to combine ingredients to make something new. She made everything her own."

Not for the first time, Zahra wondered what Maman Joon would make of her life today. Her grandmother had never been disappointed in her, had always accepted her exactly how she was, even after her dad left and Zahra was truly terrible teenage company, but Zahra knew in her bones that the life she lived now didn't look at all like the life her grandmother would have chosen for her.

When little Zahra had asked her grandmother why she loved to cook, her grandmother would explain, "When you feed people, you bring them together and leave your mark. In the kitchen, you'll never be alone." But Zahra had managed to do just that.

Abandoning that train of thought as quickly as she could, she said, "But she saved all her recipes in this incredible book. I just got it from my mom. I can't wait to cook out of it. There's this one for shepherd's pie, but my grandmother did it with all the Persian flavors. She added eggplant and dried lime, and it still had all the rich umami of the lamb but with this light, unexpected tang mixed with the traditional mashed potatoes on top. It's like this pop of flavor and texture you can't get enough of. That was one of her comfort dishes. Whenever someone died, she delivered the pie to their families."

"I'd genuinely love to try that. Your passion is contagious, you know that? You make it sound so good. And . . . how do I say this?" He squinted his eyes, searching for the words. "You make food sound meaningful, like you're talking about the most important thing in the world."

"It kind of is," she said beneath her breath as the server brought their first dishes. "It's meaning and connection and comfort and . . ." Love, she almost said, but caught herself.

Cooking, even the rote kind she did for her clients, brought her satisfaction and clarity. She described this to him. But there was so much more to it than that, so much more she'd been missing out on every time she ate alone at her counter.

Soon artful small dishes covered every inch of table space, and they stopped talking only long enough to chew. When their ankles found each other again, she didn't pull away.

34

Aurora

"You're dreaming if you think this is going to blow over two days before the Emmys," Margot barked through the speaker. The phone sat on the coffee table, practically vibrating against the polished wood every time Margot spoke. She'd already raked Aurora over the coals about lying to her, declared it a violation of their professional relationship, and when Aurora had the audacity to suggest that maybe the story would fizzle out, she'd become even more incensed. She fought back tears as Margot's disdain grew louder.

"Listen, Aurora. There's no way this is magically going away on its own," Margot said, clearly attempting to suppress the rising frustration in her voice. "It's bad news all around and the timing couldn't be worse. We have to deal with the fallout *now*. It's the only way forward, and you better believe me when I tell you things are going to get worse before they get better. But"—her voice began to cheer—"we can spin this, too. I've just gotten off the phone with *the* crisis manager for this sort of thing. He's finishing dinner with his family, but he's willing to get on a call with us tonight. He's the best in the biz, and he has some great ideas for how we can try to swing this back to our favor."

The liquor roiled and rose in Aurora's throat. The sky outside had grown dark and menacing. She had the sensation she was sitting inside a fishbowl, visible from every angle. "Spin it?"

"Dillon's two decades older than you, for one. And he's your boss, for another. We can 'me too' the hell out of him if we want to."

"But he didn't *do* anything. I mean, not without my consent."

"Well," Margot said thoughtfully, "we don't have to go in that direction. It depends on the state of the show. It's possible we can use this to boost next season. But we need his buy-in, and that might mean putting pressure on him."

"Threatening him? I don't want to hurt him. I just want to talk to him." She took Margot's silence as encouragement and hurried on. "He's not answering my texts. Do you think you could put me in touch with him?"

"Tell me you haven't been texting him."

"Only the once."

"Thank God. You can't talk to him, okay?" She softened insofar as Margot could. "I'm sorry, Aurora. Our goal right now has to be your fledgling career. Whatever . . . situation you had with Dillon is over, and the faster you can accept that, the easier this will be for you. Hollywood giveth and Hollywood taketh away."

It couldn't be over. It didn't make sense. None of this was supposed to happen. You were not supposed to be dumped by a public Instagram post.

Aurora heard the snap of fingers on the other end of the line. She could picture Margot pacing beside her desk, her assistant ready to jump at her beck and call.

"I never told anyone. I don't even understand how it got out. He said it would blow over."

"Apparently, he changed his mind."

She wiped at her nose. "What do you mean?"

"Listen." Margot lowered her voice, jamming it with a note of empathy that didn't quite suit her. "I'm sorry to have to tell you this, but I have it on good authority that Dillon's team confirmed the original blind item."

"No way."

"It's an easy way to get ahead of the narrative, redirect control so he doesn't look quite so bad. Then all he has to do is share his supposedly candid Instagram post, tell everyone it was all a big mistake, and effectively throw you to the wolves. I've seen it before."

"He wouldn't." Dillon was strategic, but he'd never outright harm her.

But then she thought of how he'd kept her like a dirty secret.

Woozy, she slumped onto the couch, the entirety of their relationship—their affair—replaying through her mind. All the times she'd believed he was looking out for her, he'd really been looking out for himself. And Serena? She was more than the savvy-business-partner-cum-wife Dillon had made her out to be. She was a woman longing for a baby, a woman either in the dark about her husband's infidelity, or worse, always wondering about the nature of his relationship with her younger costar. Aurora could easily picture Dillon construing Serena's concerns as paranoia or jealousy, weaponizing her own ambitions for the show against her so she wouldn't push back.

Aurora pressed her fists to her eye sockets, willing away this new reality.

"He already did," Margot said with an air of finality. The compassionate portion of this conversation was over. When she spoke again, she was back to business. "We're going to get on a call in . . . let's say, an hour and a half, give or take. But I need you to put on your game face, okay?"

Except for a squeak of agreement, Aurora couldn't respond, too scared that if she opened her mouth, the rising bile would choke her.

"This is a defining moment for you. Will you pull on your big-girl undies and show up for yourself? Or are you going to slink away into the night?"

All she wanted to do was slink away. It was the easiest answer. But somehow, she managed to utter a different response. "Show up," she said, wishing she could disappear.

"Good. Keep your phone on you."

The call ended, leaving her alone in the room staring at her ghost-white reflection in the window.

35

Zahra

Outside the restaurant, moisture clung to the cool night air and collected along Zahra's frizzed strands of hair. So much for Aurora's heroic efforts with the blow-dryer. It was truly a lost cause now.

Elian had bent to tie his shoe, and when he stood, he gave her a wide smile, lifting one of her hands into his.

"So, where to next?"

"Next?" She didn't want the night to end either, and it wasn't just that she didn't want to face the following day with her dad.

"Well, it's only ten something."

"Let me guess, in Seoul or wherever, the night would be getting started."

"Seoul? You can't even imagine the nightlife. But that's not really my scene."

Holding hands, they began to walk tentatively down the sidewalk. She didn't know where they were headed, and she didn't care. She was full in a way she hadn't experienced before. Not even when she was a kid. Not even with Wes. It was the temporary nature of the night, she was sure. They were never going to see each other again, and the knowledge sweetened the experience. She had nothing to fear. She could sink into this moment with the certainty that he couldn't hurt her because there was only now, this moment, and no promises for the future that could be broken. She was the one who would get back in the Volvo and leave.

"Which place have you loved the most?" she asked.

"I can't answer that."

"He won't choose favorites. Okay, fine. Where's the place that makes you feel most like you?"

He turned his head to look at her, and she met his gaze.

"Too hard."

"You're impossible. I haven't been anywhere, and here I am trying to figure out what kind of place would inspire someone to *choose* to climb into a metal tube of death for a dozen hours, and the guy who's been everywhere is no help."

Swinging her arm, he laughed.

"It's not funny. I'm serious."

"I know, I know. I'm sorry. You're almost as passionate about not flying as you are about food." He stopped them on the sidewalk, still holding her hand. "Have you really never been overseas?"

"Nope. Or across international borders. Wait, that's not true. My best friend and I drove to Mexico in college."

"So what's the other reason you don't fly?"

She cocked her head, confused. "Huh?"

"You said the trips you took to see your dad are one of the reasons why you hate to fly. There must be another reason."

"It's complicated."

Yanking his arm, she started them walking again. This was one topic she wasn't about to broach right now. But he was listening to her, listening well. He let the quiet sit between them, waiting for her to explain, and when no explanation came, he didn't pry.

"If you didn't have to fly, where would you go?"

"You mean if I could teleport myself there or something?"

"Exactly."

"God, I don't know. Everywhere. We didn't make it to Mexico City on our road trip, but I've heard the food is beyond incredible. Then there's Paris, of course. Tokyo. All of Italy. Germany, but namely because I have this intense desire to try a schnitzel that's bigger than my dinner plate." He laughed and his delight made her smile. "Copenhagen. Even without Noma, it's still such an incredible food city. Tehran, but even if I did fly, that would be tough."

The city around them had begun to blur at the edges, like she was looking at the street from the inside of a bubble. They'd turned down one block, then a few more. Letting him guide her, Zahra lost any sense of direction.

"I haven't been to Iran either. I'd love to go. Bucket-list destination."

"Aha! There's a question I know you can answer. What's left on your bucket list?"

"I'll show you," he said, tugging her toward a brick building beneath a canopy of trees. They'd found themselves in a more residential area, and as he pulled a set of keys from his pocket, she realized with a jolt they were standing outside his apartment building.

"This is where you live."

"Yeah," he said, jiggling his keys in the lock. When the door opened, he paused, and faced her. "Is this okay? I figured we could warm up and have a drink."

She hadn't been out of the game so long she'd forgotten what happened when attractive men invited you into their apartments at the end of the night. Elian had ignited something in her body she hadn't felt for ages, and maybe she needed to surrender, just for one night, to get it out of her system.

If things headed in that direction, she could text Aurora a message telling her not to wait up. She was sure her sister would understand, would no doubt encourage any extracurricular activities. Aurora was probably dying for an update. Zahra glanced at her phone. There were no messages, but it wasn't too late yet. She probably wouldn't be expecting Zahra back for another hour or two. She shoved the phone back in her bag.

"Sure," she said to Elian and followed him inside.

❦

Elian flicked a switch and the room glowed yellow, revealing the high ceilings of a loft apartment. The living room held a set of couches and a big, comfy chair, a coffee table made of wrought iron and wood, but the focal point was the main wall with a mosaic of photographs reaching nearly to the ceiling, randomly punctured by extra-large red pins.

Zahra craned her neck, trying to take in what she was seeing. At first, it looked like a giant mural of random shots, but as she examined them together, she could see the photos made up an image of a world map.

"Whoa," she said the second it hit her. The pins weren't random. They must point to all the places Elian had been. "It's like nothing I've ever seen before. You made this?"

Pulling off his sweater, he came to stand beside her. "It's a work in progress. My bucket list." He pointed to the bottom of the image. Antarctica, stabbed with a pin, but instead of a red ball on its end, there was a question mark. Her eyes roved across the map, searching for other question marks: Cuba, Uruguay, Kenya, Mozambique, Madagascar, Iran, Nepal. There were too many to count.

"So you basically want to go everywhere."

He spread his arms wide. "I want it all." Turning to her, he set his hands on her shoulders, let his fingers trail down her arms, the act deliciously intimate despite the fabric of her sweater between their skin. "Make yourself at home. I have a bottle of port open. That okay?"

She nodded and he disappeared into the kitchen. A second later music sounded from hidden speakers. Something lo-fi and instrumental. At this point she expected nothing less than cool from this guy. Normally, she would have hated that. But in Elian it all seemed so damn genuine, she couldn't help but forgive him.

The only possible reason a guy like him was single was because he wanted it that way and he'd made sure to keep it like that. It was exactly what he'd told her. Exactly what she wanted. So then why did she feel an annoying thud in her stomach at the thought?

Peeling her attention from the photo wall, she wandered the room, taking in the details. A tower of heavy coffee table books were stacked beside the couch, acting as an end table for a hurricane lamp converted into an electric light. A longer side table against the opposite wall held a clay dish with his keys and a collection of ornate liquor bottles, along with a copper shaker and a crystal decanter filled with amber liquid. Above all this was a black-and-white photograph of a woman's face.

The woman, all cheekbones and round eyes, looked past the camera, one hand resting under her dimpled chin, dark hair piled atop her head. A smattering of beauty spots freckled her face. The contrast of light and shadow made her look almost like a figment, a drawing meant to look photorealistic. Zahra couldn't tear her gaze away.

Elian interrupted her reverie to point to the decanter. "Did you want something stronger?"

She took a glass of port from his hand. "This is perfect."

He raised his glass. *"Saúde."* Raising her glass to meet his, she gave him a quizzical look. "Cheers, in Portuguese," he explained.

"When I'm with you, I don't even have to go anywhere. You're a taste of the world."

"No, trust me, the world is far better than anything I could give you. There's so much to experience. I hope you'll get to see more of it one day. When you're ready."

"Ready to face my deepest, darkest fear?"

He laughed. "It's just your irrational fear. Your deepest, darkest fear is something entirely different."

"Oh yeah? You know something about that?"

"I do," he said. "When I was younger, I actually considered myself fearless. Can you believe that?"

"Sure, sounds like most guys I knew once."

"Then you grow up and you realize there's more at stake than just dying young."

"What's that?"

"The life you *could* live."

She drank from her glass and nodded to the picture. "Do you know her?"

"I thought I did. Once," he said, gruffly, then brought her to the couch. "Come sit."

But she was hung up on his strange response. Did that make the woman in the picture an ex-girlfriend? The rush of jealousy that whipped through her left Zahra confused. She couldn't be jealous. She had no right to be jealous.

Settling beside each other on the couch, Elian threaded his fingers through hers again. The jealousy abated, and her stomach fluttered with the swift movement of a dozen butterflies, a sensation somehow familiar and entirely novel. She'd forgotten how good it felt.

"Help me remember to text Aurora if I stay over." The words escaped her lips before she'd realized how they would sound. Her cheeks flamed. "I mean, not that I am. Just if it gets later—"

He brought her hand to his mouth, and the sensation of his lips was so soft and unexpected, she could have purred. "I hope you do stay." His warm breath tickled the sensitive tips of her fingers, and when he pulled her in closer to him, nestling them in one corner of the couch, she let him, even though it was almost like snuggling. Except this was foreplay, right? Whatever it was, it felt good, and her body melted into all the small empty spaces beside his.

"You smell like jasmine," he said under his breath. Aurora must literally have been rubbing off on her.

"It's my sister's hair stuff."

"What's the deal with you and her?" he asked. "I get the sense you're not super close."

"Besides the massive age difference, we don't have anything in common."

"But siblings are like that, and they can still be close."

"We don't even have a childhood in common."

"I get that," he said. "But my older brother and I weren't close as kids, and we've still managed to find common ground as adults."

She tried to explain her feelings to him, but her usual justifications didn't have the same gusto they did when she recited the reasons in her mind. "I guess I've misunderstood her a little," she finally conceded. "But her constant positivity can be truly annoying."

He laughed. "I believe you. It's all about balance."

"Oh God, you sound like my woo-woo landlady."

"Maybe you just need a real-life example." He set down his glass and took hers to do the same. When he looked at her, her heart sped. "Like for instance, if I kiss you here . . ." He brought his lips to the most tender skin beneath her ear, and she closed her eyes, letting the feel of him soften the toughest parts of her. He used his fingertips to turn her head, then kissed her in the same delicate place on the other side of her neck. "Then I have to kiss you here."

"Is that how it works?" Her voice was muffled against his hair. "I'm still confused. Maybe you should show me again."

His mouth finding hers, she parted her lips and let him in.

36

Aurora

The night everything changed between her and Dillon, Serena had been meant to join them. At a trendy Hollywood restaurant, Aurora sat in a chair studying the man whose open face she'd already imprinted into her mind's eye, fiddling with her water glass, trying not to make a fool of herself.

Even while she silently prayed for Serena to show so the fierce intensity of Dillon's gaze would be directed elsewhere and she could breathe again, she dreaded the moment when she'd lose his full attention. The mix of desire and fear was the most exquisite drug, like being in the middle of a firework the millisecond before it exploded into a thousand shimmering lights.

At least, that's what Aurora imagined drugs must feel like, having made it to twenty-four without ever trying one for herself, unless you counted the Vicodin she'd taken after getting her wisdom teeth removed the year before, which she didn't, though it had made her feel funny.

"What do you see for your future?" he asked, running his finger down the length of his fork.

She willed herself not to squirm in her seat. In the brief second before she spoke, she considered her response carefully. "I see myself making your show a huge hit."

Dillon's eyebrows lifted and he smiled. His obvious delight made Aurora feel sexy, despite never having had sex before, or even a boyfriend, despite still feeling sometimes like she was a kid playing an adult.

She set her hand on the table across from his; they both looked down at their fingers as if daring them to touch.

"Bold words for someone without a reputation." He pulled his gaze back to her face, and his rapt expression was like the sun kissing her bare skin on a wet Seattle morning.

"What kind of reputation were you hoping for?" This time, the words were out of her mouth before she could vet them. There was no mistaking her tone, the flirting she never allowed herself. It was so much easier without her mom around. This was the kind of meeting her mom would have expected to come to if she'd known about it. But they were in the middle of negotiating a contract with a new manager, and there was no one to stop her from going alone. She'd already been cast in *You, Me, Us*, but the Kellys wanted her involved in the production. "It only works if we encourage your deep connection with the character," Serena had told her. "Sloane isn't just a role. She's a person."

Across the table, Dillon licked his lips, but the smile never left his face. "You're teasing me," he said. "But I take your point." He glanced at his phone, tapped something out on the screen. "Serena can't make it. She's . . . not feeling well."

"Oh, that's too bad." She hoped she sounded like she meant it. "Should we . . ." She wasn't sure what she was going to say. Should we leave? Should we reschedule? Should we do this another time, not over a candlelit dinner?

Aurora had been trying to win Serena over, not just professionally but as a friend, and yet no matter how pleasant their interactions, Serena kept her distance. Still, Aurora liked her, respected her, most definitely didn't want to hurt her. Aurora knew the growing urgency between her and Dillon was dangerous. She knew she should rein herself in, but his attraction hypnotized her.

Dillon saved her from finishing her sentence. "Let's order another drink." Before she could even lift the menu, he added, "You have the most stunning, clear eyes. It's like I'm looking through you."

And it was exactly like that. Like Aurora was a crystal-clear pool of water waiting for Dillon to send ripples across her surface. She didn't care to explore what hid beneath.

After dinner when he suggested they cross the lobby the restaurant shared with a boutique hotel and rent a room to continue their conversation with "more privacy," she didn't even hesitate. She didn't question what would happen next. She let him lead her.

The noise of the hotel bar filled Aurora's ears, the patrons a blur of faces and movements. Staccato bursts of laughter, the intimate tilt of two heads in conversation, bites shared, bottles shared, secrets shared.

Aurora didn't belong there, but she couldn't take another second alone in the suite, waiting for the phone to ring and her future to set a new course, while her heart broke, replaying the past.

Dillon had taken the delicate glass threads of her soul and crushed them into a powder still sharp to the touch. He'd used her. He'd used her love for him against her.

How could someone who claimed to care about you do that? How could she have let him?

Stumbling onto a stool at the farthest, darkest corner of the bar, she ordered a vodka martini and watched the bartender measure, shake, and pour. She hadn't bothered to wear her mask or her hat. Her drab hair fell flat and listless past her shoulders. Was she recognizable? She didn't even know who she looked like anymore.

"Three olives, please," she told him. Once he speared them, he handed her the icy glass. The tequila had burned its way through her system, the call with Margot deathly sobering. She craved the numbness once again, but a single sip of the martini left her sputtering into her cocktail napkin. God, that was awful. It always seemed so sexy in the movies, but here, in her reality, it was just another look she was trying on for size. A look that didn't fit.

It was so obvious now, Dillon's plea for her to leave. Get her out of the way, so he could save himself.

But the show. How could he do this to the show? That was the part she couldn't make sense of. He'd do anything for *You, Me, Us*. The show was his baby.

His baby.

The thought scoured her insides. Serena's baby was his. Serena was his. This whole time, he'd chosen his wife.

She'd never learned why Serena didn't show that night when everything changed between her and Dillon. For a time, Aurora managed to convince herself that it confirmed Dillon's claim Serena didn't really care what he did—or with whom. Now that Aurora knew that couldn't be true, she couldn't help but wonder if Serena had been sick from fertility treatments, even a miscarriage. All the while Aurora was in bed with her husband.

She thought of Zahra's lost baby, the way she walled herself off afterward, and Aurora wanted to scream thinking of what she'd done to another woman so carelessly, how self-absorbed she'd been.

And Aurora hadn't just betrayed Serena. She'd betrayed herself.

Dillon would never sacrifice the show for the sake of his marriage; neither would Serena. Aurora knew that much. But like Margot said, they could use the publicity. Aurora's character was the little sister, the secondary protagonist. She was never supposed to steal the limelight the way she had.

This was one way to put her back in her place and guarantee massive excitement for Season 2. The former bestie costars turned enemies. Sister rivalry taken to a whole new level. Who wouldn't want to watch?

But how could she ever work with Serena again? How could she bear to be in the same room with either of them?

Aurora drummed her fingers on the bar.

"Is it okay?" the bartender jerked his chin toward her glass, his gray beard a touch too shaggy.

"Fine," she said. He didn't seem to believe her, choosing instead to hover nearby.

"Can I get you something else?" he ventured.

What did she want, really? The craving came to her unbidden: the burger she'd seen Zahra eat yesterday in the café.

"A burger. Medium rare."

"Ours comes with blue cheese and grilled onions. That okay?"

She agreed. "And fries."

The martini didn't get better after the first awful sip, but she drank it anyway, knowing she really shouldn't. Margot would expect her to be clearheaded for the call with the crisis consultant. But she didn't care. It was her crisis, and it hurt like hell.

The burger arrived and she ate like her life depended on it, drips of juice leaking onto her fingers, dragging her fries through the pile of ketchup with abandon, swallowing the martini in large, foul gulps to wash the food down her throat.

She waved the empty glass at the bartender. "Another, please."

Wiping at the countertop, he side-eyed her warily. "You sure? I could make you something a little less strong."

Before she could open her mouth to protest, the deep voice of a young man spoke for her. "Give the lady what she wants," he said, taking the stool next to her.

Looking him over, she found him well dressed and decent looking. A bit bland for her tastes, with his combed blond hair and smooth cheeks, but nonthreatening. If he recognized her, she couldn't tell. His smile was straight, neutral. His eyes were a little too thirsty, but she was used to that though she'd never given in before.

The bartender hadn't moved, waiting for her response. "Another," she said, again. "Please."

Without waiting to be asked, the young man said, "I'll have the same," and stared down the bartender until he abandoned his dishcloth and picked up the shaker.

"Staying in the hotel?" he asked.

"Mm-hmm." Her plate was nearly empty, except for the detritus of onion and butter lettuce that had fallen from her burger. The residual smell soured her stomach, and she shoved the plate to the side.

"Where are you in from?" he tried again.

"Seattle." She hadn't lived there since she was fifteen, but it sounded right. If she told him LA, it would only spark unwanted questions. "You?"

"Here. I'm meeting a friend, but he's running late. Way late."

Two martinis appeared in front of them, but Aurora couldn't remember the bartender setting the drinks down. Her head had gone a little swimmy, the bar blurred around the edges, the lighting dimmed. It all felt unreal, another made-up story. Her shoulders relaxed. She'd never sat at a bar and talked to a random guy, but it was what most single twenty-five-year-olds were up to on any given evening, right? And here she was, a single twenty-five-year-old. Her heartbreak seemed to have rendered her completely average. Or maybe, like Zahra said, she'd been so all along.

She took a slow sip from her martini and turned to the guy.

"What's it like to love in Portland?" She blinked, realizing her mistake.

"Love?" The guy chuckled. "I don't know about that."

"Live, I meant."

"It's cool. Good for getting outdoors." He tapped his foot against hers. "Do you have a name?"

She had a name in more ways than one, but now her stage name was tainted. How could she ever be Aura Star again? Dillon had named her, like a pet.

"No," she said. "No names."

The guy smirked. "Okay. I can go along with that."

She leaned toward him for no other reason than she knew he wanted her to and because her legs had grown loose and limp as the alcohol pooled inside her.

They sat like that for a while, talking about nothing, about the hikes he'd taken with his friends, about how she had to try snowboarding this winter, about his recruiting job, whatever that was, and all the while, she kept inching closer, sipping her drink and letting the numbness overtake her.

Her shoulder was hitched against his when he whispered in her ear, "You're so gorgeous, you know that?"

She did, didn't she? After all, she'd been hearing how beautiful she was her whole life. Not just beautiful, exceptionally beautiful. As if there were some kind of rule about beauty she'd managed to break. But right then, she felt as beautiful as the dirty dishrag in the bartender's hand, stained and replaceable. Her body had grown slack from the alcohol and overstuffed from the food. She could still smell the grease on her fingertips. She'd never felt more disgusting and unwanted.

She slugged the last bit of her drink, and before she knew it, her mouth had found the guy's. She registered the surprise in his eyes before he closed them, and his tongue found hers.

"My room," she said, a breathy whisper when they came up for air.

"Are you sure?" But he was already pulling his coat from the back of the stool and linking his arm around her waist to guide her to the elevator bank. This is what people her age did. They hooked up. There was nothing wrong with it, as long as you stayed away from married men.

The second the elevator doors closed behind them, the guy was all over her, and she let him do whatever he liked. Let his hands run through her ratty, unwashed hair, then slide down to her breasts and squeeze. Let him wedge open her legs with his knee and press her against the wall so hard she could barely breathe. She was his doll, a little girl puppet on a string.

The sound of her phone ringing chimed like an alarm bell going off inside her. She came to like a drowned person resuscitated back to life, her mind rushing back into her body.

She didn't want this. She didn't want this guy. His hands everywhere. His hot mouth.

Even without looking at the caller ID on her phone, she knew she had to get away. To run. This time for herself. The elevator opened, and she yanked herself free, shoving the guy back through the doors.

"Hey." He looked dazed, sounded more confused than annoyed.

"I changed my mind." The elevator doors swallowed him back up, and with it, his reaction. She rushed to the room while she yanked her phone from the back pocket of her jeans. She didn't recognize the number.

Once inside, she answered, her chest rising and falling, worry sloshing against her from all sides. Margot's assistant would connect her to the conference call, and whatever was going to happen next would begin.

Except when she said hello, there was no assistant, no crisis manager, no Margot.

"Is this Aurora?" said a weary female voice.

Aurora could only imagine it was a reporter. Her gut flopped, preparing for an onslaught of questions.

"Hello?" the voice said. "Did I lose you?"

"I'm here," she chirped, still poised to hang up.

"Hi Aurora, my name's Allison Song, I'm the attending physician caring for your father tonight."

Relief came at once, followed by a slam of pressure to her chest. Her rational mind fought against the alcohol in her system. How late was it? Why would she be calling right now? "Yes? Is everything okay?"

"As you know, we've been treating your father for pleural effusion, a complication of his end-stage lung cancer."

Aurora did not know. She'd never heard those words. *Pleural what? End-stage?*

The doctor kept talking, kept using terms Aurora didn't understand, kept not saying if he was okay. Nothing she said made any sense. The whole point of this trip was to see him. They were on their way. She'd talked to him earlier that morning. He'd said he was fine. He'd said she didn't have to worry. To take her time.

"—continues to breathe on his own for the time being and respond to some stimuli, but he's entered into a state of impaired consciousness, and given the unsuccessful response to our repeated treatments—"

Why didn't she just say if he was okay? Aurora squeezed her eyes shut and tried to breathe, but her chest wouldn't lift. She couldn't get enough oxygen. She gasped, unable to take another second.

"What does that mean? What are you saying?" she nearly yelled, slumping to the hotel room floor.

The doctor paused. "Okay, let's slow down." When she spoke again, she did so firmly but not unkindly, enunciating each word as though English weren't Aurora's first language. "Your father is slipping into an unresponsive state, a coma, and once he does, he is extremely unlikely to regain consciousness."

"But he's still awake. Sometimes, I mean." Because he had to be able to talk. He was going to tell them something. Something important.

"He's had brief moments of arousal, but he's no longer lucid. I'm very sorry, but now is the time to see him. Do you understand?"

No.

No.

No.

She wanted to scream the word. She wanted to claw the word from her throat, rip it apart, rub the bloody tattered bits against the wall. She wanted to lie down and cry. She was coming undone, one layer after another, and she couldn't wait until she disappeared.

First, though, she had to see her dad. She'd promised.

"I understand," she told the doctor. "We'll be there."

As soon as she hung up, she called Zahra. It rang and rang before going to voicemail. She texted, no response. It was already eleven. She should have at least given Aurora an update. But that required her sister to consider someone else's feelings.

She tried again, the automated message from Zahra's voicemail chafing on nerves Aurora didn't even know she had. All the years of letdowns and microrejections and she'd never been mad at Zahra. Hurt, maybe, but not angry. Now, the rage collected in her fists, gathering strength.

Where the hell was she?

37

Zahra

They were fully clothed on the couch, and yet Zahra might as well have been standing in front of Elian nude. She traced her finger against the bit of tattoo poking from his shirtsleeve. "I wanna see."

"It's a chain."

"A chain?"

"A necklace. With a locket on the end." He looked at her, then away toward the photo on the wall. The jealousy reared its head again. No wonder he didn't want her to see the whole tattoo. It probably ended with another image of this woman, a permanent homage.

When he turned back to Zahra, he seemed to look right through her, straight to the panicked thoughts flooding her mind.

His mouth slackened and his dark eyes clouded. He slipped his shirt over his head and angled his shoulder toward her. The tattoo tangled its way up and over his shoulder, then came to rest above the center of his strong chest. Sure enough, the same woman with the big eyes stared back from inside the locket.

"Mallory," he said. "My younger sister."

Air rushed through Zahra's ears. But even though her relief was palpable, she could see the admission hurt him.

"You said you knew her once."

He shrugged. "It's hard for me to talk about."

Zahra knew something about that. She knew about grief. The pieces began to fit themselves together. "That bad thing that happened a year ago . . ."

"Yeah. She took her own life. She was thirty-five, and I thought she was finally stable. She'd been suicidal on and off since she was a teenager, so I knew it was possible, but I just never thought she'd really go through with it. I was in Copenhagen, not even for work, but with a couple of friends, just living it up. She sent me an email the night before. No subject line. It just said, 'I wish you were here.' I didn't write her back right away. Figured I'd call her when I got a free moment. Then my parents called me the next day." He shook his head. "I didn't get it. Depression. I didn't get why she couldn't get over it, shut down the sinister monologue that hijacked her usual thoughts. It seemed so simple to me. I wasn't always sympathetic."

Zahra thought of Wes, how he just wanted her to feel better, like there was a single switch she wouldn't allow herself to flip.

"And that made her push you away?"

"Exactly. But I didn't fight hard enough for her." He looked up at the photo hanging on his wall. "That's why I stopped taking portraits. After she died, I found myself staring at this image of her, realizing I didn't see her at all. I couldn't capture her, you know, the *real* her, only my idea of her. And what's the point of taking someone's picture if all you're really doing is projecting yourself into the frame?"

"So why do you keep it up?"

"As a reminder." He blinked hard and turned back to Zahra. "You never think the worst is going to happen."

"And then once it does, you know it can happen again at any time," she said. The fear, that bone-deep truth that none of us were safe from loss and suffering, changed the shape of a person's heart.

"Exactly. It's made me question everything."

"I know that feeling."

She pressed her hand to the locket and felt the rhythmic beat of his heart beneath her fingertips, then let her fingers trail back down the chain. He watched her intensely, then set his hand atop hers, grazing the tattoo on her own wrist.

"How do you know that feeling?"

She looked at the date inked in her skin, pressed beneath his fingertips. She didn't think she could talk about this again, but after her conversation with Aurora in the car, it was like the dam had been breached, and despite herself, she couldn't stop the words from forming. She told him about her lost baby girl, the aimless, aching years that followed.

"I've never stopped doing the math, how old she would be on this day, this year. I see other ten-year-old girls, and I think, that could be her in another universe. In that universe, I would be a mother. *Her* mother."

He squeezed her hand, but he left space for her to continue.

"And the fact that I can't wrap my mind around that, me as a mother, only makes it hurt more, like *I'm* the reason she's not here because I was never meant to be someone's mom. Because the idea is laughable."

"It's not laughable, Zahra. You would be an incredible mom. The kind that would never force her to conform. You'd let her show up just as she was. But you wouldn't take any bullshit either."

Zahra snorted a laugh even as her eyes stung.

"I'm serious, you know. You're strong as hell, but the layers you have on the outside are so thick because that's how soft you really are. Losing her changed you?"

She hadn't become a different person, but grief had sharpened her rough edges into jagged points.

"I can feel the loss in my marrow, like it's in my DNA now. But it's more than that. It made me see the world in a whole new way, all the ways you could be let down, have the rug pulled out from underneath you."

He held her close, and her face pressed against his warm skin. "I was supposed to protect her. That's what parents are *supposed* to do."

"Parents are just people. They're not perfect."

She pulled herself upright and out of his embrace, reaching for her glass of port. She drank it down in a few gulps, trying to wash away the heaviness. This wasn't exactly how she wanted the night to go.

"Now you know my life story," she said, trying not to let him hear the sudden coolness welling up within.

"I get why you've lost faith." He leaned his elbows onto his knees. "I don't blame you. But for me it's different. I told you I've been running, and I've been thinking it's time to stop. That scares the hell out of me because I think if I did settle down, I'd want it all. Marriage, kids, a house with land for a dog. I want to show up for my life. I want to be there for the good and the bad."

She flung her arms toward the map of photos on the wall, hoping to lighten the mood. "Yeah, right, like you'd give all of this up."

"For the right person, maybe."

He might as well have dumped a bucket of cold water over her head. This wasn't part of the deal. This kind of conversation. This type of vulnerability. She could cut the intimacy between them with a knife. That's what she needed, a blade to slice her way through. Pushing him back onto the couch, she pressed her hands to his chest.

"Enough talking," she said. She kissed him, and he responded, his hands coming to the sides of her face. But as she began to run her hands down his body, he stopped her again.

"Hey, let's slow this down," he said gently.

"Slow down? It's already—" She had no idea what time it was anymore. "Late."

"You're beautiful. Trust me, I want you. I want you more than anything at this moment." His voice was deep and rough with desire. "But I've done the whole one-night-stand thing, and with you, it's not the way I want it to be. I like you, Zahra. I mean, I more than like you. I want to keep talking to you."

Her body tensed, the knot around her heart tightened. "It's not like we're gonna see each other again."

"We could."

She examined his face, and the hope she saw there left her breathless. She moved away from him, then stood, head spinning. Where had she left her bag? "I should go."

"Shit. I've freaked you out."

"No, it's fine. It's just, this was a bad idea. I have a big day tomorrow and—" She caught sight of her purse and as she grabbed it, she lurched in the direction of the door. "It's not personal."

"Zahra," he said, coming toward her. He'd pulled his shirt over his head, and she wanted nothing more than to throw herself into his arms, let him hold her all night long, pressed against his chest.

"Really, Aurora is probably wondering where I am." She looked at her phone.

Oh no.

Ten missed calls, a dozen messages from Aurora. She scanned them and the panic ratcheted up another notch.

"I have to go. Right now. My dad."

"Let me at least drive you," he said.

"I'm good on my own. I'll order a car."

She rushed out his door before he could stop her, practically running down the steps to the building's front door and out onto the sidewalk. She texted Aurora that she was on her way, then tried to order a car, but before she could, Elian was behind her.

He didn't touch her, and even though she was the one leaving him, the distance stung. "We don't have to talk anymore," he said. She closed herself off to the hurt in his voice. "But let me drive you."

DAY THREE

38

Zahra

If she'd spent most of the first 80 percent of the road trip staring out at the sun-drenched scenery, trying to avoid interacting with Aurora, Zahra was spending the last 20 percent blinking into the hazy dark of middle night, begging Aurora to talk to her.

But no matter what she tried, her sister sat rigid in the passenger seat, claiming she didn't feel well enough to talk.

"I just want to get to him," she'd told Zahra, handing her the keys to the Volvo.

Elian had dropped off Zahra at the hotel just before one in the morning. Their goodbye had been awkward and stilted. Zahra had thanked him for the ride, but she hadn't let him say more even though she'd known he wanted to. It might not feel like it to him in the moment, but it was better this way. Kinder. She couldn't lead him on. And if the separation left her aching, it was only because she'd given too much of herself when she knew better. Let herself get caught up in the pleasure. Who could blame her? This road trip would leave anyone out of sorts.

As she'd raced through the hotel's lobby to the elevator bank and hit the button for the eighth floor with far more force than was necessary, the events of the night faded, and she found herself clearheaded once more. She needed to get to her sister.

Zahra had read the increasing anxiety and incoherence in Aurora's text messages and knew she was on the verge of losing it. They had to get to their dad. She had to get them there.

With an impending deadline, all the hours Zahra had spent over the last two days dreading the moment when she would finally see him seemed ridiculous. She would get to Aurora, grab their things, and race to the car.

That was the plan.

Except when she made it into the hotel room, Aurora wasn't waiting for her. Following the unmistakable cough and gag of retching, Zahra had found her in the bathroom, slumped over the toilet, heaving into the bowl. When she lifted her head, her mouth was wet with saliva, her eyes ringed with eyeliner and fatigue.

"I ate too much," she said before she was sick again.

Zahra took in her sister's droopy movements, the scent of alcohol wafting from her. She was absolutely wasted. What had she done after Zahra left? And then Zahra remembered: the call with her manager. It must have been worse than they could have even imagined.

Zahra may not have understood celebrity culture whatsoever, but acting, like cooking, was a craft. And Aurora had worked hard her whole young life, only to arrive at a pinnacle of success right as the earth gave way beneath her. Zahra knew all about that, too. How you could pour your heart into something, give it your whole damn all, and still, the universe would have other plans. In Aurora's case, the universe had taken the form of a limp prick trapped in an ongoing midlife crisis, who'd taken advantage of her disposition. Just like Zahra had always feared would happen. But she felt no satisfaction at the thought.

And now their dad. It was a poison pill to swallow, all the worse for Aurora's inability to look the truth in the face.

She knelt by her sister's side and began to rub her back. "Let it out. Let it all out."

It had taken another hour for Aurora to rouse enough to be steady on her feet. While she sipped a bottle of water, Zahra packed their things. Another half an hour later, she'd managed to get them into the elevator, down to the empty lobby, and settled in the Volvo.

On the highway, she blinked against the headlights cutting through the windshield, stealing swift sidelong glances at Aurora.

"I wish you'd tell me what happened."

"I can't."

She bunched her jacket and shoved it between the window and her head. That was Zahra's cue to shut up. So she tried one last-ditch tactic. One from Aurora's own playbook. A little dose of optimism. Not exactly her forte, but she could try.

"C'mon," she implored. "If you get it off your chest, you'll feel that much better. Won't you?"

No response. She was sure Aurora had given her some version of the same speech not that long ago. And it *had* helped. A little. Enough to get through. Enough to make it to the next thing.

Floundering, she mustered whatever positivity she could. "He could still wake up," she said, trying to find that high-pitched way of saying things that Aurora had, so even the improbable sounded possible.

Aurora made a sound like a snort. "You don't really think that."

She couldn't pretend the way her sister could. That wasn't her talent. Zahra's talent was telling it like it was.

"No, I don't." That caught Aurora's attention, and for a moment, she lifted her head. Zahra continued, "But we have a good chance of seeing him before he's gone."

Aurora seemed to find her last shred of strength. "We have to," she uttered, before her head dropped back down again and her eyes closed.

"Sleep. I'll wake you when we're closer."

With that, a weighted silence fell on the car. No talking, no music, only the rush of the tires against the road, the pounding, white noise of semitrucks as the Volvo passed.

Zahra's mind gunned as she navigated the dark highway. Moments of the night with Elian came back in kinetic flashes she couldn't shake. His mouth on hers, the press of his hands on her hips, the feel of his body against hers. In so many ways, they fit together so easily.

In another life . . .

He'd lied to her when he'd said at the café he didn't want to settle down. Or maybe he'd been lying to himself. Either way, the result was the same. It turned out he wanted something she couldn't give him, and she wouldn't promise something she couldn't see through. She wouldn't wound him the way she'd been hurt.

But thinking of her dad, dying, not in theory but at that *exact* moment, she had a harder time conjuring the bitter shell of pain that had surrounded her so much of her life. It wasn't gone, not exactly, but she didn't possess the resolute determination for an apology anymore. She wanted to see him. She wanted to get her sister to him before it was too late.

The map on her phone showed another hour on the road. Not even four in the morning, it was still the dead of night. An image of her dad unconscious in a dark hospital room came to her, and she pressed her foot to the gas. Fatigue burned her eyes, but she kept them wide open.

39

Aurora

Aurora had only feigned sleep. In her half-drunk state, the preceding hours became like a fever dream. With a wince that sliced straight through her, she remembered the guy at the bar, the sound of the doctor's voice, trying to reach Zahra and finding herself utterly alone. She remembered ignoring the video call from the crisis manager that eventually came, the heated voicemail from Margot that followed, and when Zahra didn't answer, the anger that threatened to choke her. But it was fuzzy now, like a scene from *You, Me, Us*. She'd lived it, but it wasn't hers.

As for Zahra, Aurora had forgiven her at once. She'd gotten them to the hospital in record time. It was only just five in the morning, the night sky turned grainy from the lights of the city. By the time they parked and walked to the front of the hospital, her eyes stung, her body felt like a crumpled piece of paper, and adrenaline pumped through her veins.

Without speaking, she and Zahra made their way to the ICU. She hadn't even known he was in the ICU until the receptionist in the lobby said where to find him. What had she pictured? But she hadn't pictured anything; she'd made a point not to.

They moved swiftly and soundlessly across the floor, and Aurora tried not to be scared while they checked in at the nurses' station. A young, energetic nurse, not Nicole, smiled and told them she was glad they'd made it. Aurora couldn't understand how she could look so chipper, given the heinous morning hour, before realizing she used to frequently arrive to the set before the sun, her lips made into a sweet smile to prove to Makeup and Hair how grateful she was to be there. We all wear masks. What's underneath makes us human.

At a closed door near the end of the hallway, the nurse stopped, and Aurora's heart began to pound.

Stepping inside, she rubbed the corners of her eyes as her pupils adjusted to the soft light in the room. She took in the small, sterile space before her gaze came to rest on her dad, who lay in bed, hollow-cheeked, face rough with peppered stubble, hands tucked somewhere beneath the blankets. He had shrunk since the last time she'd seen him, his burly form withered to someone unrecognizable.

Her feet stuck to the ground until Zahra nudged her forward.

"Listen," the nurse said, coming to his bedside and checking his IV. "I know Dr. Song phoned you earlier. Unfortunately, we haven't been able to rouse him since."

"He'll wake up now that we're here," Aurora whispered.

The nurse set her hand on Aurora's wrist. "It's very unlikely at this point. He's fully unresponsive."

But it's possible, Aurora wanted to protest. *Anything is possible.* Except the words wouldn't come this time.

Coma. That's what the doctor had said. But not yet. He would know that she was here. He would wait for her.

"Why aren't you doing something to help him?"

"There's not much we can do. Your dad has a DNR. Do you know what that is?"

She nodded. It was a term she'd heard, a term she associated with some far-off future that had nothing to do with her.

"I know it's hard, but we're making him as comfortable as possible. He's not in pain." The nurse squeezed the hand sanitizer dispenser by the door and lathered her hands. The room filled with the sharp scent of isopropyl alcohol, and Aurora's stomach turned. "We don't know how much he can hear. Feel free to talk to him. I'll give you guys some time." A second later, the door shut quietly behind her.

Aurora pulled the chair from the foot of his bed closer to his head and sat down. Tentatively, she placed her hands on top of the thin, scratchy blanket and felt for his hand beneath. She heard the sound of movement behind her as Zahra settled on the small settee under the window.

Wake up, she willed him. *Wake up.*

Aurora had played this role before.

In the second half of Season 1 of *You, Me, Us*, there was a three-episode arc where the grandmother who helped raise the sisters was in a car accident. Interspersed with other subplots, the sisters sat by her bedside on and off, willing her to live. She hadn't, of course, being an elderly woman and not pivotal to the show other than as backstory and an excuse to force the sisters to sit in the same room together. Forced proximity meant forced conflict.

It had taken an abysmally painful time to film those scenes, mostly because Serena kept complaining about how claustrophobic she felt in the small hospital room they'd built on the soundstage, how the eggnog white they'd painted the walls made her skin look sallow. How Aurora's character seemed to get the favorable take, the better lines.

Serena had been right about the walls. So maybe she was right about the character stuff, too. When Aurora had been filming solo close-ups beside the hospital bed, she caught glimpses of Dillon and Serena off set, his hand to her arm, her hand to his waist. Aurora figured he'd been talking her down; it wasn't unusual for Serena to get huffy on set, for Dillon to act as her handler. In hindsight, it looked like a husband comforting his wife.

But Aurora had done her part without complaint. When the grandmother blinked open her eyes for one final, bittersweet farewell, Aurora had sat weeping, imagining her own parents dying. It was the easiest way she knew how to tap into big tears. It always worked.

Until now.

Turned out that when faced with the reality of losing a parent, her eyes stayed dry. She sat by her dad, willing him to wake up, for three solid hours and didn't shed a single tear. She couldn't act her way into this. Or bright-side her way out of it. Instead, she was numb. Frozen in place. A block of stone.

At one point, Zahra had shoved a cup of coffee into her hand, but even though she drank it, the hot liquid couldn't warm her.

It was after the morning shift change that the nurse Nicole came in to find them. Her dark-brown eyes watered at the sight of Aurora and Zahra sitting there. Her blue scrubs held tight to her curves.

"I'm so sorry you didn't get to talk to him. He couldn't stop going on about you girls. What a proud papa."

Zahra sputtered on her coffee. Aurora shot her a look.

"Did he say anything else?" Aurora stood from the chair, stretching out her calves. "He has something he needs to tell us. It's important."

Nicole's brow wrinkled, then her eyes went big. She pointed at them. "Wait right here."

As if there was anywhere else to go.

Aurora sank back into her seat and slumped against the bed, spent in a way she'd never experienced before. It was her dad she wanted to call for support, her dad who could convince her she would find a way through.

A minute later, Nicole returned waving an envelope. She handed it to Aurora. "He asked me to give that to you. In case he didn't get to talk to you. I'm so sorry it didn't occur to me straightaway."

It was a plain business envelope, sealed shut, with their names on the front: *Aurora + Zahra.*

"I'll be right out at the nurses' station if you need me."

Nicole scurried from the room, and Zahra came to join Aurora at the side of the bed. Together, they stared down at the envelope.

"We should open it," Zahra said. "That's what he wanted."

"But what if he wakes up?"

Zahra gave her a sorry look. "Aurora."

Aurora took in Zahra's pity with a sickening gulp. It was happening. Her dad was dying. And she hadn't been able to say goodbye. This was no scripted series. There were no second takes. A last moment of consciousness.

She held out the envelope to Zahra. "It's your turn to read."

The paper crinkled loudly in the room as Zahra pulled the letter from the envelope. "'Dear Daughters,'" she began. "'If you're reading this, then that means I've crossed over to some great beyond. It's too bad. I'd have liked to tell you in person, but it's my own fault for not speaking up sooner. What can I say? You think you have all the time in the world until you don't.

"'So here goes nothing . . .'" Zahra took a great big breath, releasing it with a sigh. She looked at Aurora, her sister's brown eyes boring into her. "Are you sure you want me to read this?"

Aurora raised her chin.

> Aurora,
>
> I don't think it's a secret that my relationship with your mom began when I was still married. Contrary to what some may believe, I'm not proud of that fact. I had been unhappy in my first marriage for a number of years, and when your mom told me she was pregnant, it seemed the right thing to do to try and

make it work this time. And it did for a while. The restlessness I'd experienced my entire life abated after your birth. You were two years old when the young man, younger than me anyway, showed up, first at a nearby playground, then at our home.

He claimed you were his, that Lucy had lied to both of us. I scared him off; I will spare you the details of how I did so, but long story short, I threatened to ruin him. I would have, too, but as far as I know, he never came back.

Your mom said he was an ex-boyfriend out for vengeance, mentally unwell. But I wondered if he wasn't just desperate.

Either way, I didn't believe her. Maybe it takes a liar to know one. I sat with that for a while, watching you grow as the years passed, cataloging despite my best efforts all the ways in which you and I were unlike each other. I'd been disturbed when I found out that Zahra suffered the same dark moods as me, the same cynicism. That reflection unnerved me, but it turns out the opposite is worse. And when the not knowing became too much, I did a DNA test in secret. It was harder in those days but doable. I've never shared the results with another person, not even your mother. Given the tone of this missive, you can probably guess what they were.

But, Aurora, it didn't change how I felt about you. I'll be truthful and admit that surprised me. I'm not a man prone to sentiment, and practically speaking, I assumed learning you weren't my biological daughter would alter my paternal feelings toward you. On the contrary, I found myself more protective of you than ever before, more committed to fathering you in a way

I never had Zahra. By then, she was a teenager who wanted nothing to do with me, and I felt that even though I'd squandered my chance with her, I could still do right by you.

I can't say with any confidence that I did. I suspect you were always going to be okay no matter your circumstances; it's just in your nature. But I did try. And if you're wondering why I didn't choose to take this information to my grave, I do not blame you. After I was diagnosed and the outcome became clear, it weighed heavily on me whether to tell you the truth or not. It seemed there was little to gain in disclosing a secret that might cause you great pain.

But coming to the end of one's life forces a person to reflect even if they're not usually so inclined, perhaps especially if they're not so inclined. In the face of two not-so-great options, whether to tell you or not, I can only choose the one that seems most right to me. You deserve to know the truth of your existence, despite what suffering it may cause you in the short term. I do believe one day you'll be glad to know.

For what it's worth, I think your mom's intentions were, if not pure, then at least born out of a fierce love for you. It's possible she will be shocked to hear this, or not. I'm uncertain what her reaction will be, but I know she will remember the man I mentioned, and if you so choose, I encourage you to ask her his name and find him.

Roar, in case I've not been clear: you are my daughter, and I am your father, in every way except for the blood running through our veins, and if mine runs no longer, it seems less relevant than ever—

❀

"Stop." Aurora waved her arms. "Just don't." Her body thrummed, blood rushed through her head. She pressed her hands to her temples, her fingers like ice against her skin.

"It's not true." The middling sentence was all she could think to say, her mind caught like a fly between a window and screen, panicked but getting nowhere.

Zahra grimaced. Aurora had spent enough time with her sister the last couple of days to read her expressions.

"You think it's true."

All the air seemed to rush from the room, and Aurora's heart pumped wildly while she tried to inhale. She needed to sit down, she needed to count her breaths. She needed to dunk herself in an ice bath. Anything to quiet the ringing that echoed in her ears. But she couldn't access any of her coping mechanisms right then. Her skin had become the thinnest tissue paper; if she moved, she would crumple. A single touch could tear right through her.

"Why would he say it if it weren't?" Zahra shook the letter. "Why write it down?"

"Then where's the proof? The paternity test?" Yes, the paternity test. That was a valid question, and she was amazed she'd managed to think of it with her brain short-circuiting like it was. She should have been able to ask him herself. They were supposed to get there sooner. If Zahra hadn't demanded to drive the whole way. If she'd answered her phone last night.

Last night came roaring back to her. What Dillon had done. The ugly truth of their relationship. An image of the elevator door closing, and the reflection of her body hidden behind the guy pressed against her.

No. She wouldn't go there.

"It's probably at his house," Zahra said, "buried deep in a drawer somewhere so no one would ever find it. Because he didn't want you to know about it."

"If he didn't want me to know, why tell me at all?"

"Like he wrote in the letter, he felt you had the right to know."

Aurora rocked on her heels. She was aware of her dad—or the man she believed was her dad up until five minutes ago—between them in the bed, but she couldn't look at him. She wanted to be as far away from him as possible.

"Why are you, of all people, defending him?"

Zahra reared back. "I'm not. Obviously. But I'm just saying he wanted you to hear the truth, finally, from him."

"What, like that's noble or something?"

"I didn't say that."

"And I'm just supposed to take his word for it." He could have been losing it at the end. His brain deteriorating as his body gave up.

Rubbing her fingers across her eyes, Zahra shook her head. "You don't have to. We could easily take a DNA test. Then you'd know for sure. Would that make you feel better?"

She jumped to her feet but fought the urge to run from the room. Zahra was right, of course. It was obvious now how quickly this information could be confirmed. But Zahra's matter-of-fact delivery was the poke that broke through her. *Would that make you feel better?* Even now, she couldn't resist one of her sarcastic digs.

"You'd love that, wouldn't you?" Aurora lobbed back. She was breaking her own rule, letting the mask she wore slip to reveal the ugly layer beneath. "Definitive proof that I'm not your sister or your problem anymore."

Zahra's face fell. Good, she'd inflicted damage. Aurora wasn't used to the venomous wrath spewing from her mouth, but it felt good, the release of something she didn't know she'd been holding, the pop of a stage light burning out. She wanted Zahra to hurt after all the years she'd spent waiting for her sister's acceptance, a sister she never actually had.

"Aurora," Zahra said. "That's not fair. I was being sincere."

"Oh yeah, right. You, sincere?"

"You're upset, and I get it—"

"You couldn't possibly get it. You don't even care about him. You know, you claim you can't stand him and he's so awful, but you're just like him. You're both selfish and arrogant and you won't let anyone in all the way."

"Selfish" wasn't a word she would have ever used to describe her father before; he'd always been anything but. With hindsight, however, her image of him was evolving. All those weeks he spent away from the house in the name of providing when really, he was stroking his ego. He'd ended up in prison, hadn't he? All because he'd convinced himself he was invincible. All because he'd decided to do what suited him, despite the law, despite the daughter he had at home. A decision that inevitably led to the dissolution of an already fragile marriage. Just the excuse Aurora's mom needed to pack them up and move them to LA. Aurora had forgiven him, but it had never been the same.

"Except you're worse, because at least he used those traits to be successful, at least he has something to show for himself. You talk about this dream cookbook, but you'll never do it because you're too scared. Really, you're all talk when you're afraid of everything. You hide and call it confidence. But I see how insecure you really are."

Zahra opened her mouth, then snapped it shut, as if she were biting her tongue. Aurora felt her shoulders sagging with regret already.

But a half second later, Zahra seemed to find her voice. "At least I'm not delusional enough to believe a married man twice my age could actually be in love with me. At least I'm not too scared to have a negative feeling for a half second—"

"Oh, I'm full of negative feelings—"

"And for the record, I'm not the one running from a life I claim to love."

"You just live in a state of constant hostility instead. What gives you the right to take out your bad attitude on everyone else? No wonder you're permanently alone. Can't imagine why your husband left you."

The words coming out of Aurora were so cruel, but like sick hurling its way up her throat, she couldn't stop them from spewing forth.

"Anything else?"

Zahra's droll tone ignited the last shred of Aurora's anger. "You're incapable of apologizing. Do you know that? You never say sorry for anything. Ever. Just like Dad. You'll probably die alone like him, too."

Zahra glared at her. "Well, I'd rather be alone than have a bunch of people I basically have to pay to be my friend. I'd rather keep dreaming than have everything handed to me because I'm willing to sleep with my boss and lie to the world."

It wasn't the truth. But it wasn't far from the truth either, and the reality was a blow to her sternum, stealing the air from Aurora's lungs. She knew Zahra thought she was pathetic, but to hear her say it aloud left her weak. For a moment, she couldn't respond, and the two sisters stared at each other in a standoff.

"I wanted you to like me so badly, all these years, when I really should have been asking myself if I liked you. You were lucky to have *me*. But you missed out," Aurora said, talking more to herself. She coughed back tears she didn't expect, then glared at Zahra. "You're so bad at being a sister. You probably would have made a crappy mom, too."

Zahra's jaw fell before her mouth closed in a mean line. Aurora had gone too far, but she didn't know how to take it back. She was a car careening off a cliff. She braced herself for a slap across her face. That's what she deserved.

"I can't believe you'd say that," Zahra finally said. "But you're right; it's a relief to know we're not actually related. I never wanted you in my life to begin with, and now it's official. We never have to speak again."

The room dimmed and Aurora's legs wavered. All at once, she was sure she would vomit if she didn't get fresh air. She bolted for the door, knocking Zahra in the process. From the corner of her vision, she watched Zahra lose her footing and trip backward, but it was too late to stop now. She didn't look back to see if Zahra caught herself before yanking open the door and fleeing into the hospital hallway.

40

Zahra

The last time Zahra had made a journey to see her father, she'd had no clue her life was about to come apart.

Navigating SFO, she'd found her heart rate steady, even without the antianxiety pills she usually relied on when she flew. Her ob-gyn had said she could prescribe something safe for pregnancy, but for Zahra it wasn't worth the shadow of a risk. Since she'd tipped into the third trimester, the nagging worry of something going wrong had finally lifted. She wasn't about to invite it back.

Zahra could do this on her own. For once, she was going to visit her dad with something adjacent to optimism brewing inside her.

At security, people were, for the first time ever, patient with her standard fumbling nervousness as she slipped out of her shoes and pulled off her coat. The bony white woman behind her asked her when she was due.

"End of July," Zahra said, letting her hand linger on the firm knot of her belly despite how weird and clichéd she'd once found the gesture in movies and shows. She couldn't resist the tactile experience of her changing body, the growing human stretching limbs against the elastic confines of her warm, wet world. She hadn't felt much movement that morning—the past day, really—but she'd been on her feet in class and then rushing to get herself out the door.

Her dad was out. He'd been released from the correctional facility early on account of overcrowding and spent a final two months in a halfway house in Seattle. She could have made the trip to see him sooner, but they'd begun to exchange occasional letters while he was away, letters that felt to Zahra like the first step toward what could, might one day, become a relationship. At least they were communicating. Still, their back-and-forth felt as breakable as an eggshell, so she didn't suggest a visit until he was settled back home, on parole but free to begin anew. Even this offer was made tentatively, nervously. But her dad had returned her email with an enthusiastic acceptance. So she'd booked her flight before she was too far along to travel.

In the security line, the bony woman smiled, pointed at Zahra's heeled boots, and said, "You're nearing the end. Those shoes won't fit soon," and the presumptuous comment didn't even bother her. She just shrugged and laughed like she didn't know what the lady was talking about before stepping forward.

When she opted out of the scanner, a female TSA agent gingerly led her away from the crowd, gave her nothing more than a cursory pat down for show. "I miss my babies," the woman said. "They're grown men now. I loved being pregnant. I felt so full of . . . oh, I don't know . . . hope, I guess."

Hope. Zahra let the word linger in the back of her mind as she thanked the woman, collected her things, and walked to the gate. Was that the strange feeling that rumbled in her chest?

She supposed she did feel hopeful. She was going to have a baby! She and Wes would leave the kingdom of couples to become a family. A real family. In one way, it was all she'd ever wanted for herself, for the girl-child version of herself at least. To be held in the refuge of a unit. To be safely kept by the two people who had brought her into this complicated world. She was an adult now, and yet this desire had not waned. But with the appearance of her daughter, she knew it finally would.

Hope kept her aloft as she stepped onto the plane.

The low-frequency hum of pain in her lower back didn't alarm her much. Nor the spot of red blood that tore through the toilet paper when she dragged herself into the lavatory, shaking as she stood and flexed the band of her maternity pants over her quiet belly. There might have been a harmless explanation for all that.

No, what left her cold and reeking of sour perspiration thirty minutes into her short flight was the feeling of impending doom that spread throughout her body, like hostile bacteria from a single bite of rotten food. It was just the flight, she told herself as her hands wrung out the armrests.

You're afraid to fly. That's all it is.

But the plane landed without incident an hour later, and as Zahra took a taxi to the hospital, all the while telling herself she was being overly cautious, paranoid, like Wes called her when she worried over nothing, the feeling only grew. She told no one, except to text her dad that she was taking herself to the ER, as if by sharing what was happening with Wes or her mom, it would become real.

"I can't feel her move," she whimpered to the doctor by the time she was seen, hating herself for not being stronger. Her dad wasn't there when they told her there was no more heartbeat, but he arrived a few minutes thereafter, looking hulking and out of place in the small triage room they'd taken her to before they could arrange a labor and delivery suite. She tried to put on a brave face for him, the man who'd frequently told her that big girls didn't cry, but she was a pot boiling over, the tears pouring forth even as she watched her father shrink away from them, from her.

The only thing he did right was not to offer her any pointless platitudes. "It's shit luck," he said, before excusing himself to call her mother. Even in her bewildered state, Zahra noted ruefully that he would rather call his ex-wife with bad news than sit in the same room as his emotional daughter.

She saw him only once more, when he came to tell her that her mom would get there as soon as possible, that she would tell Wes and they would fly up at once.

"Hey, kiddo," he said as the nurse took her elbow and helped her to her feet. They had a room ready for her induction. "You didn't do anything wrong, you know?"

That moment had crystallized for Zahra, along with shards of memory following the smudgy, blinding smear of labor: the pleasure of feeling her tiny daughter in her arms. The magic of her perfect fingers and toes. Her closed eyes so much like she was only sleeping. If she had only been sleeping. Kissing her acorn nose and purple lips. Lips that would never part. A mouth that would never suckle from Zahra's full breasts. Breasts mapped with blue veins and swelling with colostrum. The phantom kicks that haunted her hollowed womb for months afterward.

She didn't believe her dad's parting words. She'd never trusted him, and as she walked down the hall to the new reality that waited for her and he didn't follow, she knew she never would. Just as she knew she could never fly again. That she would never be the same again.

The threadbare fabric chair beside her dad's hospital bed caught Zahra's misstep after Aurora barreled from the room. She fell into it with a thump, the letter still clutched in her palm.

Her heart pounded, her head ached, her ears rang from the fallout of Aurora's uncharacteristic outburst.

Zahra certainly hadn't seen *that* coming.

The secret in the letter had shocked her, but she believed it at once, a lost key clicking open a rusty lock. Zahra had always known her dad loved Aurora more, and here in her hands was proof. Only love could make a man raise a child that wasn't his own.

So she could understand why Aurora needed that, too—a concrete fact to hold tight to. That's why she'd suggested they do their own DNA test. Clearly, Aurora hadn't taken it the way Zahra intended.

It wasn't the first time her sincerity had been misread as sarcasm. And why should Aurora think otherwise? Zahra had given her enough reasons to assume the worst. But it stung nonetheless, a contact blister, rubbed until broken, open and raw.

A part of her marveled at Aurora's reaction. She'd finally gotten mad. Really mad. Zahra didn't begrudge Aurora her anger. If anyone understood, it was Zahra.

But another part, a small hopeful part that had recently begun to unfurl like a tender fiddlehead fern in the first warmth of spring, had been hacked at the stalk, diminished by every one of the brutal accusations Aurora had leveled at her, by their truth.

Zahra had let her sister in, and Aurora had turned on her before walking out the door. It was exactly what she thought would happen if she cared too much again.

And thus entered a third part of Zahra, the loudest part, the one she'd been carrying around like a tumor. *That* part felt vindicated. *See, see!* it hollered in her head, seething with superiority. *You were right about her. You were right to stay away. People only disappoint you.*

What was that saying she'd always found nauseatingly banal? We hurt the ones we love the most?

The ones we love hurt *us* the most, was more like it.

Zahra's palm grew damp where it held the paper, and she leaned over her knees as vertigo splashed over her vision. She could bolt, and she wanted to. She'd wanted to turn around this entire time, and now was her chance. The keys to the Volvo were in her pocket, and she could get in the car and drive back the way they'd come, or as far as the car would take her. Let Aurora hop on a private jet or whatever. Let her figure this out on her own.

Except none of this was Aurora's fault.

Zahra blamed her dad. Dragging them up here to drop this bomb on them. Checking out before he could explain himself. Or so he didn't have to explain himself. She wouldn't put it past him, guilting her into coming, knowing full well he didn't intend to show up.

And surprise, surprise, the whole letter had been addressed to Aurora. Zahra, a bystander not the subject.

Except . . . She sat up again, a jolt running straight through her core.

Zahra hadn't finished the letter; Aurora had cut her off before she could, but there was more. She smoothed out the paper and read.

> Zahra,
>
> I can't begin to imagine how you will react to this news. I know I'm a great disappointment to you, and this will surely only confirm various negative feelings you harbor against me, for good reason. But, kiddo, I come to you on my knees, to beg you not to be like me. You have never accepted Aurora as yours, and I've wondered on occasion if you could somehow sense this secret. But I think not. I think Aurora has borne your resentment toward me. It's understandable but unfair. Not just to her, but to you.
>
> I'm not good with the mushy stuff. I've already considered burning this letter more than a half dozen times. But there will be no more opportunities. You spend so much time wondering when and how your number might be called, but once it happens, the specifics hardly matter. You've arrived at the end of the road, and it's impossible not to look back to see the past winding behind you.
>
> I want to explain myself to you, Zahra, but my explanation will undoubtedly fall short. There is no great secret to justify the father I was to you, only

my personal failings. I didn't know what made a good father, and in my uncertainty, I defaulted to what I knew. And then you were so much like me, so independent and unyielding, all the traits my own father found off-putting. I convinced myself the most generous thing I could do for you was to leave you be, let your mother and your grandparents raise you before I did more damage. By the time Aurora came along, I had learned enough to know that if I made a point of it, I could do things differently. I regret the nature of our relationship, but I didn't know how to fix what was wrong, or I suppose I didn't want to because it required more of me than I was willing to give.

I picture you reading this, poking holes in my story, demanding a more thorough accounting of myself. But I'm only human with a single, imperfect life under my belt, and I can't make it make sense any better than this.

I've not been a great man, but I'd like to end my life with one decent act, and that's to bring you two girls together. You have a sister, Zahra; she needs you right now, and whether you want to admit it or not, you need her. You can tell me you're fully content with your life as it stands, but we both know it's not true. You have wanted more for yourself, and that want doesn't go away because you declare it gone. That's something I know firsthand. I'm sorry for what I said about cooking school being a waste of your potential and money. I accept now that it's a calling. You are gifted. But even a calling is not enough to fill a life. A person needs people. Take it from me. Don't let your pops ruin another good thing for you.

Whether you both can forgive me or not, I don't regret being your dad. I'm damn lucky I got to do it at all.

It's been a wild ride, kids.

Be well, Dad

When she finished reading, Zahra sat listening to the clanging of the heavy hospital doors in the ward, the sound of voices rising and falling in the hallway, the steady beat of her father's heart on the monitor turned down low.

Eyes burning with fatigue, body vibrating from exhaustion and adrenaline and caffeine, she looked at her dad, really looked at him, not at her hands or the floor or anywhere else in that dim room, like she'd been doing since she and Aurora had first walked in there.

She stared straight at him, and she saw what she'd been avoiding: Dom Starling reduced to nothing more than flesh and bone. He'd been a regular man all along. Not a myth. Not an archetype. Not a monster after all.

Gray and gaunt, his cheeks cut nearly as deep as his eye sockets. White skin peeled ragged from his dry lips, and the facial hair he'd long kept at bay with daily shaves had grown in patchy and white. Loose, spotted skin hung from his neck, and the mottled hollow at the base of his throat was so deep, it could have held a single large egg. If she couldn't see the small pulse of his heart there, the slight rise and fall of his chest, she would have thought he was dead already.

But his nose. That hadn't changed.

Even with the oxygen cannula resting over his nostrils, she could see the straight slope that led to a noticeable cleft at the tip was the same as ever, and the same as hers. They had the same curl of their lips. And they both squinted one eye when they were confused, one eyebrow always a touch higher than the other. She didn't need a paternity test to know they were related. Anyone could guess he was her father, even if their coloring was different. She'd always hated how her face mirrored his, grateful that at least her mom's Persian genes had given her darker eyes and wavier hair, browner skin, and better cheekbones.

Was it true they shared more than just looks?

With her father's final words clamped beneath her white knuckles, Zahra knew that it was. For so long, she'd fought against those traits in her dad she recognized most in herself. But instead of differentiating her, her resistance had only made her more like him. Bruisingly stubborn. Abrasive. Aloof. Principled to the point of impairment.

In the sterile light of the hospital, her flaws magnified and on display, the notion of exacting an apology seemed comical, a pitiful little fantasy she'd conjured to . . . what? Justify giving into her dad's request that she visit? Make right a lifetime worth of disappointments? To heal her? What childlike thinking.

He hadn't apologized, but even if he had, his "Sorry" would have only been a start. The first brick laid for a new foundation. In the back of her mind, she'd believed they would have more time. *One day.* Whatever that meant.

Now all she had left was a letter, a hospital room, and what remained of her dad's life.

She set her hand on the blanket, found the hard shape of his wrist, but she didn't squeeze. She didn't hold on to him, the intimacy of the moment already stretching her thin, the words she'd been saving for two and a half decades lodged somewhere deep in her throat, doubling in volume so that it hurt to breathe. But she had to speak. She had to say *something*. He might not be able to have a conversation, but maybe, for once, he could hear her.

"You're right, I *do* want more than . . ." She started without realizing she'd opened her mouth until she heard the echo of her voice in her ears. She shook the papers in her hand. "Than *this*. But it's too late for us. I'm so tired of caring and hurting. I'm so tired of feeling angry." As a fresh wave of fatigue rolled over her, nothing had ever felt truer. She'd held fast to her anger so the heavy sediment of her grief—of losing her daughter, her husband, her best friend—wouldn't drag her under. In that way, her dad had saved her, her resentment toward him a tattered life vest, keeping her afloat even as it choked her at the throat. She sat for a long time as the waves of grief and anger rolled in and receded, rolled in and receded, until the hurt had ebbed enough for her to speak again.

Taking a breath, she finally wrapped her fingers around his wrist, noting its firm fragility, then spoke to her father one final time. "I love you, Dad."

Those three words, clumsy in her mouth, rang strange to her ear, embarrassing even. She couldn't remember the last time she'd said them, to anyone. Not even to her mom. It was the kind of thing they wrote to each other in cards but didn't say aloud. She must have said them to Wes last, though she couldn't remember when. It was impossible to remember the last time you did the smallest things you took for granted, and it was usually those things you wished you could remember most.

But releasing the words now was like springing her heart from a steel trap. Her body flooded with oxygen-rich blood, a great pulse of forgiveness and love that lifted her and her dad from this room and these circumstances into a faraway place where for one brief instant there was nothing between them but potential and hope.

Her phone vibrated. An unknown number appeared on the screen, and she ignored the call, probably a prospective client. But they could wait. Everything could wait.

She'd been waiting the past decade, in a self-induced kind of limbo since her baby daughter had died. And in that time, she'd gone from a girl in her twenties hopeful that her life might turn out okay to a woman staring down forty, ignoring the fact that years of her life had come and gone while she held on to things that never were. A culinary education that might have led to a Michelin-starred kitchen. A daughter who never took her first breath. A devoted father who never existed and never would. Lives she'd never get to live.

There were no do-overs, but this felt like the closest she would come. She may not be twenty-five anymore, but there was still time.

Time to be a different version of herself. Time, maybe, for love. She had botched things with Aurora, Preeti, Elian—with everyone. But she knew how to fix things. To keep testing the recipe until it worked. To use the ingredients available to her and make something that sang.

Her phone vibrated again, and this time she looked, wondering if it might be Aurora. But the text came from the same unknown number as before. She swiped to read.

> Zahra, it's Lucy. I hope this is still your same number. I'm looking for Aurora. I need to get in touch with her immediately, and she's not answering her phone. Do you know where she is? Please call me. No one will return my calls.

The ferocious desire to protect Aurora arose in Zahra, and she wouldn't tamp it down. There was no way she'd hand over any information to Lucy. If she had any information to give.

Where had Aurora gone?

The door clicked open, and from her seat, Zahra craned her neck, fully expecting to see her sister, calm again, ready to find the silver lining. Not because she was vapid and naive, but because survival in this world sometimes required magical thinking.

"Speak of the devil," Zahra would say, and they could talk again like they had in the car. Zahra could make things right. Because that's what she wanted to do. The impulse to run had passed. She didn't want to push her sister away; she wanted to keep her close. She couldn't get through this ordeal without her; she didn't want to.

But it was just Nicole stopping in to check on them. "How's it going in here?" she asked, coming round to the other side of Dom's bed. She fiddled with his IV, touched his wrist, smoothed out his blankets.

Zahra couldn't even begin to tell her how it was going. "Have you seen my sister?"

Nicole nodded. "She ran out of here like a bat out of hell about a half hour ago. This is really hard for some people. Understandably."

Had she gone to the cafeteria? The car? She wouldn't just leave, not now.

"You must be the eldest daughter, right?" Nicole said, glancing over her shoulder at Zahra with kind eyes.

His only daughter. Zahra shook the thought from her head as if she'd been trying the idea on for size and didn't like the fit. Because it wasn't true, and a DNA test wouldn't prove otherwise.

"The super-talented chef, he said. You're just how he described you, with the dark hair and features. He went on and on about how smart and strong you are." Zahra must have made a sound of disbelief because Nicole bit her lip. "No, really. You'd be surprised. At the end, people soften. I've seen it before."

"How was he?" Zahra asked. "Did he know what was happening? Because he didn't say . . ."

Nicole stood still, considering her words. "His cancer was advanced, and he understood that we couldn't keep the fluid out of his lungs, but he talked like he was planning to go home." She sighed. "I think the timing snuck up on him."

A few days ago, Zahra couldn't imagine anything getting the best of her dad. But it didn't matter how strong you were, how impenetrable your defenses, no one escaped the human condition, the vulnerability of a last breath. Zahra's own inhale caught in her chest.

"But was he scared?"

"Oh, hon, he didn't say." Nicole's voice was laced with sympathy that for once, Zahra wanted to lean into. "He's not suffering, if that's what you're worried about."

But they couldn't really know for sure what was going on inside him. There were some things you couldn't ever know about another person, the things they couldn't speak aloud, the things they kept even from themselves.

"I know for sure he was relieved you girls would be here," Nicole said. "He told me more than once."

Zahra hoped relief was enough to carry him to whatever came next. But she knew it wasn't enough for her.

Dom Starling had come to the end of his road, but Zahra's stretched out before her. She folded the letter in her hand, shoved it in her bag, and heaved herself to her feet. "How much time does he have?"

"We can't say for sure," Nicole hedged. "Probably today sometime. It could be a matter of hours." She gave Zahra an apologetic look before stepping from the room.

She had to find her sister. Zahra looked back down at her dad. "If you do just one thing for me, hold on until I get back with Aurora. Wait for us."

But when she called Aurora's phone, it went straight to voicemail. She didn't find her in the lobby or hiding in the Volvo. Zahra popped the hatchback. Sure enough, Aurora's bags were gone.

The fallen starlet could have been anywhere, a hotel, a bar, a street corner somewhere, but Zahra had a suspicion about where she had gone, and she knew it was a huge mistake.

41

Aurora

This terminal of the airport was surprisingly quiet. Lines collected at the food stalls, crowds gathered at each gate, but people moved slowly, muted by a subdued energy.

Aurora hadn't bothered with her sunglasses or hat, but no one recognized her. She was anonymous among them, as alone as she'd ever been, bumping shoulders with the person next to her. She'd even bypassed the sky lounge in favor of waiting the three hours until boarding with everyone else at the gate.

Fumbling into a seat by the gate's kiosk, she almost took pleasure in the hard plastic beneath her, a discomfort she deserved. Outside the wall of windows, planes moved across the tarmac, workers scrambled to load and unload luggage. The wind had picked up, and their bright coats caught and ballooned. But she was as far from the scenes around her as if she were already staring down from forty thousand feet above.

When she'd stormed out of the hospital room, she hadn't planned to come to the airport. She'd raced outside, bracing herself against a planter box in case she had to puke. But after a minute, her stomach settled and her phone dinged with a text message. From Margot. Had she ever received a text message from Margot? She didn't think so. They communicated via phone, or emails between their assistants.

Texting seemed beneath Margot somehow, too ordinary. This text was anything but.

> Aurora, I understand your father is unwell and you're probably coping with some level of shock given the news from Dillon's camp, but as I've made clear, this isn't how I conduct business with or for my clients. If you miss your flight today, you will not only be going against my professional advice but also putting my livelihood at risk. That's a breach of contract, and I'll have no choice but to terminate our relationship. I am imploring you to get on the plane, get back here, and confront this head-on. Everything can be fixed, but the Emmys are two days away and we need a strategy. Please don't throw away your career. You have so much potential.

Standing outside the entrance to the hospital lobby, Aurora had gripped her phone until it hurt. In addition to being email-length, the message had the directness of a steel pole. Margot never called her by her real name, but she could hear her manager's measured approach in every sentence. Her threat was crystal clear. Aurora, the girl who never showed up late to set or demanded an extra take or called Margot without checking with her assistant first to make sure it was okay, had worn down her manager's patience.

She checked her calendar. Her current flight left after noon. She had nowhere else to go. So she found the Volvo in the parking lot, banged on the trunk until the broken latch popped open, grabbed her things, and ordered a car.

After she'd arrived at the airport and made her way to the gate, she'd texted Evangeline to update her. A string of celebratory emojis rolled in, but her assistant was probably happy because she wasn't out of a job. If Aurora had ever considered them friends, she understood now that their relationship was transactional. She powered down her phone. There was no one else to talk to. She so desperately wanted to call her dad, even Dillon, to cry on their shoulders and let them soothe her hurt feelings.

But the dad and Dillon she knew had never actually existed. She'd put her faith in them, for what? They'd both lied to her and left her. She had no one she could turn to, and the sensation was like that of a trapdoor opening beneath her, leaving her free-falling in the dark.

She could see how the love she'd had for Dillon had really been about the way he'd made her feel, and now her feelings for him had soured and gone bad. But she didn't know what to feel about her dad. For the first time, she understood why Zahra was so mad all these years. Betrayal and abandonment hollowed you, left room for bitterness to seep into the holes.

God, she'd been such an idiot. Zahra was right. Again. And the worst part was that Zahra was the only person who hadn't betrayed her, who wasn't expecting her to get on this flight, put a smile on her face, and make nice. But Zahra was the last person she could call. After what she'd said at the hospital, Zahra would want nothing to do with her from here on out.

A plane took off in the distance, and Aurora let the sound rumble through her chest. She regretted what she'd said, not because she hadn't meant it—she'd meant most of it, except for the part about her being a bad mother; she was sick with remorse about that—but because Zahra didn't really deserve it. She *was* like their dad, but Aurora liked that about her—the similarity was comforting. She liked Zahra's dry humor and snide asides. She liked that she always told it how it was and didn't fill every silence with chatter. She never had to wonder what Zahra was thinking. She never had to perform for her the way she did for everyone else.

Losing Zahra as her sister wasn't a relief. She regretted saying that most of all.

But she had, and her punishment, she supposed, was facing whatever disaster awaited her back home. She closed her eyes but couldn't sleep. What if Zahra did try to reach her and she had her phone off?

She jolted upright and turned it back on. Only seconds later it began to ring, and she sprang to answer.

But it wasn't Zahra. It was her mom, again, for the fifth time. Aurora had declined each previous call with obstinate purpose. An act of revenge for the originator of her betrayals. Her mom had withheld information about her paternity. Her mom had not discouraged her from having a relationship with Dillon. Her mom had shoved her into an acting career because that's what *she* had wanted.

Aurora's anger was a muscle she'd begun to flex, but the tissue was already strained and spent, the blunt edge of her contempt worn down to a nub. She didn't have to answer. What was another ignored call? But loneliness had her in its grip. Loneliness and confusion and heartache. She needed to speak some things aloud.

"Mom?"

"I've been calling for ages. Why haven't you been answering?" Lucy nearly screeched. "I had to text Zahra, for God's sake."

"Zahra? What'd she say?"

"Nothing. She wouldn't tell me anything but demanded things from *me*. That girl has some nerve." *Yes,* Aurora thought with admiration, *she does.* "What is going on? What did Margot say?"

But Aurora didn't have the patience for all that. "How could you lie to me for so long?"

"Lie to you? What are you taking about? Where are you?"

"Dad told me the truth. That he's not my biological father." She heard her mother's breath catch, and she continued, satisfied she'd caught her off guard. "There was someone else, wasn't there? And you knew and you never told me."

Silence fell between them, hard as an axe and long enough for Aurora to wonder if they'd lost each other. But when she glanced down at her phone, the call was still connected, the seconds ticking by.

"Well," Aurora nudged. "What do you have to say?"

Finally, her mother's voice filled the line again. "What exactly did he tell you?"

"He told me he did a paternity test but kept the results to himself this whole time. He said he thought I had a right to know. He said I should ask you about the guy, that you'd know who he was talking about. So do you?"

Lucy sighed. "I didn't know for sure."

Aurora didn't believe her. Oh, sure, she could buy that maybe her mom had never known for certain who had fathered her child, but only because she'd been deluding herself to make the facts fit the narrative she wanted. Aurora knew something about that.

"But you had a pretty good idea, didn't you? All that time, you never thought to mention it to me. You didn't think I'd find it relevant? You didn't think I had a right to know there was a possibility Dad might not be my dad? Even now that I'm an adult."

"You're not an adult, Aurora. You're practically a child still," her mother said, exasperated.

Aurora didn't argue, not because she agreed, but because the sentiment cut so deep for a moment it took her breath away. Acting had kept her from being a child when she was one, and somehow, because of that, she had never entirely become an adult, not in the way that mattered, where you controlled your own life, took responsibility for yourself. *Trusted* yourself. She didn't fault her mom, although Lucy had been the one to teach her how to shut down her own voice, to tune into the frequencies of those around her instead. Aurora had wanted to want the success and the fame, and that had been more than enough for a long time. But she wasn't sure she did anymore.

In the wreckage of this realization, an ugly thought came back to her. "You set me up. Didn't you?"

"Set you up? What are you talking about?"

"At Hannah's café. You knew I'd probably be seen there, and you didn't care. You and Hannah probably arranged the whole thing."

"You make it sound so nefarious. I didn't think it would turn into . . . this . . . this"—she stuttered—"shitshow. I had no idea about the blind item. You never told me."

Her mom was trying to lob the blame back onto her. Not this time. "And *you* didn't tell me you knew about me and Dillon."

"Technically, I didn't."

"You had an inkling, didn't you? About Dillon. About Dad?" More people had begun to gather at the gate, and she turned away from everyone, curling around her phone. "How could you lie about something so important?"

"I knew what I believed to be true until just now. Your father never mentioned a paternity test. How do we even know he's telling the truth? Did you actually see the so-called test results?"

"Are you serious?" she whisper-hissed, even though she'd briefly wondered the same thing. "Dad is lying unconscious right now. So no, I haven't had an opportunity to ask him, Mom. But it doesn't matter. He would never make something like this up."

That chastened Lucy into silence. When she spoke, her voice had a conciliatory timbre. "I'm sorry, okay? I'm sorry about Dillon and your dad, and I'm sorry this is all happening right now. I swear to you, if I ever had my own doubts about your dad, even for a second, then it was an omission meant to protect you. Can't you understand that?"

Dillon was supposed to protect her, too. Despite that, she believed her mom, she really did. But people lied to themselves. People said one thing and did another. People told half-truths all the time. *She* told half-truths. Because that's how it was when you weren't willing to look at anything head-on.

"But Aurora," her mom pleaded, "this moment is too important. There's too much at stake. You need to get back to LA."

"I am," she said, resigned. "I'm at the airport."

"Thank God. Text me when you land." A pause. "And honey, I know it feels like everything's falling apart, but we'll figure it out. We'll work through it together. Okay?"

This time, Aurora knew her mom was lying. She ended the call and turned off her phone, sure only that she couldn't sit there a second longer.

42

Zahra

The sight of the sliding doors leading into Departures left Zahra queasy. She had no intention of getting on a plane today if she could help it, but still, she hated the airport. Hated the crowds and the weird Rorschach stains on the carpets. Hated the digital signs that listed all the departing flights. All those opportunities for disaster.

Shoving all this aside, she plowed past the line, toward a desk manned by a petite, middle-aged woman strangled by a teeny scarf tied at her neck.

"Hey," someone yelled behind her. If Aurora had taught her anything, it was how to fake it so good it looked real. In this case, she turned around and waved the complainer away.

"It's fine. I was here first." She was shocked when the man piped down and no one called her out. To the woman, she said, "I need a ticket."

"Ooh-kay. Let's see if I can help you." She drew out her vowels in such a way that made Zahra want to yank the scarf right off her neck and whap her in the face with it. She didn't have time for this right now, but she'd learned from her sister a little patience could go a long way.

"Thank you. I'm grateful," she said, glancing at her phone to check the flight number. She'd had to call Lucy to get the number for Aurora's assistant, a wasted fifteen minutes of conversation in which Lucy had gone on about needing to speak to Aurora right away, as if Zahra were holding her against her will. Once she'd been able to speak with Aurora's assistant, Evangeline confirmed that Aurora had gone to the airport and, after some cajoling, provided the flight information. But by the time Zahra got there, departure time was in less than an hour.

"It's LAX bound, flight 1126," she told the airline attendant.

"Ooh-kay." The woman clacked on her keyboard, then gave Zahra an alarmed look. "Are you sure you have the right number? This flight is boarding in twenty minutes."

"I'm sure. Do you have tickets or not?" She caught herself. "If you wouldn't mind checking. Please."

More clacking.

"Hmmm . . . Nothing in economy."

Zahra's heart sped. She could buy a ticket for another flight just to get through security. But what if Aurora had already boarded by the time she got to the gate? She'd need to get on the plane and drag her off. The thought sent a chill straight through her.

"Oh, wait, I see two business class seats available."

"Business class? How much is that?"

"Um, $1,200?"

"That can't possibly be right. For a two-and-a-half-hour flight?"

The woman nodded. "Actually, it's . . . Let's see here . . . Here we go. It's $1,424."

Oof. That hurt. But it was her best option. Now she could add credit card debt to her student loan debt. She forked over her ID, eyes darting to the clock on her phone.

"Are you checking luggage? It probably wouldn't get there anyway—"

"No, no luggage," Zahra almost spat before gaining control of herself. "Would you mind just printing my boarding pass?"

The petite woman frowned but did as requested. As soon as the boarding pass was in her possession, Zahra booked it to security. Thank

God the line wasn't too long. She could feel the seconds ticking by as she waited for her turn.

She hated airports, but she *loathed* security. The arbitrary rules, the privacy violation, the urgency to disrobe and empty her pockets in a quarter second flat, not to mention the paranoia that every other person might be harboring a weapon in their bag. She shook her leg, trying to stay calm. Her stomach was roiling now, and she felt almost faint—with exhaustion, hunger, or panic, she wasn't sure.

Stay calm. You can do this. It was just the airport. She wasn't actually flying, even though her body didn't seem to believe her. Her body was in the midst of a full-on meltdown.

According to the time on her boarding pass, they'd started to board the plane. Aurora would be in business class and boarding first. At least Zahra had a ticket. She could march onto the plane and pull her right off.

When she got to the front of the security line, she slipped off her shoes and stuck them, along with her bag, into a bin. She was so close. All she had to do was step through the X-ray machine, grab her stuff, and go.

Except the second she stepped out of the machine, a disgruntled-looking TSA agent held up his hands.

"Come with me," he said.

No, no, no. This wasn't happening. Not right now. "Why?"

"You've been randomly selected for a search."

"But I'm not traveling with anything."

This seemed to give him pause as he led her to a small area away from the crowds. A female agent arrived, carrying the bin with Zahra's shoes and purse. "This yours?" she asked. Zahra nodded.

"I got it," the woman told the male agent. He sauntered off, and she riffled through Zahra's bag, took her sweet time performing a body search.

When the woman jerked her chin toward the terminals, Zahra stuck her feet in her shoes and grabbed her bag. There wasn't time to look at her phone, only to check the boarding pass for her gate number and run like hell.

Her lungs burned and her heart banged against her ribs. Zahra feared she might keel over, keenly aware that maybe it wouldn't have been the worst idea to take Preeti up on her offer for yoga sessions. She could picture the story: Professional Recipe Developer With a Fear of Flying Dies From Clogged Arteries Running Through the Airport. A fitting end, really. Her dad would find it amusing for sure.

They had that in common, too: a dark sense of humor.

But it wasn't the end, not for her.

She powered through the discomfort, cursing under her breath when she realized the gate was the last in the terminal. As she neared, huffing and puffing, she heard the tail end of the final boarding announcement. Her eyes darted wildly over the plastic seats to see if there was any chance Aurora would still be among them, but only a couple stood near the desk, struggling with their carry-ons.

Shit on a brick. She was going to have to get on the damn plane.

For a second, she considered letting Aurora go, turning around before she could watch the plane taxi and take off. But then Zahra would be here alone with their dying father, and Aurora would go back to a disaster, wrongly believing she had no one to lean on. She would get chewed up and spit out, and although if anyone could put themselves back together again it was Aurora, being beaten down too many times could break a person. First, Aurora had to stay and face their father or Zahra knew she would regret it, and the regret would taint everything that came after.

But as she neared the entrance to the skywalk where the airline attendant stood waiting to scan her boarding pass, she thought she might not make it. She might pass out. Her heart was going too fast, and she couldn't catch her breath. She doubled over, resting on her knees.

"Ma'am, are you okay?"

Waving her hand at the airline attendant's question, she tried to start the box breathing Aurora was always going on about. But it wasn't working. She couldn't tell if she was incredibly out of shape or having a panic attack. Possibly both.

Get it together. You have to do this. It's just a plane.

But she'd been lying to herself. If she got on the plane, she wasn't going to get off. They would close the doors behind her, and she'd be stuck, facing the horror of takeoff. The rumble of the engines, the rattling of the interior, then the sickening lift as they left the earth.

At least she'd be with Aurora. At least Aurora would know she'd come for her.

The attendant cleared his throat. "Ma'am, if you're well, I'm going to need you to board so the pilot can prepare for takeoff."

Resolved, she stood, ignoring her heaving chest. "I'm fine." She paused. "Is there any way it would be possible to get a drink before takeoff? Like an alcoholic beverage?"

The man gave her a strange look. "You'll have to wait for drink service to start."

"But I'm in business class. Doesn't that make a difference?"

He ignored her. "Boarding pass?"

Before she could show it to him, she heard her name.

She turned to find Aurora, blotchy faced, her strange dark hair hanging down past her shoulders, carrying an extremely large coffee and looking alarmed. "What are you doing here?" she said.

Flooded with relief, Zahra threw her arms around her sister, nearly knocking the coffee from her hand. "Thank God you didn't get on the plane."

"Whoa," Aurora said. "I needed a minute to clear my head. And anyway, I always wait until the last second."

"Which is literally now," the attendant interjected, copping a bit more attitude than Zahra found necessary.

Zahra pulled back from Aurora. "You can't."

"I have to. In case you've failed to notice, my life is falling apart. And the Emmys are the day after tomorrow."

The airline attendant's head jerked up.

"I did what Dad asked. I got us here . . ." She bit down hard on her lip. "I heard what he had to tell us."

"Wait, wait. I know you. You're"—the airline attendant snapped his fingers a few times—"You're what's-her-name. What is it?" He tapped his temple. "You're that girl on that show. *You, Me, Us.*" Genuine glee flooded his face, as if he'd struck gold. "That's it! You're Sloane. I knew you looked familiar."

"Now is not the time, dude," Zahra muttered. "Can you back off a little?" He took a few paces back, still grinning, and pulled out his phone. To Aurora, she said, "Please don't go."

Aurora opened her mouth to protest again, but Zahra raised her hand. "You said I never apologize, and you're right. But I came here to tell you I'm sorry. I'm sorry I was such a bitch the whole drive. I'm sorry we didn't get here sooner. And I'm sorry I haven't been there for you. Ever. I know what the letter said, okay? But it doesn't matter; he was your dad and I'm your sister. You're right about that, too: I'm not a very good one. But you are, or you could be if I let you. And I don't want to lose you now."

Aurora's face was impassive, a pretty frame without a picture.

"You have to stay until the end. If you don't, you'll never forgive yourself. Be angry with him but do this for yourself." They were the words Zahra needed to hear, too, but they weren't enough. She squeezed her hands tight, felt her feet on the ground. "I can't do this without you. I need you here. I really do. Please."

A long moment dragged between them in which Aurora's face didn't change. Then slowly her eyes softened. "You weren't a bitch the *whole* drive. I should never have said what I said about you being a bad mom. And you're not a bad sister. You just haven't had any practice. You did save me from the kids at the diner and held my hair while I barfed."

"So you forgive me?"

Aurora nodded. "You know I can't stay mad."

"Yeah, about that? We really need to work on your grudge-holding skills."

Suddenly, Aurora's face morphed into a squinty-eye wince. "I have to tell you something."

Zahra braced herself. *Oh no.* What else would the universe throw her way?

"I lied about there being no rental cars. Back in . . . wherever we were when the car died. You were threatening to go back to LA, and I didn't want you to leave before we'd even gotten started. But I should have been honest. This road trip meant something to me, and I should have just said that, what I felt. I don't know. Maybe it wouldn't have made a difference."

Nothing Aurora said was a shock. In some way, without giving it a thought, Zahra had already known the rental company hadn't run out of cars. She'd wanted to come, as desperately as she hadn't wanted to come. She'd needed Aurora to make it feel as if she had no other choice.

"You're right," Zahra said. "It probably wouldn't have made a difference. I hate being lied to; you know that." She was talking to herself as much as to her sister. She'd been lying to herself for a long time, digging in her heels when all she really wanted was to move forward. "But I'm glad I came. We were both a bit misguided, so let's call it even. Okay?"

Shaking her head, Aurora still looked miserable. "But I have to go. People are counting on me. If I don't show up, my career is over. Dillon has turned everyone against me. He's the one who confirmed the story about us." She paused, looped a bit of greasy hair around her finger. "I thought what we had meant something."

"You trusted him. He took advantage of your trust. He was the one in the position of power. He was the one with a wife. Then he turned on you when it benefited him to do so. You did the wrong thing, but you're a good person."

"But no one will ever see it that way unless I go back and put on a show, you know?"

Zahra's breathing had finally slowed, her heart returned to its regular reliable function. A strange calm came over her, a clarity of mind. She couldn't convince Aurora to do anything. Her sister had to figure it out for herself. Zahra had to trust she'd make the right choice, whatever that might be, then show up for her either way, just like she knew Aurora would do if the tables were turned.

"I get it. I mean, I don't really; the PR element of celebrity stuff is confusing to me. But if you leave, make sure you're doing it for you. And if you decide to stay, we'll be at Dad's side together, right?"

"I don't know," Aurora said, her voice strained with indecision.

"Take me out of the equation. Forget about Dillon and . . ." She waved her hand as if to say "everyone." "What do *you* want to do?"

"Aura Star! That's it!" the airline attendant said to a female attendant who had come to join them. He waved his phone around.

The female attendant flashed her colleague an exasperated look. "Ms. Star, if you don't get on the plane now, the doors will be closing."

"Her name is Aurora Starling," snapped Zahra.

"Okay," the female attendant said, clearly annoyed. "Ms. Starling?"

To Zahra, Aurora said, "Were you really going to get on the plane for me?"

She told her she was and watched as Aurora took this in, her shoulders widening when she turned toward the attendant. "I won't be flying today."

A relief as sweet as Maman Joon's Persian nougat flowed through Zahra's veins. She could have kissed the ground.

The woman nodded, picking up the phone at the kiosk and relaying a message.

"Let's go," Aurora said.

"Wait, can I get your autograph?" the male attendant asked.

Before Aurora could respond, Zahra gave him a death glare. "Zero chance. Read the room."

Together, they walked through the terminal, out the way they'd come. At the Volvo, Zahra climbed into the driver's seat. "I meant what I said about getting on the plane for you. But I really, really, really didn't want to," she admitted.

"Yeah, about that?" Aurora said. "We really need to work on your flying skills."

"Funny. You know, they said they wouldn't give me a drink until beverage service, even though I had a business class ticket."

"Oh, they'd give one to me."

Zahra rolled her eyes, but she didn't doubt it.

"So." She turned over the ignition. "I guess now we have to face this."

43

Aurora

Zahra navigated the Volvo back to the hospital, the car's familiar chug and rattle mimicking Aurora's bone-deep fatigue in the passenger seat. She stared at her phone, the conduit between her and her demons.

It was only a matter of time until they realized she hadn't boarded her flight. Having already burned through whatever patience Margot possessed, she couldn't keep hiding anymore.

What she'd said to Zahra, that her career would crumble, wasn't entirely true. No one likes a mistress, but it wasn't like she'd never work again. She could recover. Rebuild her reputation. Look at Kristen Stewart. And Angelina Jolie.

She'd start by groveling at Margot's feet and blame her antics on grief, talk to the crisis publicist and get media training that taught her how to appear both culpable and victimized. They'd put out a statement in which she accepted responsibility for her sins. Aurora was too new of a name for a true phoenix-rising-from-the-ashes story. She'd be lucky to get a three-page spread in *People* about putting the past behind her. She'd have to claw all the way back to the top.

The thought repelled her the way thinking of the martinis she'd drunk the night before made her gag reflexes engage. She would be happy to never drink again, and she felt the same about performing.

Aurora's intestines twisted as she powered on her phone and dialed Margot's number. Zahra gave her an encouraging nod across the car's console just before Margot's irritated voice slashed through the speaker. "Tell me you're calling from LAX."

"Margot," she said, bracing herself against what was sure to come next. "I'm verbally terminating our contract."

"Excuse me? What?"

She didn't think anything could surprise her unflappable manager, but apparently, Aurora Starling could. The power move gave her an extra surge of strength.

"I'm truly sorry. You've been an incredible advocate, but like you told me, I haven't followed through on my end of the deal. Consider this my thirty-day notice," she said. "In that time, I need to know how I can get out of the show's contract. Talk to my agency, lawyers, whoever. I want out, and I'll pay for it if I have to."

Dillon was right about one thing: sometimes you had to bust through a wall, and for the first time, Aurora was willing to make that kind of impact.

"Oh, you'll pay for it," Margot said, not as a threat but as a statement of fact. "Are you crazy? You're supposed to be walking the red carpet in forty-eight hours. We're in talks with Hello Sunshine. There are endorsement deals in the works. For God's sake, Aurora, I don't need to tell you all this. You know what you have going on. What you have to lose."

"I'm aware."

"For the record, I think this is a mistake. This is effectively burning every bridge into Hollywood. You get that, don't you? You're lighting a match in fire country."

Aurora released a shuddery breath but didn't back down. "I understand. Can you get me out of my contract or not?"

"Fine," Margot said. "But don't come banging on my door if you want back in."

"I wouldn't dare." She paused. "And Margot, let whoever needs to know that I won't be attending the Emmys. I have somewhere important I need to be."

They could hear Margot shout a string of expletives at her assistant before the call dropped.

"That went well," Zahra said.

Aurora couldn't help but laugh. Actually, it had gone better than she expected. She was shaking a little, buzzing like a timer that'd just gone off. It wasn't regret and it wasn't relief, but somewhere in between: a cloudy, hesitant knowing that she'd made the right decision without a clear idea of what she should do next.

She hadn't fully processed the news of her paternity when she stepped back into the hospital room. How could she? But she knew she loved the person she saw lying in that bed. She knew he had loved her.

"I really thought he might come to one last time," Aurora said, running her fingers over his fingerprint-smudged reading glasses abandoned on the rolling side table.

Zahra shrugged. "I know. He would have if he could. For you."

Even if it wasn't true, Aurora let herself believe the impossible one last time.

A silence fell over the room as they sat on either side of him. A few minutes later, the nurse Nicole entered. She hovered by the bedside for a few minutes.

"I think it's going to be soon," she told them, her voice thick with sympathy. "His breathing is growing slower and irregular. Press the call button when you need me."

Aurora noted that she didn't say "if" but "when." *When he died.*

She jumped to her feet, floundered for a moment, then flopped back down. She couldn't do this. She couldn't just wait to watch him go. She didn't know how to feel. What to think. What to do with her body. The lack of direction unmoored her. She bit down hard on the tips of her hair and chewed.

"Aurora."

When she looked up, her sister was staring at her with kind brown eyes. "It's okay," Zahra said. "We can do this." She reached her hand toward Aurora across the expanse of their dad's shrinking form. What had the woman back at the gas station said? There was nothing more to do; she just had to be there. *To bear witness.* It was Aurora's turn to watch the scene unfold. She dropped the hair from her mouth, fit her palm into Zahra's, and held on tight.

The end came forty-five minutes later without so much as a rattle. Only a final silent exhalation as the late-afternoon light snuck through the closed blinds and across the room. The lines of light and shadow bisecting the bed between the sisters, the boundary between life and death.

Her dad was gone. Just like that. She'd never hear him speak again, say, "Hey, Roar. How's it hanging?" when he answered the phone. He would never place his bear paw on her shoulder and squeeze, a gesture she found more reassuring than any in the world.

It was all so simple, so final, so quiet.

A strange sound rose in the room. A keening Aurora didn't recognize as her own until Zahra came up behind her and touched her head. Aurora turned to her and held hard and fast, gasping into her sister's hair.

She couldn't have stopped these tears for all the money in the world.

ONE WEEK LATER

Username: Elly Spills All

Bio: Serving tea with a side of hot goss

A close-up of popular video gossip queen Elly Belly with the GlamAnon filter obscuring her facial features appears over a green screen image of Aurora sandwiched between Dillon and Serena on the red carpet at the *You, Me, Us* premiere.

"Buckle up, Buttercups. We thought things were juicy before with the whole Aura Star / Dillon Kelly / Serena Kelly saga, but now our teacups really runneth over."

Elly brings prayer hands to her mouth and takes a dramatic breath.

"I'm genuinely freaking out right now. The video I have to show you is so, so good. But before I do, some setup: the affair rumor started last Tuesday, right around the time Serena's bump made its first appearance, and we immediately got social updates that showed Aurora had left town. We agreed the timing was weird, but nothing was confirmed until Dillon himself broke the story two days later. Still nothing from Aurora's rep at that time, but next, we hear she's backing out of the Emmys ceremony. Who could blame her for not wanting to sit next to Serena—yikes! Awwkwaard.

"And then, holy freaking drama, Aura actually wins for Best Lead Actress. The look on Serena's face during the announcement was"—Elly gestures a chef's kiss—"she did not see that one coming. I mean, I feel bad for her. Ouch. But this is the celeb gossip I *literally* live for. Which brings me to this next juicy tidbit. This is just the story that keeps on giving."

Elly issues another dramatic pause. Her blurred eyes appear to dart around.

"Guys, this is major gossip coming in hot . . . I have it on very, *very* good authority Aura's trying to get out of her contract for *You, Me, Us* and severing ties with her management team. So what the F-bomb is going on?

"According to this candid video from Seattle-Tacoma airport on Friday, Aura Star was having real-life sister drama at the same time the affair story came to life. I'm serious. You can't make this stuff up. Take a peek, then tell me your thoughts. I, for one, am glad the tides will start turning in Aura's, or should I say Aurora's, favor. Dillon's sob story about a"—she signs air quotes—"misunderstanding ain't adding up. The only thing he misunderstood were his marriage vows."

A video of Aurora and Zahra standing face-to-face appears on the green screen. The sisters speak to one another, clearly unaware of the camera so near to their faces recording their personal conversation, a private confessional in which they both admit to their wrongdoings.

After a minute of their back-and-forth, Elly interjects, "Okay, here's where it gets juicy."

In the video, Aurora says, "If I don't show up, my career is over. Dillon has turned everyone against me. He's the one who confirmed the story about us. I thought what we had meant something."

"You trusted him. He took advantage of your trust. He was the one in the position of power. He was the one with a wife. Then he turned on you when it benefited him to do so. You did the wrong thing, but you're a good person."

Eventually, the camera jumps up and down. The person behind the phone yells, "You're Aura Star!" Then a woman in an airline uniform interrupts them. Zahra responds, "Her name is Aurora Starling." The video goes dark, and Elly's GlamAnon image appears again.

"It's like a scene from *YMU*, no? Except that older sister makes Serena look downright dull. And as we all can agree, nothing is worse than boring."

Sammy_Does_Denver: Oh snap, Aura's sister is a badass.

MissSwizzle: Officially starting a petition for the *You, Me, Us* reality show, starring Aurora Starling and her real-life sister.

MiniFrens1000: I feel so bad for Aurora. Her sister tells it exactly how it is. Her married boss took advantage of her. In any other industry, he'd be fired, and she'd be compensated. #FreeAuraStar

BadGrandma: She's an adult, not a child, and she still had the gall to sleep with another woman's husband. Now she has to face the consequences. Boo-hoo.

Lindsey2688: I agree, @BadGrandma. Women like her make me sick.

Lipservicebottleservice: Y'all a bunch of haters. She's not the one who's married! Let the girl live. So tired of these public humiliation trials. Are you perfect? Are there any misdeeds in your past you'd prefer people don't know about it? That's what I thought. People are allowed to make mistakes. Full stop. Especially if they learn from them. My money's on Aurora making a major comeback.

44

Zahra

Zahra couldn't believe she was back at the airport.

What was she doing here? Why had she agreed to this?

Nothing had changed. Not the people milling about, the aggrieved TSA agents, the dread she carried as heavy as a suitcase.

A body bumped into her, and she came back to herself.

Actually, everything had changed. Dom Starling was gone. And Zahra was surprised to find she felt more than abject neutrality about the matter. She grieved for him. For the dad she never had. And the one she did.

Hers was a different kind of loss than Aurora's. Her sister had been crying on and off since they'd left the hospital and begun the process of getting on with things.

Their dad, always self-contained and meticulous, had left nothing to chance. His will and estate outlined not only the arrangements he'd made for his cremation and exactly how he wanted his assets divided—50 percent split equally between Zahra and Aurora, and 50 percent divided among his living siblings—but also the real estate agent they should contact for the sale of his home, who to hire to oversee cleaning out his things, and the organizations they were to donate various kinds of belongings to.

From their hotel room, Zahra had made phone call after phone call: Breaking the news to his eldest sister so she could tell the other siblings and remaining family members, most of which Zahra hadn't even known existed. Setting up appointments for pickups. Having his body transferred to the funeral home as directed. She asked Aurora for nothing; it was enough to know she was there.

Until two days later, when she had to unlock the house for one of the various parties her dad's estate was paying to be there.

She couldn't go alone. And not for the obvious reason of having to confront the detritus of his life. But the opposite, really. Zahra feared she might have the desire to tear through his things, see what other secrets he'd kept. She didn't want to know. And she was terrified she wouldn't be able to resist.

Plus, he'd stipulated that he'd like them each to take one, and only one, possession of his to keep.

So they went. In the rain. Aurora still a torrent of tears. Her pockets overflowed with stringy bits of tissue, and her nose and eyes were perpetually pink. Her Emmy win seemed to have only amplified her emotions, like she was wringing herself out of whatever she'd soaked up in LA.

Together, they wandered the rooms, considered the furniture, let their fingers graze his shelves. He had few knickknacks or nods to decor. The two-story home was an ironic shrine to minimalism by a man who had always wanted more.

In the end, Zahra chose the scarred bamboo cutting board he'd left on the counter, Aurora a deck of playing cards sitting by his chair in the living room. He'd used them, according to her, for languorous rounds of late-night solitaire with a whiskey by his side. A picture of pleasant solitude. Except he'd frequently called Aurora during these games, chatting with her as long as she'd let him. It didn't take much for solitude to tip toward loneliness.

Before they'd left, Zahra had let herself into his office and sat down at his desk. It was bare except for a table lamp, his laptop, and a small collection of framed photos. She'd come for the laptop, as per his request. He'd done most of the work of clearing his computer and phone, leaving behind a list of logins and passwords for the few loose ends.

But the photos caught her attention.

The first photograph was one of her dad and Aurora when she was little, in a ballerina costume, standing in front of the glass mirrors of a dance studio, Lucy with the camera in her face reflected back.

There was one of her and Aurora she'd never seen before. Aurora no more than two or three and Zahra at the peak of her angsty teenager stage, her baggy sweatshirt and jeans—and scowl—hiding the sad kid beneath. The next picture was one of little Zahra and her dad. He was bent down on one knee, and she'd propped herself on the other, like a ventriloquist dummy. They had the same expression on their faces, a smile without commitment, mostly in the eyes, one eyebrow slightly higher than the other, giving them both a look of incredulity. She recognized this one. Her mom kept a copy in a photo album Zahra used to thumb through after her dad left, trying to make sense of how a life could cleave in two without warning.

The last was an older photo, yellowed and rounded at the corners. Five children in order of height. She recognized the youngest. Her dad with his siblings. She hardly knew anything about any of them. But then, she hardly knew anything about her dad, not the man she grew up with but the other one, the man with the life that started long before she came along.

Her gaze lingered over their faces until it landed on a thin, faded ultrasound picture, curling at the edges, propped against one of the frames. A head in profile and two arms waving. A miniature person in newt-like proportions. It could have been any ultrasound, but she knew, of course, with a wallop to her gut, that it was hers. Her baby daughter at twelve weeks, according to the date. She remembered now, snipping off one of the images from the others, stuffing it in an envelope, and mailing it to her dad with a single sheet of paper that said, "Hey, Grandpa. Guess what?"

He hadn't told Aurora about the pregnancy, but he'd kept the ultrasound photo.

The inconsistency baffled Zahra. It didn't fit with the story she'd been telling herself, though she supposed it fit with what she knew of her dad. A man who never let his life fit into a single box, or a single family. A man of contradictions. A father of contradictory daughters.

The only thing she and Aurora had in common was Dom Starling. They were both fools when it came to him, in opposite ways, and no wonder. He had fathered one and raised the other. He had abandoned one and devoted himself to the other. It was true. It wasn't the whole truth. Just as Zahra was childless and a mother. An only child and a sister.

She cupped the ultrasound photo in her palm and let herself accept these twin truths she'd never allowed herself before.

Tears pricked at her eyes, and she let them fall, pressing her face to the cool, rough desk. It was only then, as she held a scrap of what might have been in her hands, another life in another universe, that she allowed herself to really feel what she'd lost. The chance she and her dad might one day have had a different kind of relationship. That he might have been the father she'd needed, and in turn, she would have been a better version of herself. It was all over now, and she recognized the duality of grief from losing her daughter, when you mourned not just the death of what was but what could have been.

Still, despite the loss—or perhaps because of it—she could feel a burning block of dry ice break from her core like an iceberg. A great, excruciating thaw.

Aurora had found her like that and asked what had happened. She'd shown her the ultrasound photo, then doubled over, shaking as she wept into her lap.

She cried for her baby. For her marriage. For a future she never had. For a past she couldn't change. For her dear grandparents and her inscrutable father. Zahra even cried for the lost cat. The accumulation of loss could take your breath away. But if she lived long enough, this was only the beginning. To survive, she didn't have to harden herself. She had to soften, make her heart spongy and pliant.

Aurora set a hand on the crest of Zahra's back, and together, they waited for the earthquake breaking her apart within to subside.

After her momentary undoing, she regained her composure, sniffling as she wiped at her eyes. "It mattered so much to me that you were closer to him. But he's gone now, and he's a mystery to both of us."

Part of what it meant to have a sibling was to share the burden of loving a parent you could never entirely know, of attempting to understand a person who would always be just out of reach, more conjecture than fact. Zahra had wasted so much time with Aurora, but as her dad had somehow intuited, they'd still come together at exactly the right moment.

Death was a lesson in regret. But regret wasn't why Zahra was walking through the airport again, taking her shoes off at security, holding her breath as she passed through the X-ray machine. No, she hadn't chosen to face her fear head-on.

She'd made a deal. A stupid deal.

Forty-eight hours after their dad died, they'd turned on the Emmys in the hotel room, each in a matching plush robe, eating overpriced and underseasoned room-service burgers and sharing a wedge salad. Zahra had abandoned her mission to perfect the Caesar. Such a thing wasn't possible, the aim inherently too subjective.

"Are you sure you want to watch?" Zahra had asked, as stunning women in flowing gowns began to grace their screen.

"I'm sure."

"It's going to hurt if you lose."

"I already know I'm going to lose."

"But it's still going to hurt to have to watch. Because there's always that point-zero-one percent holding out hope, right?"

"I guess we'll find out." Aurora sat up. "Hey, let's pretend I do win. Would you do something for me?"

"Okay. What?"

"Get on a plane. Back to LA. With me."

Yeah, right. But because God knew she owed Aurora a good deed, and also because she really didn't think she'd win, Zahra had agreed. They went back to their food while the red carpet unfurled, Aurora lobbing gossip and rumors about anyone she knew, or knew someone who knew, Zahra plucking the bacon bits from her salad.

Hours later, when Aurora's name had been announced as the winner and the camera flashed to Serena's pained face, they'd both sat in silence, stunned, until Aurora said, "That did not just happen."

Zahra leaped to her feet and began jumping on the bed, shouting, "Oh my God, oh my God!" Aurora had joined her, and the deal had been forgotten.

Until that very morning.

Zahra had mentioned taking the Volvo to a shop before she tried to drive it back all that way, and Aurora told her she'd booked them both plane tickets for a flight. That afternoon.

"You didn't," Zahra said. "Why would you do that?"

"We've been here a week. It's time to go home." Aurora shrugged without looking even a little contrite. "Plus, you made a deal."

Dammit, she had.

She refused to back down now. Even if it killed her, and she was pretty certain it would.

This time, they ambled down the terminal toward the gate with no last-minute scrambles, but still her heart began to beat a dent in her chest.

"How are you holding up?" Aurora asked, decked out in her hat, mask, and glasses again. They'd both agreed it was too risky to walk through the airport after the Emmys upset without her disguise. All

Zahra could see of her sister's face was her rosy cheekbones, but she found them reassuring nonetheless, the way Aurora was starting to glow again.

Unable to speak, she waggled her hand back and forth as if to say, "So-so."

When they arrived at the gate, they still had a few minutes until boarding. Aurora dumped herself in a chair, but Zahra couldn't sit.

She was certain she was not getting enough oxygen to her brain, and the sensation left her dizzy and blurry edged.

"I'm think I'm dying," she told Aurora.

"You can't die before we get on the plane."

But it seemed preferable to die right then and there, as opposed to when they fell out of the sky in a nanosecond of horror completely outside her control.

Except Zahra didn't want to die. She was thirty-eight years old, but in that moment, she had the sensation that her life was only now beginning, that all that had come before had been practice for whatever came next. Even this moment.

Aurora took a deep breath and waved her hands at Zahra to do the same. "Try the box breathing."

Zahra shook her head. The announcement for Group One boarding sounded over the speaker.

"That's us." Aurora got to her feet, shoving Zahra into the line. "You can do this," she whispered into Zahra's ear.

Despite the clot of fear tightening her chest, Zahra managed to calmly make her way down the skywalk and to the plane door. Just seeing its heavy metal body made her lightheaded. Her feet were cast iron as she stepped inside and found her seat in business class beside Aurora, who immediately started making herself comfortable.

Zahra shoved her carry-on in the overhead compartment and lowered herself into the aisle seat, but not before plucking out the recipe book from her belongings. She held it in her lap, hoping the weight of it would soothe her, but her brain wouldn't cooperate. They were still firmly on the ground, the plane door wide open, admitting a long line of travelers, and yet she was anticipating the ascent, the terrifying groan as the plane lifted off the ground.

Aurora squeezed her wrist. "We'll be home before you know it."

"Do you mean *home* home, as in the heavenly kingdom from which some believe we all originally came?"

"That's exactly *not* what I mean, but if such a place exists, I'm not convinced you're getting in."

Nerves aside, the dig made Zahra smile. "Well, Dad probably needs company down below anyway."

"Look at you, making jokes. Does that mean you're relaxing?"

"It's stress humor. Do you hear how I'm talking? My jaw is so tight." She rubbed at the knobs of bone in front of each ear.

Aurora reached behind her back and pulled out a mini bottle of prosecco with a plastic twist-off cap. "Ta-da! Will this help?"

"You had this the whole time?"

"Nah, I asked the flight attendant as we were boarding."

"When? How? I've been with you the whole time."

"Magic."

Zahra rolled her eyes. "Of course they gave it to you."

"You know, you catch more flies with honey . . ."

Zahra thought of the fruit flies Preeti had supposedly eradicated from her cottage kitchen back in LA with her miracle formula of dish soap and apple cider vinegar. Those little suckers dive-bombed the stuff, she'd written to Zahra in a text, assuring her, too, that she'd wiped clean all the casualties and restocked her fruit bowl, a step Zahra found unnecessary, possibly too much, really, but endearing nonetheless.

"Preeti's a good friend," Aurora had said when Zahra told her, and Zahra had to admit that she was.

"I prefer to think of myself as an apple cider vinegar, thank you very much," she told Aurora, ignoring the disturbing thumps coming from the underbelly of the plane. "A lot of tang, but still a little sweet."

"We'll make you a balsamic yet. Wait . . ." Aurora twisted open the prosecco and handed it to Zahra. "Is that the super syrupy one?"

Zahra nodded and took furtive sips from the bottle as more people filed past them. God, there were so many humans relying on this tin can, so many lives dependent on its safe arrival. Did planes have a secret weight limit? Was it better to be sitting closer to the cockpit like they were, or in the rear? The back of the plane was bumpier, but she couldn't remember which area was supposed to be safer? Probably because nowhere was safe.

Her heart ratcheted up a notch, and she took a swig, closing her eyes and leaning her head back against the seat. She could still get off the plane. There was still time to change her mind. But she knew she wouldn't.

"You're panicking again, aren't you?" Aurora guessed.

The liquid had relaxed Zahra's limbs but done nothing to quell her fears. She nodded and sighed. "Why can't you be a normal actress and carry around a tub of antianxiety pills at all times?" She paused. "And don't suggest the box-breathing thing again, because I'll just start obsessing about whether I'm breathing too much or too little."

Aurora didn't respond, and Zahra peeked through one eye to find her sister studying her. "What?"

"It's time to think of your happy place."

"Oh no, not this again."

After Zahra had spent the better part of the morning protesting at the idea of getting on a plane, Aurora had said it would help if she had a happy place in her mind. A place she could go to where she felt safe, where she trusted things would be okay. The idea made Zahra gag, and she'd said so.

Fewer people funneled onto the plane now, the flight attendants hurried back and forth, the click of overhead bins echoing from economy like a threatening drumbeat. Soon there'd be no way to escape.

Before she could make a run for it, her phone chimed from within her purse. The sound of Elian's voice passed through her mind, and she lurched to check her messages.

But it wasn't Elian. It was Wes.

> Hey Zahra, I thought you'd want to know that a cat matching the description of your guy showed up a few days ago. He's been coming by every morning and evening for food. He has fine tastes, won't eat the kibble we give our indoor cat, so I'm buying him the fancy canned stuff now. I think he's content to stay unless you want to come get him.

What followed was a photo of Sarah sitting on the front steps of their home, the cat curled up in the space between her knees and her growing belly. Zahra could practically hear him purring through the picture.

The shock of the pregnancy had worn off, replaced with a dull ache for everything Zahra had lost. Not just her baby girl, her marriage, and her best friend. But the ability to be genuinely happy for someone she cared about without a pang of envy, to not have to wonder why things couldn't have turned out differently.

"Fluff!" Aurora said, peering over her shoulder. "I'm so relieved. He looks so happy in her lap. Or wait . . ." She bit her lip and glanced at Zahra. "Do we hate her? I'll hate her if you want me to."

Aurora could no more hate a person than Zahra could suddenly decide to stop cooking, but that she would be willing to try for Zahra said enough. She'd learned that much from Aurora, that sometimes it was okay to act a part. There would always be that jealous voice inside her, but it didn't have to be the only voice. She was full of parts of herself she'd closed off, the way she closed off her life against others.

She could let her optimistic side have a turn, too, coat her thoughts in a little more honey.

The cat had been fine all along. Maybe the plane would be just fine, too. Maybe they would land safely back in LA, right on time.

His name is Fluff, she wrote back, wanting to leave some small mark on him, even if it was only that inane name. He looks like he belongs there. If he's happy, he should stay.

Zahra had experienced a potent flush of relief to learn he was okay, but he was so much better off with them and their fields of mice and birds. Their front porch and family home. After a minute she added, Thank you, and then at Aurora's urging, a smiling cat emoji.

"Normally I wouldn't rec an emoji, but in this case, it really says, 'No hard feelings,'" Aurora explained.

Zahra sent the message, her hands still shaking.

"Okay, happy place time," Aurora said. Before Zahra could protest, Aurora made the "shut your trap" sign with her hand. "Just close your eyes. It won't hurt."

For once, Zahra did as she was told.

"All you have to do is envision a place where you feel totally safe, totally in control, totally at peace. Give it detail, all five senses, then put yourself there."

At first, nothing came to her, just the black twinkling void at the backs of her eyelids, filled with an audial blur of voices and the swoosh of the flight attendants each time they passed. She smelled old shoes and Aurora's minty floral hair, and slipping faintly amid all that, the nutty, reassuring smell of coffee.

She inhaled deeply and saw her kitchen, just as she'd left it back in LA, clean and waiting for whatever came next, whatever she had in mind. She saw her reliable tools, the stocked pantry, the sink with its window overlooking the overgrown backyard. Her refrigerator hummed, and outside, birdsong hung in the citrus trees, an easy breeze wafting the scent of Meyer lemon she practically tasted on her tongue.

She could feel the smooth grain of her heavy wooden butcher block, the ultralight steel of her chef's knife.

For a long moment, she allowed herself to accept that she'd be back there in a few hours. To believe in the integrity of the plane and the pilot, in the laws of aerodynamics and the benevolence of the universe. Or, at least, the ambivalence of the universe. That sometimes the random could work in her favor.

When she opened her eyes, her heart still beat at hyperspeed, but her jaw had unlocked, her hands stilled.

The plane's door had been closed and the rustle of movement in the cabin quieted as people settled in their seats. The loudspeaker dinged and the pilot's announcement came over the speaker.

With the recipe book gripped in her lap, she glanced at her phone one last time before turning it on airplane mode. And there was a voice text. Her heart surged open, but then the plane shuddered backward, and she shoved her phone into the seat pocket, afraid that listening now might jinx her flight. When they landed—because they would—she would listen to what Elian had to say. Either way, she would apologize for leaving so abruptly. She would tell him how she felt.

Despite the fragile sliver of faith she'd found, she was still so afraid.

"Here." Aurora offered a hand. "Hold on as tight as you need to."

Zahra released her right hand from the recipe book and clamped it into her sister's left. They were going. She was really doing this. She took deep breaths through her nose, felt the strong hold Aurora had on her, her sister's soft, manicured fingers wrapped around Zahra's scarred skin. Her most recent cut from the flat-tire fiasco had healed without a scab. It had left only a small red-brown discoloration in the middle of her lifeline.

"I promise it'll be okay." Aurora raised the pinkie finger on her free hand, her blue eyes sparkling. Zahra looped her left pinkie around Aurora's right.

"Trust me," Aurora said.

And she did.

"Hey, Zahra. I know you probably don't want to hear from me, but I can't stop thinking about you, and your dad. I know how hard this time is. If you need someone to talk to, as a friend, I'm here, and that offer stands. But it's not the only reason you're on my mind.

"I know I screwed up the other night. It's not that I wasn't being honest that day we met in Ojai about not looking to settle down. I wasn't *looking*. But I didn't realize how I'd end up feeling. About you. It scares the hell out of me, too.

"I've thrown myself out of planes and visited war zones and eaten food from very questionable sources for a decade and a half, and it's only now occurred to me that the real risk is staying put. Building a life I want to hold on to. Putting down roots.

"After finishing that assignment in Southern Oregon, I decided to drive back down to NorCal on a whim. Now I'm in Humboldt County, standing in the middle of a redwood *cathedral*. And it is holy, isn't it? How these giants encircle one another. I learned from my sister that the bravest and best thing a person can do is let someone stand beside you. She tried to do that with me, and I was unavailable. I won't make that same mistake again.

"I came on too strong. I get excited when I see something beautiful, something that gives me a new perspective. This . . . occupational hazard, let's call it, has served me well. But you're not a scene to be captured. You're not a subject sitting for a portrait, and I would never ask you to hold still for me.

"I might have read you wrong, but if there's any chance you feel for me what I feel for you, well, I'm here. It doesn't have to be anything more than what we both want, but if we don't give it a try, we won't know.

"When you were talking about your grandmother's recipes, you described how two ingredients can come together to be more than the sum of their parts. They can create a whole new flavor, right? But you don't know if it'll work until you cook the dish. You have to be willing to fail.

"I guess what I'm trying to say is, I can't pretend we won't get hurt. We both know bad things happen, things you don't expect and don't deserve. But we also know the world doesn't end if the worst happens. You keep going, you make a new normal, and then, if you're lucky, something good shows up again and you're wise enough not to turn your back on it when it does just because you've learned to be more comfortable with the bad.

"I don't know. A long-distance anything isn't conducive for someone who doesn't fly. But we could talk. Like this or on the phone. It doesn't have to be all or nothing. We can make up our own rules. We've each been doing things our own way for a while. Why not try doing them our own way together?"

SIX MONTHS LATER

45

Aurora

Agile. Graceful. Smart. Thick-skinned. Social chameleon. Social climber. Grade-A manipulator. All hail, Princess Aurora.

The media had decided on a new set of words to describe the Emmy award–winning actress with the epic career pivot. But the only words Aurora cared about were the ones on her screen.

Morning sunlight cut a wedge across her bedroom, and Aurora stood in its warmth, unable to move. The light glinted over her cropped golden hair as she stared at her phone, chest fizzing with fear and excitement. She'd been expecting the news any day now, willing it each morning when she woke, but now that it was here, she hesitated.

Aurora was pro-level at handling rejection. Like a stage actor learns to recover from a fumbled line or a chef recalibrates when a dish takes a wrong turn, Aurora could nimbly adjust after even the harshest setback.

The past six months had proven that—to Aurora, most importantly. But also, to the millions of people who had followed the fallout from the Star scandal. Those who read articles, watched videos, and shitposted on social media. Those who shared hot takes and lukewarm takes, who sent her messages of support and admiration, who defended her with a passion that Aurora really wished could be harnessed for a more worthy cause. Those who spoke her legal name with reverence, and those who still refused to use it.

After all that, here she was, hovering on the precipice of a fresh beginning, itching to strike out in another direction like a river cutting a new channel. Not a detour but a different course entirely.

She wanted the change but its potential intimidated her, too. It was the same feeling she'd had when she first met Dillon, but this time, Aurora herself had spurred the change. It was a choice, not a chance encounter. A desire all her own, not one linked to the hunger her mom had taught her to crave.

She stood there, staring at the news on her phone until she heard the sound of Tibetan bells down the hall. It was time for yoga. Preeti would be waiting. Eventually, she'd come looking for her. But still, she paused one more minute, letting the moment sink in.

Her dad's death, the implosion of her career, the loss not just of Dillon but of the relationship she'd believed she'd had—it all left Aurora hurting and weak, clubbed at the knees. At first, even the Emmy win had been more like a consolation prize or a sign she'd chosen the wrong direction, and she couldn't decide which was worse.

But then she and Zahra had returned to LA, and Margot confirmed that she'd made progress dissolving her *You, Me, Us* contract but wondered if Aurora would be willing to reconsider invoking their termination clause. She'd never heard her manager sound contrite before, but apparently Aurora's agents had interest from every angle and Evangeline was fielding interview requests from basically everyone.

"I don't know how you pulled it off, but the world is your oyster," Margot had said. "What do you want to do?"

The million-dollar question.

Aurora didn't want to quit acting entirely, but she wasn't willing to hustle anymore. She wanted time to figure out what she really wanted to do. She told Margot this, agreed to a small role that paid pennies in an indie film with big awards-season potential. They'd finished shooting in Toronto a few weeks ago.

Before she'd left LA, Aurora had downsized from her pricey apartment rental. She was a feather on the wind, free-floating, unsure where she would land, and until then, she wanted something low-key. Something temporary. Thankfully, Zahra had a connection. Her landlady, Preeti, had a room for rent.

Aurora had never had a housemate who wasn't her mom, and she loved it. She loved the company without the pressure. The presence without the intimacy. The unexpected friendship.

Sure, she knew the thrill would wear off eventually, but she imagined she'd be gone by then to whatever came next. Whatever her heart desired. The future she clutched in her hand.

She glanced at the small matchbox that sat on her dresser, the teeny mirrored beads that lined its edges catching the sunlight just so, refracting a thousand miniature rainbows across the walls of the room.

She'd lied to Zahra when she'd first pocketed the matchbox. She'd told her sister she had an idea for it. But there'd been no ideas, nothing but the knowledge she should remove the object from Zahra's possession, protect her sister from whatever memories it held.

Another white lie. There'd been so many of them, she'd lost track. She didn't even realize when she said them.

She understood now that was the problem. By themselves, each lie may have been inconsequential, but they added up. It was a trick she had played not just on others, but on herself.

At first, she'd kept the box because, as Zahra said, she couldn't throw something like that away. It was too meaningful, even if the meaning wasn't hers, and it was beautiful. Delicate and clearly made with love. She liked how she could cup it in the palm of one hand, slip open the compartment with a gentle nudge of her pointer finger.

It remained unused and empty until a small envelope had arrived at Aurora's apartment just before she moved out and flew to Toronto to film her indie. No postmark, no return address. Inside, a small piece of paper with Serena's handwriting that said, "I never trusted you, but I forgive you."

It was the slap she assumed Serena meant it to be. But the message soothed her, too. Not just Serena's absolution, but the reminder that it was neither one nor the other, but both. That the line between betrayal and forgiveness was not so opaque.

Her parents had lied to her for two and a half decades. But it was an act born of love. (Though Lucy remained adamant she'd always believed Dom to be Aurora's biological father, proof that another person's conviction didn't equate to truth.) In the end, Aurora had forgiven her mom—it wasn't in her nature not to. Still, their relationship had changed, as it must: scaffolding erected around Aurora's life that should have gone up ages ago. As for her dad, she was learning to see him for the whole person he'd been, to accept both the bad and the good.

The note from Serena sat tucked inside the matchbox. Maybe she'd bury it in the woods someday. Or light a match and watch it burn. Or maybe she'd hold on to it forever, a reminder of how far she'd come.

Aurora would never understand the boundaries of Serena and Dillon's relationship, whether their love for each other even defined what they shared, but she didn't need to know that to recognize she'd had no right to bend the private bonds of a marriage. If the Kellys stayed together—Zahra gave them five years max; Aurora demurely refrained from speculation—Aura Star would be a single chapter in their memoirs. Dillon had made her believe he'd taken her seriously as a grown woman when really her interest in him had only ever been evidence of how much growing up she still had to do.

I never trusted you, but I forgive you. She could have said the same thing to herself. She had, she supposed, made her own meaning, not just from the matchbox, but from the whole experience, and for that, she knew Zahra would approve.

Heart jumpy, nerves sparking, she read the words on her screen a final time before abandoning her phone.

Floating on a cloud of joy, she found Preeti laying their yoga mats side by side.

"I got in," she said, breathless with excitement. "I'm going to college."

Preeti hopped to her feet and pulled Aurora into her arms. "You absolute genius."

Aurora laughed as they came apart. That was a bit of an exaggeration. She didn't have the academic record you needed for acceptance into most UCs, but Aurora knew she could write one hell of a personal essay. And now, her first official acceptance from UC Santa Cruz.

The two friends broke apart. "Zahra's gonna lose it."

Aurora gestured to the yoga mats. "Is she coming?"

Preeti gave her a look, her pink lips curled in amusement. "The invitation was extended, but I think she's too busy, and for once, it's a legit excuse."

They were always trying to get Zahra to join them in what she called their "hippie earth children pursuits." It worked on occasion, and nothing delighted the both of them more than hearing Zahra swear her way through a yoga session.

"Are you excited for dinner?" Preeti asked, as they made their way to the floor.

Aurora settled into a cross-legged position, bringing her hands to heart center. "Beyond."

SIX HOURS AFTER THAT . . .

46

Zahra

Zahra had been cooking for three days, all recipes inspired by her grandmother's book, altered with her own touch. Saffron tagliatelle silky with lamb sugo and fresh peas; fall-apart tender yogurt-and-turmeric whole-roasted chicken; *borani esfenaj*, a classic Persian spinach dip but with the addition of marinated baby artichoke hearts; and as a play on her grandmother's mushroom casserole, wild mushroom and rice arancini with herby ramp aioli. For dessert, labneh cheesecake with roasted strawberries and orange blossom honey.

Maman Joon's recipes had unlocked a hidden door inside herself, one that made her eager to experiment, to worry less about perfection and more about the excitement of discovery. One that made her want to share her findings.

The dinner party had been Aurora's idea. Naturally. Some things didn't change. But Zahra hadn't balked at the idea as she once would have. Instead, she'd begun to menu plan, already seeing the spread of food in her mind's eye.

It was her idea to invite Elian. Since she'd arrived home from Seattle, they'd been sharing voice texts every day, sometimes more than once a day, opting for video calls when their time zones and schedules allowed.

But they hadn't seen each other in person again. Until tonight.

She looked at the stove clock, and at the sight of the time, her heart jumped. He'd be there in less than an hour, and she was still wearing her apron and a baggy T-shirt she'd sweat through hours ago.

A double-knuckle tap Zahra recognized sounded on her french doors, and a half second later, Aurora stepped inside without waiting for a formal invitation.

"I came early to take some pics. Preeti'll be out in a bit. She's waiting for Marisol." Aurora's face broke out into a grin. "It smells so good in here."

The flowy, floral-patterned dress she wore swished as she came into the kitchen. Her short hair fanned out in messy waves that made her look older, effortless. For once, she was makeup-free, her skin clear. Her sister was "a natural." Some people came into this world as if they'd already lived a hundred lives, and for others, like Zahra, life felt more like one long warm-up, a dress rehearsal without your lines memorized. If before this discrepancy between them made her envious or annoyed with Aurora, now she found it comforting.

Yes, Zahra had experienced a mild internal panic the day Aurora moved into Preeti's house. Even though it had been her suggestion that Preeti let one of her spare rooms to Aurora, Zahra had been overcome with worry that she might start to feel suffocated, that she'd come to regret the new living arrangement that made her and her sister neighbors. In fact, the opposite happened.

She was already dreading the day Aurora would leave, ready to build her own life. Zahra wanted that for her little sister, and at the same time, she wanted nothing to change. It was how she felt about Elian, too: a desperate need to see him and the desire to shelter what they had by keeping things exactly as they were.

She'd had to find the courage to ask him to the dinner party, convinced taking another step forward might somehow ruin what they had.

"That's just a stress response tied to your long-held scarcity mindset," Aurora had reminded her.

Zahra couldn't help rolling her eyes. "Am I supposed to understand what all those words strung together mean?"

But she got the gist, and so she'd sent the invite. She was learning how to see herself a little more clearly by looking through her sister's eyes, her very own walking rose-colored glasses.

Then there was the publicity. After the airport video was shared a few million times, Zahra suddenly had notoriety—and unbeknownst to her, an online presence. Without telling her, Aurora had created accounts for her on various social media sites and even a link to a nonexistent newsletter. Zahra had tens of thousands of followers before she published her first post, a video of her trying to teach Aurora to boil eggs that immediately went viral.

They were still making videos under Aurora's direction, but Zahra was also working on a book proposal. A real one, not just the collection of notes she'd been gathering for years. She could see it coming together. She wanted to call it *Recipes from an Immigrant Grandmother's Kitchen.*

In Zahra's teeny kitchen, Aurora wielded her phone like a pro. Stage, snap, swipe. On to the next dish. Yet another thing she made look easy that Zahra could never manage on her own. But maybe that had nothing to do with their personalities and was only a matter of their age difference. It came in handy to have a member of the younger generation on your side.

"Oh, this is going to be great," Aurora said, looking at the photos and video she'd taken. "Let's get a video of you. And a selfie, too." She looked Zahra over. "Maybe you should change first."

"You think?" Zahra quipped.

Aurora rolled her eyes, grabbed a spoon, and stuck it into the dish of yogurt dip. Zahra swatted her hand. "No tasting until it's time."

"Sheesh. Sorry." Instead, she used the spoon to make a swirl on top of the dip and took another picture.

"Don't mess with anything," Zahra said, stepping from the room.

"When are you going to learn I make everything better?"

"And she's humble, too, folks," Zahra called as she climbed the short staircase to her room, but before she'd made it to the top, she heard from outside in the backyard the sound of a male voice. One she knew the way others could recognize their lover's posture from hundreds of feet away.

"Hello?" Elian called again.

He was early. For a second, she was paralyzed midstep, her lower half heading up the stairs, but her torso turned toward the french doors. Her small home seemed suddenly hobbit-like, the outdoor living area more like a tacky Crate & Barrel ad than the place for an authentic dinner among friends. And the food? What if the food was humdrum? Nothing special. Fine.

It intimidated her enough to share the recipes she'd dedicated every minute of her free time to for the last six months, but to do it on the same night she saw him again? Why had she done this to herself? What if they'd imagined whatever they thought they had? What if she took one look at him and wanted to run? What if he took one look at her and felt the same?

Aurora poked her head out of the kitchen, pulling the spoon from her mouth. "Is that him? Already?"

What if, worst of all, it was a pleasant, unremarkable evening? With pleasant, unremarkable conversation and company? With pleasant, unremarkable food?

But even as Zahra's mind whirred like a Vitamix, an ease settled over her, a certainty that everything was exactly as it should be, for at least this one single evening.

"Do you want me to stall him?" Aurora asked.

No, she didn't. She didn't want to wait another minute.

She dashed down the stairs and threw open the doors, startling Elian in the process, who stumbled back a step. He was more gorgeous than she remembered, a portrait captured imperfectly in the camera of her memory.

She reached toward him, her hand catching his forearm, bare where he'd rolled up the sleeves. Their skin might as well have spit sparks, and now it was her turn to startle.

"Hi," she finally managed. "How are you?"

He looked her in the eyes. "Never better."

Her stomach flipped. She couldn't speak, too caught up in the flash in time they were experiencing. She'd been telling herself she didn't know where their relationship would go if it were to become real, but it turned out, it already was.

"Hellooo!" Preeti's call came from her deck, breaking the two of them apart. A moment later, she appeared with Marisol, her sommelier friend. She caught sight of Zahra and Elian beneath the trees. "Oh, shoot. We interrupted the reunion, didn't we?" She nudged Marisol, who carried a case of wine in her colorful tattooed arms. "Let's go back to the deck."

"No way," Zahra said, making introductions for all of them. She'd already emailed back and forth with Marisol about the menu. She gestured to the makeshift bar she'd prepared. "You can set up the wine there. Everything's almost ready."

She turned around toward Elian, aware of the absurdly huge smile on her face. "I'll be back," she told him. "I have to change."

Inside the house, she found Aurora at the open kitchen window, watching the scene outside, a wide smile on her face.

"What?" Zahra said.

"Absolutely nothing at all." But, of course, they each knew what the other was thinking.

❦

Shortly thereafter, they were all gathered at the table, the clink of serving spoons on porcelain, wine dribbling into glasses, chatter about what was in which dish. The twinkle lights lit up the yard, candles flickered.

"It's the most exclusive table in LA tonight," Preeti joked.

Zahra's heart might as well have been laid before them, thumping madly. And yet instead of terror, honey-sweet anticipation pumped through her veins.

In the months since her dad had died, Zahra's old wounds had begun to heal, not because he was gone, but because she'd finally been able to forgive him. Accept him. And in doing so she'd forgiven herself. The anger she'd held tight to for so long had lessened, and without its overpowering presence, she experienced grief, hope, and even desire, like flavors fluttering along her palate. Her emotional scars, like the many marks on her hands from the kitchen, like the tattoo across her forearm, didn't have to exist as painful reminders, but as proof of all that she'd lived through, all that she'd loved.

Without thinking, she grabbed Elian's hand beneath the table, and shared a knowing glance when he began to stroke her knuckles. "It's stunning," he said, without looking away.

"Absolutely delicious," Marisol said. "There are so many people I want you to meet, Zahra." She looked at Preeti. "I can't believe you've been hiding this treasure in your backyard."

Elian raised his glass. "To Zahra."

Everyone raised their glasses to join. "To friendship," Preeti added.

"To love," Aurora said with a wink.

Zahra leveled a death stare that made them both laugh. "Fine. To Dad," she countered.

Dad. In the end, Dom Starling had left his eldest daughter exactly what she needed, and wasn't that better than a single apology eked out from a final breath? There were different ways to atone. To be a person. To live and to die.

Zahra didn't know where a soul went when a body stopped. She wasn't sure what a soul even was. But she knew what she wanted to believe: that somewhere, perhaps cradled among the hallowed arms of the redwoods, or higher still, among the stars, her dad was maybe, just maybe, looking out for her daughter, a last way to make his amends.

To Azar, she thought. One day soon, Zahra would find the courage to share her daughter's name aloud. For now, she held Aurora's bright-eyed gaze and raised her own glass.

"To sisters."

ACKNOWLEDGMENTS

Writing a book is a deeply meaningful pursuit, but sharing that book with a world of readers is perhaps the most incredible of all experiences. Thank you, dear reader, from the bottom of my heart for choosing this book among so many options. I'm filled with gratitude and humbled.

To my agent, Nephele Tempest with the Knight Agency, I'm still not over how you've helped me make my publishing dream come true, and I'm not sure I ever will be! Thank you, thank you, thank you.

Biggest, most joyful thanks to Melissa Valentine for taking another chance on me and giving the Starling sisters the opportunity to soar. And to Ali Castleman, for so effortlessly stepping into the role of editor mid-project and giving me all the reassurances, I'm deeply grateful. Thanks, also, to Carissa Bluestone for her brief but important role in this book's creation. I've been so fortunate to have such a dedicated, detail-oriented behind-the-scenes team at Lake Union, especially Karen Brown, Nicole Burns-Ascue, Miranda Gardner, Robin O'Dell, Kellie Osborne, Jill Schoenhaut, and Sarah Vostok. Kathleen Lynch designed a gorgeous, eye-catching cover I'll never tire of looking at. Thank you, all, for making me look so good.

Charlotte Herscher, you were unflappable and forgiving when I bungled my dev edit with a major tech error. I don't think I would have made it to the finish line without your spot-on guidance *and* generous understanding.

This book would not exist without the remarkable women of my writing group. Our friendship is hands down one of the best parts of this whole writing gig. Amy Neff, Erin Quinn-Kong, and Hadley Leggett, these few words will never be enough to say it all. I know you know that.

To the other very good writing friends who have shared so much with me and held space for my worries and questions, thank you! Special shout-out to the Lake Union '23 debuts, who have been a constant source of inspiration and camaraderie, and to Sierra Godfrey, who makes me laugh and *gets it* the most.

I finished this book at the Northern California Writers' Retreat, and it was one of the most precious gifts I could have ever given myself thanks to the wise and wonderful Heather Lazare, the lovely Dauphiene Parks, and the other fab Session One '23 participants.

Lidija Hilje, your Novel with Meaning course made the difference when it came to figuring out what I was *really* trying to say with this story. Thank you for helping me make it happen and make it meaningful.

I have some of the most exceptional friends in the world. These are the people I can pour my heart out to, but they also let me dish about the lives of imaginary characters. I love you, all. Heather and Melissa, thank you for the many (many) talk sessions. Ashley and Jolie, thank you for letting me pester you with logistical questions. Abbey, thank you for being my first nonwriter reader (for this book and in life) and opening your heart to a story that hit close to home.

Thank you to my parents, stepparents, siblings, and in-laws for being as supportive as humanly possible in my pursuit of becoming an author. Extra thanks to my sister Syd for being an early and ideal reader. My mom provided countless hours of childcare—this time for two kids!—so I could get this book done. Any mom-writer knows how invaluable the gift of time is. She would never let me repay her even if I could, but, Mom, please know: I am so thankful and I don't take your help for granted.

Matteo and Leo, you put everything in perspective and make my world infinitely better.

Mike, if any of this is possible without you, I don't want to know how. Our life is the best story I could ever imagine, even with all the scary parts and hard bits.

ABOUT THE AUTHOR

Photo © 2022 Nazaneen Ganji

Lauren Parvizi is the author of *Trust Me on This* and *La Vie, According to Rose* and the winner of the 2024 Women's Fiction Writers Association STAR Award in the Debut category. She worked for more than a decade as a digital editor and content writer, and earned an MFA from San Francisco State University. She lives in the San Francisco Bay Area with her husband and sons. For more information, visit www.laurenparvizi.com.